T0285789

DISSOLVED

DISSOLVED

A NOVEL

SARA BLÆDEL AND
MADS PEDER NORDBO

CROOKED
LANE

NEW YORK

Copyright ©2024 by Sara Blaedel and Mads Peder Nordbo

All rights reserved.

Published in the United States by Crooked Lane Books, an imprint of The Quick Brown Fox & Company LLC

Published by arrangement with Nordin Agency ApS, Copenhagen

Crooked Lane Books and its logo are trademarks of The Quick Brown Fox & Company LLC.

Library of Congress Catalog-in-Publication data available upon request.

ISBN (hardcover): 978-1-63910-595-3
ISBN (paperback): 978-1-63910-916-6
ISBN (ebook): 978-1-63910-596-0

Translation by Tara Chace
Cover design by Kenneth Schultz

Printed in the United States.

www.crookedlanebooks.com

Crooked Lane Books
34 West 27th St., 10th Floor
New York, NY 10001

First Edition: December 2023

Trade Paperback Edition: August 2024

10 9 8 7 6 5 4 3 2 1

Day 1—Friday

THE CAR DOOR window was rolled down halfway so he could listen for her. Small spots of morning sunlight were like drops of fire in the grass. It was burning, in the grass and in him. He had sat here before, sat right here in the car with his tea under these trees behind the athletic center's buildings, out of way of cameras and everyone's eyes. The garbage truck came on Mondays. The daycare workers came with their strollers and groups of toddling youngsters between 9:05 and 9:17. He had never seen them himself, but the little camera he had set up on the low addition behind him had captured everything for a whole year, and he knew what happened morning after morning down to the slightest detail. The camera had been taken down now, and he was ready.

He glanced again at the car's dashboard clock. It was 7:47. Her file lay on the passenger's seat. She came here three mornings a week before work. Her arrival time varied a bit, somewhere between 6:35 and 6:40, but she always left the gym again at ten to eight so she would have enough time to bike to work at Tallerup School and get there right before the bell rang. She hadn't been sick a single day the past year. He had noted that her husband got the kids off to school and she generally picked them up in the afternoons.

He ran a finger over her file. It was sizable. There was no surveillance on the back of the athletic center apart from the camera he had set up. The gym's own camera lens was pointed out at the front of the building, but he had neutralized it while it was still night out.

Seven forty-nine. She would be leaving soon. He took a sip from his insulated cup. His chest felt tight.

Next to her file sat a small leather-bound book, worn until it was shiny. He caressed the smooth leather before he added it and her file to the other folders in the glove compartment.

It was time. She would come out in a minute and discover that her bike was missing. Then she would look around. Time would pass. There would be less than five minutes before the school bell rang.

There she came. Her hair was up, her heavy bag slung over her shoulder, her gait casual as she walked over to the bike rack. He followed her in his rearview mirror and then started the car.

She looked around, searching, glanced at her watch and started jogging, approaching the car as she headed toward her school.

A thrill of pleasure ran through him as he turned his face toward her.

"Hi," he said as she came up alongside his car. "You look like you're in a hurry. Do you need a lift?"

* * *

The two screens in front of Nassrin hummed. Outside, the sun hung high over the old buildings across Hans Mules Gade, but a cool breeze blew in the window.

She had been sitting in front of these computers staring at faces and names since she had come in for her late shift, and she had never been so sick of her Muslim heritage as she had since completing the police academy and starting to work for the Odense Police. Face after face slid past on the screens as she inputted the new data from the cards on the desk in front of her. They had hundreds of young people with Arab roots in their card catalogs here at Funen Police, and it pretty much always fell to her to update them and keep track of their interrelationships and where they hung out. It was fine, of course. But over time she had grown sick of being the one saddled with this task. Was it because she was Muslim? Because she was the youngest? Because she wasn't good enough for real detective work? Sometimes the chore even came with sarcastic quips like *Oh, heard something new about your cousins?* Screw them.

The sound of laughter disturbed Nassrin, and she quickly glanced up at Dea Torp. Her older coworker tended to raise her volume whenever there were strong men nearby. *Pathetic!* Nassrin thought in annoyance. About seventy people worked in the Reactive Criminal Investigations Department, and she had to end up in the five-person office with Sergeant Torp as section leader.

One of the officers from the canine unit was sitting on the corner of Dea's desk with a cup of coffee. She had let down her shiny, ash-gray hair so it hung past her shoulders. The canine officer had his vest on but no jacket, so the strap of his shoulder holster was visible. He was broad chested, and the lingering flirtation between them filled the office.

Nassrin looked back at her work in annoyance. Apparently neither Dea nor the officer had to suffer through their workdays slogging through endless sequences of pictures of "ghetto gangsters."

"Here." Nassrin turned and looked up at Liam Stark. She got along well with the police inspector in Reactive and had dreamed of getting to work in Violent Crimes for a long time, but she didn't understand why he never reprimanded Dea, who had completely taken over their shared office. Some of their older colleagues called him *The Scotsman* because of his Scottish heritage and fondness for homemade haggis, which stunk up the whole department like dissolved vitamins and sheep fat.

"Do you need a cup of tea?" he continued, setting a chipped cup on her desk next to the numerous cards. "Making progress?"

She nodded slowly and took the cup. "It's just not why I came to Reactive Investigations," she said, nodding at her screen.

It seemed to take him a minute to understand what she meant, but then he gestured to the cards.

"That's the basis of good investigative work. It's one of the most important things we do."

She sneaked a peek at him, but he seemed serious.

"When we stay on top of where they are and we know what they're up to, then we have just that much of a leg up, which makes it possible for us to act . . . so you're wrong if you think this isn't important."

He had said that before, but there were other new hires besides her.

"You know they call me *Prize Perker*, right? A sort of Persian/ Turk combo slur."

"Who calls you that? Someone here?"

"No, not here . . . in town." She pointed to the screens. "These guys."

"Is that a problem for you? When you're out there?"

She shook her head and tried to swallow some of the sense of injustice she felt. "No, the problem is more that I'm so rarely out there. I'm not much of a prize anything sitting around here and staring at a screen day in and day out." She drank her tea slowly, feeling Liam's gaze on her. She burned her tongue, but at least she had managed to say it now.

Dea laughed loudly again from her desk, but it didn't seem to bother Liam. Maybe he didn't really notice it, Nassrin thought.

Although of course he was the one who had brought Dea Torp to Odense, even though it was hard to see why.

Nassrin had Googled her, and it was pretty obvious that the section leader had had her heyday on the force and was now on her way back down through the hierarchy in rapid order. She was fifty-one and had been among the high-and-mighty, a detective inspector in the old murder department in Copenhagen, but then something had happened to make her move to Greenland, where she had spent a couple of years with the Nuuk police. When she returned to Denmark, it had been as a sergeant, pretty far from the top of the Funen Police pecking order. That seemed like a demotion to Nassrin. Dea brushed it off with an "I suppose I just expected something different."

Liam had straightened up, a furrow in his brow as he contemplated her thoughtfully.

"Noted, Nassrin. I hear what you're saying, but after all, you're a constable on your first assignment, so . . ." He eyed her kindly. "We'll definitely get you out in the field as a detective. I promise. But for now, be patient!"

Over at the other desk, Dea and the canine officer had stopped laughing and stood up. A man had appeared in the office doorway. His face looked tense and pale, and he was accompanied by one of the receptionists, who explained that he was here because his wife was missing.

*   *   *

"Damn it!" Liam muttered to himself.

"Do you know him?" Nassrin asked from behind him.

Liam nodded. "That's Claus, my son's coach from the water polo club in Tommerup."

Dea was on her way over to the man, who looked around searchingly until he spotted Liam.

"It's Charlotte!" he said so loudly that his voice echoed in the half-empty office space. "She's gone. I think something's happened to her. She was supposed to pick up the kids, but she never showed up, and you know she would never leave Oliver waiting at daycare. Something must have happened to her, an accident or a crime." He rattled this all off into the silence that had come over those around him.

Dea turned to Liam, but he nodded to her, letting his section leader speak first.

"I was the one you spoke with when you called," she began, quickly gathering her hair into a ponytail. "As I tried to explain on the phone, unfortunately, we don't have the resources to move heaven and earth because your wife has been gone for a couple of hours. She's an adult, and there are so many potential explanations for . . ."

"This isn't just about her being gone for a couple of hours," Claus interrupted angrily. "She's missing. Someone did something to her. That's what I was trying to explain on the phone too, but you're not listening. I wouldn't be standing here if I weren't positive that something was wrong. She's missing!"

"Wouldn't you like to have a seat?" Dea asked, gesturing to the chair at the end of the desk. But the man walked over to Liam, holding out his cell phone to him.

"I had just sent the boys to shower off after practice when I noticed all these calls from the daycare center," he said, scrolling feverishly through his call list and messages. "She would never turn off her phone, and I can't get through to her." He sounded choked up, and his words came out sounding choppy, agitated. "She hasn't picked up the kids. I mean, I always coach the boys on Tuesdays and Fridays, you know, and Charlotte picks up Cille and Oliver on those days. I checked my email and texts, but she never told me that she couldn't pick them up."

Liam took him by the arm and led him over to one of the two armchairs by the window.

"Do you need a glass of water?"

"No," Claus said, waving the offer away with his hand. "I need you to help me find my wife."

Dea came over to join them.

"When do you think she disappeared exactly?" she asked, pulling over a chair so they were seated facing each other.

He turned toward her as if she had just flung an insult at him.

"How should I know?" he snapped. "She's gone. The kids were never picked up, and it turns out she never showed up for work this morning. So she was gone by then, at any rate."

"Let's take this in order," Liam said, taking a seat. "You said she never showed up for work this morning. Where does she work now, in Tommerup? She's a teacher?"

Claus nodded.

"At Tallerup School," he said. "Before I came over here, I called one of her coworkers, who told me that they hadn't heard from her either. She didn't call in sick. She just didn't show up. They had to get a sub to teach her classes, so obviously the school's front office has been trying to reach her too."

Liam held a glass of water out to him, which sloshed as Claus distractedly set it down on the little table.

"I've also spoken to several of her friends," he continued, "but they haven't heard from her either. You need to organize a search. She could be dead!" He started working himself up again.

"What makes you think that she's dead?" Dea asked sharply.

He scowled at her.

"Both the kindergarten and the daycare called me a bunch of times because Charlotte didn't show up to pick up the kids before both places closed. Beate—she's the pastor in Tommerup—she took the kids home with her to the parsonage, since she was picking up her own daughter from kindergarten anyway."

He turned to Liam as if he expected him to understand. "My wife would never forget to pick up our kids!"

"Could you maybe have forgotten that you had agreed you would pick them up today?" Dea suggested. "Or could she have arranged to have someone else pick up the kids today?"

Clause leaned toward her.

"Our son is three, and he was born with Down's syndrome. I'm sure you can probably work it out there in your head that a mother just doesn't abandon a little boy who's so dependent on stable routines and familiar faces. She would never do that to him. It's always us. We are always the ones who pick him up. And our daughter is only five. So you ought to be able to figure it out for yourself that something has happened to her."

His insults and grumpiness rolled off Dea. She leaned closer to him and asked when he had last seen his wife.

Claus slumped a little. What made an impression on Liam was the despair that sat as a deep wrinkle in his otherwise smooth brow. His brown hair had been brushed back, but now it fell down over his forehead because he kept fidgeting and running his hands through it. Liam knew the Laursens lived on Buchwaldsvej in Tommerup, and he knew Charlotte from the water polo club's social gatherings, but he had no idea how the couple got along or who they hung out with.

"The last time I saw her was this morning at six thirty when she left to go work out. She works out at Fin Form at the Tommerup Athletic Center three times a week. She brings a change of clothes with her, and she showers there at the gym after her workout and then she goes straight to work. When she left, she said she would do the grocery shopping on her way home before she picked up the kids." He buried his face in his hands. He was clearly struggling to keep it together.

Liam studied him, examined how his hands moved, noted where he was looking as Claus anxiously ran a hand through his hair. He tried to detect any signs of guilt or lying, but mostly it looked like fear and distress.

"She did her workout this morning at the gym. I talked to one of her friends who she works out with. Everything was the way it usually is. They said goodbye to each other after their workout, and from there Charlotte just had to bicycle a few hundred meters to her job at the school." He looked stiffly over at Dea as if he regretted his anger from before. "This has never happened before . . . never. That's how I know that something is wrong. Something happened!"

"But this happens quite often, that people disappear," Liam said. "And it almost always turns out that the missing person shows up again all on their own."

"Charlotte would never do that to her children. I'm telling you, that's bullshit! You've seen them, haven't you? Oliver has Down's syndrome. You've got to understand that this just isn't her at all, right?"

"I don't know Charlotte that well, Claus."

"No, you don't, but you have to understand that something is really wrong here." Claus dropped his face into his hands. "My wife is the victim of a crime, and you need to help me."

"And that's exactly what we'd like to do," Dea said quickly. "So, aside from not knowing where she is, is there anything in particular that makes you think we're talking about a crime?"

"We *are* talking about a crime!" Claus abruptly sat up straight and counted on his fingers as he rattled off reasons: "Her cell phone is dead, and then there's her bike. She was supposed to ride it to work, but we found it behind a dumpster by the gym."

Liam cut him off. "We?"

"Well, yeah. The pastor's husband, Peter, found it. I don't think it was there when I came out of the gym, because I looked for it too, after I finished my workout and discovered I'd received all those messages. I hurried home, of course, to see if she was there. I thought maybe she'd collapsed before she left or she wasn't feeling well and went home. I pictured her lying helplessly somewhere in the house, not being able to call for help." He teared up when he said the children were eating dinner with the pastor and her partner, Peter. "I think her bike was put out there after I left the gym."

"Couldn't she have put it there herself?" Liam asked.

"Why would she put her bike behind a dumpster and then stay away?" Claus retorted, moving around uneasily in the chair.

"There could be many explanations for that. Maybe she's picked it up by now, while you've been here."

"Peter locked it with a lock he had in his car."

Liam raised his eyebrows. "The pastor's husband, you mean?"

"Yes. He was also the one who drove me over here. He went back to his place now, because the kids are there."

"Well, then, if nothing else, she'll call when she finds her bike locked up with someone else's lock," Dea said, sounding snarky.

Liam cleared his throat. "My colleague is right," he said. "And we need to have a little more to indicate that Charlotte is missing before we can launch a regular search. But obviously, we take your concerns seriously. Of course we do, and we'll open a case stating that you have reported her missing."

"I can appreciate that what I'm saying now may seem a little harsh in your situation," Dea said. "If we were talking about a child, we would have set the wheels in motion right away, but we're dealing with an adult here. You need to be patient and give your wife a chance to come home again."

Liam nodded. He agreed, and in a way, he was also relieved that Dea with her no-nonsense style was spelling things out to Claus.

"I'm sure she'll turn up again," Liam added. "And if Charlotte doesn't come home later tonight, we'll start searching in the morning."

Claus nodded, and when Liam and Dea stood up, he reluctantly followed suit.

"But what about all that stuff about how you need to act quickly in a kidnapping, that the first twenty-four hours are the most important after a crime?" His eyes welled up again, and he clenched his fists in frustration. None of them responded, and a silence settled between them. Then Claus shook his head resignedly, stuck a hand into his pocket, and pulled out a crumpled piece of paper. "If you hear anything at all that might have to do with Charlotte, please call me. If you hear about an accident, someone knocked unconscious, anything, just call. Even overnight."

He smoothed out the little piece of paper and wrote down his phone number. Then he passed it to Dea before turning to Liam.

"You have my number," he told Liam. "Just call."

Dea was about to fold the slip of paper in half but stopped when she noticed what was printed on the back:

Allah will not forgive idolatry. He forgives whom He wants for other sins; but he who worships other gods than Allah has pulled far away from the truth.

"What's this?" she asked out of curiosity, holding the short text back up to Claus, who had already started walking toward the door. He turned around and came back.

"Charlotte teaches religion. That slip was lying on our front stoop. It must have fallen out of her bag on her way out."

"Do you have a picture of Charlotte?" Dea asked. "So we can send it around to the other police districts in case it becomes necessary to search for her tomorrow?"

Claus nodded and held out his cell phone. "I usually say she looks like Mia Lyhne."

"Mia Lyhne, the actress?" Dea repeated, looking at the little screen with surprise. "Oh, right!"

They stood in silence for a moment. Liam suddenly had a hard time just sending Claus out the door. They had known each other for all the years his son had played water polo—not that they were close, but close enough to feel connected the way you did when you were on a team together.

"Where are your kids now? Are they still with the pastor?" Liam asked, glancing quickly at his watch. He felt sorry for the man. He would have reacted the same way if his wife, Helene, had suddenly disappeared, so he could easily appreciate Claus's worry and the nagging fear.

"Beate offered to put them to bed if it got late, but if you're not going to do anything tonight, then I might as well head over there and pick them up."

"I can give you a ride," Liam offered.

"Now?" Claus said, surprised, but clutched at the straw. "Thanks, that would be great. Peter already went back home."

Liam noticed Dea's look right away but ignored her opposition to getting something started before a full twenty-four hours had passed. Those looks normally reminded him that she was a more experienced murder investigator than he was. On the other hand, she didn't have any family in the area that meant anything to her. He knew that his offer to drive Claus to Tommerup was at best a Band-Aid, given that Claus had really come here in hopes of obtaining police crime scene investigators and tracking dogs, but he actually really wanted to hear if the pastor had the same interpretation of what had happened.

Liam walked a few paces behind Claus as they made their way to the car. The coach's shoulders drooped as he walked slumped forward, his hands in the pockets of his loose track pants. If this did involve a crime, Liam thought, Claus could very well be behind his wife's disappearance, and that possibility would be the first line of inquiry they pursued if Charlotte didn't turn up by morning. And they would go hard on him. Liam had never been very fond of this part of the job—people who were scared and all the suspense of not knowing. As far as that was concerned, it didn't really matter whether Charlotte was frolicking with the local blacksmith or had run off to the Bahamas; not knowing was the worst.

He rewound back to the moment Claus had stepped into their office, recalling the worry and desperation in the coach's voice, his eagerness to get the police involved—maybe so that no one could accuse him later of having dragged his feet at searching for his wife. But once they had sat down in his car, he thought it was also possible that Claus was justified in being afraid, that something had happened to Charlotte, that she had been the victim of some crime and he and Dea would soon come to regret that they hadn't put everything they had into this right from the beginning.

*   *   *

Beate was pouring water into the big glass pitcher when she saw a car pull into the parsonage driveway. She squinted and then spotted Cecilie and Oliver's father in the car. She hurried to the door so they wouldn't have a chance to knock. If it was bad news, she wanted to hear it before the kids came racing out.

"Hi, Claus," Beate said tensely as she opened the big front door. "Everything's been going fine here, but what about Charlotte? What did the police say?"

"Liam here is with the police," Claus said, nodding at the officer beside him. "They're not doing very much yet."

"Liam Stark," Liam said, holding out his hand. "Police inspector with the Odense Police."

"I'm Beate," she said, shaking Liam's hand. "I'm the pastor here in town, and Claus and I both have daughters in the same kindergarten class."

"Claus and I know each other from water polo," Liam said with a smile. "Claus is my son's coach."

Beate nodded, and right then the door to the living room opened and Cecilie came running out to her father and threw her arms around his legs.

"Come on in, Dad. We're having meatballs!"

"We were actually just sitting down to dinner," Beate said, slightly apologetically. "The kids were hungry, and . . . you're welcome to join us if you'd like?"

"Yeah, come on, Dad," Cecilie said, pulling her father along.

"They have no idea their mother is missing," Beate told Liam. "Peter and I just said that Charlotte had to stay late at school, even though Claus says she hadn't been there; it wasn't really our place to say, was it?"

"Of course not," Liam said quickly. "It's good that the kids aren't afraid too."

Beate nodded. She liked the warmth in the red-headed policeman's eyes. There was something about him, the slightly messy hair and the red beard. She felt comfortable with him.

"Do you think something happened to Charlotte?"

"It's impossible to say at this point, but I actually came along to ask for your take on it."

"I don't know them that well," Beate said. "Mostly from the kindergarten. And, well, it is a small town."

"Do you know if Charlotte and Claus have ever picked up their kids late before, or if Charlotte has ever just not shown up before?"

"No, that's not the impression I had. Not at all, actually."

"Claus told me earlier that your husband found Charlotte's bicycle back behind the gym and that he locked it up there? Do you know what he was doing there?"

"Yes, he drove down there to look around, because Claus was so upset. And then he recognized Charlotte's bicycle, because we bump into her at the kindergarten so often. It's easy to recognize because of the color." She smiled.

"And then he put his own lock on it?"

"That's typical Peter. The bike wasn't locked up, and he just can't cope with that. He's from Aarhus, not a dinky little town like this one."

"Thanks. We're always telling people to lock up their bikes, even though—you know—we generally mean their own bikes."

She caught the joking twinkle in his eye.

Peter joined them in the front hall and eyed Liam seriously.

"I heard you talking about the bike." He greeted Liam and introduced himself.

"We were just talking about how you locked it up." Beate sought out Peter's eyes. His shaved head gleamed in the light.

"Yeah, maybe that was a little silly," Peter said. "Pure force of habit, though, when you come from a bigger city."

"Did you notice anything out there?" Liam asked with a friendly smile.

"No, nothing other than it was weird that it was behind the building. You would never park it there."

"And you were there because you wanted to help Claus search?"

"Yes." Peter nodded. "I knew someone in college who just hopped on his bike one morning and rode to Berlin," he continued, his voice sounding more cheerful.

"To Berlin?" Liam repeated, staring at him in surprise.

"Charlotte did not go to Berlin, Peter," Beate exclaimed, irritated. "Her bike is still there right now!"

"No, no," Peter said quickly, lowering his head slightly. "I just mean, sometimes people decide to do things on the spur of the moment like that . . . and the weather was really nice this morning. Anyway, I just hope she turns up again soon."

"Yes, let's hope so," Liam said quickly, then said goodbye. Beate walked him back out to the gravel courtyard in front. They needed to maintain hope, she thought, and cast a glance into the bushes and trees that surrounded the parsonage. The shadows seemed darker. There was a rustling sound to her right, as if something living had withdrawn into hiding behind a yew tree at the sound of her footsteps on the gravel.

*   *   *

Liam peeked into the office when he returned to the Reactive Department in Odense. It used to be called the Violent Crimes Unit, like in most other places in Denmark, but some group of visionary minds had come up with the idea that *proactive* and *reactive* departments sounded more goal oriented. He smiled at Dea and Nassrin, the only two people there.

"You're still here?"

"I was just thinking about going for a run, actually," Dea said, looking at the bottom of her screen to check the time. "And then otherwise just home to Netflix." She hesitated a moment. "How did it go with the guy from Tommerup?"

"I'm not sure," Liam said. "Claus seems really upset, her bike was left behind, and neither the pastor nor the folks at the gym seemed to think it was like her to be late or to fail to show up."

"So you did manage to dig into it a little today, after all?"

"She's missing, and since I was there . . ."

"I wonder who she's sleeping with?" Dea exclaimed, looking over at Nassrin.

Liam ignored her. She really sounded so much like a big-city Copenhagen kind of person when she said things like that.

He walked over to Nassrin and showed her the back of the slip of paper that Claus had given them with his phone number written on it.

"Does this text mean anything to you? *Allah will not forgive idolatry. He forgives whom He wants for other sins; but he who worships other gods than Allah has pulled far away from the truth?*"

"Nope," Nassrin replied, visibly uninterested.

"Really? Not at all?" Now it was Dea chiming in. "It's about Allah. That is your department, right?"

Nassrin shook her head and kept her eyes on her screen. Liam knew that Nassrin had been through one hell of an escape from Syria and had worked hard to learn Danish so she could get her education. The day she received her police badge, Nassrin had told him about her arduous path to the police force and into Danish society, so Liam knew all about the opposition she had faced because she was young and female and a refugee. He was well aware that Dea's comment stung.

"Are you OK, Nass?" Liam asked quietly.

Her teeth clenched, she nodded and kept staring at her screen.

"Go home for today, OK? Make an evening of it. The rest of these cards can wait before we enter them, right?"

She got up right away, taking him at his word, and started to shut down her computer. She didn't look at Dea as she packed up her things and left the office.

Liam walked over to Dea's desk after Nassrin had gone.

"I'm going to call Claus tomorrow, and if Charlotte hasn't come home yet, I'm going to go back out there myself."

"Yeah. It'll be a completely different issue tomorrow if she's still gone then," Dea said, and pulled a pair of green sneakers out of a sports bag.

* * *

The wind poured in through the open roof of Nassrin's little dark-blue Fiat 500C. She often took a scenic route on the way home when she was sick of everything going on at work. Liam was doing his best, she knew that. But Dea rubbed her the wrong way. She was mean, mean to everyone except for the men she wanted to ingratiate herself with.

She pressed her foot down hard on the gas pedal and steered the car safely around a soft curve. She had bought the car for its retractable roof, but it had dawned on her that very same day that the little Fiat also had a turbocharger, which she could switch on and off. And on the days when her temper could use a little airing out, switching the turbo on created tons of wind in her hair.

She turned her car into her uncles' driveway and pushed the button to close the roof. Her uncles' house was big, and they needed the space because they had brought mountains of books with them when they had arrived in Denmark half a lifetime ago.

The house didn't look like a used bookstore from the outside, and her uncles didn't do anything to attract customers either, but on rare occasions a customer would come from somewhere in the world to buy a certain book. Sometimes the deal was concluded in minutes, while other times it could take several days once the guest wandered into her uncles' labyrinth of books.

The smell of dust was the first thing that hit her, then Uncle Aldar's warm kiss on her forehead.

"Ah, my girl, you're home."

"Yes." She closed her eyes and enjoyed the quiet and the smells. Aldar often said that most of the dust in these books came from Damascus, because many of them hadn't been opened since Nissen and her uncles had begun living here.

"Did you have a good day?" Aldar continued, eyeing his niece over the top of his glasses. He was holding two old books in one hand, and the light from outside played over the shiny leather covers.

She shrugged.

"I don't want to bring my work home to you guys."

"No, I know that, but you also know that I always ask, because there's room here for everything, right?" Aldar looked around at the many bookshelves and stacks of books. "Can you smell my brother's baklava?"

Nassrin looked at her uncle with a smile. She could still remember when his thick hair and beard were jet black. Now they were gray, almost white.

"What's weighing on you, my girl?" he tried again.

"I'm just tired of being *the Muslim*," Nassrin said with a shrug.

He nodded slowly, giving her an understanding look.

"I got tired of that fifty years ago. But don't let it get to you, because then you just end up becoming a dusty old fool like me."

Nassrin smiled, and he winked at her.

"Nassrin!"

She turned to her other uncle, who had appeared on the stairs with crazy hair and an apron on.

"Are you bringing us cake?" Aldar exclaimed expectantly.

"No, you need to come up," Hayyan said. "I just put it on the table, and there's mint tea."

"I can smell it all the way down here," Nassrin said, and hugged him.

Hayyan nodded and shyly wriggled out of her arms.

"What are you two up to?" Hayyan asked.

"We were talking about how we've turned into two old fools here among all our books," Aldar said, grabbing hold of his brother's shoulder. "You know them all by heart. Isn't that so?"

"Well." Hayyan smiled in embarrassment. "Probably not all of them . . ."

"Surah 112, one through four," Aldar coaxed.

Hayyan bit his lip thoughtfully but then winked at his brother and recited, "*He, Allah, is One. Allah is He on whom all depend. He begets not, nor is He begotten; and none is like Him.*"

"See," Aldar laughed, proud of his older brother. They were two years apart, and to Nassrin they were inseparable. They belonged together. She had a hard time imagining the one without the other.

"I told you, didn't I?" Aldar said it as if they had just won something, something all three of them had accomplished together. He started shepherding them over toward the stairs. "Let's go sink our teeth into your uncle's dessert."

She smiled at them and followed them up as she thought about the verse that Liam had read to her. She didn't need to ask Hayyan; she already knew it was from the Quran. But if her colleagues couldn't even be bothered to try to find the text, then she couldn't be bothered to help. She didn't need to be their *Prize Perker*, ever at the ready to enlighten them the instant they encountered anything with the faintest whiff of the Middle East about it.

Day 2—Saturday

He had waited behind the workshop for about an hour. They had agreed by text that the young man would buy three grams from him. He had known the guy would take the bait because it was a good price, but he hadn't shown up. The young man's movement pattern wasn't hard to figure out in general, but when you added alcohol to the mix, his routines and appointments went out the window.

Then a text message arrived: *On my way.*

He quivered with a shiver of anticipation. He pressed himself against the wall in the dark of night, listening for footsteps on the driveway to the workshop.

He had driven to Assens three weeks earlier to park the little Peugeot in the sailors' parking lot at the harbor. It had sat there until he picked it up an hour ago; he had been meticulous about keeping his back to the harbor's surveillance camera the entire time, so he wouldn't leave anything behind other than a black silhouette. No one would notice the Golf, which was parked now for one night at a single mother's apartment.

Finally, he heard the crunch in the gravel of footsteps approaching, staggering and lurching. A hollow laugh out on the street echoed in the night, and he pulled back a little so he was standing entirely in the dark. He heard several boastful, nasal voices. According to his notes, the young man was usually alone now.

A moment later the young man and his friend walked around the corner. Their shadows danced in the glow of the streetlight.

He took a noiseless step forward, following the two of them with his eyes.

The young man stopped short then, looked around searchingly, and began yelling in a loud, bossy voice.

He quickly pulled back into his dark hiding place. A moment later the door to the workshop opened. The two men proceeded, and then inside, behind the dirty windows, a bright light turned on.

The cell phone in his pocket buzzed: *Weren't we supposed to meet at the workshop?*

He considered responding but instead crept over to the workshop's narrow back door, pressed the handle all the way down, and pushed the mildewy door open slightly. He could hear them in there. He pulled his big hoodie up around his head and stepped into the dark back hallway.

From the narrow corridor, he could make out the silhouettes of a couple of old cabinets and a footstool. He kept going and stepped around a bag of netting twine. He moved silently past a closed door and approached the strip of light being thrown on the oil-stained floor.

The voices filtered out, along with the strong smell of cigarette smoke.

"Fuck, lame," a voice with a nasal twang said from inside the workshop. He heard an empty can land on the floor and clatter as it rolled across the concrete. "I'm going up!"

He concentrated, listening for footsteps, his palms instantly sweaty.

"I'm just going to take a piss first," the one young guy said, suddenly very close to the back hallway.

"Here?" the guy's buddy exclaimed from what already sounded like some distance away.

He quickly pulled back into the darkness as the buddy's footsteps exited the workshop. He heard someone set a can on a metal table. Now the footsteps came back toward him.

He moved slowly forward, listening to the darkness like an animal. There was a clatter as a chair was pushed across the floor, and a little after that, a door opened.

The sound of piss, hitting the toilet water hard.

He moved quickly across the floor and squeezed behind the piles of tires, so he stood hidden between that door and the workshop door.

From the bathroom came the sound of an uncontrolled belch.

He stepped forward as footsteps approached the table. He would have enjoyed seeing the man's face, but there was no time. Before the young mechanic had time to react, he had placed the needle in his neck.

The young man slowly twitched before collapsing onto the floor with a gurgling sound. Then there was silence.

He placed the note next to the overflowing ashtray with a thrill of joy.

*   *   *

"If it's your mother, I'll strangle both of you," Helene grumbled groggily. "It's Saturday morning, for crying out loud!"

Liam reached confusedly for the buzzing cell phone on the nightstand. It was 6:01. He cleared his throat.

"Liam Stark here . . . Claus?"

Liam coughed and rolled onto his side so he could see Helene's back. They usually got up a little before seven, so it wasn't that early.

"Claus, you need to calm down. Yes, I understand that you've been waiting all night . . . Claus!" Liam sat up, swinging his legs over the edge of the bed. "Yes, we're coming. Yes, to Tommerup Athletic Center. I just need to gather the weekend team together. The crew hasn't come in yet, but I've contacted them. Take a breath, have some coffee, and don't drive if you haven't slept. We're starting now, full speed ahead. Yes, I understand. Yes, I see. I'm hanging up now. Coffee, OK?"

"What was that?" Helene mumbled.

Liam lay back down, rolled over, and grabbed her. They had stuck with sleeping naked for all the years they had lived together, and his cock reacted the minute he felt her comforter-warmed skin against his own.

"Work."

"At six AM on a Saturday morning?"

"You know how it is!"

Helene turned around to face him. "I dreamt that we had a three-way with another man. It was pretty hot."

"Couldn't it be with another woman?" Liam suggested, and kissed her again.

"Are you saying you think I'm boring?" She suddenly sounded more awake now.

"No, nope! You were the one dreaming about branching out, not me," he said, right into her messy hair, before he let go of her to pull on the shorts he had left on the floor. Then he took his cell phone into the living room to call the morning watch. *Where has Charlotte Laursen's cell phone been during the last 24 hours? Do we know if she or her husband have any sort of mental illness? Have we ever had any contact with either of them due to domestic disturbances?*

Check on her bank account ASAP. Then he called Dea. *We're going out there to look around. She's still missing. You want to meet there?*

*   *   *

About an hour later, he was standing out behind Tommerup Athletic Center. The signs read *Fyrtårn Tommerup*, referring to Tommerup Lighthouse. From the back it looked mostly new—new multipurpose gym, new library, new main entrance. The old section of the building was most visible from the main road. The pool extended there along much of the building's length, facing the town. Back behind the center and to the right were woods. In front of the building and to the left was the town, comprising single-family homes built of brick or wood. Tall hedges. The road to the back of the athletic center and to the parking lot ran past a couple of fenced-in backyards and the edge of the woods. You couldn't be seen there from Tallerupvej, the main road, and there were several places where you couldn't be seen from the athletic center either. It wouldn't be a hard place to catch a woman off guard and chuck her into the back of a car, Liam thought. Charlotte Laursen could very well have been the victim of a crime.

"Good morning, boss!"

"Morning, Dea. You beat me here . . ."

"Yup, and thanks for making me work."

"Were you off?"

"Are we ever off?" she said with a sarcastic smile.

"It's not supposed to work like that. I could easily bring someone else in. Nass would be thrilled!"

"No need. It's fine, Liam. I'm pretty sure my two goldfish can handle a Saturday without me."

"You have goldfish?" He stared at her in surprise.

Dea ignored his teasing and instead pointed across the parking lot.

"The dog walker confirms that Charlotte has been here."

"So far, so good. Any new clues?"

"They say that things are pretty consistent with yesterday."

"What about the woods?"

"They're just getting started out there now."

"Her social media has been quiet since she left the athletic center. The last thing she posted was a picture on Instagram from her workout. I asked IT to run a digital trace of activity on the cell phone, activity on social media, credit card. We're running the full package."

"Has her cell phone been inactive since yesterday?" Dea moved over closer to him, and Liam nodded.

"Yes, it seems like it. I tried calling her this morning, and she didn't answer. That's why I called in the canine unit." He sucked in his lower lip and regarded Dea thoughtfully. "Couldn't you try to get in touch with someone from the school where she works? Coworkers? Students? That's not so easy on a Saturday, I know." He rubbed his red beard. "If we haven't found her by Monday morning, we need to be prepared to talk to all the students she teachers. We need to get the school to help us with that." He made eye contact, hoping she would understand that that would be up to her.

Dea Torp nodded. "Shouldn't we also have a new chat with Claus about their habits, daily routines, and such?"

"Yes," he agreed, although he felt a tad reluctant. It seemed intrusive when it was a person you knew. He studied the facade of the building. "Just give me a minute to look around, and then we'll head over there." He looked at his watch. It was 7:17. "I want to have people out on the streets here by the athletic center between seven forty-five and eight fifteen. We'll stop people who come by and find out if they came by here at the same time yesterday and if they saw anything unusual; and then we need to check any surveillance footage in town, around the school, and at the closest gas stations."

"It's Saturday," Dea pointed out, even though he had just said that. "The odds of people going the same way at the same time on the weekend that they did on Friday have got to be pretty small, right?"

"I know, but we'll do it anyway . . . and Monday and Tuesday morning, we'll do the same thing if . . ."

"All right." Dea cut him off and caved. "I'll get some people on it . . ."

Liam stood for a second watching his section leader walk away while he ran through what they knew about Charlotte's movements in his head. She had worked out, showered, and gotten dressed from 6:45 to 7:45 at her fitness club upstairs in the athletics center, and then she had taken the stairs down to the common area. She had posted a selfie when she came out of the locker room, and her Instagram profile showed a happy, smiling woman who had added a couple of strong-arm emojis under her picture. No one had seen her since then. She must have walked to the door to leave the building and then around the corner by Gym 1. Her bike should have been there, but it was out behind the buildings by that point. Zero windows, zero houses. Just asphalt, a tall yellow-brick wall, dumpsters, and the edge of the woods. There was just no way that would have been a normal place to put her bike, Liam thought.

The bike was still there. He pulled on a latex glove and carefully ran a hand over the handlebars. The bell had been knocked crooked, and one hand brake cable had come loose, but it looked like normal wear and tear. The tires were full of air.

He looked around, breathing deeply and slowly. He forced himself all the way down to concentration pace. There was nothing to see on the ground, no footprints or signs of struggle. The gravel lay as the rain had shaped it. The weeds hadn't been trampled. And no one would ever park a bicycle here. Charlotte wasn't lying in bed having a tryst with the blacksmith. Something had happened to her, and she hadn't been the one who had put her bicycle back here.

"Scotsman?"

One of the canine officers had come around the corner with his eager dog. "We found the husband in the woods."

"Charlotte Laursen's husband?"

"Yes, he's sitting in the canine patrol car now. We gave him some coffee. He's a complete wreck."

* * *

Claus was sitting in the back seat of the canine unit's patrol car with his legs out the side door and a cup of coffee between both hands. His hair was disheveled, and he was wearing the same clothes as the day before. His eyes were red and puffy.

Liam studied him for a moment. His son's water polo coach already looked like a shadow of his former self. It was either fear or guilt, he thought again, before continuing all the way over to the patrol car. Either was possible. Even so, experience told him that a person racked with guilt would often take pains to appear relatively normal in an attempt to hide things. Claus was not hiding anything.

The minute Charlotte's husband spotted Liam, he leapt to his feet.

"This should have happened yesterday," Claus blurted out accusingly. His eyes seethed, and he pointed angrily out toward the search going on in the woods.

"We didn't have enough to go on," Liam defended himself. "We simply cannot launch such a full-scale effort whenever a woman misses work. I'm afraid that's just the way it is, Claus."

"But for crying out loud, I told you she didn't just miss work! I told you something happened, a crime!"

"There are no witnesses and no indication that any law has been broken," Liam continued calmly. "If we were to respond to every case of a person who's been missing for a few hours, we would need to double our police force, and that's a conservative estimate."

"But this is different," Claus exclaimed angrily. "I explained it all to you yesterday. Charlotte would never leave Oliver hanging like that, never. I knew there was something wrong, but you wouldn't listen. You didn't do anything, and today it might be too late."

"I can't say anything other than what I've already told you, and as you can see, we're going all-in now."

"Yeah, twenty-four hours too late," Claus said hoarsely. "What do you want me to tell my kids? They're asking for their mom . . . they're crying. They don't understand why she hasn't come home." He looked at Liam, distraught.

"Where are your kids now?"

"At my parents' house. They don't live that far away." He shook his head. "Cille and Oliver can tell that something's wrong."

Liam put a hand on the man's arm. "Claus, we have child psychologists affiliated with our office in Odense. You just say the word, and we'll set you up with an appointment pronto."

Claus rubbed his eyes. "Thanks, but if you could find Charlotte pronto, that would be the best thing."

Liam nodded. "We have eight officers in Tommerup now, and we're doing everything we can to find your wife, I promise."

"So now you believe me? You think something happened to her too?"

"I think something isn't right. I can't say any more than that right now, but we'll be in touch, and you need to know that we're doing everything we can to get her back home to you." Liam looked over at the edge of the woods, where one of the canine officers had come into view and was waving him over. "I'm sorry; I need to go over there for a minute. You just sit for a bit, and I'll come back."

"Did they find her?" Claus yelled.

"No," Liam said. "If Charlotte were nearby, the dogs would have picked that up right away."

Claus sat back, crestfallen, and Liam walked over to the edge of the woods. The canine officer pointed without a word to an iPhone lying on the forest floor. The glass was broken, and the SIM card had been removed. Inside the phone's clear case was a picture of two young children. The younger one had Down's syndrome.

"We need to get that to forensics right away. Thanks." He waved Dea over to him and showed her the phone while the canine officer gestured to the criminalists.

"We'll start right away looking at all the surveillance footage from around the athletic center, and then I want some people to go upstairs to Fin Form and question the people working out and the staff."

"And what about the media? Should we formally announce that we're searching for her?"

Liam eyed Dea resolutely. "Yes."

*   *   *

Nassrin let herself lean back, tightening her grip on the control bar so that her nails dug into the hard rubber. The water beat hard under her butt as she bumped along over the surface, and seconds later she braced her feet, pushing the board down into the water below her for a moment. The wind grabbed hold of the kite over her, the lines tightened, and she let herself be pulled free of the water. Scattered clouds hovered over her in the deep-blue summer sky. She felt the wind on her cheeks and the fresh air in her nose. She breathed in hard, winded bursts and then relaxed her grip so that her body sank down into the water. The water settled coolly around her, and she let herself be pulled slowly into the shallow water by the kite.

She squeezed the water out of her hair and briefly considered walking over to the public bathroom to rinse off so the salt water wouldn't have a chance to dry fully before she got home and took a shower, but she abandoned that idea and put her hair up instead. Then she shook off the limp kite, noting how sore her arms and shoulders were. The wind had been a bit too strong, but that was how she liked it best. She stowed the unwieldy equipment in the back seat of her car and glanced over at the marina's grill bar, which shone black in the sunlight. The tables out in front of the restaurant were full of people eating and drinking. The Frisko ice cream signs glowed red and white. The smell of fried foods from the deep-fat fryer, which was working overtime, hung heavy in the air.

"What's up?" a young man hollered at her. He seemed drunk. And stupid. He was wearing swim trunks and a T-shirt and seemed unsteady on his feet. She had already heard him yell once when she walked by on her way to her car but hadn't really paid any attention until now, as he was coming toward her.

"You look super wet!" he shouted loudly, chuckling to himself. He reached out to steady himself on a table. His friends laughed along with him. She looked away from them and concentrated on packing up her car.

She could hear him going on but didn't respond.

"He's an idiot," mumbled an older man, who was standing close to her car.

She smiled and nodded. "I'm trying to ignore him."

"He's a mechanic," the man continued. "A local numbskull."

Nassrin took a drink from her water bottle, which had been sitting in the car. The water was warm.

"I wonder if his bark isn't louder than his bite?" she said.

She heard laughter and hollering behind them. Nassrin turn quickly and looked over toward the grill, where the drunk man had grabbed hold of a very young woman. His face glowed red and freckly under his blond hair.

"What's his name?" she asked.

"Dennis. He's an unpleasant guy."

"Do you two know each other?"

"I don't think so."

The girl squealed again and tried a little disinterestedly to get free from Dennis's grasp. It was impossible to tell if she was afraid or thought it was funny. Every now and then she laughed a shrill laugh.

Suddenly Dennis yanked her shirt up and squeezed one of her breasts hard.

"Hey!" Nassrin yelled. "Cut that out!"

Dennis let go of the woman's breast and glared at Nassrin. "What the hell do you want, you little Perker?"

Nassrin took a deep breath.

"Yup, that's him," the older man said indignantly. "No respect."

Over by the grill, another man had stood up to say something to him, but before he got that far, Dennis shoved him so hard in the chest that he tumbled onto a bench.

Nassrin grabbed a pair of zip ties from the package she kept in her car and ran over to him. It didn't seem like Dennis had noticed what was coming before Nassrin dropped him to the ground in a quick, practiced move, pressing one of his arms up against his back hard and pushing her knee down on the guy's other upper arm.

"Fuck off! What the hell are you doing, you disgusting pig?" he shouted, trying to kick at her, but his knee and the toes of his shoes just scraped in the gravel. Nassrin rested firmly on his back.

He tried to roll free, and she wrenched his arm even farther up his back. He screamed in pain. As he floundered, she dreaded spending time later with this idiot at the Assens police station filing a report. She was off duty and wanted to get home with her gear.

For a second she regretted having gotten involved, but then she caught sight of the young woman, who was sitting on a bench, crying. Nassrin relaxed her hold a little and grabbed Dennis's wrists instead. To his loud protests, she strapped his hands together behind his back with the ties.

A couple of his friends had moved in closer, and one of them started puffing out his chest and bad-mouthing her in Dennis's defense. Nassrin turned angrily to him and stuck out her police badge.

"Just zip it, would you!"

Dennis had rolled himself onto his side. He spat at her and said, "I'm gonna get you!"

"Yeah, just try it! Maybe you ought to just go home and sleep it off instead?"

"Fuck you. I'm going to report you for this!"

"For what?" she snarled at him. "For stepping in during a physical assault? Do you want a ride home, or do we need to swing by your local police station? You need to decide now, because I've got to run."

"Goddamn it!" A little of the brutality faded from Dennis's eyes, and he let his head sink down onto the gravel.

"Well, which one is it going to be?" Nassrin asked angrily.

"Home to bed," Dennis hissed.

*   *   *

"When we get inside," Nassrin said, "I'll cut the zip tie, and you will be as gentle as a lamb. Got it?"

"Yeah, yeah." Dennis shrugged in resignation. "But couldn't you cut them out here in the car? It's not cool to come home like this."

"You should have thought of that before you pumped yourself full of drugs . . ."

"I didn't take any fucking drugs," Dennis sneered.

"Yeah, right, sure, and your pupils are totally normal. Cool, it's all good."

"What business is it of yours?"

"You mean, what business is it of the police if you take drugs, stagger around, and act like an idiot?"

He looked down. "Can we cut them off or what?"

Nassrin turned off the engine and gave Dennis a tired look. She had been looking forward to the feeling of calmness she usually got after being out on the water, but here she was with this doofus. His pale skin had gotten way too much sun and gleamed pink and sweaty.

"I don't have anything to cut them with here," she lied. He wasn't going to get off that easily.

Dennis sighed in resignation and pointed over to the workshop. "There's something in there we can cut them with."

Nassrin got out and helped him out of the car.

"Well, come on!" She nodded over at the open door of a small, dark workshop with two car lifts. Only one had a car on it, but there were several cars outside, including a couple that looked essentially totaled.

"Yo, what up, Dennis!" yelled a middle-aged, beer-bellied man in blue overalls. He straightened up and wiped his hands on a bunch of cotton waste. "Have you gotten into S and M or something?" A thin, young guy behind him laughed. The floor was stained with decades of oil spots, and the smell in the room was intensely saturated with carbon monoxide, grease, and motor oil.

An empty beer can sat on a workbench next to a crumpled-up bag from a bakery.

"Does Dennis work here?" Nassrin asked, eyeing the two, who were now standing side by side next to the table.

"Yeah," the semi-thick one said. "But it's Saturday, so he's off." There was something mole-like about his eyes. The sun that made its way into the workshop clearly bothered him. He had oil on his face and made no attempt to hide the fact that he checked her out before taking a couple of steps forward and then over to her Fiat 500 parked out in front of the workshop. "Wouldn't you like some fancier rims on that little thing?"

She shook her head. "No thanks, but if you think you could cut a couple plastic zip ties here, that would be great."

"I can get you a set of nice rims for half price," the man continued, undaunted. "If you know what I mean." He winked at her rakishly.

"Would you shut up?" Dennis exclaimed loudly. "Why the hell do you think I'm wearing these ties? She's a cop, you idiot!"

The man inhaled through his nose and rubbed his palms over his canvas overalls. "It's just something I've got lying around, that's all."

The young guy behind them laughed nervously.

"I'm off duty," Nassrin said. "Cut him free and put him to bed, and I'll be out of here."

The man grabbed a big pair of pliers from a rusty tool chest. The wall behind the chest was covered with half-naked women from muscle car calendars.

"Let's see what we can do about that," he mumbled grudgingly.

The man spun Dennis around and cut the two zip ties in one go as he whispered a little too loudly, "You ought to be a little more careful picking your lady friends."

Nassrin ignored him and looked at Dennis.

"Behave properly next time you go out; otherwise you won't get away with just a scare."

"I'm not fucking scared!" Dennis sneered without looking at her.

"What are you saying?" She took a step toward him. "You want to take a trip to down to the drunk tank after all?"

"No," he grunted.

As Nassrin turned to go, she nearly crashed into a little old woman standing there with a large handbag and a plastic food-storage container in her hands.

"Dennis, have you seen Kasper today?" the woman asked, seeming not to have noticed what they had been doing.

"No, not since I went to bed."

"He's not up in his apartment," she continued, glancing over at the exterior staircase that led to the upstairs. "We were supposed to see each other."

Nassrin looked at the worn wooden staircase, which led up to a narrow landing on top of the garage building. The whole thing had probably been freshly painted fifteen to twenty years ago with white walls and blue trim, but now there were dark algae stains on the walls and the paint on the trim had flaked off and faded.

Dennis eyed the elderly woman a bit anxiously. "He's probably asleep. Maybe he just didn't hear you."

"I don't understand why he's not answering his door," the woman continued. "He doesn't usually forget our get-togethers." She looked down at the plastic container. "I brought an apple pie."

"Well, you can just leave that here," the one with the beer belly joked. His gut jiggled inside the blue fabric.

"I have no idea where he is," Dennis said tiredly and glanced at Nassrin. "I'm going to get going."

"Do you live nearby?" Nassrin asked, looking at the small woman. Her hair was gray. Her face looked friendly and wrinkled. Her eyes were small and blue.

"No, I'm from Hvidovre," she replied. "I'm Karen. Kasper is my grandson."

"Hvidovre?" Nassrin repeated, and called Dennis back. "Couldn't we help Karen see if Kasper is asleep up there? It's a long way to Hvidovre."

Dennis nodded grudgingly. "We've got keys to each other's apartments."

He unlocked the door, and they stepped into a short hallway that ended in a fairly dark room. The curtains were closed, and the floor was covered in clothes and food containers.

There was an opened sleeper sofa against one wall, and the place smelled stuffy, like smoke, greasy hair, and old food.

Karen seemed nervous and looked around at the mess, stunned.

Nassrin walked down the hallway and pushed open the door to the bathroom. The room was empty, and the air smelled mildewy and cold.

"I'm going back to my place," Dennis said.

"Wait a sec," Nassrin said, grabbing him. "Where else could he be?" She leaned over the bed and checked under the comforter. "How long have you been waiting, Karen?"

"Oh, well, I left home at seven thirty, so I got here around eleven."

"And it's one now," Nassrin said. She looked over at Dennis. "Does he have a girlfriend he might have spent the night with?"

"No, not at the moment."

"It's not like him," Karen repeated apprehensively. "It was his idea for me to come over today so we could see each other. He was also going to drive me to the train station in Odense after we were done talking. He's always the one who handles everything with the trains."

"Was there something specific you were going to talk about?" Nassrin asked.

Karen looked at her in surprise.

"Oh, I'm sorry," Nassrin said with a smile. "I'm with the police, so I ask a lot of questions."

"Oh, no. I think he just felt like I shouldn't be alone today. It's my birthday, you know?" Karen looked around the room again. "He's usually so tidy. I wonder if maybe something's wrong."

Nassrin pulled open a curtain. "I'm heading into Odense soon. You're welcome to come along. I could drop you off at the train station."

"That so nice of you, but that's all right. I want to give him a little more time. I assume he'll show up. And I suppose I can always tidy up the place a bit while I wait."

Nassrin smiled at her and then looked over at Dennis. "Go home and go to bed." She pulled out her cell phone to check the train times and connections to Hvidovre but was stopped by a couple of messages from Liam. Apparently they had gone to Tommerup early to get the search for Charlotte Laursen started, but he hadn't written to her until an hour ago. She gritted her teeth in disappointment. She would have gladly given up her kitesurfing to work on the case, and then she wouldn't have ended up at this garage in Assens either. "Let me just give you my number," she told Karen. "Call or text me when he shows up so that I know everything is OK. Otherwise I'll help you figure out the trains."

*　*　*

Beate smiled to herself as she glanced at Silje, who was sitting on a blanket in the grass just below the large wooden deck in the yard of the parsonage. The warm rays of sunshine sparkled down through the tree leaves, dappling the ground with patches of light in the little grove of trees at the far end of the yard. Most of the trees were much older than the big yellow-brick house, which now sat in the middle of the church's land. The trees had been planted when the old parsonage was built. That building had been moved to the Funen Village open-air museum in 1950, when it had needed to be either significantly modernized or frozen in time as an image of pastoral life from the 1800s.

"Mom?" Silje exclaimed, squinting into the sun. "What should I draw?"

"How about a bunny?" Beate tried.

The girl nodded. "Do you think baby sister can draw?"

Beate put a hand on her belly. "Sometimes I think she's already drawing in there, but it'll probably take a few years before you can draw together, right? Maybe you could help her?"

"Yeah." Silje looked at her mother's belly and seemed to make up her mind. "I'm going to make a drawing for baby sister."

"That's a good idea, sweetie."

"Do you think she likes bunnies?"

"I think she loves bunnies."

Beate drummed her fingers on the stack of older church bulletins on the table. It had been seventy years since the new parsonage was built, and she was going to write about that in the next bulletin. Neither the pastor she had replaced nor his grandfather, who had also served as pastor here, had lived in the old parsonage. She had considered talking to them but almost couldn't bear to. They hadn't exactly been welcoming when she took over the church after Johannes, as if she had been the one who kicked him out the door and not the congregation, who had decided that some newer, more modern energy was needed.

She turned when Peter turned up at the back door with Claus. Charlotte Laursen's husband looked like something the cat had dragged in. The last remnants of self-care he had clung to the day before had vanished overnight. She got up and walked over to meet them.

"Hi, Claus. Is there any news?"

"She's gone," Claus said dully. "And it seems like the police finally believe it now, that it's for real."

"And what about the kids?" Beate asked cautiously. "How are they?"

A moment of quiet and then, "They're with my parents."

Peter seemed embarrassed to witness the other man falling apart. He shuffled uneasily from foot to foot and then went back into the living room.

"I'm going to get back to work," he said.

Beate nodded and pointed to the picnic table. "Won't you sit for moment, Claus?" She glanced down at Silje, who was absorbed in her drawing.

Claus sat down heavily. "I have no idea what to do now."

"Keep it together," Beate said quickly. "Both for your own sake and for the kids." She hesitated, regarding the devastated man. The muscles in his face were trembling. His hands shook. "I heard that the police were very active around the gym this morning?"

"Yes, they were there with dogs and everything, but I'm afraid that it's too late. I mean, it's been twenty-four hours since she disappeared. They were also going to talk to some of the teachers and students from Charlotte's school, as I understood it."

He hid his face in his hands and moaned, "I can't bear it if something's happened to her . . ."

Beate felt a tingling sensation in her stomach.

"If you need help, Claus, please say so. Peter and I are here for you and the kids. The kids could stay here for a few days. That's not a problem at all."

"Thank you."

Beate was startled when Peter suddenly reappeared and Claus rose from his chair.

"What is it now?" Beate exclaimed in irritation, but immediately regretted her annoyance. They were supposed to cherish each other. Always.

"Someone's here from the nursing home," Peter said. "She's at the front door." He glanced over at Claus. "I didn't know what to do with her."

"You didn't let her in?"

"She didn't want to come in."

Beate got up and walked closely past him. He smelled like detergent. He had probably wiped his face with the same cloth he'd cleaned the car with.

"You chat with Claus in the meantime," she whispered to him.

A younger woman with dark hair was waiting outside. Beate recognized her from the Sydmarksgården nursing home, where she worked as a health care aide.

"Hi." The young woman smiled shyly and looked over her shoulder. "Your husband said that I should just come in, but I wasn't comfortable doing that."

"That's totally fine." Beate followed her gaze over toward their car. Peter had left the trunk open with the vacuum cleaner's tube and nozzle sticking out. She considered saying that she and Peter weren't married but thought better of it. "Have you had a death?"

"No," the young woman said quickly. "It's not that."

"Would you like to come in?"

"No, it's not a big deal. I just needed a little air, and so I drove over here instead of calling."

Beate nodded.

"It's Olga," the young woman continued. "She's refusing to eat, and I don't know if you remember her refusing to take her pills before?"

"Yes," Beate said hesitantly, and put a hand on her stomach. "What are you thinking?"

"We've been trying for several days now, but she's just stopped eating and won't listen to any of us."

"She didn't listen to me either that other time with the pills," Beate quickly said.

"No," the health care worker said cautiously. "But maybe Johannes or Ernst could talk to her?"

Beate sighed in exasperation. "Yes, Johannes was the one who got her to start taking her pills again last time, wasn't he? Why didn't you just go see him?" Again she felt inadequate compared to the previous pastor. And the pastor before him. The grandfather and the grandchild, they had been the pastors in Tommerup for as long as people could remember. Even though she had been the town's pastor for four years now, the former pastors were still the ones people needed.

"Johannes wasn't there, and Ernst was taking a nap after dinner."

A heavy feeling of discouragement spread through Beate. "I'm suppose I'll get ahold of one of them. Olga needs to eat, of course. Johannes will come and talk to her. I'll make sure of it." She tried to smile. She would call Johannes, and if he didn't answer his phone, then his mother, Mona. But first she needed to deal with Claus. She would suggest a visit to the church, where the organist was rehearsing. Listening to that always made her feel calmer.

*   *   *

"Johannes!" Mona looked over at the two men as they sat at the kitchen table with its checkered oilcloth, each holding a cup. The sun shone in through the curtain and drew colorful square spots on the walls of the low-ceilinged living room. "It's for you. From the church."

"The church?" Johannes repeated, and looked at his grandfather with his eyebrows raised. He sounded relieved.

"I mean, really, she can't do anything by herself," Ernst said, a tad too loudly, and shrugged.

"No," Johannes agreed, and picked up the handset of the old landline phone in the kitchen. He cleared his throat. "This is Johannes . . . Yes . . . Yes, I see . . . Yes, of course . . . Yes, I'll talk to her. Don't mention it . . . Anytime."

"Well?" Ernst exclaimed, after Mona had hung the phone back up. His gray hair stuck up, and his long, bony face was thick with wrinkles. He looked insistently at Johannes. "Couldn't you say something other than *yes* to that woman?"

"It's Olga," Johannes explained. "She won't eat, and they think it might help her to talk to me."

"Far be it from me to understand what the parish council wanted with that pastor," Ernst scoffed. "She can't even comfort an old woman. No, they should have kept Johannes on." He pointed indignantly at his daughter, as if she bore sole responsibility for the parish council's decision.

"Hey, I voted for Johannes too," Mona said quietly, avoiding eye contact with her father and instead fixing her gaze on her adult son. "You know that."

"I hardly know what to believe," Ernst grumbled. "The way the two of you were running around in the parsonage, you would think you'd forgotten that my church was taken away from us."

"That's enough, Dad," Mona pleaded. She kept looking at her son, but Johannes did not come to her rescue.

She turned and walked over to the kitchen table and stood for a second with her back to them before she raised her head and once again turned to her father. "I've been the verger here in town for more than forty years. You don't want me to stop because there's a new priest, do you?"

Ernst eyed her angrily and tapped his fingertips hard on the table. "That church was ours for more than sixty years, and now I'm just supposed to sit here and accept that all we have left of my post is a verger?"

Mona turned around again, set a couple of plates a little roughly in the sink, and turned on the water.

"Are you going over to the church now?" Johannes asked his mother's dismissive back.

"I suppose it's time to go unlock it for the public," she said without looking up from the sink. "If the organist is done rehearsing, that is."

"I'll come with you," Johannes said.

"Now?" she said, letting the water drip from a plate before setting it to dry in the rack by the sink. "What about Olga?"

"First I want to hear if they said anything else to Beate before I drive over to the nursing home."

"*Beate*," Ernst grumbled with a frown. "A . . . a hippie pastor with spaghetti in her pockets. Is that really what the church has to offer nowadays? Spaghetti church services?"

Mona put a hand on her father's shoulder with a sigh of resignation. "You mustn't get all worked up like this, Father. It's not good for your health."

He stared angrily straight ahead. "And then those thin dresses. It's indecent!" He turned stiffly to Johannes. "I don't care how you do it, but you have to get the church back for us. We can't be known for having that incompetent woman bleating to our flock!"

"There, there," Mona said tiredly, and gave her father's shoulder another light squeeze. It was bony and tough. "I'll be back again for dinner."

Ernst glanced grumpily over at Johannes, who got up to follow his mother. "Make sure you're not too thorough when you read through her sermon. The parish council will notice if there are any little errors!"

"I'm doing my best, Grandpa," Johannes said quietly while avoiding eye contact with Ernst.

"No," came the firm response. "You're not, because then you wouldn't have lost the church."

"That's enough," Mona interjected. "Let's go."

Johannes stepped out the back door and looked around at the courtyard and the worn stables while Mona found her purse and changed into her outdoor shoes. One of their now too-numerous peacocks strutted by in the courtyard. It made a long, shrill cry. Two others replied from nearby. Johannes's great-grandparents had bought a pair of the exotic peacocks way back when, and they had been terrorizing the neighborhood with their cries ever since.

Mona took hold of her son's arm as they began walking between the stable buildings on the way to the narrow footpath that led back behind their house to the yard of the parsonage and the church.

Johannes walked out in the long grass while Mona followed the path that Ernst had traveled between the farm and the church for sixty years. It was a narrow track, formed by one man's heavy footsteps day after day, year after year, decade after decade.

"I don't think Father will ever forgive us for the business with the church," Mona said, feeling heavy at heart.

"No." Johannes glanced at the large slurry tank in the field to their right. Its walls were solid concrete. A thick plastic tarp was pulled down over it. The smell of the manure was a bit pungent. A couple of fat pigs lay in front of it. They had eleven total.

"If only he could be a little more like you," she continued. "You forgave the parish council quickly and are good at making things work with Beate."

Johannes sighed tiredly. The dry grass blades crunched beneath his shoes.

Mona had a firm grip on his arm. "Did you hear about that woman from town who disappeared?"

"No?"

"The sexton told me about it last night. I recognized the name. It was her, that woman who wrote about Christianity at the school for the local paper and all that."

"What's her deal?" Johannes scoffed.

"I don't know. Henning just said that he'd heard that the woman's children were at Beate's place most of the evening while Peter was out helping the husband look for her."

"Did they have some kind of falling-out?" Johannes asked.

"Yes, that's probably it," Mona said with a nod, and turned off the path. "But there was a big police turnout in town this morning."

* * *

The church rose, beautiful and white, against the gray-blue sky. As soon as Johannes stepped through the church's low doors, he heard the organ and allowed the notes to spread through his body for a moment. Then he slowly walked down the interior length of the church and sat down behind the only person sitting in the pews. He leaned forward a little. "Are you finding peace?"

Claus slowly turned to him, and there was no mistaking his ravaged face. "No."

Johannes compassionately placed a hand on his shoulder.

"I empathize with you, and I'll pray for you tonight."

* * *

Nassrin rolled her sore shoulder.

"Does it hurt?" Dea asked.

Nassrin quickly looked up. "No."

"Is that from kitesurfing?" She had done some kitesurfing herself when she was young and could still remember the stretch in her shoulder muscles and the stiffness that would settle in like a band underneath the shoulder blade.

"It doesn't hurt," Nassrin maintained.

"No, no, that's what we'll say, but I'm certainly capable of spotting an overworked shoulder when I see one," Dea said, and added, "Take care of yourself. We benefit from you most when you're in peak condition, right?"

Nassrin looked down at the desk. "As long as I'm just sitting here entering data, my condition is excellent," she retorted.

Dea was about to put her in her place, but she regarded her younger colleague for a moment while contemplating whether this was worth devoting energy to. Then she leaned over the desk a little in an attempt to get through to her.

"You simply need to understand that you have to be a little more cooperative if you want to get ahead in this system. Talk to the rest of us. Become one of us if you're planning on a career here and dream of rising through the ranks. You've got to show up, be yourself. There's something to the notion that you have to crawl before you can walk. You young people are so busy, you want everything in half the time. Have a bit of patience and observe. Learn from the rest of us."

"That's a little hard when I'm never allowed to go anywhere with you guys," Nassrin said, maintaining eye contact with the section leader.

Dea sighed and flung up her hands. "That grumpy attitude isn't going to get you anywhere. Believe me, I've tried. And look where I ended up!"

"Didn't you choose to be here?" Nassrin asked. It seemed as if she couldn't quite figure out whether what had just been unloaded on her was encouragement or a scolding.

"Yeah, you're right. Ultimately I chose to be here," Dea admitted. "I'm just trying to say that things come easier if you're amenable and cooperative. No one can stand a crabby bitch."

"And that's what I am?" Nassrin spluttered. "A crabby bitch?"

"No, no, that's not what I meant." Dea headed her off quickly. The last thing she needed was for the younger officers to start complaining about her to management for putting them down. "What I'm trying to say is that *I* used to act like a crabby bitch. You don't get far that way, at least not very quickly. So do yourself a favor and set aside the jilted attitude, then people will be more interested in bringing you along when they go out into the field." She gestured toward the window and everything beyond. "Getting to know each other might even be pretty interesting."

"How far have you gotten with the business in Tommerup?" Nassrin couldn't control her curiosity.

"That's a really messy case," Dea admitted, and turn toward her desk. She picked up a couple of sheets of paper but then tossed them down again. "Or I don't know if it's a case at all, but his wife seems to have disappeared."

Nassrin had gotten up and come over to Dea's desk.

"Liam's out there now," Dea continued. "They're talking to the husband, and then they're going to search the house . . . you know."

Nassrin nodded. "And what will you do?"

"I'll take a look at everything we have on Charlotte Laursen, even if it's not much." She pointed at the papers.

"And what do we have?"

Dea managed to restrain herself when she felt the urge to send her coworker back over to her own desk.

"They have a little son with Down's syndrome, but otherwise there's no history of illness or mental health problems in the family.

No unusual changes to their habits. No changes in their financial behaviors. No atypical cell phone history." She looked up. "There's nothing that suggests we're dealing with a planned disappearance, and unfortunately, the destroyed cell phone also points toward a crime. Liam seems more and more certain that something happened to Charlotte."

"If there's anything I can do," Nassrin offered, and it was clear that she was trying to make it sound casual, "then just let me know, OK?"

"Sure, but there's really . . . hold on," Dea said, then, "Couldn't you do the rounds with your network?"

"My network?"

"Yeah, all the boys there from the index cards. If there's someplace where the jungle drums are sounding, then it'll be in those circles. They know everything. Maybe someone has heard something about Charlotte. Why don't you try prodding them a little?"

Dea could tell that wasn't exactly what Nassrin had been fishing for, and once again she looked as if she felt she was being treated unfairly.

"I'm being totally honest," Dea said. "That would actually be a big help, and it could well bring us a lead."

Nassrin nodded, and just then her cell phone rang. Dea heard her ask if the grandmother was still there before she stepped so far away that Dea couldn't follow the conversation anymore. But a little while after that, she came back and announced that she was ready to go make the rounds asking about Charlotte. "You're right. Maybe they know something."

"Exactly," Dea said with a smile. "Taken all together, that 'cousin network' probably knows about pretty much every single criminal infraction that takes place anywhere on the island of Funen."

Nassrin didn't respond, just grabbed her sunglasses and car keys from her desk and disappeared out the door.

* * *

Just under three hours later, Nassrin was standing out in front of the little auto mechanics' workshop in Assens. She got out of her car and walked over to the doors with their little panes of glass. She had almost forgotten how worn down the place was. Either the owner was blind to the wear and tear and dirt, or he didn't care.

"Hello? Is anybody here?" She stuck her head in the open door and looked around. There was still a car raised up on one of the lifts, and the smell of oil and exhaust was the same as before.

The place seemed deserted, but the light was on. She just couldn't understand the complete lack of order. It was the exact opposite of her uncles' tidy bookstore, where they knew precisely where every single book belonged. *Mr. Potbelly and the others must waste a ton of time every day searching for tools that aren't where they're supposed to be,* she thought. An overfilled ashtray sat in the middle of the workbench, and the acrid stench of cigarette butts was overwhelming. Next to that were several crumpled-up candy wrappers and a fifty-kroner note rolled up into a little tube, which she guessed had been used to snort drugs through.

"Hey!"

She looked up and over at the open door that led to a back room.

"So, did you want new rims after all?" Mr. Potbelly laughed conspiratorially. He stuck his hands into the pockets of his filthy overalls. "Or did you just miss us?"

"No," Nassrin said with a polite smile. She hadn't gotten anything out of her visits with her "network" in Vollsmose—no one had heard of either Kasper or Charlotte. They could be lying, which they did often, but she felt fairly sure they weren't this time.

They always seemed more awkward and "ghetto" whenever they were hiding something.

Her eyes lingered on the man's filthy overalls for a minute. He was sweating. His face was shiny, and he pretty much looked like he had just climbed off a step machine or been lifting something heavy. "Are Dennis or Kasper here?"

"No," he said quickly, and pulled the door behind him shut.

"Don't you ever wear a uniform?"

"What do you mean?" She looked puzzled.

"You're with the police, right?"

"Yeah, but I'm an investigator, and we often wear civilian clothes."

He gazed overtly up at one of the naked women on the wall. Nassrin ignored his subtle provocation.

"Have you seen Kasper today?"

He itched his thick neck and shook his head.

"Just Dennis, and he's out again . . . went for a walk."

"Out drinking?"

"Yeah."

"Thanks. Do you know if Kasper's grandmother is still waiting for him upstairs in the apartment?"

"What do I care?" He shrugged.

"Fair enough. I'm going to go up and check." She hesitated a minute. "If you hear from Kasper, contact us right away, OK?"

"Yeah, yeah . . ."

She looked down at him and then went back out the door. She could feel his eyes on her body. She had secretly hoped that Kasper had returned, that his grandmother was happy, and that all was well so she could get to the marina and go for an evening spin out on the water. But there was something about this whole thing that didn't feel right.

Karen opened the door right away when Nassrin knocked on the pane of mottled glass in the door. The scent that hit her was much better than last time. Kasper's grandmother had cleaned every nook and cranny, and the place smelled like soap and cleaners.

"You came back!" Karen lit up at the sight of Nassrin.

"Yes, I just wanted to make sure that you weren't left all on your own. I understand your grandson hasn't come home yet."

"I just don't understand it. It's really not like him." Karen apologized and explained that her cell phone had run out of power. "I usually use Kasper's charger, but I can't find it." She looked at Nassrin. "It was dumb of me to leave mine at home, but it just didn't occur to me that . . ."

She stopped.

"So you haven't heard from him?" Nassrin ascertained.

Karen shook her head. Her eyes filled with tears. "I'm worried about him. Something must have happened. I don't understand where he could be."

"What do his parents say? Does he have any siblings in the area?"

Karen sighed and shook her head again. "His parents moved to Indonesia last year. I still don't understand them. Kasper didn't want to go, but his little brother is with them out there." She looked up. "They haven't heard from Kasper either, if that's what you were wondering. I had a chance to call them before my phone ran out of battery."

"So Kasper's only got you?"

"Yes." She looked away and squeezed a bit of the fabric from her dress between her fingers.

Nassrin looked out at her little Fiat, which was parked down below. There definitely wasn't going to be any windsurfing this evening.

* * *

Liam looked at the board in the meeting room, where some of the Reactive Department had gathered for a briefing. The coffee cup that said *YES PLEASE!* sat half-empty in his hand.

"We have four possibilities right now: One, Charlotte decided to disappear on her own. Two, she was the victim of an accident we don't know about yet. Three, she was abducted against her will. Four, she's dead. We've got murder, an accident, and suicide as options, of course, and if she's dead, then we'll take it from there, but at the moment there just isn't that much that points in that direction, and there also isn't much indication that she has been the victim of a crime. The only clues we have are her destroyed cell phone and her abandoned bicycle. No witnesses appear to have seen anything to support that theory." He paused and looked around at the small investigative group, which consisted of Dea, a couple of other officers, and a man from the canine patrol unit. "On the other hand, it's been thirty-three hours now since she was last seen, se we need to consider the possibility that a crime may have occurred." Liam looked right at Dea. In addition to creating an overview of Charlotte's movements and digital traces, the section leader was gathering all reports. He had realized a long time ago that the more work he piled on her desk, the less energy she devoted to trying to put herself into his managerial chair. "What's the status on the surveillance footage in Tommerup?"

"We haven't found anything unusual in the local footage, and the camera at the athletics center was gummed up with dirt and old leaves. We can't rule out that the leaves wound up there from the wind and weather, but we also can't rule out that someone intentionally covered the camera lens and made it look as if it had happened naturally."

"And no one observed any unusual movements around the camera or the athletic center's buildings? People who don't usually hang around there?"

"No, unfortunately not."

"Well then, what could have happened?" Liam got up.

"She could be with another man," Dea suggested.

"Yes," Liam said, and wrote that on the board. "Anything else?"

"She could have run off," someone else contributed.

"Yes, good." Liam wrote that down. "For that one, we just have the challenge that nothing about her movements suggests that. There weren't any atypical movements in her bank account prior to yesterday morning, and no unusual purchases recently. She hadn't packed anything other than clothes for the day. She loves her children very much."

"She could also have been assaulted," Dea said.

"Yes, that's one of the more likely scenarios." Liam wrote the theory on the board and turned to his team again. "The broken cell phone without a SIM card could indicate that something happened that someone wants to hide, but we don't know if it was her or someone else who destroyed the phone, since the only fingerprints on it belong to her and Claus and their kids."

One of the younger officers raised his hand.

"There are notes on your desk with messages from citizens, and there is actually one from someone who thinks Charlotte was unfaithful to Claus, but she couldn't give us a name of the third party."

"Good. Follow up on that."

"Now?"

"Yes, get going."

"She certainly could have run off with a man," Dea said, nodding thoughtfully. "Falling in love can make people do the most irrational things."

"Or she could have been caught being unfaithful and then accidently killed. Or killed on purpose," Liam said, thinking about the signals he had had trouble interpreting when Claus had visited the police station the previous night.

"So we primarily have our sights on the husband right now?" Dea summarized.

"Yes, we're keeping a sharp eye on him, and we'll bring him in for formal questioning tomorrow. We should also send some people around to their social circle and question anyone who might know about how things stand between Charlotte and Claus."

*   *   *

"You seem a little distracted today," the older woman in the armchair said to Johannes. "Would you like some more coffee?"

"I'm sorry, Olga." Johannes shook his head kindly. "And no thank you. I still have some." He took an adult sip of his coffee and leaned forward slightly. "What's going on with you? Why won't you eat?"

"Oh, Johannes, you're a good man, but you're so young."

"Forty-six isn't that young, is it?"

"When you're ninety-two it is, and I'm tired, Johannes. I want to be called home."

"But, Olga, that's not up to you to decide."

The old woman squirmed slightly uneasily in the chair.

"Sometimes I think maybe I was supposed to die when those youngsters attacked me."

"Olga, you mustn't think like that," Johannes said, and took her hand. Some young men had broken into Olga's place way back when, knowing that her husband had just died. After the assault, she was no longer able to manage the farm on her own and had ended up selling it. "That was a terrible blow to you, Olga, but you mustn't let it break you."

"I still think I should have been called home to God then," Olga said quietly.

Johannes released her hand and got up. "Wouldn't you like to come to the sing-along? My grandfather came along to join you all."

"He did?" Olga exclaimed, lighting up.

The aroma of coffee and sweet kringle pastry filled the large, light room. Elderly people and several staff members were seated around the tables. They had big smiles on, and in the middle of the room, surrounded by the tables, Ernst danced a very slow waltz with one of the oldest women in the nursing home while singing "The Earth Adorned in Verdant Robe."

His deep voice resonated clear and pure within the white walls. The windows were open, and the warm evening air made the light curtains flutter. Ernst helped the old woman back to her chair with an elegant flourish as he continued the hymn full force. *All flesh must die, each bloom to hay. Though they perish, the Word shall stay.*

Olga clutched Johannes's elbow, smiling at the improvised dance floor. She sat down in a vacant chair and accepted a cup of coffee and a slice of cake.

Johannes watched her with a glimmer in his eye as she began to divide her cake into smaller pieces with her little dessert fork. Her eyes on his singing grandfather, she slowly began to eat. He knew it, knew it with every cell in his body: Ernst was The Pastor, the pastor everyone had loved and still loved. Even now his mere presence had helped Olga—that was evident—and knowing that helped Johannes a little as his grandfather's clear voice crept around his throat like a freshly starched pastor's ruff: *Yea, Christ the Word breathes life from death. And love renewed greens heav'n and earth. The world, Thou Jesu makest right. In summer dawns thy endless light.*

* * *

Dea smacked her shin as hard as she could into the punching bag. Her veins stood out thickly just beneath her skin. Her clothes stuck to her body. She spun around and hammered her foot into another punching bag that was secured to both the floor and the ceiling so it offered maximum resistance.

She had been working out ever since the police academy, but it wasn't until after Mogens had died in her arms that she had started doing it so often. She hadn't been able to save his life. She also hadn't been able to be there for their daughter after his death. She was a loser. She kicked again and groaned, winded. She was a weak loser that no one could trust.

Right before her training session, she had received a text message from Nassrin, sent to both her and Liam. *I think there's another person missing, a young man from Assens. I've been there several times. His cell phone has been dead since this morning. That's the same with Charlotte too, isn't it?*

The girl's need to be seen was intolerable. Dea did a half spin and hammered her leg into the bag at full force. There was nothing that irked her like young assistant interns. Many of them had no respect for the time it took to gain experience and get to know the profession. This business with Nassrin could well become a problem she would need to discuss with Liam. She didn't have the slightest doubt that Nassrin would make a good officer; she was eager and hungry for it. It was just that no good ever came from running around and making up your own cases like that.

Breathlessly, Dea leaned over forward with her hands on her knees, panting. She closed her eyes for a second and pictured the young Syrian woman and wondered what the hell Nassrin had been doing in Assens several times that day where she would even know about the dead phone.

Day 3—Sunday

H E SMELLED THE misty morning air coming in through the rolled-down windows and listened attentively to the calm, slow footsteps approaching his hiding place. At around 5:50 AM, the old man used to turn the corner onto the deserted road. He always walked his dog on Sunday morning after he finished his night's work.

He peeked out at the wild, overgrown bush that effectively hid the car he was sitting in. There they came, the thin, slightly stooped man and his golden retriever. They walked by the bush without noticing the slightest thing. The dog was just as old and skinny as the man, but it still tugged on the leash and was happy to sniff around.

Those two had been taking the same walk for years, and for the last year they had been observed without their knowing it by several small cameras that had been put up along the route. He glanced at the three live feeds on his cell phone screen. There wasn't a soul nearby.

The house on the other side of the unpaved road was abandoned. The next building was fifty meters farther down the gravel road—a shuttered plastics factory, completely abandoned. From there the road wound onward through an open section of meadow.

On the seat beside him sat the file with the old man's data, gathered over fifty Sundays, when just like today the man and his dog had gone for their usual morning walk without encountering anyone. That was over now. In a few minutes, the dog would smell a piece of meat, and a few seconds after that it would collapse, drugged.

He closed his journal, his face expressionless, and glanced one last time at the live stream from his hidden surveillance setup before starting up the dilapidated dark-blue Ford. The car had been sitting at this abandoned house for more than twenty years, and it had taken him several days to get it running.

He slowly backed out of his hiding spot and calmly followed the potholed gravel road. Not far ahead, the man was kneeling next to his dog, who was lying on the ground. The stooped man waved his arms unhappily to get the car to stop.

He slowly pulled over to the side and got out.

"Is your dog OK? Do you need some help?"

"A cell phone . . . Do you have a cell phone?" The old man seemed shocked.

"Of course." He approached and pulled his cell phone out of his pocket. He was standing quite close to the old man now. "Would you like me to make a call for you?"

The man looked up at him, desperate, and only now seemed to recognize who he was. Then the old man nodded gratefully and bent back down over his dog.

"Who would you like me to call?" he asked, momentarily enjoying the old man's utter despair.

"That veterinarian in Brylle never answers his phone . . .
Borreby Vet Clinic . . ." It seemed like the man was talking to
his dog, but then he straightened up. "Can you find the number?
No, give me your cell phone, and I'll make the call." The old man
sounded impatient now.

He handed over his phone. The man took it with trembling
hands. When he saw the picture glowing on the little screen, he
froze midmotion and sat completely still for a moment, staring at
the screen. Then the old man looked up, confused.

"What is this?"

"The dying."

"What is that supposed to mean?" the old man exclaimed in
confusion, standing back up unsteadily, his eyes still glued to the
little screen. "Is that the woman, Charlotte, who's missing? Why
do you have . . ." He seemed to get stuck. "I don't understand . . ."

*   *   *

Liam tossed his case file on the table in a resigned motion.

"What's up?" Dea said, looking at him in surprise.

"There's a special meeting tonight for the Tommerup Water
Polo board, and guess who's on the board? Great timing, really
great."

"It's rough, having kids." She laughed, shaking her head.

"They're more demanding than fish and chickens anyway. And
if it weren't for my son, I really wouldn't care about national team
player drafts. But Andreas has been dreaming of being picked, and
he's worked hard for it."

"Your son's going to be on the national team?" She sounded
surprised.

"Yup!" For a second Liam felt a little awkward about his
own obvious pride. "He's been on U16 a few times, but the leap
to U17 is big, and they have a training session next Tuesday and

a club match on Saturday—both will determine whether anyone from Tommerup Water Polo will play on U17 at a tournament in Switzerland next month."

"Impressive." Dea found a stick of chewing gum in her bag and rocked back and forth in her chair. "And Charlotte Laursen's husband is the coach, so maybe he's responsible for making the selections?"

"Yeah. I doubt anyone will go if Claus ends up bowing out after all this stuff with Charlotte. There isn't much money in water polo, so it's not like there's another coach waiting in the wings if Claus backs out."

"So you're going to discuss that tonight?" Dea asked.

"Yes. I'm assuming that's what the meeting is about. So Andreas will kill me if I don't attend and 'fight for his future,' as he put it this morning."

Liam could tell he was blathering, but he needed to vent a little. He still hadn't managed to find a way to achieve equilibrium when his job kept him from being there for his family. He used to brush it off by focusing on the fact that his two worlds collided only now and then, but this wouldn't be the first time that he was forced to focus on an investigation.

"It's just that this week in particular is the most important of the year, according to my son."

The door opened, and the others started trickling in for the morning briefing.

Liam surveyed the faces in the room while Dea sat up straighter in her chair. Then he held up two fingers.

"Good morning. It's been two days now since Charlotte Laursen was last seen, and we are gradually coming to terms with the likelihood that she either has been abducted, is lying dead somewhere, or will turn up twenty years from now on some missing-persons reality TV show when her children track her down somewhere in

Vietnam." He drummed his fingers on the board next to a picture of Charlotte and Claus, thinking. "The husband is off the hook. He was with the daycare teacher a few minutes past eight, and there is no possible way that he—with their children in the car—could have been at the gym at seven fifty to kill or abduct his own wife."

"But that doesn't mean they couldn't have had serious disagreements," Dea broke in.

"No," Liam said. "It just means that he couldn't have committed a crime against her just before eight. Since she was seen leaving Fin Form at seven fifty, some third party could have delayed her on her way to school. If Claus did it, he would have run into her after that and committed the crime after he dropped their daughter off at a little past eight."

"OK," Dea said, "but let's assume that Claus discovered that Charlotte was cheating on him. He's furious, so he waits at the school, where she doesn't show up. He drives to the gym to look for her—on those deserted residential streets—and bam, she's lying there. She fell while riding her bike. He takes her with him. He's out of his mind and ends up hurting her, maybe by accident. Then he panics, stashes her off the road, and returns her bike to the gym."

"I think that seems unlikely, and we have no indication of infidelity or problems in their marriage," Liam said. "But let's hold on to that theory. No matter what, our suspicion that a serious crime has occurred is enough to obtain cell-site location information, so I think we ought to get going on that." He nodded at two officers. "Will you handle that?"

"So an overview of all of the cell phones registered at phone towers in and around Tommerup?" one of the officers asked. He had red cheeks and looked young and inexperienced.

"Yes, exactly." Liam gave him an encouraging smile.

The door opened, and they were interrupted by a colleague, who sent Liam a serious look. "We just received a report—an elderly man is missing in Tommerup. He disappeared early this morning while he was out walking his dog. The dog came home alone, and there's no sign of the man."

"Do we have a more precise time?" Liam asked. Everyone in the room had turned to face the doorway.

"Between five thirty and six thirty AM, according to his wife."

"No," Liam blurted out sharply as a murmur began to spread. He could clearly sense Dea's gaze drilling into him. "We have no way of knowing whether there's any connection at all between this report and Charlotte Laursen."

He looked around at his little flock, and they quieted down. "Let's keep our noses to the ground. But"—he turned to the two who were going to obtain the cell data—"let's expand the search to include a window from a little before eight Friday morning to this morning between five thirty and six thirty, OK?"

He gestured for the man in the doorway to enter and asked him to come up to the board and share what he knew about the old man who had been reported missing.

"Verner Nissen, age seventy-three. His wife, Lis, called it in."

"Did anything happen before he left the house?" Dea asked. "Was he depressed or anything?"

The man shook his head apologetically. "We haven't spoken to the woman who made the report yet. We asked her to come in later so we can open a case if he still hasn't shown up."

"How far is it from where Charlotte Laursen disappeared to where the wife thinks her husband was?" Dea asked, and when the officer couldn't answer that, she turned to Liam. "Do you know?"

"If he disappeared from down in town, it probably isn't much more than a hundred meters," he replied, picturing the area just around the athletic center.

"We'll talk to Lis ourselves," Dea decided, without looking at Liam. "We need to know everything there is to know about her husband."

Liam nodded, and he could feel the tension in the room when he expanded the morning briefing by announcing that today's tasks now involved two missing-person reports. He asked a couple of his people to pull information about the missing dog walker and quickly put together a team that would take him out to the missing man's home. Then he nodded to Dea, who was already ready to leave. As the team started exiting the room, it finally sank in that he was going to miss the water polo club's board meeting.

*   *   *

Liam looked up at the older two-story redbrick building. He had been told that at one time the lower floor had been a little grocery store, but the whole thing had been converted into a home now. One side of the building was only one story tall because the ground was so sloped. He figured the builders must have excavated to make room for the lower floor so the grocery store would be level with the street that ran through town.

A team of officers were now examining the building and the surrounding area, and Liam had sent two patrols into town to search for Verner Nissen and stop people on the street to find out if anyone had seen anything unusual.

Verner's wife, Lis, had carefully described to them the route that Verner usually took on his dog walks, and they had started by thoroughly searching the route to make sure he wasn't lying out there having had a heart attack or something.

Liam had a bad feeling. He looked down at the little slip of paper that had triggered the large police response. It now sat in a sealed transparent bag. It read:

O you who believe! When the call is made for prayer on
Friday, then hasten to the remembrance of Allah and leave off
traffic; that is better for you, if you know. But when the prayer
is ended, then disperse abroad in the land and seek Allah's
grace, and remember Allah much, that you may be successful.

"Boss?"

Holding a pad of paper in her hand, Dea was standing with Lis. A crime scene technician was behind them finishing an inspection of the front door, where the slip of paper had been wedged. Liam had ordered a thorough investigation of the whole area around the building. He didn't like that she had called him *boss*, especially not where other people could hear her, because there was no doubt that she had said it with a sizable dollop of sarcasm.

"Do you want to join in?" Dea continued impatiently, when he hesitated.

"Yes, please!" Liam ran a hand through his red hair. The sun was broiling and he was melting in his dark leather jacket, but he didn't want to take it off, because he was wearing a washed-out T-shirt underneath.

"How many years has it been since you closed the store?" he asked, walking over to Lis.

"Seven years," the grocer's wife replied quietly. She rubbed her hands worriedly, as if she had been accused of killing her husband. "The big supermarkets took all our customers, you know."

"Did your husband agree with that decision?" Dea interjected.

"Yes, for the most part. It was such a long time ago now," she replied. Her eyes wandered as she almost manically fidgeted with her wedding ring. "What could have happened to him?"

"Unfortunately, it's too soon to say." Liam tried to keep her from breaking their eye contact. There was definitely something she wasn't telling them about her husband, but he couldn't tell what it might be.

"It really isn't like him to let the dog go like that," she continued nervously. "Do you think he's dead?"

"Why would he be dead?" Dea quickly asked.

Lis shrugged reluctantly and gazed down at the sidewalk. "That other lady who disappeared last Friday hasn't turned up again either. People are saying she's probably dead. So I just thought . . ."

"It's much too soon to draw those kinds of conclusions. We can't know if the two cases are even related," Liam said quickly, stuffing the little evidence bag with the slip of paper into his jacket pocket. "It may sound awful, but people disappear all the time, and unfortunately, people have the right to disappear."

"But surely not just like this?" Lis said. She had a firm grip on her forearm. "Verner has taken Lady on that same walk for nine years. He loves that dog." Her voice was trembling.

"Have you lived here in town for a long time?" Dea asked.

Liam pulled his leather jacket out a little. Dea had been smarter than him and had shown up in more summery attire plus her standard white running shoes.

"Verner was born here," Lis replied in a reverent tone, as if it were a sign of nobility to be an authentical local.

"So he knew people in town?" Liam tried.

"Yes, certainly. From the store and because he was active in Tommerup Water Polo for so many years."

"He was?" Liam exclaimed in surprise.

Lis thought it over. "Why yes, for well over forty years, I should think. Both as a player and then as a coach."

"Do you know if Verner knows Claus Laursen? He's the club's current coach."

"Yes, he does. Claus took over from Verner way back when."

"Do they know each other well?"

"I don't think so." Lis deflated a little.

"Do you know if Verner also knew Claus's wife, Charlotte?" Dea asked.

"No, I don't think so," Lis said. "If they did, it would have been from the store, and Verner closed that years ago."

"How long did you run the grocery store?" Liam asked.

"Thirty-one years. I'm quite sure about that," Lis said, with pride in her voice.

"So Verner was a relatively familiar face in town?"

"Yes. That was also why . . ."

Liam tugged again at his jacket a bit—his T-shirt was practically drenched. "Why what?"

"Verner was angry the last few years we operated the store." Lis regarded Liam sadly. "People who had been shopping with us forever disappeared from one day to the next and only rarely came in for little things . . . or at night."

"What was that last bit about night?" Liam asked attentively, and noticed immediately how she looked away.

"Well . . . ," Lis mumbled hesitantly. "Verner liked to sell a bit on Friday and Saturday nights, and back when shops were required to be closed on Sundays, he also sold out the back door, as he put it."

"You mean illegal sales?" Dea said.

"Ye-e-e-es." She dragged the word out. "But he really wanted to help, you know, if people were out of something and it was after everything was closed. It was, you know, an extra service to the town's residents." Lis sounded as if she were reading from a manuscript. It was clear that she had heard her husband say this frequently.

"How sweet of him," Dea said dryly. "And it probably made for a nice little nest egg?"

"Oh, Verner's always handled the money," Lis said dismissively, and then suddenly looked up in horror. "What's going to happen if he doesn't come home? I don't even have a debit card."

Liam narrowed his eyes a little and studied Lis's facial expression and her hands, which were in constant motion. He quite simply could not make her out. She didn't seem particularly shaken up about her husband being gone. And yet she was visibly nervous.

They were distracted by Nassrin's little Fiat, which came into view at the top of the hill. Shortly thereafter the car pulled up to the curb right beside them. Her roof was rolled down. Nassrin was wearing sunglasses and waved at them.

"And here we have Don Johnson!" Dea mumbled, just loud enough for Liam to hear.

He started to smile but then quickly caught himself. "I'll just brief our coworker here. In the meantime, you talk to Lis about their son." He looked at Lis. "You have only one child, is that right?"

"Yes, Henrik," Lis replied. "He lives with his family in Haarby, but he's in Aalborg for the weekend for some computer something for work."

"That's great," Liam said, and patted Dea on the shoulder. It was purely reflexive. He knew she didn't like it, but here they were.

Nassrin remained in her car until a large truck drove past. Then she came over to meet him.

"What have we got?" she asked.

Liam pulled the bag with the slip of paper out of his pocket and showed it to her. "This one was stuck in a crack next to the front door, and now the man is gone. He disappeared on his morning walk with his dog. So far without any trace, like Charlotte."

Nassrin took the bag and peered at the slip of paper.

"What do you think?" he asked as she read it through, immediately sensing her reluctance. He caught her eye and held it. "Drop it, this notion that I'm only asking you because you're a Muslim. I'm asking you because you're a good police officer and I'm convinced that we need to take these quotes very seriously."

Nassrin cleared her throat. "Both quotes are from the Quran, and it looks like they were written on the same kind of paper, but it's standard, so . . . I want to say it's not one of the better-known verses."

He nodded and put the bag back in his pocket. "Charlotte taught religion, so in that case we might be able to explain why the first slip was lying on her family's doorstep, but why was the same type of note placed in this elderly couple's house?" He shook his head. "It can't be a coincidence . . . Do you think we're dealing with some type of religious crime?"

Nassrin's mind seemed far away as she looked at him, and he could tell her thoughts were racing. "I need to check on something in Assens," she said. "Is it OK if I head over there right now?"

*   *   *

The summer air was decidedly warm now. There was a dusty, summery scent of pollen. Liam had given up and tossed his jacket aside. Dea squatted in the dry grass beside the gravel road, where the tracking dogs had alerted on Verner's scent. She looked up at the driveway of an abandoned, dilapidated house across the road. She could see the top of the roof over a carport that had collapsed on one side. It was hard to imagine that someone had randomly come by and stumbled across and assaulted the old grocer right here, she thought. Farther ahead she could make out the roof of a disused plastic factory, but otherwise this was a long way from anything.

They trooped across the street to the house on the other side and walked around the now-wild hedge and then up the overgrown driveway.

"There was a car parked right there. For a long time," Dea said, pointing to a square area where the grass was stunted and practically white from lack of light. "It's been driven away, but that could have happened last night or yesterday. It won't be possible to determine for sure when it was removed. But we know that we're talking about an old, dark-blue Ford Granada. The people we talked to were really surprised that the car could drive at all, since it had apparently been parked here for more than twenty years without having been used. I'm waiting for an answer from Technical and hope that they can tell us soon if it could be the car that was parked over there, hidden in the thick brush, where they found tire imprints."

Liam nodded.

"If it turns out that the car was used in the grocer's disappearance, it's not so striking that it was chosen, is it? You can drive around in an old beater like a Ford Granada without attracting attention," Dea continued, and turned to Liam, raising her eyebrows.

"Maybe he or she wants to be noticed," he replied. "Or maybe the old car is a diversionary tactic so that we focus on it instead of looking for other cars?"

She nodded, pondering that. If that was the plan, then they had already wasted quite a bit of time out here in the dust.

* * *

Beate hung the parsonage's landline phone back up and looked at Peter. He was sitting in the armchair across from her, typing on a laptop.

She put a hand on her stomach. She felt life in there and remembered back to when she was expecting Silje.

Peter was deeply engrossed in his screen. He had scarcely heard a word of her conversation, but then, she was the one who had accepted the position as pastor, not him. She wondered sometimes if her work hadn't started to take up too much space in their lives, in their relationship as a couple. After all, they were living right in the middle of it. And she knew that the series of articles he had been so preoccupied by for almost two years now was the most important thing for him, on a purely professional level. He was convinced that it would make a huge splash in conversations about Islam and integration in Denmark, and he was working to get the articles published in *Politiken* and made into a documentary on DR2. He just didn't have any contracts in place yet, and when she read his emails, she didn't really think the interest he spoke so enthusiastically about seemed quite as overwhelming as he made it seem. His head was so full of his articles about Islam that some days it was as if he weren't there at all.

His bald head shone in the bright sunlight. His round glasses shone too. He was so thin. For a moment she was gripped with worry. Could they live in the parsonage at all while she was on maternity leave? Peter didn't generally have anything other than his unemployment, after all.

The phone rang again.

"Yes, yes . . . I know . . . Vicky called a minute ago. And Lars. Maybe we should arrange something? Gather people? I'll look into it and call you back, all right?"

Peter looked up. He looked like someone who had been completely absent. "What's up?"

"That was Bodil from the parish council. It sounds like another person is missing. Maybe it's just gossip. A retired grocer. I'm not sure I know him, but Bodil is the fifth person to call me about it."

"Missing how?" Peter furrowed his brow.

"He was out walking his dog this morning, and then the dog came home without him. And don't give me any more of your theories about how maybe he rode his bike to Berlin."

"No, no." He smiled wryly.

"Vicky thought it would be a good idea to hold a public meeting in the parish hall in Broholm to show that the church is there for people."

"That's not a bad idea," Peter mumbled, looked out at the big courtyard. "Do you think anyone will come?"

"Yes, I think so. And it will probably help, too, if there's free coffee and cake. Couldn't you help get the word out to people? It'll be tough for me to fit it all in. Plus I have that afternoon service as well." She thought it over for a moment as she gazed out the window. "Perhaps I could ask Johannes if he could do the afternoon service. His mother is always telling me how much he misses the church."

"That's a good idea. Try that." Peter had gotten up and was looking out the window. "Speaking of the son . . ."

Beate looked to see what he was looking at. "Would you be a dear and let him in?"

The former pastor was heading for the parsonage's wide front steps.

"Can't you do it yourself? He's so . . . presumptuous about his faith."

She agreed. Both Johannes and his grandfather continually made her feel like she wasn't doing a good enough job, not living up to the standard they had set for the town, and she couldn't bear their constant reminders.

"Yes, but if you open the door, then I could be sitting in here buried in paperwork when you show him in. Then at least he could see that I'm doing something."

"Beate!" Peter rolled his eyes, but he laughed lovingly and gave in.

She put on a good performance of being busy when Peter returned a moment later with her predecessor. "Johannes? What a weekend, huh?"

"Yes, that's exactly why I'm stopping by," Johannes said kindly. "I imagine you're probably overrun with worried townspeople and thought maybe I could assist or help you with something?"

"We're actually planning to hold a public meeting in the evening at the parish hall."

"Today?" He had come over to stand in front of her desk.

"Today." She glanced down at the notes on her desk. "People have been calling in a steady stream to ask what's going on."

"I've received a couple of calls myself," Johannes said, nodding. "If it would be of any help, I can take your late service today. I do know the text."

"Would you do that?" Beate smiled in relief. "I would gladly accept. That's terribly nice of you, Johannes. Thank you so much."

* * *

The old kitchen smelled of coffee. Liam took a sip and nodded appreciatively.

"Would you like some cake?" Lis waved her hand toward the kitchen table. "I have pound cake. Verner likes to have a little something sweet with his coffee."

"No thanks," Liam said, and poured a little cream right out of the carton into his coffee. "Thank you, though . . . What a lovely place you have."

"We do? My husband isn't a fan of spending too much money on the house, so it hasn't changed much in many years now."

"Is he a cheapskate?" Dea asked in her blunt fashion.

"Yes, I suppose you could say that," Lis acknowledged. "But I don't want for anything." She quickly brushed a few invisible crumbs off the oilcloth.

Dea leaned forward a little. "Have you spoken with your son? I assume he's on his way over?"

"Yes, I talked to him this morning, but he's very busy with his course, and the drive from Aalborg to Tommerup is no small matter." She fidgeted with her wedding ring.

"So he's not on his way over?" Dea persisted.

"No, not today."

"Maybe he doesn't care that his father is missing and the house is full of police?"

Lis squirmed uncomfortably and looked down. "Verner and Henrik don't have that much in common anymore."

"Did they have a falling-out?"

"No, I wouldn't say that . . . They're just not . . ." She shrugged.

"Has their relationship always been strained?" Dea did not let up.

"Verner has always been a little strict, and those years when Henrik was doing water polo, their relationship grew increasingly strained."

"When was Henrik active in playing water polo?" Liam chimed in.

"He played until he was about sixteen, I think."

"Do you know if Henrik knows Claus and Charlotte? I think you said that Verner knows Claus?"

Lis shook her head despondently. "I don't remember if they were both playing back then. They went to school together, but I don't know if they stayed in touch after Henrik moved away. And it wasn't until many years later that Claus took over from Verner as coach."

"Did Henrik enjoy playing with the club?" Dea asked.

"I think he hated it," Lis said, with surprising honesty. "And Verner was so disappointed when Henrik stopped."

"Why do you think Henrik hated playing water polo?"

For the first time in the conversation, Lis looked right at Dea. Then she shrugged again but didn't answer.

"Do you know if Verner has any enemies?" Liam asked instead.

"Outright enemies? No, I shouldn't think so," Lis replied. She seemed almost scared but thought it over. "Years ago everybody liked Verner, but I suppose there are a few who carry a grudge against him because of the night sales and such . . ."

"What is this 'and such'?" Dea asked.

"Well, not everyone is a fan of that kind of thing."

"But that was a long time ago now, so why should people still be upset about it?"

Lis stood up abruptly and walked over to the stove. "Would you like more coffee?"

"No, I'd rather hear about whatever it is that's making you so uneasy," Dea said. Then her tone softened a little. "Are you afraid of Verner?"

"No, no," Lis babbled. "I'm just confused. It's so overwhelming, the police and all these questions. Verner's always the one who usually—"

"Lis," Liam interrupted. "Do you know if Verner has anything do with Muslims?"

"Muslims? No." She thought about it for a minute. "Well, there was that one young African man from the old UngBo. He used to come into the store way back when . . . Yes, he was the one who always ran so fast, in the tight running clothes. I can't remember his name, but he was friendly and polite whenever we saw him."

"Do you know if Verner has anything to do with right-wing politics?" Dea took over.

"No, not Verner. He doesn't go in for that kind of thing. He's not really interested in politics at all."

"Boss!" One of the experienced officers, Thorbjørn, had appeared in the doorway that came up from the basement, where the grocery store had once been. "You need to come down here."

There had been no immediate indication that anyone had entered the home from outside before the former grocer's disappearance. Nor did it sound as if Lis had noticed anything unusual before Sunday morning. And when Liam had asked if it would be all right for a couple of his people to take a look around the house, she hadn't had any objections. It wasn't a search, he had emphasized. She had seemed a little anxious but hadn't objected as they split up, one taking the upstairs and the other the downstairs.

Liam stood up and quickly joined Thorbjørn. They closed the basement door behind them.

"There's a room back behind the empty store," Thorbjørn explained. "It's filled to the brim with beer, liquor, cigarettes, and such—black market. There's a book with detailed, handwritten accounts that goes back several years. I highly doubt that the government has seen these books."

Liam followed him into a mildewy room lined floor to ceiling with shelves. Vodka, gin, whiskey, schnapps—all the bottles were neatly lined up and sorted by type. Piles of tobacco occupied the rearmost shelf. He also saw plastic crates full of soda, cardboard flats of beer, and big cardboard boxes with bags of candy and chips. Verner had put together a well-stocked store for his back-door customers.

"The book ends every morning at five AM," Thorbjørn continued. "All the times and dates of the sales are carefully recorded in the transaction history he's kept up until today. There's also a cigar box here with money in it." Thorbjørn handed the cashbox to Liam.

Liam regarded the old wooden box with brass hinges thoughtfully. If Verner had run off, wouldn't he have taken the money with him? Thorbjørn had tallied it up. It was just under 4,800 kroner.

"In other news"—Thorbjørn interrupted Liam's thoughts—"we just heard that there'll be a public meeting about Charlotte and Verner tonight at five PM. The church is organizing it."

"Oh, I don't know if I'm up to that," Liam groaned. "That'll result in a hundred local busybodies breathing down our necks from the minute the clock strikes six."

"You want people out there?" Thorbjørn continued, still standing at the bottom of the stairs while Liam started back up them. Liam turned. "Yes, I think that's actually a good idea. I'll go myself and bring Dea along."

* * *

The long fluorescent tubes shined a clinical white light over the cars and the tools in the little workshop. The rain had begun pouring down steadily outside, and water was coming in under the doors and forming a puddle on the floor.

There was no answer when Nassrin called in through the door, so she decided to go in, but she sent Dennis a text at the same time and asked him to come down to her.

The dampness of the rain made its way in, and the dank air did not bring out the best in the cold workshop. The overfilled ashtrays stank more pungently than they had before, and the empty beer cans on the workbench gave off a sharp, sweet odor, like in a pub. Odense Pilsner. Without revenue stamps.

"I still haven't seen Kasper!" Nassrin looked over at Dennis, who had appeared in the doorway and now stood with both feet solidly in the puddle. He didn't appear to notice and seemed standoffish and shabby in his sweatpants and worn shirt.

"No? Well, come on in anyway."

She waited until he had come closer before she continued. "Has Kasper ever been gone for several days in a row before?"

"I don't know," Dennis said with shrug. "I assume so. I mean, it's not like we keep an eye on each other."

"But you see each other around, right?"

"Yeah, but not every day. I'm not his babysitter or anything."

She looked him in the eye. His pupils were dilated. "You're living a little hard, I think."

"So?"

"There's no one else here, so you don't need to be a smart aleck."

Dennis sighed tiredly. "I don't know anything about Kasper, OK? I think it's weird that he isn't calling back and hasn't turned up, but can't you leave me out of all this? I don't know where he is." He ran a hand over his crew cut.

"When did you last see him?"

"Right before I went to bed on Friday."

"Early? Late?"

"We were in town for a while, and then we came back here and had a smoke, and then I went to bed."

"Can you remember what time that was?"

"Around three in the morning, I guess."

"Did Kasper go to bed then too?"

"No, he was going to go take a piss, so I just headed upstairs."

"OK." Nassrin glanced at him. "Do you know if Kasper happened to know a woman named Charlotte Laursen from Tommerup here on Funen Island? Her maiden name was Wissing. Or did he know the guy who used to run the little grocery store in Tommerup? Verner?"

"We've bought beer at night from the grocery guy, but I have no idea who the woman is."

"Think about it for a minute. I'm not asking for fun . . . Charlotte Laursen? Blond and in her early thirties. She lived here near Assens before she moved to Tommerup."

Dennis narrowed his eyes a little. His jaw muscles were clearly visible beneath his smooth skin. He took a couple of steps closer to the table, stuck his hands into the pockets of his mottled-gray pants, and peered attentively down at the worn concrete floor as he slowly shook his head.

"I don't think Kasper knows her," he said noncommittally, scraping his foot over the floor in a sweeping motion. Even though he had nonchalantly tried to erase the evidence, Nassrin had seen the white powder on the floor. Not much of it, but enough for her to figure out that it was the remnants of a line that had probably been snorted on the garage workbench.

She moved over close to him and gazed explicitly at the floor by his feet, so he would have no doubt that his attempt had not succeeded. "Is that something you're dealing, or is that just for personal use?" she asked, squatting down and running her finger through what was left of the white powder. She assumed this vulnerable position in front of him very deliberately. She wanted to signal that she wasn't afraid of him but that he should begin to evaluate whether he was afraid of her.

Nassrin looked up at him inquisitively, holding her index finger with the white powder on it demonstratively up in the air. He shifted his weight uneasily from foot to foot but didn't say anything. She pulled a thin latex glove out of her pocket and put it on before sticking her hand in underneath the bottom shelf of the workbench, which was hiding the thing he had been trying to scrape away with his foot. She found a couple of beer bottle caps and the small piece of tightly rolled up paper that she had noticed earlier in the day as well.

Even though she had come specifically looking for a quote from the Quran on a slip of paper, a shiver ran down her spine as she slowly unrolled the little piece of paper.

They swear to you by Allah that they might please you; and Allah, as well as His Apostle, has a greater right that they should please Him, if they are believers.

Without taking her eye off the piece of paper, she pulled one of the little evidence bags she always kept with her out of her inner pocket.

"Where did this come from, Dennis?"

She had stood up, and he was looking desperately at the slip of paper. It was clear that he assumed he needed to explain the white powder and not the short text.

"How the hell should I know? This place is full of all kinds of shit."

"Yes, but this isn't shit," Nassrin said sharply. "You knew it was there, right?" He stared at her blankly and pulled away a little. With one quick step she was in his face, waving the little bag with the slip of paper in it in front of his nose. "If you tell me when this showed up, then I won't ask you what you used it to snort."

He straightened up. "I have no idea where that stupid paper came from. It could have come out of a Kinder Surprise egg. I have no idea. And you can't fucking stand there tossing out accusations. I'm not the only one who comes into this workshop. Everyone comes in here. Everyone comes in here for beer after work. There were maybe fifteen of us in here last night. How about you go after them instead?" His cheeks had some color now from getting worked up.

"Can you remember if you noticed this slip of paper right after we discovered that Kasper was gone?" Nassrin asked calmly. But he was incensed now, and he thundered on with his self-righteous self-defense speech.

"Was it there when you and Kasper smoked your good-night smoke?" she interrupted.

He made a point of looking up at the ceiling.

"Dennis, I can easily get a warrant to search your apartment, and if you have so much as a gram of anything that's white and in powder form, I'll find it." She closed her eyes. She didn't have time to play this game with him. "Dennis," she repeated slowly and clearly, "when did this slip of paper show up? It's important."

"Oh come on, I don't know! Yesterday, I think? Our boss, Pio, read it, and we laughed at it. We don't really go in for that sacred stuff."

"So it wasn't there when you and Kasper said good-night to each other?"

He looked at her, disoriented, but then shook his head.

"No, I don't think so. I cleaned up down here on Friday after we closed—we take turns—and the workbench was totally clean when I left. I had yesterday off, but Pio brought breakfast over, and while we were eating that, that's when he read that stuff about pleasing and being a messenger. He thought he was the one who was pleasing us by being a messenger, because he had stopped in at Mønsterbageren Bakery on his way." Dennis laughed dismally.

Nassrin tried to picture it. The slip of paper had already been lying there when she drove Dennis home from the grill the day before, when he had been drunk and making a nuisance of himself. She pulled out her cell phone and called Liam.

"Hey, boss . . . I found a slip of paper in Assens . . . also a quote from the Quran . . . Positive . . . Yes, I'll bring him in with me . . ."

She put her phone back in her jacket pocket along with the evidence bag containing the quote.

"OK, Dennis, here's the deal. I'm going to ask you to come back to the police station for proper questioning, but since I'm here alone, I need to ask you to come with me voluntarily. Would that be all right?"

He nodded despondently. "Am I under arrest?"

"No. You just need to repeat your explanation at the station so it won't just be me listening to what you say. And then the police's forensics technicians are on their way out here to go over your workshop with a fine-toothed comb."

That startled Dennis, and he glanced nervously over at the rattling metal cabinets that stood along the opposite wall.

"No, it's too late," Nassrin said, reaching out a hand to stop him. "We're waiting for the forensics crew now. You can't call anyone or remove anything."

"Bitch," he snarled under his breath.

Just then Nassrin's phone buzzed. It was a text from Dea. *Dennis was once accused of breaking into Charlotte Laursen's place. We need to bring him in for voluntary questioning ASAP. Don't tell him anything else about the case without us.*

* * *

"Three days, three victims." Liam looked at the board, where pictures of Charlotte, Kasper, and Verner were now hanging. The mood in the room was tense, like a breath held for a long time. Beneath each photograph hung the quote from the Quran that had been found in conjunction with each of the three people's disappearances. The names of their immediate family members hung there too. Underneath those read *DENNIS* in all caps, with arrows pointing from his name to their three names.

"It turns out that Dennis Sørensen can be linked to the three people who are missing," Liam said, pointing to his name. "Nassrin, tell us about Dennis."

"It's a bit of a coincidence that I ran into him, but he works with Kasper at the auto workshop in Assens. The two of them are friends and they both live upstairs, over the workshop. It turns out that he was with Kasper right before he disappeared. They'd been out on the town, and when they came home, they sat down in the workshop and had one last beer before heading upstairs. Dennis claims that he went up shortly before his buddy. He says he tumbled into bed and fell asleep with his clothes on. He didn't see or hear Kasper come upstairs."

"Dennis Sørensen is a known entity," Dea took over. "We have quite a bit on him: breaking and entering, assault, and robbery.

He's a charming guy. And it simply doesn't hold up that he doesn't know Charlotte, because he was convicted of breaking into her place. He was actually also accused of theft and aggravated assault against an elderly woman from Assens a few years ago, and guess who his alibi was in that case, resulting ultimately in the case being dropped? The missing Kasper! In addition to this, for years Dennis was among the clientele who made use of the old grocer's back-door sales. So in other words, he has direct connections to all three of the people we're looking for."

Liam nodded. "And right now he's waiting for us in Questioning 1."

"So are we considering Charlotte, Kasper, and Verner's disappearance as one case?" Nassrin asked with a glance at the board.

Liam nodded. "Yes, I think everything suggests that. We need to get ahold of everyone one more time. We need to ask about these passages from the Quran and any conceivable relationship with Islam or radicalized groups: Do the three individuals have any particular relationship with Islam? Is there anything that connects these three people? Shared interests, attitudes in common, common enemies? Is there anything at all that ties these three people together—beyond Dennis? Why are we finding these verses in the locations that we have to assume are crime scenes?"

"Shouldn't we talk to a theology expert?" Thorbjørn suggested. He reported that he had a source he had relied on in the past. "He's with the University of Southern Denmark."

"Talk to him," Liam said, and then turned to Nassrin again. "Do you have anything to add about Kasper?"

"I haven't found anything at all that would suggest the slightest connection to any Muslims. But if Dennis and Kasper buy drugs often, which seems pretty likely, then there's definitely a chance that they have gang contacts. They might even have debts."

"Ooh, good thought! Will you follow up on that?" He hesitated for a second. "Wasn't there something about a grandmother too?"

"Yes," Nassrin said. "Karen . . . I think she spent the night at Kasper's apartment. I'll get in touch with her."

Liam gave her the thumbs-up.

Dea shook her head slightly and looked away.

"Who was the woman that he assaulted before?" Nassrin asked.

"An Olga Andersen," Liam said. "She lives in a nursing home in Verminge now, near Tommerup." He put a hand on Nassrin's shoulder. "We need to send someone out to see Olga. Can you take that?"

"Of course. I'll drive over there after we're done here."

"It needs to be right away," Liam said. "We need to gather everything we can scrape together about Dennis and Kasper."

"But what about the questioning?" Nassrin tried. "I was the one who found—"

Dea cut her off. "We'll take care of it, don't worry."

"Whoa, wait!" Liam said, and turned to Nassrin. "I almost forgot. There's a public meeting in the parish house tonight. I would really like to have you attend that." He hesitated for a second. "But try and see if you can fit in the nursing home and the grandmother before that, OK?"

* * *

"Do I need a lawyer?" Dennis asked. He sounded tough, but it was also obvious that a lot of that was an act.

"You haven't been charged with anything," Liam said nicely. "We just want to talk to you, and then you'll be allowed to read our account of this conversation so you'll know what you're signing your name to."

"Is this being recorded?" Dennis continued in the same tone of voice, watching Dea.

"You've done this several times before," Dea said dryly, thinking of the time she had questioned him herself after the assault on Olga Andersen. He had been a real hard-ass and impossible to sway one way or the other once he realized that they couldn't prove he had been the one who broke into the old woman's house and left her helpless on the floor of the bedroom. "So you know how this works, right?"

Dennis snorted dismissively. "I don't know what you're talking about, but if you're charging me with anything, I want a lawyer."

"You're here as a witness, because you've been Kasper's best friend for many years. You were the last one to see him before he disappeared, and we hope that maybe you know something— whether you realize it or not—that could help us find him, OK?"

"Why the hell is it so important where he is? You make it sound like he's been beamed up into a UFO. He's been away for a couple of days; so what?" He flung his hands up in irritation. "And what's the deal with him and that Muslim stuff on the piece of paper? Just what is it that you think he's done?"

Dennis angrily whipped one leg back and forth so that the whole table was rocking.

"We don't actually think you've done anything," Liam replied calmly. "But we suspect that your friend isn't just out of town for the weekend. We think something might have happened to him. That's why you should tell us everything there is to know about Kasper."

Dennis had opened his mouth to say something, but it appeared to take him a second to understand what Liam had said. Then he said, "What do you mean, something happened to him?"

Dea leaned in over the table. "Do you know Verner, the guy who used to run the little grocery store in Tommerup?"

Dennis nodded reluctantly and repeated that he regularly stopped by the grocer's basement in Tommerup when they were on their way home from a night in Odense and everything else was closed. "But what the hell does that have to do with Kasper? He's just hooking up with some woman. It's just a little awkward to tell his grandmother that when she shows up with a cake."

"Is that something you know he's doing or something you think he's doing?" Dea asked pointedly, trying to temper her annoyance with the fact that, just like that time with Olga, he thought he could worm his way out of trouble with his flippant attitude.

Dennis's freckles glowed orange on his pale face. He rested his elbows on his knees and ran both hands over his crew cut. "It's something I think."

Dea looked at Liam and nodded that it was time for him to apply pressure.

"I'd like to talk to you about Charlotte Laursen," he began, and turned to Dennis so they were sitting directly across from each other. "What was your relationship to her?"

"What?" Dennis said, flinging up his hands. "I don't have any fucking relationship with her. I don't know who she is. OK?"

"But that doesn't add up," Dea interrupted dryly. "You've been in her house."

"Give me a break," he yelled, so angrily that Liam leaned across the table and put a hand on his arm. "I heard on the radio that you guys were looking for her, but I have no idea who she is."

Dea set a picture of Charlotte on the table in front of Dennis. "Just take a look."

He looked at the picture for a second and then shook his head. "I have no idea who she is," he repeated.

"Dennis, man . . ." Dea cleared her throat in irritation. "Before Charlotte moved to Tommerup, where she lives with her husband and children now, she used to live in Ebberup, and her last name was Wissing. Does that mean anything to you?"

Dennis's leg stopped shaking. "No."

"Yes," Dea said. "Because you broke into Charlotte Wissing's house on October twenty-third, 2014, and you were convicted for that break-in, weren't you?"

"I have no fucking idea who that bitch is!" Dennis snarled. He closed his eyes, clearly trying to get himself under control again.

"Knock it off. You've met her before, because she was home the night you broke in," Dea continued, unmoved. "You knocked her down and emptied her house. Just like you did with Olga Andersen."

"I'm not saying any more." Dennis made a show of pressing his lips together tightly.

"Do you really expect me to believe that you don't want to confirm that you once assaulted the Charlotte we're currently searching for? We know that. You were convicted." Dea stubbornly continued looking him in the eye.

"I'm not saying any more without a lawyer," Dennis said.

"You're not under arrest," Liam quickly interjected. "You can walk out the door right now if you want."

Dennis eyed Dea coldly and sniffed self-righteously. "Good." Then he got up and walked over to the door.

"I'll join you," Liam said, following him.

"Just one last question," Dea added from over at the table. "Would your ever hire a Muslim at the workshop?"

Dennis turned and looked at her in surprise, but then he thought it over before shaking his head. "Nah . . . no, I don't think so. It's too much of a hassle with them, right? I mean, it's all the same to me, but Kasper and the other guys aren't so fond of *Perkers.*"

Liam let his hand sit on the doorknob so Dennis couldn't exit. "I just need to speak to my colleague out in the hall for a sec before you leave, OK?"

Dennis nodded reluctantly and moved the cigarette he had tucked behind his ear into his mouth so he would be ready to smoke as soon as they let him go.

Out in the hall, Liam lowered his voice.

"I'm considering charging him."

"Do you think it would stick?" Dea asked. "He definitely has an ugly history of assault and violence, but would the prosecutor be with us on this?"

"I'm not sure," Liam said, scratching his beard. "But we know that he was convicted when Charlotte was assaulted. The motive could be revenge. He's been a steady customer of Verner's. It could be about money."

"But Verner wasn't robbed," Dea reminded him.

"True." He nodded. "And then there's Kasper. Dennis claims that they're best friends, but after all is said and done, hard drugs are rarely the best basis for a healthy friendship."

Dea nodded and agreed that it was striking that Dennis had a relationship with all three of the missing people. "But is it enough to be able to get a judge to remand him into custody in twenty-four hours, just based on this?"

Liam stood there in the hallway staring into space for a second.

"We'll have Chief Constable Dybbøl breathing down our necks if we fail," Dea continued. "Isn't it better if we let him go and keep an eye on him?"

"You're probably right," he admitted, frustrated. "We'll keep an eye on him and expand our investigation to look into his actions in recent weeks, phone information, and social media."

"But let's get a search warrant so we can start tapping his cell phone," Dea said, realizing she was allowing herself to get carried away by Liam's desire to put much more pressure on Dennis Sørensen. "Do you think he has something to do with this?" She looked at her boss appraisingly. Sometimes he seemed weak and ever so slightly insecure, and that triggered the old boss gene in her. She had a tremendous urge to bulldoze right over him and lead the way, but she had promised herself that the era was over when she would lead anything or anyone at all.

Liam nodded. "I think he knows more than he's telling us. But again, you're right—we don't have enough to hold him right now. So let's find out some more!"

*　*　*

Beate glanced over at Ernst, who stood in the middle of the packed meeting room in the parish house at Tommerup's Broholm Church. More people had come than they had chairs for, but luckily the rain had stopped a few hours earlier so they could leave the doors open. Ernst sang "I Am the Oats, I Have Bells On." She didn't fully comprehend that choice, but for once she was relieved that he was there and singing. There was something about the gentle song and the interlude that felt soothing.

The older women who always came to church had whipped up big plates of fresh warm kringle and plenty of coffee. The parish house had place settings for seventy, and all the china was in use. A few of the last guests to arrive had to make do with paper plates.

Ernst finished his song and bowed ceremonially to his audience.

Beate stepped into the middle of the room where he had been standing. She looked at the old man, who was greeting people warmly left and right on his way back over to Johannes, who stood talking quietly with a small group of older people. Grandfather and grandson, both former pastors in her church. They both seemed so calm and relaxed, as if they were both so comfortably secure in their faith that they trusted that in the end everything would be fine.

Beate was sad. Johannes had not turned up for the service he had promised to lead, so the small number of people who had come had waited in vain, and everyone blamed her. Karen from the parish council felt that Beate was taking the "modern church" thing a little too far when she let people sit alone in the church without a sermon or anything. Johannes had apologized and excused himself, saying that he had been forced to help Ernst, who had fallen, but Ernst seemed to have recovered miraculously well.

The room grew silent around her. "Thank you for showing up in such numbers at such short notice," she began. "I know that you're here because you're worried, and a situation like this is precisely when the church can be a place for us to gather in safety." She looked up. "And thank you, Ernst, for the lovely song. It was . . . so . . . well chosen." Her eyes fell on Lis and Claus, who had both shown up and were standing side by side. The grocer's wife looked like her usual self, but Charlotte Laursen's husband looked even more run-down than he had the day before.

"Is there any news?" a woman called loudly from the last row of chairs in the back.

"I don't know any more than you." Beate spoke loudly as well so that everyone could hear her.

"Then why bring us all here for a meeting?" someone else asked.

"It is my hope that we can stand together and be here to support each other. When uncertainty makes us fearful, talking together helps."

"Is it true that the police presence in town is because Charlotte and Verner were murdered?" a man shouted in a hoarse voice. He wore a white and dark-blue cap pressed down over his head.

"They're just missing," another person yelled.

"Says who?" called a woman's shrill voice. "I can't imagine the police hunting high and low for days on end in a little town like ours if it didn't have to do with murder."

Beate felt a sense of pressure in her chest. She tried to take control of the conversation but was interrupted by another woman standing along the wall. The woman thought something had happened in Assens as well, because she had heard from her sister that the police had also been all over an auto workshop there.

"Quiet!" Johannes cut through with his firm voice. "If we're all shouting over each other, no one will be able to hear anything in the end. And that will just increase our worries." He had stood up and was looking around at the many who had gathered. "I think that we—"

Just then Ernst placed a hand so heavily on his grandson's shoulder that Johannes lost his balance for a second. "Johannes is right," the grandfather interrupted in his deep voice. "It is important that we not let ourselves be carried away in a panic, because that won't help the missing or us. As we all know, a couple of our beloved fellow citizens are missing. But let's agree that it is far too early to resort to fear." He paused for an unctuous moment, patted Johannes emphatically on the shoulder, then sank back down on his chair and continued in a slightly quieter voice, "We owe both Lis and Claus the consideration of not allowing ourselves to get carried away whipping ourselves up into a needless frenzy, which will take attention away from their worries. And their missing partners. Remember that they are going through something much worse right now than the rest of us. Not knowing is suffering."

"Couldn't you chair this meeting, Ernst?" an elderly woman with bluish-gray hair asked.

Ernst nodded and then turned to Beate. "Perhaps you could begin, Beate, by telling us what you know? Then our guests can continue if they have anything to add."

"Yes." She stood up hesitantly. She definitely felt like she had been hung out to dry, but she pulled herself together and raised her voice. "Thank you, Ernst, but . . . as I said, I don't know any more than you do. On Friday morning, as you all know, Charlotte disappeared without a trace from the Tommerup Athletics Center at around eight o'clock in the morning, and she hasn't been seen since."

"The police aren't doing a darn thing about it either," a bony man snarled loudly.

"Well, that's not true," Beate said. "There has been quite a police presence out here, both Saturday and Sunday."

"But they should have already been out searching on Friday when I told them my wife was missing," Claus declared, distraught.

Ernst walked over and placed a hand on Claus's shoulder and gave it a gentle squeeze. "Hold on to your faith, my friend."

Claus hid his face in his hands. A woman whom Beate recognized as one of the mothers from Oliver's daycare put an arm around him. He leaned against her shoulder and sobbed.

Lis looked away and sipped her coffee. It was hard to read her, but as Beate regarded that reserved face, she wondered if the rumors of Verner's tyranny toward both his wife and their son were perhaps not as exaggerated as they might have sounded.

A debate flared up about the police and whether it was dangerous to be out alone, given the scope of the search that was underway. People gesticulated and debated, and the quiet public meeting Beate had envisioned was evolving into a collective panic attack.

"If I might make a suggestion," she began, raising her voice again. It grew quiet, and everyone suddenly looked at her. She put a hand on her round belly a little self-consciously and took a deep breath. "We could split up into groups and then search for them ourselves—all the way out to the brickworks, along the railroad, and around the athletics center. We know our town best."

"That's not a bad idea," Ernst hurried to say, looking around at those assembled. "If we break up into groups of five to six men, that will give us about thirteen or fourteen groups full of alert eyes."

"And once we've searched for a couple of hours—or until we've found something," Beate continued, encouraged, "we'll serve spaghetti and sausages back here for everyone so we can round the evening off together!" She could tell that the idea of sharing a meal together didn't sit well with Ernst, but he kept nodding and smiling.

A young Muslim woman who worked for the police appeared in the back of the room, by the double doors. She stood with her hands in her jacket pockets, leaning against the doorframe. Beate wished she had come sooner so she could make a statement on behalf of the police about how far they had come. Now Beate would try to get her to join one of the search groups instead so that it would be clear to everyone that the police were behind what she'd started.

* * *

Nassrin instinctively waved back when the pastor waved her over.

"Wouldn't you like to join the search group over there?"

Nassrin hesitated a little and looked over at the small group Beate was pointing to. It was five people: an elegantly dressed woman with her hair up high on her head, two men in windbreakers, an overweight woman in her forties with lively eyes and a shoulder bag over her shoulder, and a short distance from the others, a younger woman standing by herself.

"The young woman's name is Luna," Beate whispered. "She's had a bit of a troubled past. Then she came and did some community service, and I try and look after her a little."

Just then the woman with the blond updo called the others together and asked Nassrin if she planned to go with them.

Nassrin nodded and joined them.

"I suggest that we take the route along the tracks," the woman continued, with an attitude that said she thought it was inevitable that she would be the one to take charge. "Although it would probably make the most sense to walk through everyone's yards."

"We can't do that," Nassrin interrupted. "That's private property."

The woman held out her hand to Nassrin. "You're with the police, aren't you?"

"Yes." She nodded and took the woman's hand. "I'm Nassrin. I'm a detective with the police in Odense."

"So you guys are the ones who should be searching everyone's yards," the woman continued. "I'm Karina. My husband and I live in Haarby, but I'm here because Verner is my father-in-law."

"Oh," Nassrin exclaimed sympathetically, regarding the energetic woman with renewed interest. "So you're Henrik's wife?"

"Yes, that's right," she replied, and straightened her red silk handkerchief.

"And Henrik couldn't come?" Nassrin prodded.

"No, he's taking a course in Aalborg. And with his position, it's not so easy for him to just skip out. If Verner were dead, of course, he would have come."

"Maybe your husband isn't so worried about his dad?" Nassrin continued. Behind Karina, Luna tossed a glowing cigarette butt onto the sidewalk and stepped on it. They had cut across Kirkevej and were on their way down a little path toward Svanevej. The air smelled fresh after the rain shower that had passed over Funen a little earlier.

"Verner and Henrik don't see each other very often, but I'm sure a lot of families are like that."

"Everyone loves Verner," the overweight woman broke in. "Hi, I'm Ruth." She was already sweating quite a bit. "Verner was a good shop owner, plus he coached both of my boys at water polo when they were little."

"Me too," one of the men in a windbreaker said. "Verner was my coach for four whole years."

"And everyone loves Verner?" Nassrin repeated, looking around at the group.

"Well, I don't know about that," the other man in a windbreaker continued. He said his name was Lars. "You can count on Verner, but we do also know that he can be heavy-handed, if you know what I mean. That was why he had to stop coaching way back when, after all."

"Oh, I'm sure it wasn't that bad," Ruth said promptly. "And I wouldn't be surprised if you kind of deserved it!" She smiled and winked at him.

"Sure," Lars admitted, and turned to Nassrin. "But as I recall, Verner dished it out pretty good at home too."

Nassrin asked Karina, "Is that why they don't see each other?"

"I wouldn't know anything about that," she said, sounding dismissive.

"He took a lot of beatings," Lars continued unabashed. "His wife too."

"Were you there?" Karina hissed, turning to him.

"No, but I've run into your mother-in-law at the store afterward."

Nassrin sneaked a peek at Karina, wondering how Liam would have handled this situation. "Do you know if Henrik knows Charlotte Laursen, who's also missing?"

"No, why would he? We live in Haarby—I already told you that."

Nassrin noticed a change come over the woman's eyes. She sort of tilted her head back a little, and her voice sounded different when she continued, "It must be nice for you, not having to wear a headscarf."

"You mean because I look Muslim?" Nassrin said, firmly holding the woman's gaze.

"Yes! There are a lot of you struggling with oppression and that kind of thing, but maybe you've liberated yourself? Or is that only while you're at work?"

The group went silent. Nassrin wondered for a moment if she shouldn't give her the whole spiel, explain that she used to be Muslim but was no longer practicing and that that was why she didn't see her parents anymore but remained close to her uncles. Instead, she shook her head.

"I don't feel oppressed, but thanks for your concern."

"But that's the way a lot of your men are," Henrik's wife continued. Her voice sounded indignant, as if this were an issue she felt strongly about. "They oppress women, and soon they're going to take over everything. I mean, just look at how busy the police are out in Vollsmose—it's getting so that the mailmen and the animal welfare people won't even dare to go out there anymore. I'm surprised you even have the personnel to search for my father-in-law."

It was as if a valve had opened up, allowing the words to hiss out of her.

"It's baffling to me that they're allowed to be here, since they very clearly don't want to be a part of our society."

"Seriously?" Lars blurted out. He had taken a step back. "We're here to help search for your father-in-law, so just spare us your political propaganda!" He eyed Karina standoffishly. "If you don't like the young lady here, who's just doing her job, or police efforts in general, then maybe *you* ought to scurry off home. We can certainly carry on searching without you."

Karina stared icily at him for a moment and then turned on her heel without a word while the others stood watching her in silence.

"Knock it off," Ruth exclaimed, hoisting up her shoulder bag, which had slid down onto her arm.

"She was a candidate for the New Right party in the last election," Lars explained, after Verner's daughter-in-law had left. "Sorry you had to listen to all that."

Having lit a fresh cigarette, Luna muttered a gloomy "Fuck her."

"The New Right is onto something that could use a little nudge," Nassrin said quietly, regretting having pushed Verner's daughter-in-law away. "But hatred and anger have never been a good place to start anything." She could hear it herself, how she sounded like her uncle Aldar.

Ruth shepherded the team onward, seeming to quickly forget that Karina had left the group. They had spread out a little as they proceeded, forming a chain and searching in various directions. The guy in the windbreaker who wasn't Lars had walked around to the other side of the tall hedgerow they were following. Nassrin could hear his footsteps but could no longer see him.

Ruth ran into someone she knew and laughed so hard her whole body rocked.

"Do you think something happened to them? Do you think they're dead?"

Nassrin felt a light grip on her arm. It was Luna. Nassrin looked into the young woman's grayish-blue eyes. There was something about her eyes that made Nassrin think the woman had not had a loving childhood.

"So, what happens if we find them?" she continued. "If they're suddenly just lying somewhere and we pass by?"

Even though Luna was half a head taller than Nassrin, Nassrin put her arm around her shoulder.

"It's good if we find them," she replied, and then quickly added, "But there's no reason to think they're dead. They could be injured and need us to find them and get them help." She wished Liam were here. They hadn't had time to prepare a joint statement to go public with. "Do you know Charlotte and Verner?"

Luna shook her head. "I know Beate. She called and asked if I would come to the meeting. I think she was afraid no one would come. That wouldn't look good, since the meeting was her idea."

Nassrin considered her for a moment.

"How did you get to know Beate?" They kept walking.

"It was several years ago." Luna stopped, suddenly seeming embarrassed. "I was a health care aide for her mom."

"So you know Beate's parents?"

"Yeah, but . . ." Luna walked a few paces away to look into an overgrown yard with a low fence. "I don't work as an aide anymore."

Nassrin sensed that Lars was circling around her a little as if he had more on his mind, and now he approached and picked up his previous thread. "That stuff about the water polo . . ."

"Yes?" Nassrin said expectantly.

"Henrik was playing back then too, but he was too scrawny. I've never seen anyone get clobbered so much. And then also by his own father. I think he swallowed several liters of chlorinated water every week to keep from drowning."

"Why did he play at all, then?"

"It was a different time back then, and Verner wasn't someone you said no to."

Nassrin nodded in understanding, even though she had no idea what life would have been like in a little town on Funen thirty years ago.

*   *   *

The evening sun had finally broken through the last of the rain clouds, and it smelled like wet soil and summer as Liam and Dea walked up the driveway. Liam spotted Nassrin in the distance. She was standing in line at a long table, which had been set up in the grass as an improvised buffet.

Liam pulled Dea over there with him. He had hoped he would be home in time to sink his teeth into the lamb shank he had seen in the fridge, but that was not to be.

"Hey, Nass, did you find anything out there?"

"Not really, but I got to talk to a lot of people."

They left the buffet and moved off to the side with their full plates.

"There seems to be something about Verner being prone to violence," Nassrin said softly, "plus I found out that their son, Henrik, is married to a woman who ran in the last election as a New Right party candidate. She seems pretty worked up about Muslims and Islam."

"How worked up?" asked Dea, exerting great effort to get her spaghetti to obey.

"Enough to go after me, anyway, and storm out of our search group in a huff."

Dea looked up in surprise from the plate in her hand.

"OK, we should take a closer look at that," Liam said. "Did you hear anything else about Henrik?"

"Someone there said that Verner forced Henrik to play water polo when he was a kid, even though Henrik hated it and was terrible at it, and Verner also reportedly used to lash out at people physically. At home too."

"He kind of sent a signal when he chose not to come home when everybody else in town is freaking out about his father being missing," Dea said, and gave up on her spaghetti to eat her sausage instead.

"Dea?" A middle-aged man was coming toward them in long strides, moving eagerly. He was tall and gangly, with dark hair and brown eyes.

"I knew it," Dea whispered, and then scooted a little closer to Liam.

"Dea!" the man repeated excitedly, spreading out his arms.

Dea was stiff as a board but allowed herself to be hugged.

The man let go of her and took a couple of steps back. "It's so great to see you." He said it very warmly, as if they had known each other all their lives. Then he turned to the others.

"I'm Dea's second cousin. The name's Johannes," he said, introducing himself. "I was the pastor at the church here for many years." He looked back at Dea. "But it's been quite a few years since we've seen each other."

Dea stood as if someone had unplugged her as the former pastor obliviously explained that Dea had come to see him at the church after her husband's death.

"It was such a joy for us to know that we could be there for her and support her during that rough period. That we could stand together before God and feel his salvation. In the darkest hours it can be hard to see the light and the will of God when death strikes those we are close to."

All the overwhelming concern made Liam want to put an arm around Dea and pull her away, because he knew exactly how she felt about it. She hated it.

"And of course it's completely normal to seek solace in the church when you lose someone you're so close to," Johannes concluded solemnly, but by then Dea had already turned around and was on her way back over to the buffet to clear her plate.

Nassrin and Liam eyed her questioningly when she returned.

"I should never have come to see them then. That was a mistake. But I was all alone. They were my only family. My father and Ernst were brothers. My father died years ago, so I went to see Johannes and Ernst, because I didn't know what to do with myself." She stopped suddenly, as if she regretted having talked about her personal life. Then she straightened up and looked expression-lessly from the one to the other. "Johannes and Ernst are so darned holier-than-thou, and I had my fill of the two of them a long time ago. The only normal one in that family is my aunt; that would be Johannes's mother. She's very down-to-earth. I don't understand how she puts up with them." Dea started walking. Liam stood there with Nassrin and watched her go as she stomped down to the garden path and vanished around the hedge.

*   *   *

Liam slammed his laptop shut dejectedly.

"Did you get the minutes from the meeting?" Helene asked, patting his arm.

"Yes, and it's a load of hogwash, to put it mildly. I thought the water polo meeting was about Claus and the coaching situation, but bad news usually brings company. It appears that the club is losing a large part of its income this year and next year because the club's main sponsor, a lumber company, has filed for bankruptcy. The club already received a three-month deferment on its payments, so it's in the red, and the bank won't give it any more time."

"Does that mean that the club might have to file for bankruptcy too?" Helene asked. "Why didn't you know anything about this, Liam? What will happen to the kids if the club closes?"

She had sat down across from him, and he was suddenly over-come by a feeling of tenderness for her and reached out his hand.

"Well, for starters, there won't be any practices or games for a while, and the U17 team is probably doomed. It means they'll have to be selected based on their U16 matches. Andreas is not going to be happy."

"But it's not totally out of the question, is it? Isn't there still a chance that he'll get onto the team?"

"I don't know," Liam replied, shaking his head. Their son had devoted so many hours to the workouts and had such lofty dreams. He kissed his wife on the forehead. "I'm going to go sit out in the yard and have a beer. You want to join me?"

"No thanks; I'm going to take a shower so my hair has time to dry before bed."

*   *   *

Liam sat watching the rooster and the chickens his parents had given them. They couldn't fly. His mother thought it was animal cruelty, but his father had clipped their wings anyway. The chickens lived in Laura and Andreas's old playhouse. If he was lucky, a fox would come by before too long.

He took a swig of his beer and turned his face toward the faint pink of the evening sky. He thought about Dea and had a hard time interpreting her reaction at the parish house earlier. She had just suddenly seemed so fragile. She had told him that her husband had died under traumatic circumstances, and he had pieced together that her life had been thrown into a long period of crisis afterward. But there had been so much discomfort in her eyes—or maybe shame, to be more precise—when the former pastor came over to say hello. He couldn't remember having seen her like that before. Not even when they were younger.

He drank a little more of his beer and thought back to the time before he had met Helene. He and Dea had taken a weekend training course at Nyborg Strand. Several of them had ended up in a little dance club in the hotel's basement, and the next morning he had woken up naked in her bed. They had been in their twenties then and had stayed in bed until they were kicked out of the room.

He smiled and finished his beer. They had missed everything on the program for the day's seminar. After that, they said goodbye and didn't see each other for many years.

When he had been asked if he wanted Dea Torp in Odense after she returned from Greenland, he had said yes right away. And he knew very well that it wasn't just because she was the world's best detective; it was also because of that sweet memory. Not that it would ever turn into anything more, and she wasn't exactly what you could call easy to get along with. She occasionally had real trouble controlling her temper. He had also been informed that she had been forced to leave Greenland because she had caught a man in the act of raping his nine-year-old niece. Dea had punched the man's nose so far into his head that he'd had to be airlifted to the hospital in Iceland to have it pulled back out again. But Liam liked her. He respected her, and he trusted her.

Liam felt a buzz in his pocket and took out his phone. It was Nassrin, who had sent a picture. She'd texted that it was a picture of her Uncle Hayyan's Quran. A number of scattered verses had been circled, including the three they had found.

Liam answered right away. *Bravo, Nass. Can you stop by with that?*

Now?

Yes, I'd like to look at it before the morning briefing.

Day 4—Monday

D EA KICKED OFF the comforter in frustration and rolled over onto her back. A new wave of heat from her body's internal radiator made her skin flush and her irritation rise at the eternal reminder that she was no longer young.

She swung her legs tiredly over the side of the bed and slowly got up. She stared despondently out at the day through the crack between the curtains, then she pulled them aside all the way. It was early and the sun was low. She stood for a bit looking at the mist and the grainy morning light.

It wasn't just the hot flashes that were keeping her awake. When she was nine, she'd started suffering these sleepless nights. Night after night she had persistently tried to struggle her way back to sleep. Over time her insomnia had improved. For long stretches she had even stopped thinking of nighttime as a necessary evil in her life. But running into Johannes again had knocked her back to the starting line.

She pulled on her clothes while promising herself that she would never again stand around listening attentively to Johannes's monologues about the will of God and nonsense. His self-important faith that everything happened for a reason, that there was always a bright side, made her sick.

They had been at the cabin when Mogens died. She had gone for a jog, and when she came back, he was lying on the floor, lifeless. She knew what to do, but she couldn't save him. She failed right when she was most needed. Up until that day, she had lived in the belief that she would always be able to protect her husband and daughter from everything—even death—but as Mogens died in her arms, she realized that that was an illusion. She had become aware that she couldn't protect anyone from anything.

How the hell could Mogens just up and die on them so brutally? she wondered heavily, and turned away from the window. And then there was Johannes and all his rubbish. They should keep their mouths shut, all of them. Liam too. Especially Liam. She couldn't stand seeing him behave so protectively toward Nassrin, and she was going to have to go to great lengths to keep from headbutting him the next time he familiarly called her Nass.

She shouldn't have come to Funen. It was a huge mistake. She was fully aware of that, but she hadn't had anywhere else to go, because she never wanted to go back to the Copenhagen police. There were too many people there who had seen her crack and become a wimp. Liam knew her history, but he hadn't actually witnessed her crumbling, and he didn't need to know how miserable she had been.

Dea walked over to the dresser by the door and unplugged her cell phone. She had written to her daughter the night before when she came home from the police station, but she hadn't received a response yet. True, it was only a little after five in the morning, but she had been hoping there would be some sort of message. She decided she should probably lower her expectations when it came to her twenty-seven-year-old daughter. Even so, she sent off another heart before moving on to the kitchen and boiling herself two eggs.

*   *   *

"Good morning." Liam looked at the time. It was ten o'clock. They were pretty much all there. The sun shone in through the windows of the big meeting room and made the furniture look a little dingy and worn. He took a sip of his steaming coffee and gazed back at the many faces looking up at him. Some of them appeared a bit livelier than others.

"As you already know, we are working off the theory that the three disappearances are most likely connected. A slip of paper with a verse from the Quran was left at each of the three locations where the disappearances are presumed to have occurred. As you're also aware, we have not approached the media with information about the short Quran quotations. This is the most important part of our investigation right now, and that's why word has come down from on high that we will not be making the public aware of this—both because it would arouse the public's fear of terrorism and because it's information that could very easily muddy and pollute our investigative work."

Liam paused, waiting until everyone in the room had nodded at him. Sometimes he was accused of not being clear enough, and other times people whispered that he made things a little too clear. There would be no mistaking this.

"We have, of course, asked the folks at the auto mechanics' workshop in Assens and their relatives if anyone knew anything about these little slips of paper," he continued. "But no one has been able to explain where they came from. So let's keep our focus on the Arabic quotations to ourselves."

The mood in the room was focused and tense, with several people whispering. Serial crimes were rare, and that seemed to be making the detectives pay more attention, Liam thought as he watched them before turning his gaze to the forensics team.

"What can you tell us about the little slips of paper—beyond the text that's printed on them?"

The forensic specialist came up to the whiteboard, where he hung up blowups of the three quotes.

"We've analyzed the ink, font size, font, and paper, and it appears that all three verses were printed on the same printer and on the same type of paper. Unfortunately, it's a standard paper type that can be bought anywhere. A font called Arial Narrow was used, and all three of the Quran quotes were written in flawless Danish. It's most likely an HP printer, but we'll know more about that later."

"Did you find any DNA, fingerprints, or other evidence?" Liam asked, his gaze still on the forensics technician. "Or is it too soon to say?"

"The analytical results aren't back on the last one yet, but so far no evidence. On the other hand, we *can* say that the slips of paper were cut so straight that we assume a paper cutter with a large blade was used."

"So we're looking for an HP printer and a paper cutter?" Dea interjected, a bit snidely.

"We're putting together a profile." Liam took over, unaffected by Dea's tone. "Right now we're interested in what type of people use Arial Narrow. The font is available in Microsoft Word, but a person would need to actively go in and choose this particular version of Arial. So we're looking for a person who's familiar enough or interested enough in Word to do that. Plus we're looking for a person who can spell and punctuate properly and is familiar with the Quran."

"I don't think younger people are the first thing that leaps to mind," one of the other team members volunteered.

Liam agreed and again looked around at the flock of faces.

"Right now, one of our priorities is finding out if there's any link between the missing people, something that ties them together, maybe something they weren't even aware of themselves: common acquaintances, family relationships, shared interests, and so on." He hesitated a moment. "The big task that awaits us today is systematizing all the data we're receiving. We have a team in Assens. They're searching the auto workshop and Kasper's apartment. Thorbjørn is leading efforts down there and talking to the shop foreman and the other employees. I have a man in Hvidovre to talk to Kasper's grandmother, who filed the report that he was missing a day after he was last seen." Liam nodded appreciatively to Nassrin. "Beyond that," he continued, "we only have the Quran passages and the missing Ford Granada, which may not even be relevant to the case, so every bit of information counts." He singled out one of the detectives. "Can you share what you know about the car?"

"The Granada was spotted in Verninge by several witnesses and in Glamsbjerg by a patrol car with an ANPR camera," the detective replied, referencing the camera's automatic number plate recognition capabilities. "We just weren't aware of it at the time, so the officers didn't respond. We only have the information because the officer who noticed it is a car buff and reacted when he heard there was an APB out for it. Our assumption is that it was driven through Verninge and Glamsbjerg to Assens, and the times when it was spotted fit the time window for when Verner disappeared. There were plates on the car, but we have to assume that they were stolen, since the car hasn't been registered since 2003."

"Thanks," Liam said. "We're sending extra people out to look around between Glamsbjerg and Assens."

The detective nodded. "I should add that the Granada was not seen in the areas where the two other people disappeared, either before or after their disappearances."

"Were we lucky enough that the presumed stolen license plates were picked up by a surveillance camera?"

The officer shook his head.

A woman raised her hand, and Liam nodded to her in confirmation.

"Where do we stand with the press?" she asked. "The story is out and there's a lot of interest, and we're not going to be able to keep people from showing up in person. I think we probably want to take charge?"

Liam took a skeptical view of the matter. Most of the big newspapers had discontinued their crime beat columns ages ago, but there was always a reporter each from both DR and TV 2, and *Ekstra Bladet* usually showed up too. And then many of the other outlets would pick it up from them. The team had already discussed how there was no keeping the rest of the Funen media from assigning people to the case, and Liam had made it clear to the crew in communications that they would have a hard time utilizing the local press with this case. But he had also notified them that they could release only the information that came directly from him or from Chief Constable Dybbøl—not a word about the verses from the Quran, and no one was to answer a single question from a journalist before they had vetted it with him.

"Three missing people in three days is a lot," the woman continued reluctantly.

"I have full confidence in you," Liam said. "But yes. There's a delicate balance between informing people and spreading fear. The most important thing right now is for us to control the media and not the other way around. And we also don't want to risk having so much information get out that the culprit or culprits can just watch us over our shoulders while we do our work. Just play your hand close like you're doing now and stay chummy with the press."

The woman nodded, and Liam looked over at the forensics tech who was working on surveillance.

"Is there anything new on Dennis since our last meeting?"

She cleared her throat and nodded. "We know that not only Dennis but also his sister, whose name is Luna, have several convictions for burglary." She waved a photo of a slender young woman in a blue puffer jacket.

"Hey," Nassrin blurted out. "That's the same Luna I met in the search group I was in yesterday."

"Great," Liam exclaimed. "Good that you were there, Nass."

Dea subtly rolled her eyes and shook her head at her boss before leaning forward and asking, "Do we know any more about this Luna?"

"She has been living in Tommerup for a year, but she comes from Assens like Dennis and Kasper. She's never done any jail time, but she was sentenced to community service after being on probation six times for theft. So far we also know that she used to work as a health care aide but lost her last job because of a theft charge. Unlike his sister, Dennis served time for the burglary at Charlotte Laursen's house. Their father is dead. Their mother is known in the local community as an alcoholic and a drug addict."

"OK," Liam said, and then pulled a small brown copy of the Quran out of his bag, the copy that Nassrin had brought over the night before. "Right now it's high priority that we figure out exactly what the quotes mean to Muslims and whether there's any connection between the three quotes that have been found." He stood up. "So with that, let's get out there and find these folks. Alive."

"Yes," everyone chimed energetically before they all left the room. Liam was well aware that several of them had already begun to speculate as to whether the three people were still alive, but no one had actually said it yet.

Dea sat down on the table quite close to him. "What about us?"
He struggled to suppress a yawn. "We're going to go see Lis
again."

"And Nassrin. She'll go to the nursing home?"

Liam nodded. "Yes, and then she'll meet up with us later."

"Is it true that Henrik's wife is a racist?" Dea flipped through
the small Quran.

"I don't know, but according to Nass's report, she ran as a New
Right candidate in the last election."

"Rin!" Dea blurted out.

Liam stared at her blankly, confused.

"The girl's name is Nass*rin*!"

He was not going to be corrected and ignored her. "When they
were out searching, Verner's daughter-in-law made it clear that she
was not particularly enthusiastic about Odense's Vollsmose neighborhood or the people who live there.

"Is that enough to bring her in for questioning?"

He shrugged dubiously. "She probably has a large political network, and we would pretty quickly run the risk of having their
party chairman blow up the case," he replied. "Let's talk to Lis first
instead so we can find out what she knows about her daughter-in-
law's involvement." Liam smoothed down his blue shirt. His iron-
ing job had not turned out as well as he would have liked.

"Hey, I see you dropped the leather jacket for today," Dea
teased.

Liam smiled wryly and started gathering up his things. "Yeah,
that was a silly idea at this time of year."

"Scotty?" An older officer had poked his head in the door.
"The police in Kolding just sent around a missing-person report
for a fifty-four-year-old woman. She went missing during an early-
morning run, and the search is already underway, since she needs
to take medication for a psychiatric disorder."

Liam glanced quickly at Dea and could tell that she agreed with what he was thinking. "We need to get a person to Kolding to investigate whether a slip of paper was left either in her home or somewhere along her running route."

* * *

Beate glanced around at the parsonage's backyard. At the far end they had let a wide swath of grass grow tall so it could go to seed.

"Are you looking at birds?"

She smiled at Peter. "No, I'm just sitting here for a bit." She pulled her feet up underneath her in the armchair and gathered the blanket around her. The ocean air was still a little chilly.

"I found a dead bird one time," Peter said. "I thought I would taxidermy it, but then it flew away."

"So it wasn't dead?"

"No, I don't know. Maybe it was in some kind of trance."

Beate looked out at the yard again. Silje was with her father this week. They generally traded off on Sundays between her two sermons.

"Is your work going well today?"

"Yes," Peter said enthusiastically. "I'm becoming more and more convinced that I can prove that Allah and the Christian God are the same if I can just get my hands on the right information." He looked at her triumphantly.

"What do you need?"

"I dream of getting my hands on one of the supplements to the Quran, where Muhammad speaks of the fellowship among Muslims, Christians, and Jews, because that sura dates back to Muhammad's lifetime and he is supposed to have written it himself, but as far as anyone knows, there are only three extant copies. There are Muslims who would give their lives to be able to destroy that sura so no one would say it out loud if they knew of a copy."

"Why would someone want to destroy it?"

"Because it presents a completely different openness and friendliness toward other faiths than the Islam practiced today does, and that's why my series of articles will be an important work." He smiled at her expectantly.

Beate suddenly felt discouraged. She couldn't bear to listen to any more about this series of articles. She seriously doubted he was ever going to finish it and be satisfied with it.

"What did you do this morning?" She changed the topic, turning toward him.

"What do you mean?"

"I woke up at four thirty and you weren't here."

"I couldn't sleep, so I drove down to the water." He seemed uninterested in this shift in their conversation.

"For over two hours?"

"I wasn't paying attention to the time. I went for a walk on the beach. It was a really beautiful morning, and there was a fog over the peat bog on the way over there."

"Peter, would you tell me if you got tired of me or tired of our life here at the parsonage?"

He squatted down beside her chair and looked seriously into her eyes. "Why would you say that?"

"I don't know. I feel fat and ugly, and now you're suddenly gone half the night. And during the day you're hiding behind your computer."

"It's work, Beate." He kissed her on the cheek. "You're busy with your work too. And with your parents, right?"

She looked down. "You know I need to help my father."

"I just wondered if they couldn't get some more outside help, your parents? Surely it can't all fall to you, the whole thing?"

"They need me," Beate said defensively, her eyes welling up with tears. "My mom can't be moved into a nursing home, and my father can't be left in the house alone. If that's what ends up happening, I've been wondering if we couldn't maybe offer to let him move in here and live with us. We have enough room, after all."

Beate put a hand on her pregnant belly and added that it might not be such a bad idea to have a grandparent in the house after the baby came. She said it mostly to irk Peter a little, but it occurred to her that it was true: having her father here wouldn't be such a bad idea. After her mother had been diagnosed with dementia three years earlier, things had gone downhill rapidly, an upheaval her father had had a hard time adjusting to, since her mother had been the driving force in their social lives. Her father mostly sat around at home now, and Beate could hardly bear that, so she stopped by their house daily.

"We need you here too."

She clenched her teeth firmly, sensing a headache coming on.

"I'll try to do it all, OK? I'm working myself to the bone for all of us, and one of us needs to earn some money."

She regretted her harsh tone immediately, but Peter had already stood up. He nodded stiffly and mumbled something or other she couldn't hear.

"I'm sorry," she continued, backing down. "I didn't mean it like that."

"I know," Peter said. "I'm stressed about the money too, and I'm trying to spend as little as possible."

Beate looked at him with a gentle smile. "You don't spend very much money . . ."

"And things *are* tough with your dad," he continued, without waiting for her to finish talking. "I also understand that you really want to help, of course I do. But he could come over here sometimes, too, so that you're not constantly having to drive there and back . . . Has he even come to visit us at all this year?" He paused and walked over to the window, then stood with his back to her. "He doesn't like me."

This wasn't the first time Beate's boyfriend had expressed that he didn't feel welcome in her family. It had been the cause of a couple of exhausting arguments, but Beate wasn't taking the bait anymore.

"You're not the only one who feels hurt that my dad never comes here," Beate said, determined not to let him get away with driving a wedge between her and her parents.

"I'm going to get back to work." Peter turned around resolutely, but before he made it to the door, he softened a little. He turned to face her, and there was a new spark in his eye. "I found a source who might be able to get me the text I've been looking for."

There were equal parts excitement and anticipation in his voice, and Beate let the words hang there for a moment before she leaned toward him a little, impeded by her pregnant belly.

"Peter!" She took the first step. She had been taking the first step for years, but she really needed to get it said now before it wormed its way into their relationship and ended up splitting them up before the little one was born. "You know full well that I have supported your article series, and I also definitely appreciate that it's important to you. But I am gradually starting to think that so much time has elapsed that you're going to need to give yourself a hard and fast deadline for these articles."

He had taken a step toward her, but now he stood completely stiffly in the middle of the room as the excited look faded from his face.

"Couldn't we agree that you'll use the next two months to finish? And if the project can't be finished in that time, then you're going to need to find a job."

"Two months?" he exclaimed. "You can't be serious!"

"Look, I wrote my dissertation in two months," Beate maintained. "With Silje climbing all over me and a boyfriend who ran off to America."

*   *   *

And your Lord has commanded that you shall not serve any but Him and show goodness to your parents.

The slip of paper had been stuck to the bottom corner of the kitchen window. Once it was clear that a verse from the Quran had been left at the house, Liam and Dea had immediately driven to Kolding, where they were met by a team of technicians and the officer who had taken the missing-person report about Lone.

"We took up jogging when Lone got cancer," her husband said quietly. "She found out that she only had a year to live at the most." He sat upright with his hands folded tightly in front of him.

"How long ago was that, Karsten?" Liam asked.

"Five years ago. So the doctors were wrong, or maybe Lone just ran it off." He smiled sadly. "I didn't know. She was so headstrong," he said. "But anyway, she's been running ever since."

Dea let Liam steer the conversation. She had taken a seat over by the window and was watching the husband, who had reported his wife missing earlier in the day. Karsten was about sixty years old, with thinning hair, skinny, freshly shaved. He looked like what he was: an accountant nearing retirement.

"I know that you already spoke with our colleagues from Kolding, but I would still like to ask you to run through your morning one more time."

Karsten nodded willingly. "Lone always gets up first. Then there's coffee and running clothes. I ran with her every morning for the first year, but now I only go two or three times a week, which is fine with her."

"Doesn't Lone work anymore?"

"No, gave up her job at Trapholt Museum when we thought she was going to die."

"So she has an arts background?"

"No, she was a salesclerk in their gift shop." He cleared his throat. "But it ended up being nice that she quit, because our eldest daughter had her first child that year. My wife had been so excited about becoming a grandmother—well, we were both excited about becoming grandparents, but then Lone was able to step up when our daughter and son-in-law needed help."

"Did she go running this morning too?"

"Yes." Karsten meticulously straightened his shirtsleeves. "There's nothing unusual about Lone being gone for a couple of hours, but without exception she has always been back by the time I leave for the office."

"But not today?"

"No, not today, and now"—he looked at his watch, an older Omega—"she's been gone for more than four hours."

"Do you know where she usually runs?"

"Yes, she has three different routes she alternates between. I've checked them all myself, and your colleagues have been there too."

"And your daughter, does she live nearby?"

"Yes, but she hasn't seen her mother either, and she's been very worried since I called her to ask. Lone needs to take her medicine, and of course that's making us extra nervous. So when we're done here, I'm going to drive over to our daughter's place. Your forensics people said earlier that it was best that she not come here until they were done."

Liam nodded and glanced quickly over at Dea to get a sense of whether she had anything to add, but when she subtly shook her head, he proceeded. "I understand that Lone's mother lives in a nursing home on Funen Island?"

"Yes, that's right," the man replied. "Lone's from Funen, and her parents have always lived there. It's only her mother who's alive now, and she moved into the nursing home a few years ago."

"Have you visited her recently?"

"No, it . . ." Karsten straightened his sleeves again. "We haven't been there so much since Lone got sick. We've been busy with our own things." He looked up. "Why are you asking about that? Are you referring to that slip of paper in the kitchen window? About that last part where it said that Allah decreed that you show kindness to your parents? Does this have something to do with my mother-in-law?"

Liam sensed how Dea had straightened up attentively.

"I'm asking because all relationships are relevant," Liam explained. "And because your mother-in-law lives in a nursing home in the area where two people have recently been reported missing, and your wife originally comes from the town where a third person has also disappeared. So I'd really like to know if there's anything, even the slightest thing, about Lone and her mother that I ought to know. Or if your wife had any other ties to the area she's from."

Karsten let out a long sigh, as if speaking were suddenly an insurmountable exertion, but then he pulled himself together. "When my father-in-law died and my mother-in-law, Olga, later decided to sell their farm, that did cause some conflict between Lone and her brother about how to divvy up the money from the sale. Which is to say that obviously it was Olga's money, but she wanted to share it with her children. My mother-in-law ended up taking her son's side, because over the years he had helped them out on their farm with all the bigger things. My wife, on the other hand, had always stepped up to help with the more personal and practical matters. Lone was very hurt that her efforts obviously hadn't been valued as equally important when it came time to divvy up the money. The conflict resulted in my wife deciding to cut off contact with both her mother and her brother. So we haven't seen any of them for several years now."

Liam could tell that the husband was struggling more to maintain his composure than he had at first assumed, so he decided to move on from the family conflict for the time being.

"One last question before you head over to your daughter's place: Do you or Lone have any sort of connection to Islamist circles or to the far right?"

Karsten looked up in surprise and responded emphatically. "No, we do not, and on that one I can also answer that the same is true for Lone's brother."

"Whom you haven't seen in a really long time?" Dea interjected from the window.

"Yes, but I know him well enough to know that he doesn't. We're more left-wing and definitely not friends with any extremists of one kind or the other."

* * *

"I think we're starting to close in on it now," Liam said, climbing into the car.

Dea got into the passenger's seat. She opened her phone and a bit absent-mindedly started scrolling through the surveillance report on Dennis. "Yes, but it seems like we can rule out Dennis. He couldn't have had anything to do with Lone's disappearance," she said, after she had compared timelines for the morning Lone was taken.

"I was thinking more about how we haven't had coffee since we left Odense."

It took her a moment to understand what he meant. She smiled. "There's a Starbucks at the mall in Kolding."

He nodded with a laugh and started the car.

Dea pulled out the evidence bag with the new slip of paper and studied the short verse. "What the heck is up with these verses from the Quran?" This one was printed the same way as the first three. It was the same size as the others, and the paper had been left behind in a place where they would definitely spot it if they looked for it. Just like the others.

Liam was lost in thought as they stopped at a red light but began talking once traffic started moving. "Nass came over to my place last night with a Quran. It's one of her uncles', and several verses were marked in it, among them the four that we found."

"Marked in what way?" Dea asked, letting his use of *Nass* go this time.

"Some of them have been outlined in pencil. I guess her uncle marked them for us, and maybe they're connected somehow. He also marked the quote we found today."

"So out of the many hundreds of verses in the Quran, the quotes that we've found were circled?" Dea exclaimed, looking insistently at him.

Liam nodded.

"And the quote from today too?"

He nodded again.

"But you said that she dropped the Quran off at your place last night? And the verse that Karsten found here this morning was already marked then?"

He turned to face her now and nodded for the third time. Then he recited the new verse thoughtfully. *"And your Lord has commanded that you shall not serve any but Him and show goodness to your parents."* The light turned green. "Lone does not show goodness to her mother . . . She doesn't actually pay attention to her mother at all."

Dea's voice was sharp now. "But if that quote was already marked in her uncle's Quran before Lone disappeared, then we

should bring her two uncles in for a chat! What does Nassrin have
to say about the markings?"

"Not much yet."

"Oh, for crying out loud, Liam!" She looked at him, shocked,
and wondered just what kind of relationship he actually had with
Nassrin since he hadn't gone after her uncles the minute he discovered that the new Quran verse was one of the ones that had been
outlined in the book.

"We'll bring them in, of course," he said placatingly, having
clearly picked up on her irritation. "Let's just concentrate on the
quotes we've found. The one that was left at Charlotte Laursen's
place said something about not associating anything with Allah."

Dea nodded and pulled out her phone. She was so annoyed
that she made up her mind to go to the chief superintendent if
Liam kept protecting Nassrin like this. She scowled at him.

Liam ignored her piercing look and asked her to read the first
three verses out loud.

"*Allah will not forgive idolatry. He forgives whom He wants for
other sins; but he who worships other gods than Allah has pulled far
away from the truth.*"

He nodded and asked her to continue while he thought about
the picture of Kasper, a broad-shouldered guy with a dirty-blond
fade haircut, cut very short on the sides and back but longer on top,
where he'd applied a generous amount of wax. He also thought
about the young man's grandmother from Hvidovre and the auto
workshop that had been turned upside down.

The forensics team had transported a lot of dirt, garbage, and
cigarette butts back to their headquarters. They had secured sole
prints, tire prints, and fingerprints. They had done a thorough job,
but he was prepared for it to take them a long time to get through
all of it, because so many people had walked through the workshop. Martin from Forensics had told him it would be like finding

122 SARA BLÆDEL AND MADS PEDER NORDBO

a needle in a haystack if they managed to find a clue that helped move the investigation forward. And it would take time.

"They swear to you by Allah that they might please you; and Allah, as well as His Apostle, has a greater right that they should please Him, if they are believers."

Dea read on. The old grocer was the one Liam had the hardest time connecting to the other victims. On the other hand, it wasn't hard to understand that the quote referred to Verner's back-door sales.

"O ye who believe! When the call is made for prayer on Friday, *then hasten to the remembrance of Allah and leave off traffic; that is better for you, if you know. But when the prayer is ended, then disperse abroad in the land and seek Allah's grace, and remember Allah much, that ye may be successful."*

"We need to know exactly how those quotes relate to the missing people." Liam drummed his fingers on the steering wheel.

Dea moved on from her irritation and nodded. "If you try to view it this way, that the quotes are a set of instructions of sorts for how one should ideally behave, then maybe their disappearances could be interpreted as a punishment for something they have or haven't done?" she suggested.

"You mean that they disappeared because they didn't behave the way the passage instructs?" Liam turned to her with interest now. "Good thinking. So Lone is being punished for not showing goodness to her mother?"

Dea nodded enthusiastically. "Yes, and Verner did not leave his trafficking in goods on the day of prayer. He probably didn't say many prayers, since he was busy selling things from the back of his shop on Sundays."

"What about Kasper?" Liam asked.

Dea shook her head. They could see the mall in Kolding now. "I don't know."

She pointed to the Starbucks sign, but now he seemed so animated that his need for coffee appeared to have evaporated.

"Of course, terrorism does come to mind because of these Quran quotes," he said, concentrating on passing a semi and heading for Odense. "But can we just agree that none of us will say that word yet? Because the minute it's said out loud, we'll have the Police Intelligence Service breathing down our necks and the prime minister will be on TV going off about the whole case. We've got enough on our plates right now just coordinating with the South East Jutland Police."

"What if it *is* terrorism?" Dea asked, eyeing him somberly. "Isn't it too risky *not* to say the word out loud? There have already been big local actions around the country, even in smaller towns, that were not connected to acts of terrorism or preparations for acts of terrorism in any way."

Liam stared out the windshield, focused on the traffic.

"You're going to have to be open to the possibility," Dea said.

They drove for a little while in silence before he nodded reluctantly. "I just don't believe it," he said. "This slow, patient, seemingly carefully planned and relatively discreet process with one disappearance at a time does not seem to fit at all with Islamic terrorism, which always and without exception is looking for a big bang and tons of attention."

Dea was inclined to agree with him. If this turned out to be terrorism related, this would be a highly atypical approach.

Liam pulled into the police garage and turned off the engine. Dea was about to get out when he stopped her. "Four people missing in only four days. It's hard not to be afraid that another one will disappear tomorrow."

She nodded, having had the same thought herself.

*   *   *

Claus poured some milk into a tall glass. He turned to put the carton back into the fridge but missed the shelf and instead dropped the milk on the floor, where it splashed and then spread into a big puddle. He quickly grabbed a dishrag from the kitchen table but then realized it wouldn't be able to soak up the whole mess. He pushed it aside and left it lying in the puddle of milk and slumped down onto the floor instead. The cold tiles felt smooth against his cheek. It was quiet in the house. He looked at the dishrag in the milk. It was stained with dirt and food scraps. Charlotte was usually the one who swapped out their dishrags and kitchen towels. Everything was filthy now.

"Dad?"

Claus quickly got back up into a sitting position and grabbed the milk-laden rag. He gave Cecilie an apologetic look.

"What are you doing on the floor?" Her high-pitched voice sounded worried.

"I dropped the milk," he said, making a face as if he were the silliest clown in the world.

"There's a man here," Cecilie continued, and started laughing at him as he continued clowning around with the dishrag. "He's standing in the hallway. Can Oliver and me have something yummy?"

Claus had gotten to his feet and nodded absent-mindedly. The girl excitedly opened the cookie drawer and got out a whole package of cookies. Claus tossed the rag into the sink, which was full of dirty dishes, and sighed. He wasn't up to people, didn't want to talk to anyone. He thought it was probably the police again. Or someone from water polo. They kept calling to try and get him to coach the boys as usual and take them to the game. It was as if they didn't understand that his world had collapsed.

Claus stopped abruptly when he spotted the man who was standing in his front hall. "What are you doing here?"

"You're not answering your cell phone, so I just wanted to see how you're doing. And see if there was anything I could do for you?"

"You can't come over here," Claus exclaimed vehemently, quickly pulling the door closed behind him. The kids were sitting on the sofa in the living room, engrossed in a cartoon, munching on cookies.

"I know, but then you need to pick up. I'm worried about you!"

Claus jerked his head away when the man reached out for his face. "We can't do this . . . It's over. You need to understand that I mean it. I can't keep saying it. It won't do. It's over!"

"I thought maybe now that your wife is gone, there could be something else . . . couldn't there?"

"Keep Charlotte out of this," Claus interrupted him angrily.

"But . . . you don't need to go through all of this all by yourself."

"Just leave me alone," Claus continued dismissively.

The man reached out for him again and this time made contact. Claus twisted slightly, but in the end allowed himself to be pulled into the man's arms. And once he was enveloped by the warmth of the other man's body, he broke into a flood of tears and snot, which dripped down onto the man's dark-blue jacket.

"There, there," the other man said, very close to Claus's ear. "You'll get through this. We have each other. Always."

*   *   *

Nassrin pulled off the little one-lane Degnegyden, "Parish Clerk Alley," onto a patch of grass behind Ernst and Mona's farm. To the right of the farm sat Johannes's house. It was white and actually looked nice, even though it didn't appear to have been renovated since the 1970s.

Liam had called shortly beforehand and told her about Lone from Kolding and the fourth quote. And then he had sent her out here to see the former pastor. She leaned her head back against the headrest and looked up at the blue sky. He had sent *her*. She was on the case.

The air smelled of fields and summer and manure. She sat for a moment in her own world and jumped when she heard a rasping scream very close to her. At first she couldn't figure out where the scream came from, but then she spotted a peacock sitting in an oak tree with its blue, green, and gold tail pointing backward. It screamed again, and another peacock answered from nearby. She looked around for it, but she could only see the fat pigs in the field.

When Johannes answered his front door, he regarded her tensely.

"I'm sorry to bother you," Nassrin began quickly. "But I have a couple of questions about Olga Andersen. Do you have a minute to answer them?"

"Has something happened to Olga?" He sounded instantly concerned and took a step closer to her.

"No," Nassrin quickly replied, explaining that she had come to talk to him about Olga's daughter.

His shoulders drooped a little, and his eyes grew kinder, but he remained in the doorway without making any sign of inviting her in. "Well, if I can somehow help, go ahead and ask me already."

"I understand that Olga's daughter hasn't visited her mother very often since she moved into the nursing home. Is that true?"

Johannes cocked his head to the side and looked upward, contemplating. "I don't think I've ever run into Olga's daughter at the nursing home or heard that she had been out there to visit. It's only her son who comes."

"Is that normal?"

"Unfortunately, it's not abnormal that old people rarely get visitors. But for Olga it's a great source of sorrow that her daughter never visits."

"Do you know about the assault that sent Olga to the nursing home?"

He nodded slowly. "I was the pastor in town when it happened. And it was a terrible incident both for Olga, because she was so badly knocked about that she subsequently had to sell and move away from the farm that had been her home for more than seventy years, and also for our little community. From one day to the next it became unsafe for the elderly who live all on their own out here in the countryside."

Nassrin asked if he had had any contact with Olga's daughter back when the assault occurred.

Johannes nodded. "After the assault she used to come out regularly to take care of her mom. But I never saw her again after the farm was sold and her mom got a bed at the nursing home."

He seemed sad for a moment, Nassrin noted, studying his dark, compassionate eyes. But then he continued. "In the beginning Olga had a hard time settling into the nursing home. As you would expect, she missed her farm and everything familiar. The rest of us circled our wagons around her, and her son was also good about coming, even though he lives all the way up in Hundested. But we didn't see her daughter, and do you know, it's been a long time now since I've heard Olga mention her."

Nassrin was about to thank him, but she suddenly heard herself ask what had actually happened when Dea's husband died.

She could tell that the former pastor was taken aback for a moment at the abrupt change in topic, but then the look in his eyes softened. "She entered into a very dark spell," he began, his gaze slipping out over the countryside, as if it were important to him that what he wanted to say come out correctly. "I feel so terribly sorry for her, because it's so obvious that she's still carrying a tremendous amount of anger and grief over what happened to Mogens."

"Why anger?" Nassrin followed up curiously, knowing quite well that it was unprofessional of her to pump him for information. But she couldn't forget Dea's strong reaction after the public meeting.

Johannes closed his eyes briefly as he thought it over, and then he looked straight at Nassrin. "Of course there is anger at the departed, because there is so much grief in being left behind. That's completely normal. But she's also very angry at their doctor. Her husband had been complaining about chest pain for a long time, but their family doctor kept playing down their concerns. In the autopsy, it turned out that Mogens had a heart defect that could have been detected and remedied if the doctor had taken his pain seriously." He shook his head sadly and folded his arms in front of his chest. "I don't think she'll ever completely get over that: that the doctor could have prevented his death if he had responded to the symptoms. I do feel, though, that she took some solace from the time she spent staying with us."

Nassrin's cell phone rang in her hand. It was Dea. Nassrin jumped as if she'd been caught red-handed and embarrassedly thanked Johannes for taking the time to speak with her. Then she hurried back to her car with the illogical feeling that Dea had overheard the last part of their conversation.

"Hi, Nassrin." Dea sounded perky. "We brought your uncles into the station for a little chat. It's probably best if you come in too."

* * *

"As you already know," Liam said, "you're here for questioning because of the Quran that Nassrin brought me last night. You're being question exclusively as witnesses, not as suspects."

"Naturally, we are at your disposal," Aldar said formally, and smoothed his mustache with his thumb and forefinger. "But I still don't quite understand what it is that my brother and I can help you with?"

"To begin with, you can tell us why your brother circled these specific verses in his Quran," Dea said, nodding at the leather-bound book that sat on the table between them.

"My brother writes in all our books," Aldar replied immediately, holding up his hands. "Sometimes if I'm going to sell a book, I need to go through and erase it all."

Hayyan hadn't said a single word since they had been picked up for questioning, but now he leaned forward slightly and began chanting in Persian.

"What's he saying?" Dea hurriedly asked.

"He's reciting some verses," Aldar reported, and watched his brother attentively.

Liam reached out and took Hayyan's worn Quran and opened it. "Are they the verses that are marked here?"

Hayyan looked startled when Liam pushed the book over to him. Then he drew it toward himself and stroked the brown leather. He flipped through and pointed to the four verses they had found at the victims' homes. After that, he continued to browse through and pointed to two more.

"No, they aren't," Aldar said.

"Do the verses your brother is pointing to mean something particularly important to Muslims?" Liam asked.

"No, there are many other verses that mean more," Aldar replied.

Liam looked into Aldar's eyes. "If I tell you that I think all the verses your brother has pointed out have to do with punishment in one way or another—have I understood that correctly?"

Aldar gazed calmly back at Liam. "At heart, both the Bible and the Quran are about making people live in fear of God's wrath and punishment." He glanced over at his brother. "No form of government is more effective than fear."

"What verses was your brother reciting just now?" Liam asked pleasantly.

"There is a sacred text that is said to have been written by Muhammad himself. It is a text in which Muhammad orders Muslims to be good to Christians and Jews. In other words, a text that refutes the idea that Muslims should perceive infidels as enemies."

"Can I get that text?"

Aldar smiled indulgently. "You can get the short fragments we are aware of, but no one can give you a complete version, since no one knows where the three preserved copies are."

"Let's just stick to this copy of the Quran," Dea said dryly. "Why does your brother have a Danish translation of the Quran at all?"

"We never have only one copy of our books, and we've had a Danish Quran handy since we've lived here. Since 1973."

"But it appears that he uses—"

The door to the interrogation room opened with a bang. "Hayyan can't do this!"

Dea stood up quickly. "Relax, Nassrin. This is a calm conversation, and we're almost done."

"You're done right now is what you are!" Nassrin eyed Dea defiantly.

Both uncles sat completely still, looking down at the table.

"Hayyan has severe PTSD," Nassrin hissed, staring at Dea.

Dea's facial expression was icy as she took a step closer to Nassrin.

"Stop!" Liam warned her, taking hold of Dea's arm. He turned to Nassrin. "Just take your uncles home now. We were finished."

As soon as Nassrin and her uncles were out the door, Liam collapsed onto a chair.

"Sorry," Dea said. She was still standing in the middle of the room, ready for a fight. "She made me lose it, but—"

"Just stop. I can't deal with your rivalry right now."

Dea stomped out of the room without a word and slammed the door behind her.

* * *

Liam handed her a cola as he pulled a chair over to her desk. "Are you OK?"

Dea accepted the soda and shook her head. "No," she admitted. "But I don't feel like talking about it."

She felt his gaze on her and sensed that he was getting ready to say something.

"Dea," he began. "I need to know if you have a problem with working with Nassrin."

"No, of course I don't!" she replied quickly. "Today's just a shitty day." She rubbed her forehead hard before turning to face him. For a second, she sat there staring straight ahead. "You know it was my fault back then, with Olga. My fault that Dennis wasn't convicted for the assault."

"Stop," Liam said, holding up his hand, but she brushed him off.

"The minute we walked in the door in Kolding, I had this feeling that Lone's husband could see it in me."

"It wasn't your fault," Liam said insistently.

Dea closed her eyes and sighed deeply. "If anyone starts digging around into it because of Lone and the other disappearances, then it will come out, and you totally know that." She had set down the unopened soda.

"There's nothing to find out. You don't have anything to hide," Liam exclaimed, leaning forward toward her. "Drop it. You did your job, and you know very well that part of the job description is watching criminals go free sometimes because we can't prove they committed a crime. And that's how it is."

She wished he were right. Wished it were as easy as he made it sound. But it just wasn't.

"Liam, come on! I showed Olga Dennis's testimony. I was so furious at what he had put the old woman through that I ran through the whole process with her. I wanted that idiot to be convicted. I wanted her to say the right things during the trial."

There was something fatherly about the way he reached out and put his hand over hers.

"Dea, stop now! Olga had already been questioned. She had given her evidence. She had explained what she remembered. You didn't put words into her mouth, and—"

"I went too far"—she interrupted him—"when Kasper turned up out of the blue and gave his buddy an alibi, which we all knew was a complete lie. I got her to say that she recognized Dennis."

Liam let go of her hand. "Dennis got away with it. There were no consequences to what you did, so there's no reason for you to keep wallowing in these self-recriminations."

"I gave false testimony in court when I said that Olga had singled Dennis out as her assailant. I'm not worried about him deciding to blab, because he knows that he only got off because of Kasper. But if someone starts talking to Olga now with her daughter missing, then it's possible it will come out."

* * *

Liam raised the glass of whiskey, an eighteen-year-old Longrow that his father had brought over as a kind of peace offering after his mother had expanded the population of chickens in the yard by another two. Helene had been furious. Over time he had given up. He let the alcohol fill his mouth and closed his eyes for a moment, enjoying the flavor.

He adjusted his position in the pillows and kicked the comforter aside a little so one leg was out. This was absolutely his favorite time of day. There was something almost sinful about a nightcap enjoyed in bed after the sharp taste of the toothpaste had worn off a little.

He set his glass down and reached for the daily reports lying on his nightstand. Then he leaned back, pulled the reading light closer, and picked up the topmost report. It was from their colleagues in Kolding. In the field at the top, in addition to the case number, it said *Lone and Karsten*.

Liam skimmed the first page but looked up when Helene came in from the bathroom in her light nightgown.

"Is that work?" She came over and took a sip of his whiskey.

"Yes, there's a lot right now." They had already talked about it. He had played his time-out card. That was something they had eventually come up with many years earlier. There were cases that required so much time that he did best if he was honest about bowing out and saying that the family simply couldn't rely on him while they were going on.

"And there's still nothing new?" She walked over and opened the window facing the yard.

Liam shook his head.

"Why were they the ones who disappeared? Who are these people?"

He picked up the whiskey glass and brought it to his lips, then paused.

"Ordinary, boring people, to put it bluntly," he began. He could tell Helene anything; he didn't need to dress it up. "There's nothing about their lives or their immediate background that sets them apart or makes them in the least bit interesting. Or predisposed or vulnerable, for that matter."

"So maybe that's why they're disappearing?" She had lain down on her side of the bed and was looking at him, her head resting in the palm of her hand.

"Because they're . . . meh?" Liam said, surprised.

"Yes, in the grand scheme of things. Not to their families, of course." She reached over and took his glass from his hand and sipped again. "What about those verses from the Quran?"

"When you look at these verses, that's when these people stop being so unremarkable, because the verses are like a brightly lit arrow, pointing directly at specifically them."

Helene rested her head on his chest. "Do you think they're still alive?"

He took his glass back and finished it before answering.

"Yes, we're working off the assumption that it doesn't really make sense to dispose of four people without leaving behind the slightest trace unless there's some additional point to it. And that fact, that they're probably being kept locked up somewhere, is now causing us some new problems. Lone, who disappeared today, is bipolar, and she can seem schizophrenic if she's not on her medications, which she probably isn't, because she went missing during her run without her medication with her." He paused and then glanced at his half-naked wife. If a fifth person disappeared tomorrow, this would probably be the last night he had time for Helene before they wrapped up this case.

Day 5—Tuesday

IT WAS EARLY morning. Beate had stopped by the bakery and handed the bag of fresh bread to her father. The living room smelled stuffy, so she walked over and opened the window. When she looked around the room, she noted that her father still had not done much of any tidying, let alone actual deep cleaning. She immediately felt the familiar sense of guilt that she wasn't helping out more herself.

"How are you, my girl? You seem a little sad." Her father asked from the kitchen. He came into the living room a moment later carrying cups and two small plates.

Beate looked at her father. He was completely right. She felt sad and burdened.

"You would know more about my life if you would just come visit us once in a while."

She could tell instantly that the remark pained him, but she still hadn't shaken off her argument with Peter.

"You know how it is, my girl," her father hastily said. "I can't just drive off and leave your mother on her own. You know that, right?"

"You didn't come before she got sick either," Beate continued. She realized she sounded like an unreasonable, petulant child. She quickly disappeared into the kitchen to get the coffee.

Her father didn't look at her as he leaned forward in his chair to pick up his coffee cup. "Maybe it's time for us to consider looking for a nice home for your mother, where people can take better care of her than we can."

Beate sipped her coffee. She knew what was coming.

"But then there are moments," he continued, as expected, eyeing her intently, "when she's completely herself, and I don't have the heart to have some staff member at the nursing home explaining to her during one of her lucid moments that we've given up on her. Each time that happens, it will feel like the first time to her. It will shake her over and over again that we gave up on her."

"I know that, Dad, but when my baby arrives, I'm not sure I'll be able to take care of my job duties, Peter, the kids, and also visit you and Mom so often."

"You're not taking care of Peter, are you?" he exclaimed.

Beate gave a strained smiled. Her parents had both retired years ago. They had been in their late thirties when they had her, and she was their only child. Her father had always called her a miracle, because they had tried and hadn't been able to have a child and had given up on that dream. She'd grown up in the independent residential school for teens where her parents had worked as house parents. The school had shaped their lives in every way—it had been the center of their world until they left it behind. Now they lived in a smallish house in Verninge.

"Yes, yes, I wasn't trying to nag," her father continued. "And you do know that you can use the car out there all you want." He pointed to the courtyard.

Beate cleared her throat and smiled wanly at him. "I know, and that's a big help too."

"Is it Peter?" he continued. "We did advise you to stick with Mathias. Plus you two also had Silje, so maybe it would have—"

"No, Dad." She cut him short, annoyed. "And you know that too. When Mathias extended his contract in New York, I lost my only chance at that." She still felt the heartache when she said it out loud.

"It was his job," her father said, defending his former son-in-law. "You don't turn down an embassy job when you're climbing the ladder."

"But what about me? Was I supposed to just hang out at home taking care of Silje, interrupted only by going to Pilates twice a week?"

"No one was saying that," her father objected, his brow furrowed. "A person like you would surely have found something to dig into."

"Dad, Mathias left us, and I made it clear right from the beginning that I wanted to stay in Denmark with Silje."

She shook her head, resigned. She was so tired of this conversation. Tired of having to defend her decision even though she had gotten divorced years ago. When Mathias was offered the job in New York, she had known right away that he was going to take it, and she had cried pretty much every day when he wasn't sending half as much love to her via Messenger and text as she was sending him. He was busy, he said, and when he extended his contract the following year, she made up her mind. She had met Peter right after that, and that had pushed the grief away. He was good for her, and he was good with Silje.

"What's he doing now, Mathias?" her father continued, brushing the crumbs from his pastry off his chin.

Beate gave him a resigned look. "I think he's a trademark lawyer in Odense. I don't remember the name of the company."

"Yes, I think that's right." Her father looked up at the ceiling. "Mathias was so fond of your mother. They had good chemistry together." He shrugged. "We never see Peter."

"Well, you don't come visit us either!" she repeated stubbornly.

"Isn't he unemployed?"

Beate gave up with a sigh, regretting that she hadn't spent the morning at home in the kitchen enjoying some fresh bread and hygge and her family.

"He's working on a series of articles that could change a lot of people's ideas about religions, and I'm proud of him."

She was interrupted by her cell phone, had a short conversation, and then got up from the sofa after she hung up.

"A death?" her father asked out of curiosity.

"Yes." Beate nodded. "One of the old women at the nursing home. Olga."

"Oh, those nursing homes are so sad. I really don't think that would be right for your mother," he said, as if this one death settled the matter. "Couldn't you just squeeze in a quick visit before you go, just to say hello to her? We could just peek in and see if she's awake."

*   *   *

Liam snapped his briefcase shut after the concluded briefing. There hadn't been any problems getting extra staffing allocated. Fifty police officers were working on the case involving the missing people. He had just assigned investigative tasks and shooed them out the door. The whole system ran like a well-oiled machine, but in truth, he had no idea what direction they should go. The next step was calling in the Police Intelligence Service. There was no way around that.

"What do we know?" Dea asked, pointing to the wall with the photographs and the Quran verses after the others had left.

"Come on! Four people are missing. What are we thinking?" She looked questioningly from Nassrin to the psychologist, who had also remained in the briefing room. No one said anything. "We have to assume now," Dea continued on her own, "that the missing people didn't disappear of their own free will. I mean, it would be beyond weird if the Quran passages we found just happened to be lying around at the disappearance locations by coincidence."

The others nodded, and Nassrin mumbled, "Check to that!"

"They were obviously put there and contain a message that we still have not fully grasped but seems to be personally connected to the missing people. So we're working from the assumption that four crimes have occurred, and we're looking for one or more perpetrators. So far, so good."

Dea walked all the way up to the board. "We've been through all the local surveillance footage several times but haven't stumbled across anything unusual." She looked over at the psychologist. "What can you tell us about the missing people?"

Liam had tipped his chair back and was enjoying having his section leader take over.

"There's such a lot of variation between them," the psychologist began, his hand resting on the white cafeteria mug, "that it hasn't been possible yet to piece together a common profile. We're working on finding commonalities, but to the extent there are any, they're pretty well hidden."

"And what about the perpetrator or perpetrators? Do you have anything for us to go on there?" Dea continued.

"Regardless of whether it's one person or multiple people," the psychologist said, "whoever it is is incredibly thorough. It's clear that nothing has been left to chance. For example, we haven't found the slightest trace of any fingerprints on the slips of paper with the Quran quotes, not even on the quote that was stuck on the windowpane. So, we're dealing with people who know what they're doing."

"Do you think the missing people are still alive?" Liam interjected.

The psychologist nodded slowly, set down his cup, and instead folded his hands. "Yes, I do, actually. I don't think the passages from the Quran would have been left if the missing people had been killed. Someone wants to tell us something. Maybe those passages are a kind of a riddle that can lead us to the missing people."

There was a murmur of agreement.

"We need to get out there and get some perspective," Liam said energetically, using his hands to mime a helicopter. "We've been poking around with our noses all in the same mudhole. Let's take one more round through the other police districts. Has anyone else run into Quran verses like this? Do we think there's a sexual motive? Is this terrorism? The families of the missing people haven't received any ransom requests, no blackmail. The search teams still haven't covered a number of lakes in the area. Word is that the military doesn't have enough divers to cover such a large area in such a short time frame."

"What about the two Syrians you brought in for questioning?" the psychologist asked.

"The uncles are protected," Dea mumbled, so quietly that Nassrin couldn't hear it.

Liam cleared his throat and gave Dea a stern look. "We discussed with them what the four passages might mean in this context, and one of Nassrin's uncles pointed out that both the Bible and the Quran are collections of verses, like poems, about how people should behave and live their lives. Our working theory is that the people who are missing violated the commandment or rule that's on the slip of paper that was found at each disappearance site."

The psychologist nodded approvingly.

"We had a religious scholar look at the four passages, and he confirmed that they are less well known verses and thus not something that a Muslim would be likely to have tattooed on his arm or hang over his door."

Nassrin sat very still, staring at the four quotes on the board in concentration. Then she suddenly leapt to her feet. "Could I just borrow my uncle's Quran?"

She stood, bent forward, focusing as she flipped back and forward, alternately looking at the book and at something on her cell phone. Then she straightened up and in a clear voice read the four quotes.

Everyone watched her.

"If we think further about your theory, then Charlotte's crime was *associating anything with Allah*, which would be essentially idolatry. She shouldn't have any other gods, right?" she continued, after she finished reading.

"Yes, it would appear that way." Dea had sat up again.

"And Kasper swore, but maybe only to please Dennis and not to please Allah . . . in other words, he lied." She kept going without waiting for any response. "And Verner did not leave off his trafficking on the day of prayer. He did not heed the call to prayer or hasten to remember Allah, because he was selling black-market goods at all hours."

"And Lone did not show goodness to her mother," Dea blurted out. "We know that already!"

Nassrin ignored her, eyeing Liam with focus. "Can't you see? Maybe these quotes aren't related to the Quran at all. Maybe these are the Ten Commandments from the Bible."

Liam got up without a word and left the room. A few minutes later he was back with a printout of the Ten Commandments.

1. Thou shalt have no other gods before me.
2. Thou shalt not take the name of the Lord thy God in vain.
3. Remember the sabbath day, to keep it holy.

4. Honor thy father and thy mother.
5. Thou shalt not kill.
6. Thou shalt not commit adultery.
7. Thou shalt not steal.
8. Thou shalt not bear false witness against thy neighbor.
9. Thou shalt not covet thy neighbor's house.
10. Thou shalt not covet thy neighbor's wife, nor his manservant, nor his maidservant, nor his ox, nor his ass, nor any thing that is thy neighbor's.

Liam hung the printout on the board and stepped back a little as he regarded the piece of paper.

"Impressive, Nassrin! I think you're right!" He looked over at the others. "Are these people being abducted as punishment for breaking the ten Christian commandments?"

Dea appeared to have forgotten her irritation and leaned eagerly over the table. "So those verses from the Quran are the Muslim version of Christianity's Ten Commandments?" She turned to her young colleague, impressed.

Nassrin felt her cheeks grow hot with equal parts pride and shyness.

Liam hesitated for a moment before putting a finger in the middle of the Ten Commandments. "Do you know what that means if it's actually true?" He looked around seriously at the three people sitting across from him.

"Yes," Nassrin said with a nod. "That today someone who committed a murder will disappear."

* * *

"I think we should invite Dea over here someday," Mona said, pouring coffee for Ernst.

"Why in the world would we do that?" he grumbled distantly, his eyes lingering on the marble cake over on the kitchen counter. "She was the one who turned her back on us."

"Turn the other cheek, Dad." She looked to see what he was looking at. "She was going through a difficult time."

"Why would she even want to see us?"

The morning sun shone in through the low farmhouse windows.

"I've always been fond of her. Even though she's so much younger than I am, she's still my cousin."

"You didn't have to put up with her father your whole childhood!"

"Dad! You can't blame her for that!" Mona sat down at the table and carefully dropped a sugar cube into her coffee. "Dea and Johannes got along well together when they were kids. They were always out playing. I can picture them so clearly as they ran over to Alfred and Anna's and got slices of bread with honey on top, even though your father didn't want them to go over there."

"My father was opposed to most things," Ernst said, and suddenly seemed more cheerful. "Even summer, I think."

Mona smiled at him. "Do you have any plans for today?"

"I think I might like to ride my bike over to the nursing home."

"Will there be singing today?"

Ernst raised an eyebrow, but he had a twinkle in his eye. "No, but that makes it a good time to stop by for a chat and a cup of coffee."

Mona enjoyed the days when he wasn't constantly on the war path, when he wasn't cranky and argumentative with everyone around them. The days when he was just pleasant and they could have a proper conversation together.

Silence settled over the kitchen, while her father ate the warm cake. He carefully brushed the crumbs off his chin with the cloth napkin and pushed his plate away. It had just started to rain outside.

"Did Johannes get off OK to the convention in Fåborg?"

"Yes, he left this morning. It was nice of Beate to let him do it so he could get away. He's so happy about those gatherings."

"*Nice of,*" Ernst sneered, and Mona instantly regretted having mentioned Beate. "Without a doubt it was just because our incompetent pastor couldn't be bothered to go herself. But then, what would she have had to offer? After all, Johannes is better qualified."

*   *   *

Nassrin cast a curious glance at the man walking out the gate in front of Claus and Charlotte's house in Tommerup as she and Thorbjørn made their way in.

"Wasn't that Lis and Verner's son?"

Thorbjørn nodded. One of their colleagues had questioned Henrik, but Nassrin recognized him from the picture hanging under Verner Nissen's relatives on their bulletin board. The sky was dark and brooding over them, and thunder rumbled on the horizon. The rain poured down in sheets on the windows of the house, and the trees and bushes in the yard shone wetly.

Claus opened the door with a cigarette in his hand. He still looked disheveled but not nearly as shabby as before.

"Do you have a second?" Nassrin asked. Even though there was always some risk of rejection when they trooped in unannounced, it was often advantageous to drop in on people when they least expected it.

"Of course," Claus said through the smoke. His face seemed rigid and his movements slow, but he immediately stepped aside to let them in.

They followed him into the living room.

Claus put out his cigarette in an overflowing ashtray. It kept smoking and sent a thin column of grayish-white smoke up toward the ceiling.

"Is there any news?" he asked.

"We came to talk to you about your wife's perspective on religion," Nassrin said quickly instead of answering.

"Religion?" Claus repeated, taken aback, suddenly seeming a little more present. Another thunderclap rumbled in the distance. "She's a religion teacher, but hopefully it didn't take you five days to figure that out?"

"No, but we have become aware that religion may be a factor in her disappearance, and—"

"You're thinking about that slip of paper I found?" Claus interrupted, taking a seat on the sofa. "You think that maybe Islamists took her?"

"Claus?" Nassrin watched him calmly. He seemed tired, exhausted, but he had showered and his clothes weren't as grubby as the last time she had seen him. "Has Charlotte had any kind of conflict with anyone?"

"You've asked me that a hundred times," he objected despondently.

"Yes, but could you think about it again? Whether she's had conflicts with anyone specifically about something religious? The conflict could easily have been something that seemed insignificant when it happened."

"Yeah . . ." He sighed heavily. "A few years ago when the school wanted to change its Christianity classes into religion classes, there was a little op-ed war between Charlotte and the pastor, who was angry that such a big change was being made . . . cultural heritage and stuff like that . . . I don't remember clearly."

"Was that in one of the local papers?"

"Yes, in both *Lokalavisen* and *Stiftstidende*."

"Do you have copies of the op-eds here?"

"No, I don't think Charlotte saved them. And there wasn't really anything in them other than that they disagreed."

"And Beate was the pastor?"

"No, it was the guy before her . . . Johannes. He was the one who baptized Cecilie, and he's all right. It was just that Charlotte was taking the heat for the school's decision, but she also felt like she had to go to bat for it since she was teaching the Christianity classes. But she also agreed that it was a more open and inclusive approach to the subject to call them religion classes instead of Christianity classes. She'd been teaching about all of the religions the whole time, not just Christianity."

Thorbjørn took over now and changed the subject.

"We just saw Verner's son walking out your front gate when we arrived, didn't we?"

Claus looked down at the floor and said, "So?"

"Do you know each other well?"

"We come from the same town."

"So you've always known each other?"

"Yes, from school and water polo and stuff . . ."

"Stuff?" Nassrin asked, eyeing him inquisitively.

Claus shrugged. He was looking at a point just over her head.

"It's a small town. We grew up together. Everyone knows each other."

"What did he want today?"

"Just to find out if there was any news about Charlotte."

"Do you socialize together, you and Charlotte and Henrik and his wife?"

Claus continued to look stiffly at that spot above Nassrin.

"No . . . it's just me who knows Henrik from way back when."

* * *

Liam looked around at Lis and Verner's kitchen. Since Charlotte disappeared, they had been looking for any conceivable clues. They knew a little more now, but still not enough to be all that targeted in their investigation.

Henrik set a cup of coffee on the table in front of Liam.

"We have to offer you something," Henrik said, and put a comforting arm around his mother.

Dea got straight down to business.

"We're here to ask you to think carefully about whether Verner has any connections to anything religious. And we'd also really like to know if anyone in particular has expressed dissatisfaction with Verner conducting his back-room grocery sales."

"No," Henrik said, dragging the word out a little, but then he seemed to decide that he had better say something after all. "Well, he still runs the little grocery, which can be open when the other shops are closed. I think everyone benefits from that."

"Surely not everyone?" Liam said.

"That's just something people say, right?" Henrik said with a shrug.

"Yes, although not usually to the police during an investigation," Liam chastised him. "In this situation, we need to find the exceptions. That's what we're looking for, so think it over carefully."

"I don't know," Henrik said, and looked over at his mother questioningly. "I don't have that much contact with my father."

Lis shook her head. It seemed as if she had completely lost the courage to speak.

"Lis, do you know anyone who doesn't like Verner's basement sales?" Liam continued.

"No, not that I recall." She paused. "Although that's not really something I've paid attention to either."

Dea leaned forward toward Henrik and held his gaze. It didn't seem so easy for him to look people in the eye.

"You work for the Tax Administration, don't you?" Dea asked.

"Me?" Henrik exclaimed. "Uh, yeah . . . I thought I had answered that question."

"Yes," Dea said, "I'm sure you did. I just can't help wondering how you—given your job—feel about your dad earning a pretty penny every year on black-market sales from his basement."

Henrik's eyes wandered.

"Now don't tell us you don't know about that," she added.

"Fine," Henrik snapped, straightening up. "My dad earns money under the table, and he has never given a damn about legal business hours. When I was a kid, I took enough beatings for a whole town. Many years ago I gave up believing I had any influence on what my father did. But that doesn't mean that I murdered him and stuffed him in a freezer or anything."

"Henrik!" His mother woke up now. "What are you saying, the freezer? Your own father!"

Liam looked at him. His shirt was nicely ironed. His shoes gleamed, neatly polished. His cheeks were as smooth as a baby's butt.

Dea cocked her head to the side, and her tone softened a little. "You're still afraid of your father, aren't you?" she asked.

"I'm a grown man now." Henrik's voice sounded dull as he answered. "I live all the way in Haarby."

"That would make sense if you were scared," Dea pointed out.

"We've looked into your wife's background a little." Liam changed the subject. "And it appears that Karina was convicted twice of anti-Muslim hate speech when she was a New Right candidate. When she was younger, she was also convicted in a racially motivated assault on a girl. What do you think about that?"

"I don't care about the hate-speech convictions," Henrik said cockily. "White people aren't allowed to say anything about other people these days, and if you just step aside a little, then the whole squad of official do-gooders swoops in on you in no time. Completely ludicrous convictions, if you ask me!" Henrik raised his chin.

"But convictions all the same," Liam said. "Does your wife still have a similarly strained relationship with Muslims?"

"Strained?" Henrik blurted out, his cheeks taking on a little more color. "I'll tell you what's a strain. What's a strain is how they come pilgrimaging up here to drain our treasury while at the same time not giving a hoot about our laws and culture! It seems like they're allowed to behave however they want, but the second a Dane says one wrong word, all hell breaks loose. Talk about that if you want to talk about things that are a strain!" After releasing all his hot air, he seemed winded.

Liam calmly took a sip of his coffee and let Henrik calm back down.

"One totally different item, Henrik," Liam said. "When I talked to your mother the first time, I got the impression that you didn't know Claus and Charlotte. But you went to visit Claus this morning. So you do know the couple?"

A pink blotch spread across Henrik's face and then down his neck at lightning speed.

"Mostly Claus . . . We played water polo together growing up. I stopped by to see if there was any news about Charlotte."

"At nine o'clock in the morning?"

"I wanted to fit it in before work."

"I was told that you seemed shaken," Liam said.

"Did I? I was late. It was probably just that." He drummed on the table. "Was there anything else you wanted? Otherwise I'd like to be getting home."

* * *

As soon as they were outside on the sidewalk, Dea pulled out her phone. "Check your phone. The team sent a summary. Here in

Assens alone they've found five people who've been convicted of murder, and this case does appear to revolve around Assens, so if we believe our theory, one of those five people is at risk of disappearing today."

"Have people been dispatched to them?" Liam asked while he read through the message himself. "Two of the convictions are from more than thirty years ago, and the most recent one is from 2016. He's the only one of the five who's still in jail."

"Thorbjørn is on his way to the former convict in Haarby," Dea said, and looked at Liam. "We'll take the one in Aarup?"

Liam nodded decisively.

"Call Thorbjørn and find out how far out they are."

Dea followed him over to the car while she made the call. It was pouring, and she felt the wetness making its way down the back of her neck and underneath her collar.

"They just left," she said, and climbed in. The feeling that they might be able to get there in time, might be able to stop the next disappearance, left her quiet and focused, while Liam chatted away behind the steering wheel as they sped along the narrow country roads.

"Has anyone requested protection for these ex-cons?" she asked.

Liam nodded and launched into a torrent of speech about how the security measures were coordinated from the command room at the police station. Dea wasn't listening. She leaned her head back against the headrest and sincerely hoped they would manage to get there first.

About fifteen minutes later they pulled up in front of the house in Aarup. The woman at the address had once killed her uncle. She had claimed it was self-defense, but it had not been possible to substantiate her accusations against the dead uncle, and the premeditated murder charge had stuck. There hadn't been any doubt that she had plunged the knife into her uncle's throat. The only doubt was whether she had been defending herself against a sexual assault or whether she, as the prosecutor had claimed, had been searching his house for valuables, because there was purported to be a large amount of money there. According to the prosecutor, the uncle came home and surprised the niece, who found the knife in a kitchen drawer. According to the police report, the murder suspect maintained the whole way through that she had been visiting her uncle when he assaulted her. The money had never turned up, not in the house and not in her account.

Dea looked around. It was a row house, with flowers and a green hedge, and everything looked peaceful. Two older women stood chatting not far from them, each under her own umbrella. They stared back at Dea and Liam with at least as much curiosity as was directed at them.

"This is the first time I'm trying this," Dea said, as they walked up the front walkway.

"What?" Liam was less talkative now too. She could sense the tension in him.

"Trying to rescue a murderer!" *That's pretty messed up*, she thought, realizing how nervous she felt. It was quiet around the house, and nothing seemed to be moving behind the windows.

"You know what they say: you should never be afraid to try something new," Liam said, and knocked on the door. "But what do we actually say to her?"

She was about to answer when the door was opened surprisingly quickly by a woman about their age, who sized them up.

"Yes?"

"Hi, I'm Liam Stark, and this is my colleague, Dea Torp," Liam said, showing her his badge. "We're with the Odense Police."

"Yeah, I figured that much out already," the woman said.

"Are you Søs Kellermann?" Dea asked, eyeing the woman with curiosity. She had short hair without much body. She wore a smart-looking boiler suit with a colorful scarf tied loosely around her neck.

She nodded curtly.

"Could we speak with you?" Dea continued.

"What about?" Søs Kellermann had crossed her arms in front of her chest and was leaning against the doorframe. She cast a quick glance over at the two women, who were still standing in the street and following the scene.

"Have you heard about the current case involving missing people?" Liam asked.

Dea heard how patient his voice sounded and felt her own anxiety level decrease. They had made it. The woman in Aarup would not be the next victim.

Søs Kellermann nodded, but even more curtly now.

"What's that got to do with me?" she said.

"Hopefully nothing," Liam said quickly, and smiled at her. "To put it briefly, we're here because we anticipate that another person is going to disappear today. Unfortunately, we can't go into any more detail about the specific reasons we're afraid you might be at risk as the perpetrator's next victim."

"The *victim*?" Søs exclaimed. "But I don't know anything about the case apart from what I've read in the paper." She looked over at the hole in the hedge by the walkway. The two older women were still standing out there staring in. "OK, come inside for a minute."

Once they finished shaking off the rain, she showed them to a low sofa. The living room was full of green plants, family photos, and porcelain decorations.

"Why would I be the next victim? Is it because I killed my uncle?"

"We can't go into details," Dea said, and placed the photographs of Charlotte, Kasper, Verner, and Lone on the coffee table between them. "But it's important for us to find out if you know any of these people in any way."

Søs studied the pictures carefully before shaking her head.

"I don't know who they are."

Just then, Dea's phone rang. She stood up apologetically and walked back out into the front hall to speak. She heard Liam ask from the living room if Søs had someone who could come and be with her in the house, or if it might be possible for her to stay somewhere else for a couple of days.

"Yeah, my boyfriend will be home around four thirty," she replied as Dea came back into the room and gestured to Liam that they were leaving.

"We'll keep you posted, but I just received information that means we no longer fear that you're in any danger," Dea announced. The woman had gone pale and had pulled her legs up underneath herself in the deep armchair, as if she were protecting herself by making herself as small as possible. "A patrol car is already on its way out here, and they'll keep an eye on you and your place for the rest of the day. But again, there's no indication that you're in any danger. It's being done exclusively out of an abundance of caution."

"But what about now?" she asked. "Until they get here? I mean, if you're leaving? Couldn't you stay and wait with me?" she called from the living room.

Dea felt a bit guilty as she dragged Liam outside. Once you had aroused someone's fear, it wasn't so easy to dispel it. But there was no easy way to tell the woman that they had just been informed that a different former convicted murderer had disappeared.

"Haarby," she said, and heard the lock in the door being turned as soon as it was closed behind them. "The man Thorbjørn went to go see is missing. His wife thought he was in his workshop, but no one has seen him for several hours." She looked into Liam's eyes for a moment. "On the other hand, they found a new verse from the Quran there. Just like in Assens, it was left on the workbench in the shop: *Do not kill the soul which Allah has forbidden*."

"Haarby?" Liam repeated, already on his way to the car.

"Yes, the techs and a team are on their way to the workshop, and a canine patrol unit is coming up from Svendborg."

"Let them know we're on our way." The tires squealed over the asphalt as Liam turned around on the residential street and turned on the flashing blue lights.

Dea felt a tug of disappointment. They had known what they were looking for, but they had been too late.

*   *   *

"Damn it," Liam muttered as he stepped out of the car into a big mud puddle at Kent Hansen's house. It was located on the outskirts of Haarby and looked like it had been a business at one time. Wrecked cars and car parts sat in the mud surrounding the house, and both the house and the rest of the property seemed bleak and dilapidated. It was pouring. He looked over at Dea, the water flowing down her face, but her eyes were concentrating, focused on the family's house, and she made no move to wipe away the rainwater.

"Do we have people out in the area?" Liam asked.

"Yes, they're searching the whole town. I just got a text that the canine unit will be here soon. We have a witness who saw a gray Peugeot drive away from here about an hour ago. You can call Thorbjørn if you want to talk to him yourself. He's in charge of the search."

Liam shook his head, then slapped the roof of the car in frustration, creating a splash of droplets.

"If Kent Hansen turns out to have been taken away in that gray Peugeot, then we were only a couple of hours away from being able to stop it."

Dea nodded, and the raindrops in her eyelashes gleamed. "What do we know about him?"

"People call him Red Kent. He paints cars, has an auto body workshop there." She pointed over at a building that had once been yellow, but the paint had now peeled all the way down to the underlying brick. "And there's rumors of untaxed income and black-market car sales. Although not much around here looks like it even runs."

"No," Liam said, looking around. "But as far as I know, there's good money in scrap too. Is that his wife?" He looked past Dea at the crying woman approaching them. She had messy bleached-blond hair and was dressed in black from head to toe. She was carrying a redheaded child in her arms who was about two. She moved slowly due to her pregnant belly.

"Yes, her name's Maria," Dea said quietly. "According to Thorbjørn, she hasn't worked in the last eleven years, and we don't have anything on her."

"Are you the boss?" the woman asked through her tears. She addressed Liam in a nasal voice and dried her eyes on the child's shabby cotton shirt.

Liam nodded and walked over to her.

"Can't you tell me what's going on? Why are you here asking about Kent? I don't know where he is, but I know he hasn't done anything!"

"We're here to find Kent," Liam said, and tried to put a comforting hand on her shoulder, but she twisted away from him.

"I don't like you coming here. You started out oh-so-friendly that time you put him away for murder too!" The rain trickled down the child's pale skin. Dea wanted to take off her jacket and put it around the little one, but the woman didn't seem to notice that they were both getting soaked.

"We want to know all about Kent and his comings and goings. Maybe we should go inside?" Dea suggested. "It's a little cold out here in the rain. Your son looks like he's freezing."

The woman shook her head. "Forget it," she said, readjusting her son's weight. "We'll talk right here."

"Fine," Dea said quickly. She received a nod from Liam, so she assumed he agreed that getting into the house was not a big priority at this point. What mattered was whether Kent's wife had anything to tell them. "You understand that we're here because we're trying to find your husband, right?"

She waited a second, but the woman didn't say anything.

"We're afraid that something may have happened to him," Dea continued.

Still no reaction, so Liam took over.

"I know that this isn't pleasant to talk about, but we need to," he said. She just stared at him stiffly. "A couple of our colleagues have been down to the local bar, asking around a little about Kent. People say that your husband has a temper. And it seems like there's a few people around who don't like him all that much. Is that true?"

"I knew that," she mumbled quietly, but she didn't answer the question.

"You're going to have to talk to us," Dea added. "Otherwise we can't help you."

"We didn't ask for your help," came the prickly response.

"No doubt you've heard about the people who've gone missing in the last week?" Liam said, and then without waiting for her response, he continued, "We're afraid that your husband might be another victim in that case. That's why we need to talk to you about the murder he once committed."

That brought some life into her eyes.

"He didn't kill anyone. That was an unfortunate accident. We told the police that."

"No, just stop," Dea cut in. "The man who died was walking on the sidewalk, and Kent drove up onto the sidewalk and hit him."

"It was an accident," Maria repeated firmly. Liam noted that the woman didn't ask why the police thought her husband might be a victim in the case that had been in the news. He studied her for a moment and concluded that that must be because she hadn't been following the news and probably didn't know anything about the case.

"Several of Kent's pals at the bar had a somewhat different take on what you're calling an accident." Dea was making her move.

"I have no idea what you're talking about," Maria said dismissively.

"Isn't it true that the man Kent hit and killed with his car had tried to rape you behind the gas station earlier that same night?"

"Stop!" The outburst was so vigorous that it scared the child in her arms, and he started to cry. "Would you just leave already? I promise I'll call when Kent comes home."

Liam looked at the drenched toddler and the desperate woman and suddenly felt a surge of tenderness. He had no doubt that she had no idea what they were talking about. He decided to stop and hold off on telling her about the slip of paper with the verse from the Quran that had been found in the shop until they officially added Kent Hansen to the list of missing people.

He thanked her for her time and noticed that Dea didn't agree with his decision to stop now, but the little boy was crying. His pale cheeks were bright red now, and he was soaked to the skin.

Liam and Dea walked back to the car in silence and got in. They were both drenched, and Dea was shivering. Her teeth were chattering, even though she was trying to control it. They both sat staring out the windshield. Neither of them had any doubt that the auto body painter in Haarby was the perpetrator's fifth victim.

*   *   *

Nassrin stared at the screen and typed in the last of her daily report. She didn't think they had gotten very far with Claus. She glanced over at Dea, who was sitting at her computer. She looked so confident with her unwavering gaze, upright posture, and tight-fitting clothes.

"Have I grown horns or something?" Dea asked without look-ing at Nassrin. "I can feel you staring at me."

Nassrin was about to answer but was interrupted by Liam, who walked into the office out of breath.

"The papers are running with it now . . . damn it!"

"I saw that," Dea said with a nod. "People have started keeping their kids home from school, and there's been a frenzy of activity in various Facebook groups. There's no helping that, but we risk the whole thing getting out of control."

"Excuse me?"

All three of them looked toward the door, where the chief con-stable stood watching them.

"Chief Dybbøl," Liam said cheerfully, straightening his back.

"I thought you'd probably still be here," Margrethe Dybbøl said. "I read the online newspapers."

"Yes," Liam said. "It's out everywhere now."

Dybbøl cleared her throat. "Do you have all our people on it?"

"Yes, everyone who can be spared from other duties," Liam said, standing up. "I have a good forty people out in the field right now."

"And what do you have from today? I haven't seen any reports yet."

"They're almost done," Liam said. "We were at the address a few hours after the fifth person disappeared. We're gaining on them. We know what our perpetrator is after. The problem is that the contents of the Ten Commandments or the selected verses from the Quran can fit a broad selection of people. Today's was about not committing murder. Luckily, there aren't too many mur-derers, so that narrowed things down, and we were able to quickly narrow in on the people we should probably concentrate on. The man we're assuming is our latest victim was previously convicted of murder. He was released four years ago. While he was in jail, his wife gave birth to two of their five kids. We spoke to her."

"Does that mean that you've made a breakthrough?"

Liam looked into her eyes. "No, unfortunately not."

"That's not what I want to hear. I want these disappearances to end. I fully understand that it may be difficult without bodies or crime scenes, but you've been given free rein to call in all the manpower you need, and I need there to be progress. The people demand it."

"I know . . . Dybbøl, jeez," Liam said, frustrated. "We're working our butts off around the clock, and I know the pressure's on. Besides, there's nothing we would rather see than a break in the case. Fear is spreading everywhere, and I myself want these people brought safely back to their families. But what the hell do you want us to do beyond turning over every single stone? Plus"—he had gotten so worked up that a little drop of spit had landed on the chief's jacket collar—"we're trying to prevent more people from disappearing by attempting to figure out what the perpetrator's next move will be."

"The perpetrator?" Dybbøl repeated. "Does that mean that you've now working off the assumption that we're dealing with one individual working independently?"

Liam shook his head.

"We don't know anything about that yet. I just said that for the sake of expedience. There could easily be multiple people. There probably are multiple people. We have different vehicle registrations that we're connecting to the case."

"So what exactly do we know?"

"We don't know anything for sure, but we're pretty confident that the culprit or culprits or whoever it is doing this will go after a person tomorrow who has committed adultery or broken a marriage." He tried to get his frustration under control. He shouldn't get worked up, and he could tell that Nassrin and Dea were staring at him. He pulled himself together and continued in a calmer tone of voice, "We're also pretty sure that in the coming five days, five more people will go missing, people who have broken commandments six through ten in the Bible. If we can't stop this, that is!"

The look in Chief Dybbøl's eyes changed. For a second Liam was afraid that she was going to pull him in and give him a comforting hug, but she just reached out and put a hand on his arm.

"Listen, I understand that you're doing what you can, and I also know that you're putting in a lot of hours. It's just that when the media connects these disappearance cases with the Ten Commandments, then the municipality of Assens and possibly the entire island of Funen will rev up into a panic, which is understandable, of course. That's why I need to have something that I can use to calm them down." The chief paused for a second, thinking. "I'm looking for people from other departments," she decided. "If we don't have information to reassure the population with, then we at least need to be a visible presence out there. What about military divers? Do we need help searching lakes and bogs?"

"We're working on it," Liam said.

"We need to get this under control, Liam," Dybbøl continued, authoritatively and unnecessarily.

Nassrin's cell phone rang, and Dybbøl left the office, her heels clacking solidly against the linoleum.

"That was my uncle," Nassrin said, her phone still in her hand. "Hayyan just told me that the markings in the Quran go all the way back to last year, when Peter stopped by the bookshop and asked for his help on a writing project he was working on."

"And he didn't think it was relevant to mention that until now?" Dea exclaimed, looking from Nassrin to Liam indignantly.

"We're going to have to talk to your uncle about that, Nass," he said. "You know that too, right?"

* * *

Liam sat on a bench inside Tommerup Athletic Center by the big swimming pool. The air smelled strongly of chlorine, and his eyes stung, but he thought that might just as easily be because he hadn't gotten anywhere near enough sleep the last several days. It had turned out that Peter didn't remember the specific markings in Hayyan's Quran. He'd explained that he had talked to a lot of people and used many different sources in his work on the series of articles. And neither of Nassrin's uncles could explain any more about why Peter had requested Hayyan's help than they already had. On the other hand, their explanations seemed believable.

Liam had taken a stroll through the café at the athletic center before taking a seat in the bleachers to watch his son play water polo. Now his crumpled hamburger wrapper sat on the floor beside him, and he kept catching his eyes slipping shut even though there were yells from the pool and the game was nearing an end.

He turned his head when the door from the lobby opened and Henrik looked in. His and Liam's eyes met briefly, and then he quickly withdrew, closing the door again.

Liam quickly got up and followed him. "Wouldn't you like to come in?"

"No, I'm just going to have a hot dog in the café," Henrik said, and kept walking.

"Did you visit your mom?"

"What?"

Liam jogged to catch up with Henrik and kept going until he was slightly ahead of him.

"What are you doing here at the athletic center on Tuesday right at the end of the workday? Don't you work at the tax office in Odense? And live in Haarby?"

"Yes, I stopped by to see my mother."

"Henrik, stop walking!"

Henrik reluctantly stopped and looked at Liam. "Look, I'm tired and I want to be left in peace. My mom's not doing that well. She's sad and very worried, and now journalists have started showing up at their house. I don't like her being there all on her own, but she doesn't want to move to our place while all this is going on. She wants to stay in the house in case my dad comes home."

Liam nodded in understanding. "I'll make this fast then." While he had been sitting and eating his burger, he had received an email with the phone records from Henrik's and Claus's cell phones, and it appeared that the two men had often been in the same place. Dea had been the one to notice the overlaps, where the cell tower data had recorded their two phones in the same geographic area. She had put together a simple summary showing clearly that the two men had met alone at rest stops, in the woods, and at a couple of cabins that were owned by the tax office and could be rented out by employees.

Liam regarded Henrik calmly. "If I come over to talk to you and Karina tomorrow, will you be able to explain to me then why your phone has frequently been in the same place as Claus's over the last year?"

Henrik looked like someone who had been punched. "I don't understand what you're referring to."

He had taken a step back and was staring defensively at Liam.

"Then let me ask more directly: Are you and Claus having some kind of relationship?"

"I didn't have anything to do with Charlotte's or my dad's disappearance." Henrik once again had red blotches on his neck.

"I didn't say anything about that either," Liam said, and asked him to answer the question.

Henrik looked right at him now. "It's going to kill Claus if this gets out."

"But neither of you felt it was relevant to mention this when his wife disappeared? That could be the reason she left him, couldn't it?"

"Claus's coaching career is over if people start gossiping," Henrik continued, as if he hadn't heard what Liam had said. "He would also have to move. People will think all kinds of things and turn against him."

"Yes," Liam said, "the more that's at stake when you hide something, the farther you'll go to keep it hidden." Henrik squirmed uncomfortably and was taking a breath to say something when they were interrupted by Andreas, who came running over to them.

"Dad! Is it true that the club is filing for bankruptcy and we might not even compete in the game this weekend?"

Liam hesitated, and Henrik took that opportunity to say goodbye.

"Seriously?" Andreas continued, his angry outburst tinged with desperation. "You've got to do something. We've made it so far. We can't just give up on getting onto the national team!"

Liam put his arm around his son and walked to the locker room with him.

"I can promise you that every conceivable effort is going to go into fixing this. It'll probably all work out and you'll end up playing, of course."

* * *

"You're sitting in here alone?" Dea heard from the doorway. "Dybbøl!"

Dea looked up from her computer screen, where she was skimming through her daily report before handing it off to Liam.

"Yeah, it's just me right now."

"Well, you're the one I wanted to talk to." The chief constable walked over to her desk. The hard click of her heels echoed in the deserted office. She sat down on the very edge of Thorbjørn's desk.

Dea glanced down at her screen.

"I'm just putting the finishing touches in the report on Kent and Maria Hansen, and then Liam will send it on to you ASAP."

It didn't seem like Dybbøl had come to speed up the day's reports. She eyed Dea somberly.

"What are you doing to prevent a sixth person from disappearing tomorrow?"

Dea looked puzzled and shook her head in confusion. Dybbøl eyed her expectantly, and Dea tried like crazy to think why the chief constable would have come to talk specifically to her about something that obviously should go through Liam.

"Liam will brief you on all of that." She studied Dybbøl.

"Yes, I'm aware of that. I just wanted to hear what you thought. You know what the focus is now, right? Adultery and unfaithfulness."

"Yeah, that's basically like saying we know a person over the age of twenty-five will disappear," Dea said. "A lot of people have been unfaithful or lived together without being married."

"Plus it's not something you'd want to shout from the rooftops, I would imagine?"

Dea couldn't make out what the chief constable was getting at and suddenly had the sense that Margrethe Dybbøl might just really want to feel like she was involved. Maybe that was all it was.

"Would it make your day any easier tomorrow if all the adults out there spent the day being afraid they would become the next victim?"

Dea caught the hint of a smile at the corner of the chief's mouth.

"I wouldn't exactly say that," Dea admitted. "But it would make my day easier if we had a breakthrough."

Dea could tell there was more coming and leaned back expectantly.

Dybbøl gave her a searching look.

"You butted heads with Nassrin?"

"It was nothing," Dea replied dismissively.

"So there are no problems between you in the group?"

Dea shook her head.

"You have a somewhat problematic history," Dybbøl continued, alluding to what she had described at Dea's hiring interview as her "hefty baggage from Greenland."

"There are no problems between us." Dea looked calmly into her eyes.

"I'm glad to hear that. I felt like I needed to see that, though, because I don't need any divisiveness in my main group right now. Nassrin is mad that you questioned her uncles without her knowing about it. Is that so?"

Dea smiled tensely. "As I said, it was nothing, and there's nothing that would compromise Nassrin's work—quite the contrary. She'll be sitting in your seat someday, and that's what's so freaking exhausting about her. She's set her sights high, and I bet she'll darn well achieve it too!"

Day 6—Wednesday

IT WAS STILL dark when Beate opened her eyes. Something in the night had pulled her out of sleep. She listened attentively but couldn't detect anything other than the usual house sounds: the heating pipe that clicked in the living room, a branch scratching against the edge of the gutter outside. She thought the baby in her womb must have woken her.

She tried to settle down and sink back into sleep. She rolled over onto her side and reached for Peter, wanting to feel his soothing heartbeat against her check. And it was only then that she realized he wasn't lying in bed beside her. For a second she was overcome by a heartbroken longing, then she pushed the comforter aside and let the breeze from the open window flow over her hot, pregnant body.

It was his insomnia. He was gone so often in the early-morning hours that she should be used to it by now. She ran her hand over his side of the bed, thinking that perhaps he had just woken her up as he got out of bed. But his side of the bed was cold.

Beate fumbled to switch on the bedside light and lay there for a moment adjusting to its brightness before she got up and put on her robe. It was just starting to get light out, and the horizon glowed a very faint pink against the black of the night sky.

Downstairs in the kitchen, the clock on the stove said *4:12*. For a second she stood in the silence looking out the window at the courtyard out front and the yard. She longed for the intimacy she and Peter had shared early in their relationship—not just the sexual attraction, which had been so hard for her to understand, because he was so different from Silje's father. She had felt at home with him from the moment they met, a chance encounter at a restaurant in Aarhus. One of her girlfriends had just gotten divorced and needed to unload. Peter had been there with an old classmate. Such a cliché. She thought about it often when she met with couples before their weddings, thought about that inexplicable connection with another human being, which between her and Peter had been so strong that she hadn't doubted even for a second that she wanted to spend the rest of her life with him. But she was afraid now that he was pulling away from her.

She had just turned and was about to open the refrigerator when she spotted a small, neatly folded slip of paper on the kitchen counter next to the keys to her father's car. Peter didn't usually write little notes. She picked it up expectantly and slowly unfolded it.

And go not nigh to fornication; surely it is an indecency and evil is the way.

Beate's brow furrowed, and she didn't understand the meaning of the words at first. Her eyes lingered on the brief message for a long time. Then with her hand over her mouth, she tossed the note aside, taking a shocked step back. For a second she was struck by a paralyzing fear and felt dizzy as adrenaline coursed into her blood. She grasped for the counter and tried to get her breathing under control. She felt as if all her senses were exploding. She stood completely motionless, listening attentively into the silence, but she could hear only her own heartbeat throbbing in her ears.

Then something moved. She was sure she heard footsteps in the living room, the very distinct sounds of another person walking across the creaky, worn floorboards.

"Peter?" she tried hopefully, her voice timid. There was no response. The footsteps stopped. She glanced wildly around. She wouldn't be able to reach either the front door or the patio. She pulled her robe closed over her bulging belly and tiptoed slowly and laboriously toward the staircase that led upstairs. Her cell phone was on the nightstand. She had time to think that it was good that Silje was at her dad's place. Then she felt the grip around her neck. In a sweeping motion that came out of nowhere, she was yanked backward and landed heavily on the floor.

She twisted her way free and got up. Then, catching a fleeting glimpse of a man in a hoodie, she kicked out in a panic and hit him so hard he collapsed.

Her heart pounded in her chest, and there was a buzzing in her temples. She felt dizzy. She wouldn't make it out the front door, she thought, but maybe she could hide upstairs. Although maybe that was stupid and she risked being cornered if she tried to hide.

She ran for it anyway. Out of the kitchen and up the stairs.

It was dark. She heard heavy footsteps right behind her. She gasped for air and darted into the bathroom. Her belly grew hard with a Braxton-Hicks contraction, and a sharp pain shot across her pelvis. She slammed the door shut and wanted to turn the key, but it was gone. For a fleeting instant she imagined that Silje must have removed it. She leaned heavily against the door.

The man reached the top of the stairs. She heard him pass the bathroom and continue to the bedroom. She knew that she wouldn't be able to sneak out of the bathroom and make it downstairs. It was too short a distance, and she wasn't fast enough with her pregnant belly.

She felt defenseless as she grabbed a nail file and hopped into the bathtub. She had considered the window, but she didn't dare. She pulled the shower curtain closed now and crouched in the tub.

It was silent out on the landing. Beate could hear her own panting as she tried to hold her breath. She heard footsteps just outside, and then the door to the bathroom slowly opened.

She looked around in a panic in the darkness. A little moonlight shone in through the skylight right by the sink, and through the shower curtain she was able to see a silhouette standing in the doorway. The shadow moved and slowly came into the room.

She bit down hard on her lower lip and fought to keep her breathing calm. She jumped when the man grabbed the curtain and yanked it aside in a violent motion. Her scream tore through the silence. She stabbed at him with the file and felt his weight as he leaned in over her. She felt his hot breath on her face, felt paralyzed and sluggish as he brutally yanked her out onto the floor and bent over her. He held her tight. He was stronger than she was. She screamed again and realized she was going to pee. It felt warm under her thin nightgown. He grabbed her hair and yanked her head back.

*   *   *

The cold coffee sloshed into the car's cupholder. Liam gazed sadly at the black surface of the liquid in the cup. The Tommerup morning outside was dead quiet and misty, awaiting the new day. He hadn't been able to sleep, tossing and turning uneasily until Helene had asked him to take his comforter and go sleep on the sofa.

There were five people missing. They had disappeared on his watch. Five families had been left behind and now hoped for comfort and answers that he couldn't give them. He scratched his beard, tried to recall the timeline on the wall of the meeting room. There *had* to be something they had overlooked, *had* to be some point in the last five days when a mistake had been made, when an opening had been left that they could descend on.

He made a face as he drank the last of the bitter coffee from the cup. They didn't have shit. That was it. The only clue that the various cases had in common was that the people who had disappeared each had some tie to Tommerup. That was why he was sitting here.

It was a little past seven, and the co-op on Tallerupvej had just opened. He had seen the light turn on and watched the girl who worked in the bakery put out the sign. He got out of the car and crossed the deserted main road.

"Good morning," the young woman behind the bakery counter said with a wide smile. "What can I get for you?"

Liam was so surprised at how friendly she sounded that he decided to indulge himself, even though he had actually only gone in to talk to her.

"I'll take a slice of your brunsviger coffee cake," he said. "And if you have real cream, then I'd also like a large coffee."

"I do," she said energetically, and turned to the coffee machine as she informed him that he could have three slices of the cake for the price of two.

"Oh, one slice of brunsviger is plenty," he said. "How have people been reacting to the disappearance cases here in town and in the area over the last several days?" he continued, but noticed that she stiffened. "I'm with the police," he quickly added, and showed her his badge.

She examined his badge closely and thoroughly studied him, as if she wanted to memorize his red beard and longish hair. Then she set the disposable cup with its plastic lid on the glass counter in front of him. Her welcoming smile was gone.

"So you're here because of the Quran Case? Did something new happen? Are more people missing?"

"Are people calling it the Quran Case now?" he asked casually, inwardly cursing that news of the quotes had apparently gotten out. At the same time, he was a little impressed that they had managed to keep it in the bag for five days, given the scope of the case. He didn't answer her questions, although her fear was so palpable it vibrated around her.

She gestured to the newspaper stand. "Well, that's what *Stiftstidende* is calling it this morning, anyway."

Liam walked over and took a paper. He quickly skimmed the subheading. There were pictures of Charlotte, Kasper, Verner, and Lone, but nothing about Red Kent. He set the paper on the counter and asked to buy that too.

She had placed his coffee cake in a bag, which she closed neatly.

"Yesterday several of our customers filled up their shopping carts as if there were a war coming or a big storm. I've heard of people barricading themselves in their homes. Some of my parents' friends have left town. I even heard about people renting summer houses in Jutland to stay in until all this is over. It's not very fun to have to be here, but I have a job to do, even though I'd prefer to get out of here too."

She put her hand over her mouth, as if it had occurred to her that she was babbling.

"It makes sense to me, that you want to get out of here," Liam said.

"Only nine of the kids in my daughter's class were at school yesterday. Parents are keeping their kids home, because they're scared."

The fear they had predicted would strike the small community had apparently set in. Not that he was surprised. He had foreseen this himself, and he was fully aware that he was responsible for making sure panic didn't spread like a prairie fire.

"If anyone else disappears here in town or on Funen Island in general, than I think people will completely lose it," she continued. "My brother told me yesterday that some of the men where he works are talking about forming a neighborhood watch." She did something with her eyebrows that made Liam feel like he was being accused.

"To be completely honest, it doesn't really seem like you guys are doing anything to prevent more people from disappearing. It shouldn't be possible for so many people to disappear without a trace without your being able to put a stop to it."

Liam restrained himself, but he did have time to regret not having just stayed home in bed under the covers. Instead, he was here getting chewed out.

"I'm sorry you see it that way," he said sincerely. "Maybe this just sounds like empty words, but we actually are doing everything we can. To be quite honest, the problem is just that we don't really have anything to go on."

"But you get the impression that it could happen to *anyone*. How are we supposed to feel safe, if that's the case?" she asked indignantly. "Charlotte is my daughter's Danish teacher. She's Katrine's favorite teacher. She's super nice and really organized. I mean, what did she do to deserve this? You've got to understand that we're scared. People are scared. Just look at that old man who was simply out walking his dog."

"We understand that," he replied calmly. "We understand that quite well, but I'm glad you're saying these things. And you have my word that we're doing everything we can so that all the residents, both here in Tommerup and throughout the rest of Funen Island, will be able to feel safe." He almost wanted to ask her to stay home for the next five days, but instead he paid and took his coffee and his bag with the slice of warm brunsviger cake.

"Hey!" the clerk yelled, just as the sliding glass was closing behind him. "I don't know if this is useful for anything, but my nephew found a little thingamajig in a tree over there where you had things roped off the other day, out by that abandoned house where they say the old grocer was attacked. Kristoffer's eleven, and he's still nuts about that Pokémon Go game. He was out there looking for some more Pokémon for his collection when he spotted it. It's a little camera that was attached to a branch, my brother said. But Kristoffer couldn't get it to work."

"When was that?" Liam came back inside and over to her.

"It was the day after the grocer went missing."

"It would be a big help if I could have your brother's cell phone."

* * *

"Hello?" Mona scanned the large backyard behind the parsonage. There wasn't a soul in sight. The sun had regained its strength after the previous day's thunder and rain and was now shining warmly on the well-maintained lawn. She lifted her dress a little and started walking up the steps to the patio. The door into the sunroom was ajar.

"Hello! Anyone here?" she called, and walked in. The light poured in through the big mullioned windows.

"Yes, I'm here." Peter appeared in the doorway and smiled at her. He seemed windblown and looked fresh, with a jacket over his arm. "Can I help you with something?"

He set down his jacket and invited her in.

"I was supposed to meet Beate half an hour ago, but she didn't show up, and she's not answering her phone," Mona said. "It's just not like her."

"No, you're right about that," Peter said, and set his car key down in a bowl. "I'll just check upstairs. Maybe she went up to take a little nap."

Making herself at home, Mona wandered into the kitchen to put on a pot of coffee. If Beate was asleep, a cup of freshly brewed coffee would probably be just the thing.

The machine was spluttering when Peter came back down again. He shook his head.

"She's not here, so she's probably over in the church. Did you try there?"

Mona nodded and said that's where they were supposed to meet.

"Then she probably just forgot."

Mona shrugged a bit apologetically. Now it seemed almost pushy of her to be standing here puttering around in the pastor's kitchen, she thought.

"I'll come back another time," she said quickly.

"You can just wait. I'll text her, and she'll probably turn up."

"I suppose she could have nipped into town to do a little shopping. She'll probably be back soon," Mona said, as if it were up to her to explain where the pastor was. "I saw her dad's car parked here last night, but now it's gone."

"She usually lets me know if she's going to drive somewhere," Peter said, after he sent the text. He sat down at the kitchen table and accepted the steaming cup of coffee Mona handed him. He gathered up the sections of the newspaper, which had been scattered across the table, and glanced at his phone again.

"Has she responded?" Mona said, still standing by the coffee machine.

"Not yet." Peter absent-mindedly ran his hand over his bald head. "I'm sure she'll be here any minute."

He and Mona were rarely alone together. She wasn't sure what to talk about and felt awkward.

Instead of waiting for Beate to respond to the text, Peter called her and sat for a moment with his phone to his ear before hanging up and setting it down.

"It says her phone's not available."

He tried again with a deep groove in his forehead.

"Her phone must be either turned off or it ran out power."

He was the one who seemed apologetic now. He told Mona he was sorry she was having to wait when they had arranged to meet.

"As long as nothing happened—with the baby, I mean. When did you last see her?"

"Last night. I couldn't sleep, so I got up at around three thirty and went for a drive. She was asleep in bed then."

"At three thirty?" Mona repeated, surprised. "That's early."

"I'm struggling with that," Peter said with a nod. Then he abruptly got up and went out into the hall. When he came back, his windblown, red-cheeked look was gone, and he was pale. "None of her shoes or sandals are gone, and she would never leave the house in just her bare feet."

"I think we should call Johannes," Mona said, starting to feel worried because Peter was worried. "It might be good if he came home from his convention, if she's sick or if something happened to her—" She had just gotten up and was on her way into Beate's office to call her son when Peter called her back, his voice hoarse. She turned around and came back into the kitchen.

He didn't say anything as he let her read the little note that had been hidden underneath the Culture section of the newspaper.

*   *   *

"Jan!" the stocky man introduced himself, smiling. He stood waiting at the abandoned house, where Liam and Dea had arranged to meet him. "Right here, this is where my son found it!" Jan nodded so enthusiastically that what little hair he had flopped back and forth.

"Could we see the camera?" Dea asked, eyeing the stocky man. His smile grew so huge that for a second she was nervous his face might rip clean across, he was so proud to be able to assist the police. He dug around purposefully in his jacket pocket and pulled out the little camera. It was in a clear plastic bag, but Dea had no doubt that both the man's and his son's fingerprints were all over its small surfaces, probably to such an extent that any other traces were long since gone.

She took the bag and held the camera up in front of her. The little box was about four by four centimeters, with a long rubber antenna sticking out one side.

"Can you call for a car to bring this over to forensics right away?" she asked, looking at Liam.

If they were lucky, they might be able to secure the data and photos from the camara. If nothing else, they could have their colleagues at the National Forensic Service try to find out where the camera had been bought. And by whom.

Liam nodded and walked a little farther away while Dea focused once again on the man.

"Can you show me where the camera was when your son found it?"

Jan pointed enthusiastically into the trees.

"Was the camera up in a tree, or did he find it on the ground?" Dea asked, but stopped him as he went to walk into the forested area.

"It was attached to a branch a little way up, and then—"

"How was it attached to the branch?" she interrupted.

"Uh, with some of that camouflage-colored tape. It was taped on."

"Do you know where the tape is now?"

Jan shook his head doubtfully, and his happy grin vanished.

"He probably threw it away. He was only interested in the camera. He told me about the tape because it was like the kind we use when we set up wildlife cameras out in the bog."

"And where do you buy that kind of tape?" Liam asked quickly. Dea had the sense that he was ready to dispatch a patrol unit over there immediately.

"We get ours in Odense at Jagt og Fritid. They carry a lot of hunting supplies, but I think you can buy it lots of places. You can order it online too. I've done that several times."

Liam stepped a few paces away to make a phone call.

"When we're done here, I'm going to ask you to go to the school and pick up your son," Dea said, eyeing Jan with urgency. "We have a crew on their way over here, and when your son arrives, they're going to retrace the route he took from here back home to your place, OK? If you son threw away the tape on his way home, we hope that he can maybe help by showing us where he threw it away."

"We're ready!" Jan said, once again beaming like a shiny coin.

"Something has happened," Liam said, after he wrapped up his phone call and pulled Dea off to the side a bit.

"What?" She was struck by dizziness for a second, but it passed.

"A slip with the sixth passage was left at the parsonage."

"The one about infidelity?" she asked.

"Yes," Liam nodded somberly, "and Peter can't find Beate."

*   *   *

"Damn it!" Claus said in sympathy, pulling Peter into a hug. At first Peter resisted, but then he gave in to it. "But Beate is a pastor. Plus she's pregnant. Are you really sure that she disappeared the same way as Charlotte?"

He made it sound as if there was just no way that could be possible. For a moment Peter was completely confused.

"I'm not sure of anything at all," he mumbled, pulling awkwardly free of Claus's embrace and walking into the parsonage's office. "But you're probably the only one who understands me right now. That's why I called you . . . I can't stop thinking what could have happened to her and wondering where she is. And what about our baby? How have you even been able to cope with this since Friday?"

"I don't know," Claus admitted, and sat down across from Peter on the love seat facing Beate's desk. "But I've made up my mind. I'm going to keep believing she's alive and that she's coming back home to us."

"What have the police told you? It's been five days. Have they said anything at all?"

Claus shrugged slightly.

"They're not saying much—almost nothing, actually. Aside from that, they're bringing in more officers, pulling out all the stops. I've been mad at them and chewed them out, but it didn't do any good. They didn't take it seriously in the beginning; you heard that yourself. But now they do. Of course I keep thinking that if only they had acted right away when it first happened, then maybe they could have stopped it, prevented more people from disappearing."

Peter averted his gaze, couldn't bear to see the despair that was eating away at Claus.

Out in the hallway and in the kitchen, the forensic techs were making noise. Claus and Peter hadn't been allowed to come in and sit in the office until now. Ever since Peter had sounded the alarm, the pastor's residence had been invaded. Every single little nook of the downstairs had been examined. The crime scene investigators had spread throughout the many square meters of the residence like a carpet unrolling, securing evidence, scrutinizing every detail. They were still working in the kitchen where Peter had found the slip of paper. And Peter had been told several times that he could not enter the living room, or the hallway, or use the door to the patio. If he needed something in the house, he should let them know, and it would be brought to him.

Liam came in to join the two men in the office and sat down on a chair facing Peter. "I just have one question I need to clear up." He glanced at Claus, who was already standing up.

"You don't need to leave on my account," Peter said quickly.

"We can see from the parish house security camera footage that your car left the courtyard in front of the parsonage at three thirty-eight and returned again at seven thirteen. Is that correct?" Liam eyed him expectantly.

"Yes, that's correct," Peter replied, straightening up. He noted the surprise in Claus's eyes and regretted having encouraged him to stay. "Sometimes I have trouble sleeping, and when I wake up early, I like to drive out to the beach and sit in the sand and watch the sunrise."

"OK, and when you got up at three thirty, Beate was asleep in your bed?" Liam asked.

Peter nodded.

"So you didn't notice that your girlfriend was gone until Mona came over asking for her just before nine?"

Peter nodded again and looked down at the table.

"Yes, I always come in and sit down at my computer right away when I come home. I'm focused then and ready to get down to work," he explained. "If I go upstairs, I just risk waking her up. She's a very light sleeper now that her belly has gotten so big. And I assumed, of course, that she was in bed up there."

*   *   *

Liam looked at the brick house ahead of them. At one time it had been one of the bigger small farms in the area, but at some point it had been renovated into a modern home. They were between Tommerup and Verninge, closer to Verninge.

Dea knocked, and Liam took up his position beside her in front of the wide main door. A pair of glazed cobalt-blue pots of half-withered flowers sat on either side of the door.

The door was opened right away, and a gray-haired man with a questioning look on his face appeared in the doorway. The house seemed dark behind him, and he brought a faint smell of frying with him from the kitchen.

"Liam Stark with the Odense Police," Liam managed to say before Bent Møller Nielsen interrupted him.

"Is there any news about Beate? Have you heard from my daughter? Is she back?" The questions rained down on them before the elderly man caught himself and apologized.

"Come in," he said, stepping aside. They were shown into a living room with a low ceiling, where only a scant amount of light made its way in through a row of small windows, their sills crowded with neglected geraniums.

The man apologized right away. "I'm having a hard time maintaining the house. My wife came down with dementia a few years ago, so it's all on me."

Bent Møller Nielsen cleared his throat and pointed by way of invitation over toward the two checkered Børge Mogensen sofas.

"Just help yourselves."

Liam reached for the coffee. "Have you lived here long?"

"We moved in about eight years ago when we stopped serving as house parents at the residential school we taught. We moved out of the house parents' residence but kept working there as teachers until Anne Grethe got sick." Bent poured himself some coffee. "Tell me, what do you know about Beate? Are you sure that she disappeared as part of this case that the newspapers have been writing about? Did someone kill her?"

Liam quickly shook his head.

"We don't know anything for certain yet," he said in an attempt to reassure the worried father, even though he didn't have anything to reassure him with.

"That first woman who went missing from Tommerup," Bent continued, "she's been gone for six days now. I worked for the police for a few years when I was younger, so I know very well that six days without any sign of life is a long time to be missing."

"You were a policeman?" Dea exclaimed.

Beate's father nodded, but there was something dismissive about the look in his eye.

"For a few years, but it wasn't for me."

"Bent," Liam proceeded, "have you noticed anything unusual going on with Beate recently? Has her mood changed? Has her behavior been unusual in any way?"

"No, she's as happy and upbeat as she's always been. Sometimes she seems a little stressed out, but that's how it is for most young working parents these days."

"Did you see her yesterday?" Dea continued.

"Yes, she stopped by with some things, and we had a little breakfast together before she went upstairs and sat with her mother for a bit."

"And she didn't say anything that gave you reason to believe that she planned to be away for a few days?" Liam continued.

Beate's father sat for a moment, staring down into his coffee cup before he looked up again. "You found a note, didn't you? Peter called and told me about that."

He regarded them by turn until Liam nodded.

"And go not nigh to fornication; surely it is an indecency and evil is the way." Beate's father referred to the sentence as if it had been

burned into him. "I can't help but think that it's because she's a pastor and she's expecting a baby with a man she's not married to. Is that how you interpret it?"

Bent's face slumped into sad folds, but he seemed calm, content.

Liam nodded. "Yes, we're also afraid that that's how it ties in, but we don't know anything for sure yet. That's why we need to hear if anything happened that might give you reason to think there could be some other explanation for her disappearance."

Bent Møller Nielsen shook his head. A woman's voice called out from upstairs.

"I had also hoped there was some other explanation," he said quietly, glancing over at the staircase in the front hall. "I was just imagining that you had come to say that this didn't have anything to do with the Quran case. That the note was a misunderstanding and there was a good explanation. But of course I knew that was just wishful thinking."

There was another call from upstairs.

"You'll have to excuse me," he said. "My wife is awake. I need to go up and check on her."

Dea stood up. "Thank you for your time."

Bent got to his feet with surprising agility. Liam looked at the aging man. He looked strong, with muscular arms and broad shoulders.

"Why didn't police work end up being for you?"

Bent hesitated a moment. "I was young back then. I lost my temper late one night in Odense. That resulted in an assault conviction," he explained matter-of-factly. "But that was fine. I deserved it. And I enjoyed my life at the residential school."

*   *   *

"Welcome to this very quick briefing," Chief Constable Dybbøl announced authoritatively, looking around at those assembled, who consisted of the best people they had in Odense in addition to the steering committee, lead officers from the South East Jutland Police, and a captain from the Home Guard.

People nodded and murmured, and she continued.

"As you all know, it's a big problem for us in law enforcement that we have not been able to find the six missing people." She paused for a moment. "Between three forty and nine this morning, our sixth victim disappeared, a pregnant young pastor from Tommerup. In addition to that, she is a woman we know and have had contact with. It is unacceptable that she can simply disappear from in front of our noses, and this does not look good in the press. It is also a problem that the press had dubbed this the Quran Case, because that makes people think of terrorism." She glanced at Liam. "Do you still think we can rule out the possibility of terrorism?"

He nodded tensely, annoyed at being put on the spot like this. And he also had no doubt that Dybbøl was keeping the Police Intelligence Service waiting in the wings even as she reported to her superiors that the case was not currently being viewed as terrorism.

"It is our clear impression that the notes with the quotes we've been finding are to be viewed primarily in connection with the Ten Commandments in the Bible, but of course we don't know that for sure." He stopped and made a point of holding his ground by not breaking his eye contact with the chief constable.

"Why use verses from the Quran if the message is the Ten Commandments?" Dybbøl continued.

"Maybe to mislead people," Dea broke in. "Or to send multiple messages at the same time."

Dybbøl nodded and looked around the room. Then she turned on her heel without any further comment and left the room. She left relieved silence behind her.

"Our thanks to Chief Dybbøl," Liam said, smiling stiffly at his team. "There's something I'd like you all to mull over today . . ."

People seemed tired, he thought. It was more noticeable in some than in others. But when he raised his voice now, everyone turned their attention to him.

"When Beate's boyfriend found the slip of paper with the Quran quote on their kitchen counter, the paper was curled or maybe previously crumpled up in a way that caused the forensic techs out at the site to take notice. The paper was sent to the Forensic Genetics Lab, of course, but as always, it will take at least twenty-four hours before we have a DNA result. But what's interesting here is that it looks like Beate herself may have found the note. Maybe it was on the counter where Peter later found it. Or she might have brought it into the kitchen." He paused for a moment as he tried to visualize the events. There was no sign of a struggle downstairs, but in the bathroom upstairs, the shower curtain had been pulled down and was lying on the floor. "Beate was very aware of this case," he continued. "So I assume that the minute she saw that quote, she realized that the perpetrator was in her house. Or had been there. There wasn't anyone else in the house when Peter returned from his drive. So there's no reason to think that anyone other than the perpetrator or Beate crumpled up the piece of paper. And that's where this gets interesting."

He looked around at the many attentive faces.

"Before this, it appeared that the slips of paper were placed at the scenes *after* the victims disappeared. But this time it seems like the victim was supposed to find the passage herself. So here's my question: Considering how painstaking you would have to be to make six people disappear without a trace, we should maybe wonder whether the person or people behind this crime wanted Beate to leave behind some clue. Is this a signal to *us*? Or was this put there to frighten her, because she was aware that the short passages were a warning of something bad?"

Several people around the room nodded.

"Why this development?" Liam asked the group. "How is Beate different from the other victims? Is the perpetrator starting to get bored?"

The room filled with murmuring as the detectives discussed whether the perpetrators had started slacking on their approach versus whether it had been done intentionally. If they were heading into a new phase of the crime, what would that entail?

"What about the Wi-Fi camera?" a detective from the steering committee in Kolding asked. "Any news there?"

Liam shook his head. "Unfortunately, not really. We still don't have any proof that the little camera that was found where Verner disappeared is connected to the case. The National Forensic Service is working on tracking the signals and looking into the app that we presume was used with the camera."

"Do we know if any similar cameras were found near the other disappearance sites?" asked a female investigator who had been called in from Svendborg.

"We still haven't found any," Liam replied, "but we have personnel from the Home Guard literally climbing around in trees and on roofs right now looking for traces of the type of tape that camera in Tommerup was secured with."

A murmur spread once more. Liam clapped encouragingly and looked around.

"Thanks. That'll be all for now. This meeting is adjourned. Let's go find these poor people."

*   *   *

Everyone aside from Dea left the large meeting room chatting.

"Where's Nassrin today?" Dea asked, once they were alone. "Did you give her the day off?"

"No!" Surprised, Liam looked up from the table, which was covered with all the reports and photos from the search of the parsonage. "Why would you think that?"

"Because she didn't attend the meeting," she replied tersely.

He could tell that Dea was dying to say more, and for a moment he felt like chucking her out the window. He didn't feel like dealing with any more of their conflicts and was starting to feel more and more like Dea had decided Nassrin was a problem. He ignored it and concentrated instead on the material in front of them.

"Do you think Beate was intended to be the sixth victim right from the beginning?" he continued, "or do you think she wasn't chosen until later because she has a connection to several of the victims and has made the church into a sort of gathering place with respect to this case?"

"Are you thinking of the public meeting and the large-scale search she started?"

"Among other things." He nodded. "She took care of Claus's kids when Charlotte disappeared. And she's visited Lis."

Dea nodded.

"My sense is that this was so well planned that I'm inclined to believe Beate was meant for day six all along."

Liam studied the documents on the table in front of him one more time. There was no sign of break-in at the parsonage. Nothing was missing from the house. The little slip of paper was the only thing that led them to believe Beate's disappearance was part of a larger crime.

They were interrupted when Thorbjørn entered the room in long strides.

"We have a new witness," he announced, sounding harried, as if he had just been running around trying to find them. "Early this

morning someone out walking their dog heard what he describes
as a riding mower in the parsonage's large yard. The man is home,
and he's ready to talk to us. I'm heading over there now. Or do
you want to?"

* * *

"It was in there. That's where I heard it," the man said nervously,
nodding toward the yard of the parsonage. "It sounded like one of
those riding mowers that the sexton uses."

"You're familiar with the sound?" Dea asked, looking in the
direction the man was pointing.

The man nodded quickly.

"Yes. When I walk Sally, I often pop in to chat a bit with Henning when he's at work. We play in the forty-plus soccer league
together."

"And that was around four thirty this morning?" Dea said.

"Yes. I'm a baker in Vissenbjerg, so I'm up early. And I need to
fit in a walk with the dog before I leave for work."

"Did you notice anything else this morning?" Liam took over.
"Anything unusual aside from the engine noise?"

"No, it was just the riding mower, but the engine stopped as
I crossed the road, so I didn't really think any more about it. It
had been light out for a while by that point, so I figured they were
just getting started early. But then I heard about the pastor, so I
decided to call you."

The forensic tech came walking toward them from the yard.
"A small construction machine drove across the lawn recently,
and we're bringing the cemetery's riding mower in with us for
examination."

Dea thanked the witness for his time and followed Liam as he
pulled the forensic tech off to the side. "We need to have all the trees
in the area here examined for cameras and tape. The construction

machine's engine was turned off just as the dog walker crossed the road."

"So you think the perpetrator saw him on a surveillance camera?"

"We don't know," Dea replied quickly. "But we're considering the possibility that he might follow his victims that way."

She looked out at the lawn and considered whether it was possible that Beate had been carted away on the riding mower. The trailer it pulled was big enough for a person.

Liam looked to see what she was looking at and nodded at the gate leading into the yard, where the sexton usually crossed the road between the church and the parsonage.

"He could have brought her out over there."

Dea nodded. Again she felt a shiver under her skin. Again they were one small step closer.

"We found traces of something we think could be urine in the trailer," the tech continued.

Dea turned to him quickly as a wave of hope spread through her. "If it was Beate's urine, that means the perpetrator may take the victims with him alive."

Just then, Liam's phone rang. He turned back to face her as he listened. Dea brimmed with hope as she realized they were going to hear something new. Without exchanging a word, they started walking back to the car.

"Well?" she asked, as he concluded his conversation and she fastened her seat belt.

"Beate's cell phone was traced to Thorø. According to IT, it's in an empty house on the north side of the island."

"Empty?" Dea repeated.

He nodded.

"The owner of the house died six months ago."

"And who owned the house?" She had rolled down her window a little and now leaned her head back against the headrest. It had been a long day, and now she regretted not making sure she had gotten something proper to eat.

"Peter's grandmother lived in the house until she died."

* * *

It was dark when Beate opened her eyes. She felt both battered and weightless. It took her a minute to realize that she wasn't lying on the floor of the bathroom. Then came the fear, encircling her and squeezing the air out of her. A lukewarm grip had a hold of her body. She screamed in panic as it dawned on her that she was down in some kind of stinking, claustrophobic pit. Water closed in around her. Something was holding her up. It was tight around her chest, and she started flailing her arms and kicking around to find some footing.

The water filled her mouth. She gasped for air and for a second thought she was being pulled down. She felt her feet scrape against something, and she straightened up and got her shoulders and head free of the water.

She shivered and at the same time felt warmth inside her skin. There was an acidic burn in her chest. The air was heavy and dank and the stench pungent and sickening. She held her breath and tilted her head back a little, trying to keep her face above the water. She clutched her stomach and gasped for air.

She tried to comprehend what had happened. All she remembered was that Peter wasn't there. His side of the bed had been empty. And then there was that slip of paper in the kitchen. The man. The bathroom. Her cold, wet hair stuck to her cheek, and the water pressed against her ribs. Waves of nausea trembled through her, the smell of rancid urine was overwhelming, and she tried feverishly to think of something else.

She closed her eyes and tried to calm down. Concentrated on her breathing. Despite the stench, she inhaled deep into her lungs, then forced herself to keep up the big, slow breaths, which sent oxygen to her brain. Where was she? Had she been raped?

Then she noticed it. Something was moving right up against her.

She screamed into the darkness, terrified, her blood pumping so hard throughout her body that it throbbed in her head. Her mouth was once again filled with filthy water, and it was impossible for her to see anything. She pulled away a little from the movement, feeling the baby turn around in her belly.

"Shh," a hoarse voice said from right beside her.

Beate tried to pull away more and scraped her back on a sharp projection in the raw concrete.

"You mustn't be afraid of me," the voice said. "I'm Kasper. I was the second one to come down here. You're number six."

Beate held her breath and stared into the darkness. It sounded as if it was an effort for him to speak. It sounded as if he was suffering. She knew who he was. But she couldn't see him.

* * *

"This place sure is out in the middle of nowhere!" Liam observed, looking around in the light summer evening. They had driven over a narrow wooden bridge from Thorø Huse and then down a gravel road to reach this desolate house on the little island of Thorø. "Who owns all of this?" He turned toward some trees that blended into the island in the late-evening darkness. The waters of the Little Belt strait gleamed pale behind them in the moonlight.

"The Copenhagen Teachers' Union," Dea said. "They bought the place after a director went bankrupt and shot himself. The union actually bought the whole island back then, and they used the three biggest of the island's four buildings to run camps for schoolkids. But according to an old contract, the last building was owned by Peter's maternal grandmother and her father before her. The father was apparently friends with Plum, the guy who shot himself."

"And Peter's grandmother died six months ago?"

"Just under that, but yes."

Liam waved to Nassrin, who was already there with Thorbjørn.

"Have we gotten ahold of Peter?" Liam asked. They hadn't been able to reach Peter since they had searched the parsonage.

"We're looking," Nassrin replied.

"And Beate's cell phone?"

"It was turned on and lying in the bushes over there, but so far the dogs haven't smelled anything."

"Have it sent to forensics for examination immediately."

"Boss! Come around back," Thorbjørn called from the corner of the house. "There's an escargot farm here . . . They're shut up in a bunch of wooden crates with lids."

"Wait, snails?" Liam exclaimed in disbelief, and followed his colleague around the corner of the old house. He was immediately met by a number of wooden crates fastidiously stacked up along the wall of the house. "Did you guys push those lids off?"

"Yes, there's salt in the boxes. People use it to pull the mucus off the animals. That's sheer animal cruelty, that is."

Liam was about to object, but Thorbjørn didn't seem to have considered that this might not exactly be the optimal time to launch his own animal welfare campaign.

He made do with saying "OK." Then he regarded the snails, which were on their way out of their boxes heading every which way. It surprised him how quickly such slow animals could move once they caught a whiff of freedom. He bent down by one of the wooden crates and determined that the vegetables inside looked very fresh. Someone had been here not long ago.

He was starting to walk back around to the front of the house when he heard that the tracking dogs had arrived. The lights inside the house were on now. The investigators were going through the whole house now for evidence of Peter and Beate, and soon the dogs would be deployed in a line to search the little island from end to end.

Wearing a forensics body suit and a hair net, Dea signaled from inside the house that they had found something. Liam made his way over to the blue back door and waited for her to come out.

The house didn't look like it had changed at all in the last fifty years. He peered in the windows. The kitchen, light fixtures, cups, and furniture were clearly older than he was.

"You have to see this," Dea said, when she came to the door and handed Liam a notebook. "Peter's grandmother kept accounts. She sold snails and sea kale in the summers—both to the general public and to restaurants."

Dea started pulling off her protective suit so she could get out of the way of the forensics team inside while Liam flipped through the pages. There was nothing else written in the book after the grandmother's death, but the snails would not have been kept alive if the business were not still operating.

"What do you think?" she asked.

"I think that Peter is still running his grandmother's business and probably earns a pretty penny alongside his unemployment."

"Well, then we know what he was doing on his morning outings."

"Yeah, maybe." Liam drew that out. "I don't think Beate had any inkling of this, and the question is, why did he keep it a secret?"

"Maybe she didn't even know he had inherited the house."

Liam sat down on an old lawn chair by the wall of the house. It collapsed underneath him.

"We need to get a helicopter up in the air and set up road-blocks. Peter is our first priority right now." He jutted out his lower lip, thinking. "Beate's cell phone didn't just turn up here all on its own after having been on standby mode since she disappeared, right?"

Day 7—Thursday

"Boss?"

Perplexed, Liam blinked and glanced around his office. His back ached and his T-shirt clung to his skin under the dust-gray wool blanket.

"It's seven thirty-three," Nassrin said, "and I thought you might need some coffee before the morning meeting?"

"Yes, damn it. Thank you." He accepted the steaming coffee. They had been so late getting back from Thorø that he had just lain down on the sofa in his office and gone out like a light.

The coffee was far too hot, but she had remembered cream.

"Is there anything new from the last couple of hours?" he asked.

Nassrin handed him a couple of pages of notes.

Peter apprehended close to Tommerup at 7:23 a.m. He was brought in for questioning. He'll be ready in a minute.

Luna disappeared in Tommerup sometime between 10:30 p.m. and 6:00 a.m. We don't know yet if it's related to the case.

As we all know, Luna has several convictions for theft, but it was news to us that one of them was for robbing Beate's parents—they reported her just over two years ago, and she lost her job as a health care aide. Beate and Peter may very well have known this.

Peter's car was spotted near Luna's house last night and a witness saw a man "last night," who could be Peter, walking right behind a woman whose description matches Luna. But it was dark out.

We need to untangle all the interrelationships between Luna, Dennis, and Beate's parents ASAP.

DNA evidence, urine, and fingerprints from the parsonage? Where are we with those?

A gray Peugeot was spotted driving out of Assens the night Kasper disappeared, but it had a different license plate than the one seen around the time of Kent's disappearance.

* * *

"G'morning!" A couple of minutes later, Liam clapped the way he usually did to get everyone's attention as he walked into the large meeting room, which was packed with people. He recognized a few people each from the Police Intelligence Service, the drone team, the Police and Mental Health Joint Response Team, and the canine unit; a couple of military personnel; and colleagues from the Criminal Investigation Centers in Odense and Kolding.

"Things are happening now!" Liam said.

He quickly briefed the entire group and then released a string of people from the room so they could get down to work before continuing with the key members of his own group, mostly from the Violent Crimes section of the Reactive Criminal Investigations Department.

"Is it true that we detained Dennis?"

"Yes," replied one of the officers from Surveillance. "He flipped out when he heard that Luna was missing. Plus he was so high that we didn't see any other way than to bring him in. He was a danger to himself, pure and simple."

"Good, as long as he knows that he isn't being charged with anything." Liam drummed on his thigh with his fingertips. "Do we have people searching the parsonage again yet?"

"We've been working out there for half an hour now, yes," another officer said. "Eight men and dogs. Peter's car is being transported to Forensics. They've called in more people from the National Forensic Service, and we already have his computer."

"Do we have enough to detain him?"

"We will!"

"You have twenty-two hours left, and then we'll need to go before the state prosecutor." Liam looked around at the thirty or so people remaining in the room. "In terms of the car, we're pretty sure now that the gray Peugeot, which we've linked to the abduction of Kent Hansen, was also seen leaving Assens at four thirty-seven AM on the night when Kasper disappeared, but with different license plates. And those plates belonged to an older man in Broby who uses his car about as often as it rains frogs. We're pouring through his acquaintances now. It's also noteworthy that the Peugeot was caught by surveillance cameras in Assens three weeks ago, and in all likelihood hasn't moved since it was used to abduct Kasper and later Kent. Anything else to add?"

"We know from the surveillance footage, as you say, that the car was parked at the harbor for three weeks, and we know that it was picked up by a man in a hoodie on Saturday night at three twelve AM, but we don't know who that man is, and we have no witnesses who saw him pick up or drop off his car."

"But from his height and build, he could be Peter Løve, right?" Dea asked.

"He could, yes."

"Thanks," Liam said with a nod. "As I understand your reports, we don't have any other repeats aside from the gray Peugeot?"

"No, so far there haven't been any other cars that have warranted further investigation, and the same is true for phone data. We haven't managed to trace a specific telecom signal that tracks with either the Peugeot or the old Granada during the hours in question."

"Does that mean the person in question doesn't have a cell phone?" Dea looked around at the others in the room incredulously.

"He or she had to have turned it on to be able to track their private surveillance of the crime scenes, based on our current view," the telecommunications specialist said. "So the person in question doesn't bring a private cell phone along on these trips but swaps out the unit for each crime. We also need to assume that these devices are hidden relatively close to the crime scenes so that we don't have the opportunity to pick up a unit in the vicinity being turned off, and yet not so close that the dogs could detect it."

"How did you get to be so clever?!" Dea exclaimed, sounding almost impressed.

"This level of insight you have into our work—and how the perpetrator hides from us—is right up there with what I'd expect from some aging biker," the officer said with a little chuckle.

* * *

The water was black and stagnant. Beate had her arms around Charlotte. Charlotte's head was covered in wounds and swollen splotches, as if she had been horrifically sunburned. Her body felt too cold, her forehead and breath too hot.

"Here." It was Kasper's voice.

Beate felt a plastic bottle hit her arm and fumbled after it.

"Do we get clean water every day?"

"I think so, but I don't have any sense of time."

"How do you get into the water?" Beate asked. She could feel Kasper moving closer.

"Every time the hatch opens, they throw a new one down."

"You mean a new person?" Beate said in disbelief.

"Yes . . . There are two dead people here, and then us two . . . and Lone and Charlotte."

Beate opened the bottle and carefully tasted the liquid before she groped her way with her fingers to Charlotte's mouth and poured in a little water between the woman's lips. Charlotte swallowed with difficulty.

"She'll die if we can't escape."

"I know." Kasper's voice was thick, like that of someone with a fever. She could smell his breath. It was acidic and a little rotten.

"She's been here a day longer than me, and we haven't eaten since we were put down here," he continued.

Charlotte's skin felt raw and porous against Beate's. It was so waterlogged it couldn't hold another drop. The body tried to protect itself by thickening and wrinkling up the skin. It was worst in the hands and feet. They bulged and cracked.

Beate was doing a little better than she had been when she first woke up in the water. She had pounded on the rough wall with her hands until they bled, and she had thrown up in the water because of the horrific stench of piss all around her. She was calmer now but could still only get her head and shoulders out of the water. Verner was dead. Another man—they had no idea who he was—was also dead. He had been dead when he was thrown in, Kasper said. Verner had lasted a day but had been confused and distrustful.

Beate listened to Kasper's breathing in the darkness. He must be crushingly hungry, but he didn't complain.

"Let me hold her a little."

Beate carefully let go of Charlotte's body and guided her over to Kasper.

It was silent for a moment in the darkness.

"Can you help me lift her out of the water and tie her up?" Kasper continued. "I don't have the strength to do it myself anymore."

"Why don't you just let her stay up there?"

"It hurts, hanging up there, and we need to move around a little to survive."

Beate tried to get a sense of him in the dark, tried to picture what he looked like.

"You've been in here for five days." She could hear from the little ripples that he was moving a bit in the water. The stench of urine and rot felt less overwhelming than it had for the first few hours, but she could still smell it, and her breathing felt labored. "How did he get you?"

"It was at night . . . I was in the workshop. My friend and me, we were drunk. I went to go take a piss. Dennis had gone up to his apartment. I don't know what happened, and I didn't have time to see anything. Suddenly there was just someone there, right behind me."

He stopped.

Beate stared into the darkness with her face turned toward his voice.

"And then what? What happened then?"

"He stabbed me."

"I felt a jab, too . . . in the neck!"

"And then you woke up here?"

"Yes . . ."

"That's what happened to Charlotte too. She was snatched out by the gym in Tommerup. And Lone and Verner were also poked right before they fainted."

"And it was also a man who attacked you?"

"Yes, but I didn't see his face."

"What about the others?" Beate asked.

"Lone caught a glimpse of his face, but she didn't know him. Verner didn't remember anything, just that his dog collapsed. I've tried to get Charlotte to remember. She saw him, but she's confused and incoherent. She doesn't know what happened. I think she's in shock. Think about it; she was the first. She was completely alone down here. She didn't know that more people would come. Did you see him?"

"Not at all. I was alone in my house, and it was dark when he . . . when he came in to where I was . . . He smelled like the same cologne as my boyfriend, but I think he was older than Peter."

"He was in your house?"

"Yes, he grabbed me in our bathroom."

"Whoa." Kasper exhaled heavily.

"I knew it was my turn," Beate continued. "It sounds like the rest of you didn't know what was going on, but I knew."

"How?"

"I'm number six," Beate said, searching for the words, "and I've been following the case, so I knew that each time one of us down here went missing, the police found a note with a quote from the Quran. When I woke up this morning, one of those notes was on my kitchen counter." She paused and then continued weakly, "They're pulling out all the stops for this case, but the police aren't getting anywhere." She shivered. "They're not even on his trail, Kasper."

She could hear Kasper moving again. The thought that they would slowly die in this fetid black water took her breath away.

"Why are you whispering about me?" a shrill voice yelled, suddenly close to them.

Beate flinched and moved closer to Kasper.

"That's Lone," Kasper said reassuringly.

"Don't talk about me!" Lone cried, still yelling. "You're going to kill me! I know it! You're the ones doing this . . . Where are you?"

There were loud splashes in the dark. It sounded like hands hitting the surface of the water hard. Big surges of the disgusting water hit Beate in the face.

She clung convulsively to Kasper's arm.

"She'll stop again," Kasper whispered. "This is how she's been acting from day one."

Lone kept pounding the water. "Get your hands off me!"

"What if she gets hold of us?" Beate whispered.

"She won't. It's just . . . I don't know. She has these fits, and then she'll be quiet again for a long time."

"Get your hands off me!" Lone yelled.

Beate felt her hands. Her skin was more wrinkled now. Her fingers felt like they were asleep, like they belonged to someone else, as she rubbed them together.

* * *

"It's nine twenty-seven," Liam said, looking up from the interrogation transcript that now sat on top of the case file. "Present in the room are the accused, Peter Løve, Sergeant Dea Torp, and myself, Police Inspector Liam Stark." He paused briefly. "Peter Løve, you stand accused of unlawful restraint. I need to ask you to state your name, your date of birth, and your address."

"Yes," Peter said. Short dirty-blond stubble covered his bald head. It made him look helpless. "Peter Løve; March seventh, 1986; Kirkebjerg 2, 5690 Tommerup."

"Thanks. Peter, you are under no obligation to say anything more here at present, but I hope that you can help us shed some light on this case."

"I'll try," Peter said. "It's my Beate." His voice sounded vulnerable. "And my baby."

"Do you confirm that you know you're entitled to have a defense attorney present and that you have waived this?" Dea said.

"I don't have anything to hide." Peter shook his head. "It doesn't make any sense that you're saying *I'm* accused of anything!"

"You're being *charged*," Liam said calmly, "because there are a number of circumstances regarding you and your person that have resulted in our needing to speak with you." He glanced down at his papers. "Have you seen Beate's cell phone since she disappeared?"

"No, I've been calling and calling, but I haven't been able to get through."

"So you don't know why it was turned on last night?" Liam said, watching Peter's eyes attentively.

"It was turned on?" he said, and stood up halfway. "Did you find her?"

"No," Dea said. "And please remain seated. We found her cell phone but not her."

"Where did you find it?" Peter sat back down, his jaw clenched.

"You have a habit of taking long drives early in the morning"—Liam took over—"and neither Beate nor anyone else knows where you go?"

"Yes, I told Beate that I drive to the beach to get some air. I do a fair amount of work at night."

"You're unemployed," Dea said caustically.

"Yes, but that's only temporary. I'm doing a lot of work on this series of articles I'm writing."

"Help me understand this," Liam continued. "You're writing articles about similarities and differences between Christianity and Islam?"

"Yes, I am," Peter said, leaning forward. "I'd like to reform Islam."

Liam nodded. A little of Peter's nervousness disappeared when he discussed his work.

"What do you mean by 'reform Islam'?"

"My focus is on the way Islam is interpreted today. If you go back only forty to fifty years ago, people lived with a lot more freedom than they do today in a number of Muslim countries. Women were allowed to go to school and wear short skirts in both Iran and Afghanistan, whereas today they need to be completely covered up and stay at home. That's what I want to do away with. We in the West need to find the courage to dare to criticize this oppressive interpretation of Islam; otherwise we'll end up like Iran, and that's something everyone here in the West should be opposed to. But what do my articles have to do with Beate? She didn't go missing because I'm writing about—"

"I'd like to know"—Liam interrupted him—"why you asked Hayyan Khalil to suggest which verses in the Quran could correspond to the Ten Commandments in the Bible. What were you going to do with them?"

"The Ten Commandments?" Peter repeated, taken aback. "Well, that was a long time ago . . ." He shook his head. "I . . . I wanted them because I was working on similarities and differences between Islam and Christianity. In one sura, which has been lost, Muhammad is said to have personally written that Muslims should be good to Jews and Christians, but very few orthodox Muslims today want to accept that."

"But you want to convince them to do so?" Dea glanced intently over at Peter.

"The Christian faith was reformed for the better. If the Inquisition could give way to loving thy neighbor, then maybe sharia could be reformed too?" Peter's cheeks were flushed.

"I can see that you're very passionate about this," Dea said, "but we mustn't forget that you're here because your pregnant girlfriend is missing. What went wrong there?"

"What do you mean by wrong?" Peter asked, disoriented.

"Did she see too much?"

Not understanding, Peter stared blankly at Dea without making a sound.

"When you found Charlotte's bicycle a week ago"—Liam took over—"it turned up in a place that had already been thoroughly searched. How did that happen?"

"I have no idea," Peter said quickly. "It was just sitting there!"

"It was just sitting there?" Liam repeated, nodding thoughtfully. "And then there are your little daily morning trips to the beach."

"Well, it's not every morning . . ." Peter looked from one to the other of them in confusion and gulped a couple of times. "Can I ask what this had to do with anything?"

"Peter, where were you last night and in the early hours of this morning? We've had several patrol out searching for you, but you weren't easy to find."

"I was driving around looking for Beate," Peter said. "She's missing, and she's pregnant with my baby! What is this?" He rubbed his eyes. "What are you imagining?"

"Why didn't you want to be found? Why didn't you answer your phone?" Liam asked.

Peter shook his head, seeming defeated. "I wasn't thinking all those thoughts. I was just crushed. I'm crushed."

Someone knocked on the door of the interrogation room, and both Liam and Dea got up and walked over to the officer who poked his head in. Then they nodded and came back over to Peter.

"We caught your car in Tommerup last night on a surveillance video. It was seen during the same window of time when a young woman disappeared from the town. What did you do while you were out driving?"

There was an almost-invisible reaction that crossed Peter's face, as if he didn't quite understand that what was being asked had to do with him. Then he flung out his hands disarmingly.

"I went by the parsonage to see if Beate had come home, but all the lights were off in there!"

"The young woman's name is Luna." Dea took over. "We're sure you've heard of her, because your father-in-law filed charges against her for theft a couple of years ago, and she has gotten to know Beate since then."

Peter shrugged.

Liam drummed on the case file. "So you're saying that you drove past the parsonage, drove around town a little, and then drove back out to the water again? But you were caught by the surveillance camera at the market getting gas from the OK pump at eleven forty-five PM. So it could appear that you had stayed in the Tommerup area for two hours."

"Yes, if you say so. I wasn't paying attention to the time."

"But what were you doing in that little town for so long?" Dea cut in.

"I wasn't doing well," Peter mumbled. "I have no idea what I was doing."

Liam opened the thin folder. "Peter, when you were young, you were an ardent left-wing activist, weren't you? And you have a couple of convictions behind you for vandalism and assaulting a police officer?"

Peter looked up with an expression of astonishment. "You can't mean it. That was, like, a hundred years ago."

Liam drummed hard on the tabletop with his fingertips and changed tack again. "Did anyone see you while you were out driving this morning?"

206 SARA BLÆDEL AND MADS PEDER NORDBO

"How would I know? I don't go for drives to see people. I do it to get some peace."

"Do you have peace?" Liam asked, studying Peter's eyes attentively.

Peter looked away and shook his head.

Liam caught his eye again. "You never told your pregnant girlfriend about your grandmother's house and the black-market money when you inherited her little racket. Why not?"

Peter looked at Liam in dismay.

"Why did you keep that a secret, Peter?"

Peter didn't say anything for a long time.

Then he said, "Because I was embarrassed about it."

"You were embarrassed?"

"Yes, damn it," Peter yelled.

Liam was startled. This was the first time he'd detected any sincerity in Peter's eyes. This was genuine. This hurt.

"Why?" Liam asked.

"I'm thirty-five years old," Peter said, agitated. "I live for free with my girlfriend in her residence that she gets through her job, and I've been unemployed for almost two years. I'm a loser, and she knows that my articles will probably never amount to shit, because we're living in a time when everyone is so damned scared of offending Muslims . . . Am I supposed to also tell her that I earn money under the table selling snails from my dead grand-mother's house?"

"Yes?" Liam said. "That's a big thing to keep hidden, and I wonder if Beate wouldn't have understood the problem if you had told her."

"Maybe she found out about it?" Dea added tentatively.

"So you think," Peter exclaimed angrily, "I supposedly killed my girlfriend, who is carrying our child, over some fucking snails?" He slumped back in his chair, exhaling noisily.

"We don't know if Beate is dead," Liam said quickly. "Why do you say *killed*?"

With a sigh, Peter let his head flop down onto the tabletop. "I can't do this anymore. I waived the lawyer because I don't have anything to hide," he mumbled down at the tabletop. "But I don't want any more of this now! *My* Beate is gone! *My* unborn baby. This is over. Over! I'm not saying another word without legal counsel by my side."

Liam looked up. "It's ten fifty-six. The interrogation of Peter Løve is suspended in order to procure him his state-appointed counsel." He got up and regarded Peter, who was still resting with his face down on the tabletop. Then he followed Dea out of the interrogation room.

She grabbed his arm. "You have to see this!" She stuck her phone in his face.

It was showing Facebook's page for *5690 Tommerup*. There was a picture of Peter, and underneath it, the caption read that the police had detained Peter Løve and that he was the main suspect behind the disappearance of seven people. The post had already been shared 237 times and had 489 comments, the vast majority of which were filled with anger and hatred directed at Peter.

Liam skimmed the first several comments. People were scared.

*   *   *

Beate was aware of the hunger gnawing at her. She felt exhausted and discouraged. The baby moved restlessly in her belly.

Kasper drifted in and out of sleep. She had felt his arms; they were bumpy, like he had a rash and sores. He had taken off his clothes and used them to tie himself to the pipe that ran across the tank over the water. It was better to be cold than to feel your skin slowly decomposing in the water.

They had helped each other do the same with Charlotte so she could have a break from the water as well. Her skin was also swollen and full of soft little lumps. Beate had tried to get through to Charlotte the whole time, to find out what she had seen when she was captured, but she was either completely out of it or very distant.

Beate had not heard anything from Lone for a while. She had moaned for a long time, then quieted down. They hadn't been able to tie her up. She'd gotten hysterical when they tried. Her skin must have broken down completely.

Kasper didn't moan, but he was talking less and less. Both he and Charlotte felt hot, as if they had high fevers. He had been in the black water for five days without food, but he was handling it better than the others. Maybe that was because he was young and muscular. If he died, she would be completely alone in the disgusting, putrid water. She had already thought many times how easy it would be to sink down and let the water into her lungs, but the thought of Silje stopped her from doing that. Silje's smile and her happy eyes. Her eager little body as she ran around playing in the living room.

The baby in Beate's belly also kept her from giving up. How long did it take a fetus to die if the mother's body died? How long would the baby survive after her? Would it suffer? She couldn't bear thinking about it. She clung to the iron pipe. The thick, heavy denim fabric she was tied up with cut painfully into her skin. Kasper had taken the jeans off Verner and the other dead man. Beate only had the thin nightgown, which couldn't hold her up at all, so she was hanging in dead people's clothes.

She didn't have the strength to hang there anymore. It hurt. Kasper was right; her body quickly grew cold and overstrained when she was out of the water. She had been freezing and shivering this whole time, even in the water, although the water was warmer than the air. Her hands shaking, she untied the clothes she was hanging from and allowed herself to slide back down into the water.

They had tried to explore the tank they were floating around in and had found a box down on the bottom. It felt like it was made of a wide-mesh iron net—a sort of cage. Every now and then the water in the box started to move and heat flowed out to them.

She jumped when something metal rattled above them. Then there was light. It stung her eyes.

"Let us out! Hey? Let us out! I'm pregnant . . . Please let us out of here!" she sobbed, and for a brief instant she could see Kasper in the light from above. His skin was blotchy with bluish-black patches, and he was covered in red blisters. She gasped. A tremendous splash close to her sent a wave over her face, and she got water in her mouth. Then it was dark again.

*   *   *

Dea looked around the elongated park that stretched along the river between the police building and her home. It smelled like hot summertime. She ran that way every day to clear her mind and burn off her irritation. She knew she was a pain in the butt to many people, but of course they didn't realize she could easily be so much worse. She controlled herself, gritted her teeth, sat on her hands, ran it off.

Her feet churned quickly beneath her. The evening sun cast dark shadows in the gravel. Farther ahead on the path, a man was bending over with a hand up in the air, as if he wanted to say something. He looked like a junkie, dressed in dirty pants that were too tight and a scruffy hoodie. She slowed down a little and stopped a few meters from him. He clutched at his heart with his right hand and slumped over even farther.

"I think . . . I . . . think I'm having . . . a . . . My heart . . . Help me!"

"Your heart?" she exclaimed, out of breath, taking a couple of steps closer. "Lie down, and I'll call for help."

He reached out to her, but she was standing too far away, so he sank down onto his knees instead.

"I . . . can't . . . breathe!"

"Lie down!" Dea repeated, and took out her phone. "Don't put your energy into talking."

"Hello?" An older couple with a little dog on a leash were headed across the grass toward them. "Is everything OK?"

The drug addict bowed his head forward and gasped for breath.

"It's better now."

"No, no," Dea said, bending over a little to peer into the big hood, which completely obscured the man's face. "You need to be seen at the hospital . . . I'm making the call now!"

Suddenly the addict leapt adroitly, extremely close to her now, and knocked her down with a forcible shove.

"Hey!" Dea yelled angrily. "What the hell are you doing?"

The older couple had stopped as the shabby man abruptly broke into a run and vanished between the bushes heading toward the footbridge toward Christiansgade and Valdemarsgade.

Dea lay on the ground, speechless, and contemplated setting off after the man, but she was too shaken. When she tried to get up, she discovered that she had hit her head on one of the rocks along the edge of the path.

The elder couple finally made it all the way over to the path.

"Did he take anything from you?" the man asked.

She had made it up into a sitting position and patted her pockets. "No, I have everything. He said he couldn't breathe, but then he ran like crazy when you showed up."

* * *

Nassrin knocked on Dennis's door just before five. There was still activity in the workshop under his apartment. She had been near Assens when it was confirmed that Luna was the seventh victim in the case, and she had offered right away to pay Dennis a visit to find out what he could tell her about Luna and her movements for the last twenty-four hours.

When Dennis opened the door to her, his eyes were red from crying. All his toughness was gone. He smelled like sleep and pot.

"I'd like to talk to you about Luna." Nassrin took a step back and leaned slightly against the worn blue wooden railing; suddenly it felt too intimate to go inside with him.

Dennis sniffled and came out onto the covered landing with her, then closed his door behind him. "What do you want to know?"

"What happened back when Luna lost her job?"

At first he didn't seem to understand, but then he nodded.

"She was working as a health care aide back then and had been sent out to see some old fool who lived out in the boonies. His wife was messed up in the head . . . couldn't remember shit. They had a real haul of expensive stuff lying around, so one day Luna snatched a pair of figures to sell, but the old man caught her, so she was fired."

"And then after that, she moved to Tommerup?"

"Yeah; then she had to do community service at the church in Tommerup. That's how she got to be friends with that woman pastor up there."

"Beate?"

"I've never met her," Dennis said with a shrug. "But it was kind of messed up, because it turned out that the pastor was the daughter of the old fool Luna had stolen from."

"Do you know what Luna did yesterday?"

He pulled out his cell phone. "No, but she sent me a ton of text messages. You want to see them?" He handed his phone to Nassrin with a sheepish smile. "Excuse all the hearts and all that. Luna's always like that."

Nassrin smiled warmly at him and scrolled back through their texts from the last couple of days, but there wasn't anything of interest.

Dennis pulled a cigarette out of his pants pocket and lit it.

"You haven't by any chance happened to notice an older gray Peugeot or an old Granada lately? With your job, I'm sure you notice car makes that you wouldn't typically see driving around the area." Nassrin continued.

"Yeah, I would definitely notice an old Granada," Dennis exclaimed, "but I haven't seen one."

"Dennis, now I'm going to ask you about something that you're probably going to bristle at, but it's important that you give me an honest answer, because we need to know everything there is to know if we're going to figure out whether it was a specific theft that put Luna in the sights of our perpetrator: Has Luna ever stolen anything or helped steal something that the police never found out about?"

A large seagull flew over the roof, startling them both. Dennis smiled briefly and took a deep drag from his cigarette and then exhaled with a nod.

"Yes."

"Could you make a list for us? Where you also note who she stole from?"

He closed his eyes. "If you find her, you'll prosecute her for all those cases."

"If we don't find her, you may never see her again."

* * *

By the time Nassrin stepped back out onto the landing, two hours had elapsed since she'd knocked on Dennis's door. His list of

Luna's robberies had gone on forever. They had gone into his small living room, which was tidier than she had imagined. She had sat there in an armchair, completely quiet, as he concentrated hard and worked his way back through time.

She had been struck by how much love went into his efforts to remember everything and get it all written down. It was a part of the intimate life the two siblings had shared.

She would go back to the police station now and compare this list with the case data. There might be a connection somewhere that could lead them closer to solving the disappearances.

When she got back down in front of the workshop, a big, slightly dirty, older Golf with temporary plates was parked so close behind her that even from a distance she could already tell she was going to have a hard time getting out. She groaned, annoyed, and got into her car. She tried to coax her way out, inching forward and back many times and trying to get the back end angled out. But ultimately she gave up. The Golf had blocked her in.

Nassrin cursed loudly as she got out. She slammed her car door and walked back to look into the Golf, thinking that maybe the owner had left the key in the car if it was waiting to be driven into the workshop. But there was no key in the ignition. The car was locked. There were a couple of folders on the passenger's seat, but it was the little slip of paper next to the folders that caught her eye. With a start, she instinctively took a step back, tensely looking around in all directions. *Thou shalt not bear false witness against thy neighbor.*

It was the eighth commandment from the Bible. She recognized it right away from the whiteboard in their meeting room. And she also immediately realized that it corresponded to one of the verses her uncle had marked in his Quran.

The courtyard was quiet in front of the workshop, which was now dark and closed up. Nassrin felt short of breath as she took a

picture through the Golf's window and sent it to Liam and Dea.
She also sent a picture of the car's temporary license plate.

Dea called back right away. *That looks like one of our notes? Is
there anything else in the car? Nassrin! That car must not be allowed
to drive, OK? Don't lose it. I'm in Tommerup. I'm leaving right away.
Contact Liam so he can send reinforcements. And be careful, right? Do
you have your sidearm with you?*

Nassrin hung up. Unlike Dea, Liam asked her to pull back
from the location and leave the rest to the team, which was coming to assist her. She could hear him running down the stairs as
they spoke. He was on his way and said he would call a team of
crime scene investigators as well. And he was right, she thought.
She ought to leave the location and wait for her colleagues. If the
Golf left before the reinforcements got there, they had the license
plate. They could put out an APB on it.

Even so, she stayed waiting by the car. Dea wasn't far from
Assens. She would be there soon.

Nassrin tried to memorize all the details from the parking lot,
tried to remember if anything seemed different from when she had
arrived. She looked around to see if she could spot one of the little
cameras that they knew the perpetrator used. Suddenly it hit her
that the door to Kasper's apartment right next to Dennis's was
open. It definitely hadn't been when she arrived. *Stay by the car,*
rumbled through her thoughts.

* * *

Twenty-five minutes later, Dea pulled up in front of the workshop
in Assens. Darkness had fallen. The sky was heavy with bluish-
gray clouds. The black Golf Nassrin had mentioned was nowhere
to be seen, but Nassrin's little Fiat was still there. A wave of irritation ran through Dea's body. Wouldn't it be just like that little
wannabe detective to let the car get away?

She zipped up her jacket and started walking over to Nassrin's car. Liam had called a couple of times after he left the police station in Odense, but it would be at least ten more minutes before he arrived. She pulled her phone out to call him back but stopped abruptly. There was someone sitting in Nassrin's car, and it most definitely was not Nassrin.

Dea raised her gun and aimed it at the car door.

"Come out!"

Nothing happened, and she took a step closer to the car door. She tightened her hold on the gun's grip.

"Come out now. This is the police!"

Still nothing happened. The figure inside didn't move. Dea proceeded around the car until she got close enough that she could see the person's profile.

"Dennis?" she yelled, walking all the way over to the car door.

She quickly ran her eyes around the seam between the door and the vehicle frame to see if it was a trap, but there was nothing to be seen. She yanked the car door open, and Dennis spilled partway out. He was unconscious.

"Damn it!" she mumbled, looking quickly in all directions. There was no one around. She stuck her gun back in her shoulder holster and squatted down next to him.

"Hey, wake up!" She slapped him gently on the cheeks and managed to get him up into a sitting position.

He shook his head slightly before finally focusing on her.

"What the hell?"

"What are you doing in Nassrin's car? Where's Nassrin?"

Dennis put his hands over his eyes and grimaced in pain. The whites of his eyes showed, and then they closed again.

She patted his cheeks again cautiously. "Dennis, you need to tell me where Nassrin is."

Dennis moaned and turned away from Dea. "I don't know."

"Oh, come on, you're sitting in her car! Are you on drugs? Talk to me!"

"I . . ." Dennis squeezed his eyes shut tight, as if it took his full concentration to respond. "She was here a minute ago . . . The man that was here . . . I . . ." He shook his head and made a face.

"Take a deep breath and think about it!" Dea yelled.

"There was a black Golf parked here," Dennis muttered. "I was on my way to my mom's place, and he was sitting there in the car . . . yeah . . . and then I saw Nassrin. She was lying inside . . . on the back seat."

"You saw Nassrin in the Golf? Was she awake? What was she doing?"

He shook his head.

"She was lying down . . . crouching . . . I couldn't tell if she was moving . . . I wanted to . . . he was just sitting there, the man, staring at me. Then he got out of the car . . . He was, like, emotionless . . ."

Dea studied him. He seemed woozy, like he was in shock. Sirens were approaching from a distance. She wanted to get Dennis away from the car and tried to grab his shoulder, but he pushed her away.

He faltered a little as he unsteadily got out of the car, then his eyes opened wide.

"Hey, yeah. What the hell? That man, yeah, he held his phone up to me! There was some kind of movie on it, and he wanted me to watch it . . . then he said, 'Say hi to your sister.' And when I leaned in closer to the screen to see what that idiot was talking about, he stuck something sharp in my neck."

The first police cars came into view out on the road behind the workshop, and the sirens and the bright emergency lights cut through the quiet night air. Dea's heart pounded in her chest as she grabbed his arm.

"What did you see on the screen?"

He shook his head uncertainly, suddenly seeming afraid.

"What did you see on the screen?" she shouted right at his head.

He shrugged, scraping the toe of his shoe across the dirty pavers.

"I only caught a glimpse. There was water. It looked like a dark room. But water . . . I could see some figures, but I couldn't see Luna . . . The video was maybe taken with a night vision camera or a GoPro? Yeah, I think so. That's what it looked like."

He dug around in his jacket pocket and found a crumpled pack of cigarettes. When he finally worked the pack free of his jacket, a little slip of paper came out along with the pack and fell down on the pavers.

Dea snatched the little note up and recognized it right away from the photo Nassrin had sent. She heard multiple car doors slam and sensed Liam running toward them. As she held out the slip of paper, she had a hard time looking him in the eye.

"Nassrin's gone. She's the eighth victim."

*   *   *

The meeting room's artificial lighting was bright. The night outside was black, and Liam could see his own reflection in the windows. The darkness gave his cheeks a black outline. He leaned forward over his notes from questioning Nassrin's parents and her two brothers. They hadn't had much to contribute. He already knew from Nassrin herself that she didn't have the greatest relationship with her parents and brothers, which was why she lived with her elderly uncles. Dea was the one who had informed the two uncles, in their used bookstore, of Nassrin's disappearance; they were inconsolable, and she had promised them that someone from the police would return the next day.

There was a bang from a door down the hall, and then the door to the meeting room opened.

"Boss, are you in here?"

It was Dea. He looked at his watch. It was one twenty-seven AM.

"Is there any news?" she continued.

Liam shook his head. When they had finished up in Assens, he had expressly asked her to go home and sleep so she would be fresh and alert for work in the morning.

"What about the license plates?"

"The temporary plates were reported stolen from the DMV just under six months ago." He looked around tiredly. "I sent everyone from the daytime team home to sleep so we'll have fresh energy on all fronts starting at seven in the morning. They're pulling a list of everyone who owns a black Golf. It's an older model, and they'll bring the lists out to us, and then we'll assign a big team to locating the car." He stopped for a minute, seeing that she wanted to say something. "No, we don't have any reports of a black Golf that's been reported stolen. But we're going to find it."

To put it mildly, Dea looked like shit. He studied her, taking on some of his colleague's fear as if it were contagious.

"We should probably both get some sleep," he said, adding that the night team from Forensics had taken over. "And we still have patrols out, of course." He smiled encouragingly at her. "But maybe you're working a twenty-four-hour shift now?"

"I can't just sit around home. Damn it, Liam!"

"Nah," he said. He also doubted that he would be able to sleep until they had found Nassrin and the other seven victims.

Dea came over to his desk.

"Have you been through everything from today?" She pointed down at a series of prints from various surveillance cameras.

"Surveillance cameras captured the black Golf at two locations driving into Assens the night Kasper disappeared, with the same license plates. It left the town again the following morning and then came back again in the afternoon, which is when Nassrin saw it at Assens Auto."

"Same plates?"

"Yes, so it's also possible that the car isn't listed in the motor vehicle registry, and then it will be hard to know where we should look. We definitely have other features that will identify the vehicle if we find a black Golf without plates. The man in the car wore a hoodie pulled way down over his face."

Dea stared at the grainy black-and-white pictures from the surveillance cameras for a long time.

"So Forensics is saying it's the same car?"

"Yes."

Dea walked over to the board, where the main points of the case had been outlined. She erased a couple of now-obsolete theories and started writing.

"We're looking for a man. We don't have any real description because of the hood, but Dennis is positive that the man is older than he is. We know that he's used a black Golf with stolen temporary plates at least twice and an older Peugeot and an ancient Granada. We know that he's really good at keeping his phone from being tracked. Based on the movie clip Dennis saw, we think the victims are still alive and that they're in a dark space with water in it."

"Exactly, and the results from the National Forensic Service show that it was Beate's urine that we found. So she was alive when she was abducted."

"How long can a person survive in water?"

"I asked Forensic Medicine," Liam said with a shrug. "I expect an answer in the morning as soon as they come in."

Once again they heard noises out in the corridor, and then Thorbjørn opened the door. He stopped abruptly when he saw them. He rubbed his face tiredly.

"Not one of us got any sleep tonight, huh?" he said, and tossed a report down in front of Liam.

"What've you got?" Dea asked, walking over to the table.

"As you know, Beate's father, Bent Møller Nielsen, is a former policeman," Thorbjørn said, sitting down on the corner of the table. "To be sure, he was only in the job for a few years, and back then he went by Hans Henrik."

"So he changed his name? Why?"

Thorbjørn shrugged.

"It happened shortly after he got out of jail, where he served time for a violent crime."

Liam took the report and skimmed it. His eyes burned, the fatigue wrapping around him like wool. He circled a couple of passages before passing the report back but was too tired to take in anything else.

"Dive into that tomorrow," he instructed. "If you can get to it before our morning briefing, that would be great. Right now, I either need a bucket of coffee or an hour's worth of sleep, and since we're out of cream, it's going to have to be sleep."

* * *

Liam woke up. His eye itched and he had to sneeze. He shook himself free of the blanket and got up.

Dea was still sitting at the table in the big meeting room. She looked up, her face ashen with exhaustion. She had spread the indistinct screenshots of the Golf out in front of her.

"Did you find anything?" Liam growled, then cleared his throat. It was only then that he noticed the big photograph of Nassrin that had been hung up on the board next to the other victims.

He stood there for a moment, lost in thought, as he looked at it. He was startled when Dea started speaking.

"It's the hoodie . . . Liam. I think it was the same man who abducted Nassrin."

Liam looked at her in confusion and thought that they all would have been better served if he had made sure to get a few hours of proper sleep instead of staggering around in a stupor like this.

"I'm not following you," he admitted, rubbing his face before he sat down next to her.

"I was attacked in the park out here, by Christiansgade, this afternoon when I was out for my run."

He looked at her in astonishment.

"You didn't think to mention that?"

"At the time I didn't think it meant anything. I assumed he was just a junkie on the prowl. He faked that he was having heart problems, and then when I went over to help, he shoved me to the ground. But he ran off when he realized that he and I weren't the only ones in the park."

"And what do you think now?"

"I've been sitting here staring at these surveillance images from Assens of the man in the hoodie, and this could be the same guy who pushed me over."

"Are you sure?"

"Almost." But then she shook her head. "But how can I be positive? I just can't help thinking that maybe the plan was for me to be the eighth person to disappear?"

Liam tried to say something, but he couldn't collect his thoughts.

Dea leaned forward. "What if I was intended to be victim number eight, Liam, and then he took Nassrin instead because he screwed up with me? It shouldn't have been her at all."

He was struck by the despair in her voice and had to look away to prevent it from rubbing off on him.

"I'm sure there are plenty of people who would think I've given false witness against them." She blinked a couple of tears away in irritation.

At first he thought that sounded crazy and that she must be imagining things. But then he thought better of it. He couldn't let himself rule anything out.

"What time were you assaulted?"

"Around five PM."

"And we know from Nassrin's texts and from Dennis that she was abducted around seven fifteen PM, so that gives our madman a good two hours to locate Nassrin, drive from Odense to Assens, and force her into his car before Dennis came downstairs to the Golf around seven twenty PM. Not much wiggle room there."

He shook his head as he tried to picture the route the perpetrator had taken. But the only thing that kept pushing its way to the front of his thoughts was whether Nassrin had been forced into the car or if she'd already been unconscious when she was placed in the back seat of the Golf.

"It takes forty minutes max to drive from Christiansgade to Assens Auto," Dea continued. "And who's to say that he hasn't had multiple people in his sights the whole time? Maybe that's why he gets away with it? Timing, a big portfolio of people, and surveillance? He's one step ahead the whole time."

Liam nodded hesitantly.

"I can't let this go," Dea continued, and grabbed her phone. When she set it down again a few minutes later, she had woken up the manager of the forensics group and ordered her out of bed and into the park behind Christiansgade—immediately. She looked at Liam. "I'm going down to the park so they know exactly where to look: DNA, camera, tape, the whole shebang."

He nodded to her. It was worth a try. If they were lucky, the perpetrator wouldn't have been so thorough at removing his DNA because his attack had failed and he'd had to hurry to get away.

Dea put on her jacket and turned to him. "Are you coming?"

* * *

There were shouts coming from the hatch. Beate untied the clothes and let herself slide down into the water. Her skin burned all over her body. She clenched her teeth. There was yet another shout. She heard Kasper rummage around and then glide down into the water.

She groped for him in the dark and got ahold of one of his arms. His skin was bumpy and rough. He no longer felt like a human being.

"We haven't heard that kind of noise before, have we?" Her voice shook.

"No." She could tell he was listening carefully.

They heard tumultuous footsteps on the cover of the tank and a high, desperate woman's voice yelling again. It sounded like she was struggling mightily. It echoed down to them in the darkness as something hard hit the hatch with great force.

"What's going on up there?" Luna whispered, right behind Beate.

That startled Beate. She hadn't heard Luna moving closer.

"I think someone is fighting up there."

"Can we come out?" Luna sobbed. She started gasping for air.

Beate instinctively put her hands on her belly. She wanted to go up there, to Silje. To bring Charlotte out while she was still alive.

There was another loud shout from above. They could hear a man's voice as well now. He made a complaining sound.

The hatch was being opened. They recognized the sound. The clanking sound of iron against iron and squeaky hinges.

Luna grabbed Beate's arm as the hatch gave way and a little light made it down to them. It was night up there, but there was light. Maybe it was moonlight.

A woman with a grimace on her face stuck her head in the hatch opening and stared down at them.

"Help us," Kasper yelled wildly.

"Can you climb up on your own?" the woman yelled back. She had black hair.

"You're the one with the police," Luna yelled shrilly.

"Nassrin?" Beate said tentatively. She felt an almost euphoric relief.

"I'm alone," Nassrin continued frantically. "So I need to know if you can climb out on your own when the hatch is open? How far down are you?"

"Too far," Kasper said through his exhaustion.

They could hear the man up there groan.

"I'll find a rope," Nassrin said quickly. Her head disappeared.

Beate regarded Kasper in the light that made it down to them from above. He looked like a living corpse. The skin from his face had come loose from his cheekbones in a weird way and was covered in sores.

Their eyes met, and she could tell from the look on his face that he was seeing the same things she was.

"Can we lift Luna up?"

*   *   *

"I'm going to help you!" Nassrin yelled, glancing over at the man, who lay motionless a few meters from her. He was facedown on the rusty iron.

Voices called up to her from down below, desperate and distressed. She couldn't make out much down there, but she could see people submerged in water, their faces and hands severely damaged.

The night was black around her. The only light came from the Golf's lights.

"Are you there?" one of the frightened voices yelled from down below.

"I'm going to find a rope," she yelled back. "Or something else I can use to bring you up with." She jumped down from the tank.

Her phone, badge, and handcuffs had been gone when she woke up, groggy but able to sense the man in the darkness. She had been awakened by the noise from the manure conveyor belt—a rusty, dragging sound. Then she saw the tank, big and close by. He was standing bent over the lid of the tank when she ran up and jumped him.

She attacked him with a rusty iron bar she had found on the ground, smashing it into the back of his head with all her might. He was on the verge of gaining the upper hand and she was balancing on the edge of the tank when she managed to land a blow that hit him cleanly in the gut. He'd fallen over and stayed down.

"Rope, rope, rope," she muttered to herself as she ran past the car and over to a building she could make out in the dark. There was a bunch of junk on the ground but nothing that could be used to bring the missing people up out of the water.

She was surrounded by absolute darkness now that she'd moved away from the beam of the headlights. She stopped to let her eyes adjust. An old barn stood in front of her. She felt her way to two large doors, which were both closed. Her body was still weak, but the thought of the missing people in the water kept her going, and she put all her strength into it as she forced the one door open and squeezed through the gap. She fumbled around in vain inside for a light.

Her heart pounding, she ran into the barn's impenetrable darkness to find something that could help the trapped people get out. She stumbled and lost her balance for a second. A power cord ran across the floor and out the door. She thought that maybe it was connected to the conveyor belt that led up to the top of the tank and pictured the unconscious bodies being transported on that. She grabbed the cord and yanked, pulling it out of its outlet somewhere in the darkness.

Again, desperate cries broke the nighttime silence. She looked down at the power cord. It wasn't enough, but it was all she had. She thought fleetingly that it would be enough to tie the man up, and then she could tell the people in the water that she was running for help. She wanted to promise them that it was over, promise that she would get them up out of there. She thought about running over to the nearest house, finding a phone and some rope.

She ran back past the car and over to the tank. She ran up the conveyor belt in a few quick bounds. She stiffened when she realized that the man was gone.

*   *   *

There was a throaty scream and then a muffled thud. Beate held her breath and looked up at the narrow strip of light that made its way down to them. An oppressive silence prevailed over them. Detecting a dragging sound above their heads, she stiffened.

"Nassrin!" Luna's voice cut through the silent summer night. The dragging sound stopped, and Nassrin's head appeared up by the edge of the hatch. Her eyes were empty, her face covered in blood. It dripped down into the water and onto them.

Beate sensed a shadow behind Nassrin's unconscious body. Then the young woman fell heavily down into the water next to them. The hatch slid shut, and it was dark again.

The sound of their screaming was swallowed by the thick concrete walls. Beate gasped for air, shocked, and tried to protect her
face from the wave of rotten water set in motion by Nassrin's body.
She groped in the darkness, trying to find Nassrin's hand, which
had bumped against her as the young police officer started to sink
toward the bottom of the tank. She heard Luna's sobs as she and
Kasper dove down to grab the unconscious woman so she didn't
drown.

Day 8—Friday

ALDAR SMOOTHED HIS mustache with two stiff fingers and stared vacantly out the window at Hans Mules Gade. He was the one who had called and asked if he could meet with them at the police station rather than having them come out to him and his brother. He had boiled it down for them very succinctly: Hayyan suffered from anxiety. Liam felt a tremendous amount of empathy. Nassrin was the center of her uncles' world.

"Are you completely certain that our little Nassrin has been abducted?" The uncle's voice was dry. He seemed distant as he sat there shaking his head despairingly.

"Yes, unfortunately . . . I'm so sorry to say."

"It's just not like her to allow herself to be caught unawares like that. I'm having a hard time understanding how she could have let that happen." He was controlling himself, but his grief radiated from every wrinkle in his careworn face.

"Aldar, you already know a fair amount about this case, so I can tell you that in connection with Nassrin's disappearance, we found a slip of paper with the Bible's eighth commandment."

Aldar nodded and leaned in closer to Liam with an intense look.

"Are you absolutely sure these verses are that important?"

"Yes, but so far we don't know much more than that."

"But you know that he would know that kind of thing about her?"

Liam nodded and said they had to assume that.

"Right now, we're hoping to figure out what or who could connect her to that accusation. So I'm going to come right out and ask you now, even though it might be unpleasant: Has your niece ever borne false witness?"

At first Aldar seemed dismissive, but then the stern glint in his eye softened. He took a deep breath and leaned back in his chair. Then he nodded.

"Nassrin has a sister who traveled down several years ago to fight against ISIS. When she returned to Denmark, the Danish government confiscated her passport, because they weren't sure which side she had fought for." He searched for the right words. "In that situation, Nassrin gave her sister alibis and backed up all her stories, because even though most of it was made up, it was the right thing to do for her sister's sake. That caused a lot of trouble, and Nassrin was threatened and shunned by many of the Muslims in Vollsmose."

"Why?"

Aldar smiled bitterly.

"You have no idea how unbelievably many of my immigrant peers actually want Muslim dominance and sharia. It is a thorn in their eye that neither Nassrin nor her sister agrees with them. Since then, Nassrin has been decried as a 'whore of the West,' to use the words they use about her."

"Even when she has been out there patrolling?"

"Always," Aldar said. "She's one of the most hated women in Vollsmose. So imagine how it's been for her all those times you've sent her there to keep track of the Arabs."

The old man shook his head, and Liam looked down at the floor. "I understand."

"Do you?" Aldar asked pointedly. "I don't think you do."

Liam absorbed that, and there was a brief silence in the room while they both let the last comment sink in.

"Aldar, how likely is it that the perpetrator could have this knowledge about Nassrin when I didn't know anything about it? It must be a very small circle of people who could have known this."

There was an indulgent snort from Nassrin's uncle.

"If you had had the slightest inkling," Aldar said, "then you would have thrown her out of the police. She lied to Allah to protect a warrior who fought against ISIS's caliphate, and she also lied to the Danish government and thereby broke her oath as an officer. I want you to appreciate that working for the police is Nassrin's dream. It's the only thing she wants. It's what she's passionate about. To you, I'm sure she's just one of the gang, but my niece is ready to go all the way for you. That's why she chose to keep this hidden. And she put up with it when you pushed her out into those situations that could so easily have exposed her."

"How do you think the perpetrator found this out?"

"It wouldn't take many hours in Vollsmose; if you made the rounds a few times, I'd imagine you would find someone who was willing to say anything."

"Do you think folks out there would describe this willing person to the police if we went around and asked?"

"I would think so. My ethnic roots are in a very lively, thriving gossip culture, where nothing is sacred, as long as it's about the neighbor and not yourself."

Liam wrote a note on the top sheet of paper, and then he pulled Thorbjørn's case file out of a stack and turned to the short summary his colleague had written about Bent Møller Nielsen and his assault conviction.

"There's one other thing, Aldar. It's about your brother, Hayyan."

Nassrin's uncle raised his bushy eyebrows quizzically.

"We have learned that not long after you arrived in Denmark, your brother was brutally attacked, and that his attacker went to jail."

Aldar nodded reluctantly. "It's been more than forty years since I've heard about that case, and I had hoped never to hear about it again," he said, seeming slightly irritated.

"The attacker was a man by the name of Hans Henrik Møller."

Nassrin's uncle nodded again but still didn't seem to understand what Liam was getting at with this. "We came to Denmark in 1973, just before they halted immigration. Those first few years, we lived in a little room in a high-rise apartment building that served as a sort of reception center, I guess you could say. We were guest workers, as people called it back then, and there was a group of charitable locals who tried to help us get settled. It was so many years ago that I can hardly recall that time. But that was where my brother fell in love. They fell in love with each other, and many times I have had the thought that I almost wish they had run away together back then. That is the only time I have ever known my brother to find love, and I don't think he has ever gotten over her."

"Has your brother had any contact with the woman since then?"

Aldar quickly shook his head.

*   *   *

After they said goodbye, Liam stood out in the hallway and watched him leave. The old man shuffled away, shoulders drooping. Just before they parted, he had once again asked if the police were sure his niece was the victim of a crime. He had started listing all the different places where she liked to go windsurfing and had asked if it would help if he drove around looking for her himself.

Liam thanked him for his offer and explained that the police had a network of detectives spread across Funen looking for her. He failed to mention the little movie clip Dennis had seen. Nassrin's uncles didn't need to imagine their niece fighting to survive down in the dark water.

"Was he able to help?" Dea's voice asked from behind him.

"There's a sister," he replied. "Nassrin lied pretty heavily to protect her, so we need to find this sister. According to Aldar, she's more or less homeless, lost her mind in the fight against ISIS. We also need to get people out to Vollsmose and ring some doorbells. Aldar thinks our madman may have learned what he knows about Nassrin and her sister by asking around out there."

"Should I get both of those started?"

"Yes, but we need to be a little cautious with the sister. She's fragile. Have Thorbjørn lead that search. He's good at that kind of thing." Liam glanced at his watch. "And remember the press conference with the minister in an hour."

*　*　*

By the end of the press conference, no one in the Kingdom of Denmark had any doubt that the Odense Police were searching for a black Golf. Dybbøl had insisted that all the prints from the surveillance videos be shown on TV. Every single detail was emphasized, from the scratch on the left door to the little dent in the bumper right over the trailer hitch.

After the press conference, Dea followed Liam into the large meeting room, where by this point the case was taking up all the walls and whiteboard space.

"Well, at least she didn't actually use the words *Quran Case* with the media."

"The minister? She's not that stupid," Liam said. "The police and the minister operate in very different worlds, but we do agree to bite our tongues if a case smells a little like terrorism."

"This doesn't smell like terrorism," Dea said, looking around at the case details covering the walls. "But what the hell does it smell like?"

Liam nodded somberly. The room actually smelled a little like bacon and coffee from down in the building's cafeteria.

"We need to get Nassrin back," Dea said quietly. She felt hollow inside as she slumped down in a chair across from him. "Her loss is on me."

"You both did the right things, Dea."

"I made her stay out there on her own." She had gone over her last conversation with Nassrin in her head countless times and regretted it even more times. She had cursed and sworn and castigated herself for putting the responsibility on Nassrin out of her own eagerness to end the insanity they were flailing around in.

"Neither of you could have known he had targeted Nassrin as his next victim, and you did the right thing. You got right in your car and headed straight there. We all got there as fast as we could."

"We would have had him if I had gotten there faster," she continued.

"There's no point to all these what-ifs, Dea." Liam studied Day 7 and Day 8, as they were called in their summary. "I don't understand his suddenly opening the case to us this way. What the hell is his goal here? We have pictures of the Golf. Dennis met the man face-to-face. We found the sedative in Dennis's blood. We've gained this insight into how he abducts his victims. Why?"

"Maybe he wants to be seen," Dea suggested. "He's almost to the goal line if he's planning to stop at the tenth commandment anyway."

"He couldn't have planned on Dennis leaving his apartment to go visit his family."

"No, and according to Dennis, it actually sounds like the man was sitting there and waiting with Nassrin in the back seat. He could just have driven away."

Liam put up a new sign on the case summary for Day 7.

"He waited for Dennis and left a little piece of his world behind in Dennis's blood in the form of the anesthetic propofol."

"That's supposed to work really fast, right?" Dea couldn't shake the image in her head of Nassrin in the back seat of the black Golf.

"Yes, and I supposed that's why he succeeded in abducting Red Kent, because otherwise, if the local witnesses are credible, Kent is the closest they've ever come to having a T. rex in Haarby."

"Big and ugly, but slow." There was nothing jovial in Dea's words, even though it was an attempt at humor.

"Day 3," Liam continued. "We know that a car was parked behind the trees at the abandoned farm. And we're assuming that the perpetrator waited for Verner there. After he attacked and anesthetized Verner, he took off in an old Ford Granada, which was subsequently spotted in Verninge and Glamsbjerg—thus heading southwest. Since then, the car has vanished. On Day 2, we're confident that the perpetrator drove to Assens in the black Golf that we're looking for now before abducting Kasper. Then he left town in a gray Peugeot 205. And then last night after he abducted Nass, the same black Golf was used to get away from Assens."

"Could you please stop calling her *Nass*? Her name is Nassrin, right? It annoys me, and you're usually such a stickler for language." Dea's anger was like an explosion, erupting inside her. She tried to pull herself together and took a deep breath and closed her eyes for a minute.

"Uh . . . yeah . . . OK. I just forgot," she heard him say.

"Sorry," she said. "Just proceed."

Liam started in on Day 5. "We know that he drove an older gray Peugeot. That must be the same one he used on Day 2. We just don't have anything on either the cars or the man behind the wheel, because he's sharp as a straight razor when it comes to covering his tracks and hiding."

Dea took a dispirited breath. Cars, information, surveillance. They were groping around blindly, even though Liam kept steadily clutching at all the straws that lay before them. If they did end up catching the perpetrator, it would no doubt be thanks to his stubbornness, she thought. Right now, she was hovering somewhere close to zero. She didn't even really believe they would succeed.

"But this stops now." Liam broke into her thoughts, referring to what the minister had said at the press conference. "We've gathered all the ALPR data from the whole area between Tommerup and Assens, and even a mosquito couldn't slip through if he didn't have a clear conscience." He glanced at Dea. "Did we get the results back from the DNA evidence at the parsonage while the minister was entertaining the press?"

She nodded and pulled out a printed email. "They were fast with the urine, but they've gotten a handle on the rest now, too . . . I told them you really appreciated their running all the analyses through so quickly."

"Yes, yes." Liam read the dense text in the email. They had sent in everything they could find in terms of unwashed cups, mugs, silverware, and plates as well as all the parsonage's hand towels and dishcloths, the cushions from the living room, and the pillows from the bedrooms. "Beate, Peter, Claus, Mona, Silje, Claus's children, the ex-husband, Johannes, and Henning, who's the sexton." He looked at Dea in disappointment. "Fingerprints?"

"The same people."

"We need to find out where he got the propofol from."

Just then the door opened with a bang, and a female colleague, whose name Dea couldn't quite remember, eagerly interrupted.

"We just received a call from Bent Møller Nielsen, who says he owns a black Golf that looks like the one we just announced we were looking for."

*   *   *

This was the second time in only a couple of days that Liam and Dea were driving down the gravel road to Bent Møller Nielsen's house near Verninge. Even before they had pulled all the way up to the house, Beate's father appeared in the doorway and came out to meet them with his shirtsleeves rolled up, gesturing at his car.

On the left side of the courtyard in front of his house in the shade of a large linden tree, the black Golf was parked with mud splashed on its sides.

The first thing Liam noticed was that the car bore a license plate starting with the letters *AC*.

Dea was already standing by the car. She had taken out her phone and was comparing it to the Golf in Nassrin's photo.

"Is there any news about Beate and the others?" Bent asked as he held out his hand to Liam.

"Unfortunately not." Liam walked all the way over to the car.

"I was sitting inside watching the press conference, and I called as soon as I saw the pictures of the car. It was the dent and the scratch in particular that I noticed."

Dea squatted down behind the car and took a picture of the dent and the bumper, then turned to Bent and asked for the car keys.

He had them in his hand and held them out to her. Dea opened the car's hatchback and leaned in to inspect the bottom edge of the opening. The way the dirt was smeared made it likely that the straps of a temporary license plate had been held in place there by closing the trunk.

She didn't say anything as she took pictures of both the area surrounding the lock and the bottom edge of the opening. Then she turned and gave Bent a quick nod.

"Could we go inside and have a chat?" Liam asked. He was already walking toward the door before Bent had a chance to answer. They were shown into the living room, and Liam regretted coming in when he spotted Beate's mother in an armchair over by the window.

"Maybe we should go into the kitchen?" Dea suggested, after removing her shoes in the front hall.

Beate's mother nodded politely, but she didn't say anything as they walked through the living room. She had some knitting in her lap but mostly ran her fingers through the yarn as she watched a little tit that had flown into a small round glass birdhouse that had been set up outside the window.

"We'd like to talk to you a little more about your car," Dea began. "And I also need to prepare you for the fact that it will be transported to Odense for a forensic examination. In addition to that, we'd like to search your home here, and as you know, that can be done either by your granting us permission to search the house or by our obtaining a search warrant."

Bent had taken a seat across from them. He suddenly seemed confused and a little bewildered. "I don't understand this! You don't think I have something to do with my own daughter's disappearance, do you? I called you because I want to help, because I thought then at least you could cross one Golf off your list."

There was a soft humming from the living room.

"We strongly suspect that your car might have been used last night in Assens, where yet another person was abducted," Dea explained. "Obviously, we can't say for sure until the forensic testing has been carried out."

"I wasn't in Assens yesterday." His eyes flitted over to the front door.

"And I'm not saying that you were, but is there any chance that your car was?"

He shook his head no.

"Where were you last night at around seven PM?" Liam asked.

Bent straightened up a little in his chair.

"I was here with my wife and her sister. We had dinner together. That's a standing tradition that we've stuck to ever since my wife got sick. Ellen comes and eats with us every other Friday."

Bent stood up and walked over to the kitchen counter, where he got a piece of paper and wrote down his sister-in-law's phone number.

"So your car was not out driving around yesterday?" Dea concluded, and Liam sensed the energy drain out of her.

Bent set both of his hands palms down on the table and looked down at the checkered tablecloth.

"That I don't know actually," he said. He had gone pale, and there was some sort of reluctance in his eyes when he looked up. "To put it bluntly, I didn't notice if it was parked out there. We keep the key in the woodshed, and sometimes Michael takes it. That's the neighbor's son. Whenever his car is in the shop, I've given him permission to borrow mine."

"OK, so you keep your car key in the woodshed? Does anyone else know that?"

"No, I don't think so. I don't use the car very often anymore. It's mostly Beate."

"So Beate uses your car too? Does she also take the key from the woodshed?"

"No, she has her own key."

Dea hesitated. They needed to follow up on the neighbor's son and Beate's car key. She felt pretty sure they hadn't found a car key in the parsonage the morning Beate disappeared, so now they would have to go through the whole place again.

She looked out the window at the courtyard, where more police cars had turned up plus one other one. She recognized the man who got out. He was from *Ekstra Bladet*, one of the tabloids. The press was paying attention now, and they had definitely noticed the police sending multiple cars out to Beate's father's place. In five minutes there would no doubt be a breaking news story on the newspaper's homepage.

*   *   *

Peter woke up to someone knocking on the patio door, and he hurriedly jumped up. Everything in front of his eyes went black, so he had to support himself on the back of the sofa.

Then there was another knock. He pulled the curtain aside and found himself staring at Mona. She had a dish in her hands.

"Yes?"

"I just wanted to check on you," she said, a bit apologetically. "I brought you some apple crumble."

"I don't think I can eat anything."

"How about I make you a cup of coffee?" she suggested. "You look like you could use one."

He stared at her blankly after he had opened the door. "I'm not up to visitors, Mona."

"No," she said, and pushed him resolutely out of the doorway. "But it just won't do, you sitting here all alone. It's not good for you. I have eyes, after all." She proceeded past him toward the kitchen. "Have a seat, my friend. I'll be back in a sec with the coffee."

Peter looked down at his hands. They were shaking. He got out his phone. He had 178 unopened emails, and more were arriving all the time. All of them probably from complete strangers and just as hate filled as the ones he had already seen last night before he gave up. The little number on his Facebook page showed a large number of notifications. He had thirty-seven unanswered calls and almost as many text messages, some from journalists, but also some from people who just wanted to drag his name through the mud.

Murdering lowlife scum, I hope you die!!!

Where are they, you psycho?

You sick fuck, we're going to fuck you up, you fucking psycho!

"Do you take milk?"

He dropped his phone on the sofa. "It doesn't matter."

"I'll put a bit of milk in it."

Mona returned with two cups.

He eyed her skeptically.

"I know what you're thinking," she said. "So, no. Of course I don't think you're guilty. Otherwise I wouldn't be sitting here."

"So what are you doing here?"

"I feel awful for you, Peter. We all love Beate, and you must feel worse than—"

She didn't have a chance to say any more before Peter burst into tears.

"What have I done? Why does everyone think I'm a criminal?"

Mona got up and came over to sit beside him on the sofa.

He reached out to her like someone would reach for a life preserver after a shipwreck. He shook and sobbed hoarsely as he buried his face in her dress like a little kid.

"It's my Beate," he cried. "My baby. I've lost everything, Mona. Everything, and I don't know what to do. I can't even go anywhere in town because everyone hates me, even though I'm the one who's lost everything!"

* * *

Dea pulled her silver-blue Passat onto the pea-gravel-covered drive-way at the parsonage in Tommerup. They had left Bent shaken but calm. His alibis had all seemed to hold up, and there wasn't much else to do besides continue to keep an eye on the man, for his own sake if nothing else.

There were already a couple of cars waiting in the driveway.

"Wow, the press is really on top of things now," Liam grumbled. "Pull all the way up to the church, and we'll lose them." A local security guard had detained a man and locked him in a room in the church. That was what Mona had reported, but she hadn't seen the man. Peter had run off—on his bicycle. He had thought the security guard was after him.

Dea stopped the car and they hurried into the church, which was cold and smelled dusty.

"Ah, there you are, finally!"

"Here we are, yes," Liam said dryly, eyeing the group of agitated men, who were waiting in the nave for him. "Odense Police. I'm Inspector Liam Stark, and this is Sergeant Dea Torp. Generally we're the ones who investigate crimes and detain relevant suspects. Who are you?"

"I'm Lars," the man said, "Lars Smed. I feel like we haven't seen you making many arrests. Plus you guys let Peter go again right away."

"It's quite normal for us to let people go when they're no longer suspects," Dea replied, eyeing him steadily.

"So maybe you don't think Peter reeks of guilt?" He made such a show of checking her out that she wanted to go over and give him a wedgie.

She made do with saying, "I wasn't aware that guilt could reek."

"No . . . but that's a saying, right?"

"Well, then it must be true." Dea sighed. "I can see that you're really on top of all this," she continued, her sarcasm flying right over Lars's head. He nodded officiously. "But since you're sure Peter is guilty, then why did you detain someone else?"

"He was suspicial, so we—"

"Suspicious," Liam corrected him, pronouncing the word with exaggerated clarity. Dea smiled at him. Backup came in many forms when you were dealing with Liam Stark.

"What?" Lars said.

"Forget it . . . What did he do, your prisoner?" she asked.

"He was breaking into the parsonage," another man chirped.

"How?"

"He was about to break open a window." Lars took over again. "There was no doubt."

"And so you brave boys thought you'd detain him?" Dea contemplated them.

"Yeah . . . I mean, you're not doing shit!"

"And what does the man himself have to say about all of this?"

"He says that he's the pastor's daughter's father and that he wanted to pick up a teddy bear, but why the hell would anyone break a window open for that?" Lars waved his arms energetically toward the house. "Hell, I can show you! There are marks on the window!"

"Thank you. We'll take a look at that in a bit." Liam held up his hands. "Shouldn't we take a peek at your *suspicial* man first?"

"Yes, he's in the church porch," Lars said, gesturing for them to follow.

Dea followed Liam, who turned to Lars and said, "We'd like to speak to your prisoner alone for just a moment."

By the time they returned from the porch with Silje's father about five minutes later, Johannes and Mona had shown up. Johannes seemed agitated.

"What's going on?" Liam asked, and nodded as Dea prepared to follow Silje's father out of the church.

"I'm sorry about all this," Johannes said. "I would never have let it happen if I'd known. Mother came and got me." He clapped his hands together. "I can only apologize. We had no idea that it was Mathias who had been apprehended."

"Hey!" Lars interrupted them. "What happens now? Aren't you going to take him with you?"

Dea had just returned as Liam slowly turned to face Lars.

"That man is Silje's father and the pastor's ex-husband. He wanted to get into the house to pick up his daughter's favorite teddy bear, but it was locked, and since he didn't want to disappoint his daughter, who is already crushed because her mother has been abducted, he tried to open a window."

"What?" Lars interrupted him. "You can't just take his word at fair value! We caught him red-handed."

"At *face* value," Liam corrected him, annoyed. "Try to hear what I'm saying," he continued, enunciating very clearly. "I'm not up to trying to explain this to you better, but I can assure you that if I see one of your tiresome faces again—here or in a newspaper—then you're the ones who will be detained, immediately, and I won't hesitate for one second."

Dea's phone rang. She listened, hung up quickly, and didn't even look at Lars and the others as she cut Liam short.

"Boss!" She pulled him away, out of the others' hearing. "We need to get over to Claus's house right away. Claus allegedly hit Peter in the head so hard that he's unconscious on their living room floor. We're the closest. They just called from the emergency call center. Claus's daughter phoned it in."

"Isn't she only five or six years old?"

"Yeah."

"Poor girl," Liam said. "What the hell is going on?"

* * *

"Hi there!" Dea said, squatting down in front of Cecilie, who was sitting on the front stoop. The girl seemed scared, and her whole face was wet from crying. "I'm so impressed that you called us. Did your dad teach you how to do that?"

"No, Silje's dad did," the little girl squeaked in her high-pitched voice.

"Is he in there now?"

She nodded, wide-eyed. "He's lying on the floor. He hit his head."

"Where's *your* dad?"

"He went out in the yard."

Liam smiled at Cecilie and pushed the door open. "Is your brother with Silje's dad or out in the yard?"

"He ran upstairs. He's scared too," the girl hiccupped.

"Do you want to come find him with me?" Dea suggested cheerfully.

Cecilie nodded and eyed Dea with curiosity. Then she took Dea's outstretched hand.

Liam continued over to the doorway into the living room. It was unnervingly quiet. Peter lay not far from the door. Liam quickly secured the room and then ran over to the man on the floor. He was unresponsive, but he was alive and had a stable pulse. There was a baseball bat lying next to him.

Once the ambulance picked Peter up, Liam went out into the yard to find Claus. He could hear Dea and the kids' voices from upstairs through the open window.

Claus was sitting on a freshly painted bench in the yard and looked like he was waiting. He had considerable stubble on his chin and a wild look in his eyes.

"Did I kill Peter?" he asked. Claus sat up straight and turned to Liam. "The first few days after Charlotte disappeared, I was at my wit's end, alternating between feeling crushed and believing she would turn up again, but now . . . Eight people are missing now. I have no faith left that she'll turn up. I can't keep it together, and I don't know what came over me."

*   *   *

"Lone's not doing so well," Kasper said under his breath from down in the water. "She's been quiet for a long time."

"What about Charlotte?" Beate said.

Kasper moved but didn't say anything. There was a little splash. Then it was quiet for a bit.

"She has a pulse, but it's weak."

Then it was quiet again. The ripples died away.

"Beate?"

"Yes . . ."

"Lone is dead."

"Are you sure? Couldn't we try to lift her up here? She can have Nassrin's spot for a few hours. I can hold Nassrin in the water."

"She's dead, Beate."

"Lone? You can't be sure of that," Beate exclaimed. She wanted to move toward Kasper's voice but didn't want to pull the new one with her through the water. "I want to check for myself!"

"Don't, Beate." He had come over close and grasped her arm.

"I want to talk to her, Kasper. She can't be dead."

"Beate, damn it! She's completely bloated. Her skin is covered in sores. I feel like I can stick my fingers into it. She's . . . decomposed."

"Water," Charlotte whispered, barely audibly. Beate turned her eyes toward the sound. Charlotte was tied to the pole and had been for some time. They had to take her down soon. She must be in a tremendous amount of pain. When Nassrin and the new man had been dumped in, no bottles of water had been tossed down to them the way they usually were, so it must have been at least twenty-four hours since they'd had any water.

Beate pushed herself through the water over to Charlotte, while Kasper took over the new one. Beate felt her way to the woman's body and face. She put her swollen hands against the skin on the woman's face. It was cracked and covered in sores.

"We don't have any more water right now, Charlotte."

"Water," Charlotte repeated, but her words died away in the darkness until in a clear, bright voice, she suddenly whispered, "Beate?"

"Yes."

"When I dream, it's bright. Do you think that's what it's like when you die?"

"Yes," Beate whispered, her throat choked with tears.

"You . . ." Charlotte moaned with effort. "Take care of my kids if you get out . . ."

"Yes," Beate sobbed. "But Claus is there too, not . . . Claus and Peter. They'll take care of our kids . . . I promise."

"Will you pray for me?" Charlotte turned her head slightly.

Beate had never watched someone die before. She started to pray with her lips close to Charlotte's peeling skin. "Merciful Father . . ." She groped for the words, which felt so empty in their stinking grave of rotten water.

*   *   *

"Wait a minute," Liam said, when Dea started the car. "I just heard back from Forensic Medicine about how long a person can stay alive in water."

Dea looked at him expectantly.

"They write that there are a lot of factors involved. Is it fresh water or salt water? What's the temperature? Is the water clean or dirty?"

"Well, we don't know, but what if we assume it's dirty fresh water?" she said. "I mean, they would have to go to the bathroom in the water."

DISSOLVED247

Liam concentrated on reading his cell phone. "They write a lot of things, but one of them is about osmotic pressure. That means that the water penetrates the skin because there's more pressure in the water than there is inside the body. That's what they say."

"I remember osmosis from school," Dea said. "All free water molecules move to where there are fewer water molecules. What does that mean for our victims?"

"They say that a person can survive for up to ten days in fresh water. And during that time, the person will lose feeling in large portions of their body, develop a rash, peeling skin, blisters, and liver problems." He gulped and paused for a second. "The skin begins to break down after just a few days in fresh water, and sores and infections will arise—especially in dirty water. If you stay in water for a week or more—it varies depending on the person—the skin will decompose and the victim will be extremely susceptible to infections. They'll get sick . . . and ultimately die."

He jumped as his phone started vibrating in his hand. It was Thorbjørn. Liam put it on speakerphone so Dea could listen in.

"Hi." Thorbjørn's voice sounded loud in the car. "It appears that Johannes' alibis from that convention in Fåborg are not as bulletproof as we thought at first. The woman at the front desk, who seemed so sure that she'd seen him, isn't sure after all."

"What do they say now?" Dea asked, a little annoyed.

"So Johannes was there. The other attendees agree on that. He attended meetings and spoke with many of the other people. But no one can say with any surety that they were with him at the specific times when Red Kent and Beate disappeared. No one remembers having seen him at breakfast on the morning when Beate disappeared, and when Kent disappeared, Johannes had gone to his room with an upset stomach. He was gone all morning, and no one actually saw him again until dinner."

"But they already confirmed several times that he was there?" Liam said, irritated.

"Yes, and they're sure, too, that he was just in his room. But no one specifically remembers seeing him during those hours that we have now asked about more precisely."

"Thanks," Dea said, and gave Liam a questioning look. "Will you follow up on this yourself, Thorbjørn? With Johannes?"

"Sure."

Liam nodded in confirmation.

Dea started the car. "Back to the police station now or what?"

*   *   *

It was late before Liam got home. The front door was unlocked, and the light was on in the kitchen, but that was often the case. They lived a peaceful life on a quiet residential street in Dalum, but he could still imagine the headlines in the local paper: *Police Inspector Leaves Door Open to Burglars.* He tossed his jacket on the kitchen table and contemplated having something to eat. His stomach was growling, but it seemed like so much effort.

A shadow moved out in the yard somewhere. He tensed, but then he thought it was probably one of those silly hens from his parents, flapping around in a tizzy.

He opened the fridge after all and pulled out a piece of fried *medister* sausage. Helene was showing him a little love. He considered taking a shower but dropped the idea. He stood there at the kitchen counter and ate it right out of the plastic container. He wished he could just lie down and be asleep without all the traffic he had in his head. But that was probably wishful thinking. He sighed tiredly. No matter what, it would be nice to lie down with his head on a soft pillow.

He decided to close things up and brought the plastic container over to the dishwasher. He had just opened the door to the dishwasher when he saw the slip of paper. He stiffened, and it took all his self-control not to pick up the little piece of paper with his hand.

And do not stretch your eyes after that which We have provided different classes of them, of the splendor of this world's life, that We may thereby try them.

That was the verse from the Quran that corresponded to the Bible's tenth commandment, which he knew in his sleep by now: *You shall not covet your neighbor's wife, or his male servant, or his female servant, or his ox, or his donkey, or anything that is your neighbor's.*

"Helene?" he screamed, and ran to the hallway that led to the bedroom. "Kids?" He yanked open the bedroom door. "Helene?" No one was there. The bed was empty. "You won't do this to me, you monster!" he screamed at the top of his lungs and ran back to the living room. He could tell that Helene had been sitting on the sofa with a blanket. There was a half-full cup of tea next to a book on the coffee table. The light was on. The blanket had been tossed aside, and the book was open to the page she had gotten to. She had been caught unawares. "No, no, no!" His breath came in rapid, sharp bursts.

"Dad?"

Andreas had appeared in the doorway.

"Dres!" he yelled, far too loudly. "Is your sister OK?"

"Yeah, she's just peeing. Why in the world are you yelling?" Andreas looked at him in confusion.

"Do you know where Mom is, Andreas?" His voice was shrill and still way too loud.

"I think she's in bed reading."

Liam shook his head and took out his phone, his hands shaking as he dialed. "This is Liam Stark. Come right away . . . the verse for Day 10 is on my dining table, and my wife is gone!"

"Dad, what are you talking about?" Andreas had gone pale and wide-eyed with worry.

"We're going to settle down now," Liam said, trying to get himself under control.

Just then the front door opened. Helene's eyes widened in surprise when she saw them.

"You're both awake?"

"Helene, what the hell!" he exclaimed, pulling his wife to him. "You scared the shit out of me! Where were you?"

"I just took a little walk down the street. I went over by Lis and Henning's place and back again."

Liam hugged her tightly.

"I was only gone half an hour. Did something happen?" She pulled herself free so she could see his face.

"It simply won't do, you starting to go out for walks on your own in the middle of the night!" He was overcome by anger and he couldn't stop himself, even as she pulled away from him in fear.

"I'm sorry!" she said sarcastically. "I didn't realize you'd put us under some sort of curfew here."

Liam grabbed his phone, then hesitated. "Do any of you have the slightest idea where that slip of paper came from?"

"No . . ." Helene looked at the table. "It wasn't there when . . ." She stopped abruptly and looked at him questioningly as the color drained from her cheeks.

"Was he in our house?" she whispered. "Here? In our kitchen while the kids were sleeping and I was just outside?"

Liam nodded tensely. "I'm afraid so."

"He must have just been here then."

"Who?" Laura had appeared, looking sleepy and with a bad case of bedhead.

"That psycho guy from Dad's Quran Case," Andreas said. "He was standing right here in our kitchen."

Liam wished all three of them would hurry off to bed. He needed to think, needed some peace and quiet. And most of all he needed to get his own fear under control so he could protect his family.

"What did he want?" Laura asked, standing in front of him. Her sleepy face looked scared in the brightness from the overhead light in the kitchen. "Did he want to take one of us?"

Liam slowly shook his head and put his arms around her.

"I don't know."

His thoughts were spinning in circles. Why was it the tenth commandment and not the ninth? Why his house? Should he be afraid? What had he desired that didn't belong to him? Or was it Helene or the kids who had broken the tenth commandment? He called the switchboard again.

"My wife turned up, but we need a full Forensics response out here. And canine units ASAP. And then I want an armed guard at the house until we've caught this guy. Thanks."

*   *   *

"Can I see?" Aldar asked, leaning closer to his brother. They were sitting in the comfortable chairs in the reading nook upstairs over their bookstore.

Hayyan had asked earlier in the evening if he should put something on the stove to cook, but neither of them had felt hungry. They just sat there for a long time, side by side in complete silence.

Hayyan passed his brother a photo he had been holding.

"Is that her?" Aldar asked, curious. "I thought you had gotten out the pictures of Nassrin."

"I did, but then I found this. It's the only one I have."

She had blond hair and was smiling as she stood in a pale-yellow summer dress. The colors had faded long ago, leaving the old photo looking brownish.

Aldar sat for a bit, looking at the happy face and the hair, which was fluttering in the wind, before handing the photo back.

"I had hoped that we would never hear about this case again . . . for your sake."

He had felt a deep sorrow when his brother's face appeared on the homepage of the *Fyens Stiftstidendes* online paper that afternoon. The newspaper included the whole story about the old assault. Aldar had called the newspaper's offices and asked them to remove Hayyan's name. It was so many years ago; no one could be interested in that old story. He had tried, but it hadn't done any good. The woman at the newspaper told him that they had already talked to Hayyan's attacker, who had given his version of the story. In that interview it had come out that Bent Møller Nielsen's fiancée at the time had gotten pregnant. And when it turned out that the baby wasn't his, he had broken off the engagement and attacked Hayyan.

"They're digging this all up because his daughter, Beate, is one of the missing people, the same as Nassrin," Aldar explained, even though he doubted his brother was listening. "It's obviously interesting, because there's a connection between you and you both have a family member who has disappeared in this terrible case."

Hayyan nodded, as if he wanted to show that he had understood, but he didn't take his eyes off the picture of the young woman.

"Do you think they'll see me?"

On the newspaper's homepage, they referred to the woman as Bente, but they explained in parentheses that the editorial staff did know the woman's actual name.

"Brother . . ." Aldar closed his eyes. "If Mona decided not to tell her son about you, then do you really think it's wise to go contacting them now, after so many years?"

"Can you believe it? I have a son," Hayyan whispered down at the photograph.

They both heard a loud noise from downstairs in the bookstore.

"Didn't you lock the door?" Aldar glanced over at the stairs.

"I left it open in case Nassrin comes home."

"But she has keys, Brother!" Aldar tiredly got to his feet. "I'll go down and look. Maybe the door just came open."

Hayyan nodded and watched his brother disappear down the stairs with heavy footsteps.

Then all the lights went out.

"Aldar?" Hayyan peered around blindly in the dark space. "Aldar, are you there?" He waited, listening in the darkness.

There was a clicking sound from the bookstore.

"Aldar," Hayyan again called into the dark. He had stood up but was unable to get his bearings as he approached the staircase, taking small steps.

There was one more sound from downstairs, but Aldar didn't respond.

"Why aren't you answering me?" Hayyan had reached the foot of the stairs and squinted in the dim light that came in from outside. "It looks like the streetlights are working, so the power is only out here. Did you check the fuse box?" He groped his way forward shelf by shelf toward the closet, where their fuse box was located behind a curtain.

"Aldar? I'm scared . . ." Hayyan's voice sounded small in the darkness.

The lights flickered back on for a brief instant, and then it was dark again. Hayyan jumped. The light blinked on again.

"Aldar?"

"No," a strange male voice replied.

"Who are you?" Hayyan whispered, trembling.

"God's punishment."

Then he felt the needle in his neck. His throat swelled up. The air felt heavy. He tried to speak but couldn't. Everything went black.

Day 9—Saturday

"How long do you think you were unconscious for?" Dea asked, looking around at the many shelves and the almost endless rows of dusty books. Nassrin's uncle seemed frail and disoriented as he sat in the armchair, one side of his face covered in bruises.

"I'm not sure," Aldar replied uncertainly, rubbing his neck. "When I came to, my brother was gone." His dark eyes were red from crying, and his gaze kept returning to the doorway, as if he still hadn't quite grasped that both Nassrin and his brother were gone.

"You told my colleague that you can't remember what happened?"

Aldar nodded. "The doctor found this little mark in my neck." He held his neck over closer to Dea and pointed. "He says I was probably drugged. They took some blood tests, but I haven't heard any more than that. I was downstairs, because the power had gone out, but I don't really know how it happened . . . I think I fell. It was completely dark in here."

Dea looked at Liam. "There weren't any reports of power outages in the area last night, and the lights were back on when Aldar came to."

Aldar nodded in agreement. "Right after the lights went out, we heard a noise downstairs. We hoped it was Nassrin and that she'd come home. That's when I went downstairs to check if we blew a fuse."

"And you didn't find a quote from the Quran?" Liam asked again. They had already investigated the whole downstairs, but the crime scene investigators hadn't found one of the little slips of paper anywhere downstairs or upstairs.

Nassrin's uncle shook his head. There was a small stack of old photographs on the little end table between the two armchairs. The one on top was of Nassrin as a child in front of a blanket that had been spread out on the ground.

Dea turned to Liam and lowered her voice. "If Hayyan is the perpetrator's ninth victim, that may indicate that he's starting to feel so much pressure that his plan is slipping. Either he didn't bring a quote this time or he forgot to leave it?"

Liam thought about the note he had found at home in his own kitchen and agreed. Something was beginning to fall apart for the perpetrator. And he feared their perpetrator had started doing things not according to plan, which would make his movements even more impossible to predict or prevent.

"Is there anyone we should contact who could come and stay here with you?" Dea asked as they prepared to say goodbye to the elderly man.

Aldar shook his head. "I'd like to be alone for a bit," he said. He reached for the stack of photos and then set them in his lap. He showed them the picture of young Mona and explained that Hayyan hadn't had any idea he had a son. "And now maybe the two of them will never meet."

"We can also offer to find you somewhere else to stay for a couple of days," Dea continued.

He shook his head again, politely declining the offer. "I'd prefer to stay here."

*   *   *

"It's been a living hell for us," Ernst said, his face severe. "I don't understand how stories like this end up in the newspapers without journalists doing the necessary fact checking first!"

"You don't think the press has a correct understanding of what happened in the case?" Dea asked. Aldar's despair still stuck with her, even though they had stopped to get gas and buy a sandwich before driving to Tommerup to talk to Ernst and Mona about what had happen back when Mona was engaged to Bent.

Liam took a sip from the steaming cup of coffee that had been placed on the table in front of him. He nodded appreciatively to Mona and set the cup down.

"I think," Ernst continued, "this is a private matter, which is not the business of the entire country."

"The question we in the police are facing," Dea maintained, "and that surely people in the rest of the country are curious about too, is: What's the truth behind the whole story about Bent, Hayyan, and your daughter? Since Hayyan is missing, we only have Bent's version. That's how we've ended up here, to talk to you, Mona."

"We don't want to go into the past," Ernst grumbled dismissively.

Dea watched Mona, who seemed nervous. She sat at the table, keeping her eyes down and her hands together in her lap.

"We understand that, but unfortunately, you're going to have to," Liam interjected. "We're working on a case involving nine missing people. As you know, Hayyan was abducted from his home last night, and we need to determine if his disappearance could have anything to do with events from the past. In other words, no one can get out of discussing anything if we consider it to be relevant to this case."

Liam turned to Johannes, who sat across from his grandfather with the day's newspaper spread out in front of him on the table.

"Were you aware that Hayyan Kahlil is your biological father?"

Johannes returned Liam's gaze and then glanced uncertainly at Ernst.

"What possible benefit can there be to dredging up events from forty-six years ago?" Ernst continued in his booming voice.

"Were you aware that Hayyan has lived so near you all these years?" Dea looked attentively at Mona.

"Odense isn't really all that close," Ernst broke in again.

"I'm talking to Mona," Dea said coolly. Liam could tell she was starting to feel annoyed.

"Everything's always been difficult with you," Ernst continued, shaking his head as he looked at Dea. "Your father also turned his back on the church, as soon as he could get away from home."

Liam put a placating hand on Dea's arm.

Ernst's old, wrinkled face twisted in contempt. He stared caustically at Johannes.

"Even my own family has treated our faith lightly, *and* our responsibility to the church."

"That's not true," Johannes exclaimed sharply. "We have always stood behind you and your faith, but it's never been good enough!"

"I didn't get an answer yet to my question about Hayyan," Dea said, ignoring the bickering and focusing on Mona.

There was a rumble from Johannes's cell phone, which he was holding in his hands. Liam saw the screen light up. It looked like a notification from an alarm app.

"What do you want my daughter to say?" Ernst asked, a little more subdued. "She hasn't seen that man in forty-six years!"

"We're asking Mona," Liam said. Johannes's cell phone rumbled again. He quickly stuck it in his pants pocket.

"Mona," Dea continued urgently. "Please answer our questions. Otherwise we'll be forced to bring each of you in to the police station in Odense for formal questioning." The old pastor began to protest again, but Dea interrupted him. "It stops here, Ernst. We'd like to hear about Mona's relationships with Bent and Hayyan now. Mona, did you know that Hayyan lived so close to you?"

Mona slowly shook her head with a sad look.

"Did you know that Bent—that's Hans Henrik—is Beate's father?"

Again, Mona shook her head.

"I had no idea until it was in the paper," Mona said, picking anxiously at her apron. "Like my father said, it's been more than forty-six years, and I've tried to forget everything that happened."

"That's what I'm saying," Ernst crowed triumphantly to himself.

Dea ignored him and continued, "Would it have made any difference to you if you'd known that Beate's father was your ex-fiancé?"

"I don't know what difference it would make," Mona said with an uncertain shrug. "I suppose I might have had to withdraw from the church. I might not have been welcome."

Silence filled the kitchen for a moment, then Dea cleared her throat and leaned toward Mona again.

"I'm sorry to have to ask you this question." She reached out and took her cousin's hand. "But right now we need to know everything we can about your relationship with Hayyan back then. Did he rape you? Was that why your fiancé had such a violent reaction?"

The older woman sat for a long time without answering, then she looked seriously into Dea's eyes and shook her head.

"Hayyan is the only man I've ever loved. I dreamt of a life with him, but that was not to be."

An agonizing silence hung in the kitchen. Then in an abrupt jerk, Johannes turned to his grandfather.

"So it's not true? You lied to me?" His outburst was so explosive that Liam didn't have a chance to intervene before Johannes had yanked his grandfather up out of his chair and shaken him so violently that the old man lost his balance and fell forward. "You claimed that I was the result of a disgusting rape. How could you say that kind of thing if it's not true?"

Sobbing, Mona looked at Johannes. "I loved your father."

"You were just giving yourself away," Ernst said hoarsely, having regained his balance and groping unsteadily for his chair, which had tipped over behind him. "And you brought shame upon our family," he added, his lips twisted in disgust.

Liam's cell phone beeped, and he made eye contact with Dea. "Could we just step outside for a sec?"

* * *

"Ugh, so much drama!" Dea said disparagingly, as soon as they were out in front of the house. "Maybe now you see why I'd rather not have anything to do with them?"

Liam held up his phone eagerly. "We got the DNA results back from Bent's Golf, and they show that the following people have been in the car: Bent himself, the neighbor's son, Beate, Luna, Nassrin, and another three people in addition to that that they haven't been able to identify, since they're not in the database."

"That makes it sound almost like a car-sharing vehicle!" Dea watched him expectantly when she realized that there was more.

"And there's one more person who used it," Liam said, and looked over at the house. "Johannes. His DNA was found in the driver's side of the car."

"Johannes?" she exclaimed in surprise. "Why would he have driven Bent's car?"

They started walking toward the house to ask when Dea grabbed his arm and stopped him. "There has always been something unhealthy between Johannes and Ernst," she began. "And I've always had the sense that Johannes was trying to live up to his grandfather's expectations, that he spent a lot of time seeking his approval. I don't think he wanted to become a pastor when he was younger. We saw a lot of each other back then. As kids, we spent summer vacations together at my grandparents' house, and then we saw each other at family gatherings after that. We were never close, but he was really different back then, happier and more fun. But it was as if nothing he ever did or wanted was good enough for Ernst, and then he began to conform to the expectations. That was no fun to watch." Dea rubbed her nose. "He changed and became more and more like his grandfather . . . also in terms of his faith in God."

* * *

"Where's Johannes?" Liam asked, as they walked back into the kitchen.

"In the bathroom," Mona said, as if apologizing for her son's absence.

Dea walked over and sat down across from her uncle. "Did you make the decision to keep the truth hidden from him for forty-six years?" she asked, trying to make eye contact with his watery blue eyes.

Ernst made a point of looking past Dea.

"You need to fill in the details for me about how that story about the 'disgusting rape' came about when Mona just told us that Johannes' father is the only man she's ever loved."

"I don't have anything to say," Ernst said darkly, still refusing to look at her.

"Either you explain what this is about, or I charge you and bring you in for formal questioning."

"Charge me?" Ernst blurted out, sounding almost like he was enjoying himself. "For what, if I may be so bold?"

"Accomplice to the imprisonment of nine people as well as suspicion of murder."

"Oh, please." He shook his head indignantly so his thin hair bristled. "You have absolutely no evidence of that."

"Yes, she does, actually," Liam interjected, looking up from his phone, where he had just received an email from Thorbjørn, who was outside with the team from the National Forensic Service. "We were just informed that the little Wi-Fi cameras we suspect the perpetrator of using in this case were purchased from Austria thirteen months ago. And they were sent here to the parsonage in Tommerup and paid for with *your* Visa card, Ernst."

"What do you mean?" the old pastor exclaimed, seeming genuinely confused for a moment.

"That's true," Mona said, coming to her father's rescue. "Johannes helped us set up an alarm system here."

"Ernst, damn it, stop being so stubborn. You're going to end up in jail if you keep resisting," Dea exclaimed. "Can't you just tell the truth?"

"I'm almost ninety," Ernst growled. "You should appreciate me while I'm here."

Liam ignored him and turned to Dea. "Don't you want to just go get Johannes so we can talk to him about the surveillance cameras and the car?" Dea nodded and hurried out into the hallway.

Mona put a hand on her father's arm. "I want to know what you said to Johannes, Dad."

Ernst closed his eyes and slumped a little. It was as if some-thing inside him relented at the gentle touch from his daughter. "I was sick a little over a year ago." He looked up at Liam. "I thought my time had come. We all did."

"That's true," Mona said. "Dad had pneumonia, and we were afraid he wasn't going to recover."

"I felt it was wrong to die without Johannes knowing."

Mona stared at her father in horror.

"So you told him that his mother got pregnant from being raped?" Liam tried, watching the old man to see how he reacted to this provocation, but Ernst just kept looking into his daughter's eyes.

"I told him the truth, yes."

"But, Dad, it wasn't like that," Mona exclaimed, distraught. "You've always known that!"

"You were a confused young woman," Ernst stated. He had found his booming voice again. "You lost a good man because you were raped, and you had your bastard. That was and remains the truth!"

Dea came back in then, her cheeks red. "Johannes is gone!"

*   *   *

Dea raced off across the uneven grass, trying to catch up to Liam, who was heading toward the whitewashed house where Johannes lived at full speed. She tried to imagine the hatred Johannes must feel toward his grandfather now that he knew about his mother's love for Hayyan and regretted not having asked Mona if she knew whether her son had a gun in the house before they ran off.

Liam cautiously opened the unlocked door and called to Johannes. They were met by a sweet, mildewy smell, but the place was clean and tidy.

"You take the upstairs?" he said, concentrating and proceeding into the living room with his hand on his gun holster.

Dea slowly climbed the stairs to the second floor. There was woodchip textured wallpaper on the walls, and the furnishings had a 1970s vibe to them.

There were four doors upstairs. One led to a bathroom with shiny brown tiles and a gray-green sink; two of the others led to half-empty rooms with synthetic rust-colored carpets. Liam yelled from the living room downstairs that there was no one down there, and then she heard him leave the house.

Dea grasped the doorknob on the fourth door. It was locked. She rammed it powerfully with her shoulder a couple of times, and on the third attempt the lock gave.

She stood for a second in the doorway as her eyes adjusted to the dark. A couple of orange embroidered curtains were closed over the room's only window, and unlike the other two rooms, this room was fully furnished with a blue velvet sofa with pillows and a comforter and various shelves full of boxes, crates, plastic folders, and books. There was a big desk in the middle of the room with two new computer monitors, a computer, and several thin file folders in a neat pile.

She pulled open the curtains. She saw Liam coming out of one of the side buildings out in front of the house. Dea rapped hard on the windowpane to signal that Johannes wasn't upstairs either, but Liam didn't hear her and continued around the corner into the side yard.

She stood for a moment looking around at the packed little room. She was on her way back over to the door when her eyes came to rest on the top brown folder on the desk. A picture of a middle-aged woman was attached to the cover. Dea put on a pair of the blue crime scene gloves before picking up the top folder and holding it up to the light so she could see the picture.

It took a second before she realized, as if in slow motion, that it was a picture of her.

Dea stiffened and felt her palms grow damp inside the tight gloves. She slowly opened the thin folder. It was the same type as the ones the police kept case files and reports in. There was a small stack of pages inside. A yellow Post-It note on top said *Unsure*.

She pushed the top pages aside with frantic hands, and then for page after page, she saw her life described down to the slightest detail. Her normal work hours. Her standard running routes. The places she liked to shop. When she usually worked out. Her address. Which damned bench she liked to sit on when she thought she was sitting by herself thinking about life out in the gardens behind St. Canute's Cathedral. Even her closest coworkers were described in detail: Nassrin, Liam, Thorbjørn.

She looked in the next file. There was a picture of Luna on top. The system inside was the same. He knew everything about that young woman. About Dennis, about their mother, about how she was connected to Kasper and Beate.

She could hear that Liam was back in the house and called to him. She could hear how her own voice sounded strangely weak, as if the room had squeezed all the air out of her. He came running up the stairs a moment later, yelling her name.

"What's going on?" he asked, winded, as he entered the room.

She turned to face him, pale, and pointed to the desk. "It's Johannes!"

In a couple of quick strides, he was over at the desk. Dea showed him the folders and pointed to her own picture. He sank down into a squat beside her and quickly skimmed the contents before he started flipping through the next several folders.

Dea pulled the chair in closer to the desk and turned her attention to the two computer screens. Behind her Liam began pulling boxes off the shelf. She heard him talking on the phone. He called in reinforcements with brief orders. The area needed to be searched and the house cordoned off. There was no mistaking the seriousness. The hunt was on, for Johannes and for the nine people they needed to find.

She turned on the computer. One screen on the desk lit up and asked for a code. Dea sensed that Liam had come over to stand behind her chair as she positioned her fingers on the keyboard. He leaned in over her shoulder as she entered Johannes's birthday. That was wrong. Then she tried Mona's. Wrong again.

Dust motes danced in the rays of light from the window.

"How about Ernst's? Do you know his birthday?" Liam suggested.

She shook her head. She could only remember her father's, even though he had died a long time ago. Dea interlaced her fingers a couple of times, focusing all her attention on the computer.

She closed her eyes, trying to picture Johannes and remember him from back when she had sought comfort with the family and stayed with them in Tommerup. Then she happened to think of the verse over the altarpiece in the church. She remembered that it had meant a lot to her uncle. *I am the resurrection, and the life: he that believeth in me, though he were dead, yet shall he live. John 11.* She Googled the verse and quickly found it. The Gospel According to John, book 11, verse 25. Or in Danish: Johannes 11:25.

She took a deep breath and put her fingers on the keys. *Johannes1125.* She stared at the dots in the password field. That wasn't it either. She deleted the whole thing again and wrote *1125.* That was enough. Four digits. Then she hit enter.

Both screens came on at the same time. One showed a normal Windows keyboard with a ton of folders. The other was flickering, dark and grainy.

Liam had gone back over to the shelves, so she called him over and scooted aside a little so they could both see the dim screen.

"A video?" he suggested.

"Maybe surveillance video filmed with a night vision camera?" she guessed, pushing a folder over to him.

He opened the file. There were several overviews that showed the exact locations of cameras. It was easy to recognize the location where Verner had disappeared, because the abandoned house was visible in the background. And out behind the Tommerup Athletic Center, they could see a camera discreetly placed right under an eave, where it wasn't visible unless you were looking for it.

"Son of a bitch!" Dea leapt up from the chair and leaned in right up to the screen. "It's them, damn it!"

Liam stuck his head in close to the screen. They stood in tense silence, staring into the darkness, which moved slowly back and forth.

"Water!" Liam said. Two people had come into view.

"Is that a pool?" Dea asked with bated breath. Body parts gleamed pale in the darkness. The outlines of people, several of them.

Liam took the mouse and clicked on the bottom corner of the window, enlarging its size. It looked as if some of the people were clinging to a pipe running across over the water. Dea heard Liam's breathing, loud, right up against her ear. Neither of them said a word. Indistinct bodies moved on the video, and then suddenly Beate's face came into view very clearly. There was no doubt.

"And that's Kasper," Liam said, pointing to the figure behind Beate.

"And Luna." Dea could almost feel the pool's darkness closing in around her in a claustrophobic grip. "Can you see Nassrin?"

Suddenly the dusty silence in the room was ripped apart by sirens. An emergency response team was coming down the road by Ernst and Mona's farm, but Liam's eyes didn't budge from the screen.

"When was this recorded?" Dea asked, looking at the concentration on his face. "Do you think they're still alive?"

"This isn't recorded," Liam replied in a low voice, pointing to the upper right corner where a counter was running, showing the year, month, day, and time. Liam looked at his watch. Three fifty-seven PM. "What we're seeing is happening in real time. This is happening right now."

*   *   *

Within a half hour, a forward command center had been set up in Johannes's house. The house quickly filled with white-clad technicians from the National Forensic Service, the National Police's IT support department, and several of their own investigative teams from Odense. The pasture outside between Johannes's house and Ernst's farm had been transformed into an anthill of police in uniforms and street clothes. Even Dybbøl had stopped by before hurrying back to the command center to handle the press, the politicians, tactics, and strategies. She had asked Liam to make his presence known and report frequently and regularly to the strategic group in Odense.

After Dybbøl left again, Liam accompanied Martin from the National Forensic Service back to the room upstairs, where a couple of younger computer technicians had started setting up a camera to film the screen, which was showing the surveillance of the victims. They would need their own recordings so they could go back later and document the sequence of events.

"Several of them are definitely still alive," he heard someone from the National Police's supporting department say somewhere behind him. Liam thought it wouldn't surprise him if the minister of justice turned up soon too. But right now he didn't care, as long as he got to run his operational teams out in the field and locate the nine victims before it was too late.

"Is it possible to trace the connection from this computer back to the camera that's filming?" Dea was standing behind the IT investigator, who was sitting in the dusty chair in front of the computer. He had placed his own laptop plus and an extra laptop beside Johannes's computer.

"We're trying," he said, engrossed in his work. "Right now this live feed is the only connection we have, but if the pastor doesn't want us to find them, then he can just cut the signal. Then there will be no contact with the victims. We're setting up a trace and we're betting that the surveillance was set up with Bluetooth or some other wireless connection, but we don't know yet."

The outlines of a head appeared on the screen. Dea had just enough time to think that the black-and-white video looked like something right out of a horror movie.

"If Johannes had planned to cut the signal, he would have done that already," Liam said, sounding confident.

Two forensic specialists finished emptying the boxes off the shelves. Everything would be brought in for investigation. There were seven small surveillance cameras in one of the crates and several boxes containing new ones that hadn't been opened yet.

Liam turned to see if Frank from Forensic Medicine was still there.

"What do you think?" Liam asked, and pointed to the screen. Then he made room for the forensic specialist to move in very close.

"Of course it's hard when I can only see the victims on a screen, but as you already know, there's a big difference depending on whether they're being kept in salt water or fresh water. The water temperature is also a big factor, and how clean the water is will also affect their chances of survival."

Liam watched him impatiently. "What else?"

"If it's fresh water, the water penetrates their skin, and they will develop sores and infections." Frank stopped himself and looked Liam right in the eye. "It's been nine days now, so if the first victims have been in the water since they were abducted, they can tolerate another twelve hours max. If they haven't already died—"

Liam pounded his fist on the desktop in frustration.

"Time is getting away from us!" he exclaimed, frustrated, and looked out the window. The road was crowded with people. The press had arrived, plus curious locals, the Home Guard, and groups of their own personnel.

Dea came over next to him. Then suddenly she turned and clutched Liam's jacket hard. "The slurry tank, Liam. It's right outside!"

*   *   *

Dea ran down the stairs with Liam hard on her heels. He waved over a couple of officers in full uniform, motioning for them to follow them.

"They might be in the tank out in the field," Liam panted. "Get ambulances out here STAT!"

Dea jumped over the fence and ran around a couple of chubby pigs that came squirming hungrily over to meet them.

"Hello?" she called out.

The slurry tank was old and gray and had been made of rough concrete a lifetime ago. A thick, rubbery cover was stretched over it, and they couldn't see from the outside if there was anything underneath the thick covering.

"We need to get someone up on top of this thing right away!" Liam yelled. The two uniformed officers had reached them.

"I'll go," one of them yelled, and his partner put his hands together and gave him a boost up. He quickly crawled across the rubber. "This cover is soft . . . Wait!"

There were a few strained sounds from up there.

"I'm going up too," Dea said, impatiently nudging Liam. "Help me, would you?"

He put his hands together to hold her foot and helped boost her up.

Dea quickly rolled over to the officer who was cutting a hole in the thick rubber cover. She reached for the small flashlight in the officer's belt. Then she tore the hole in the rubber big enough that she could squeeze her face into the opening along with the flashlight.

The stench turned her stomach. She pulled free of the hole and rolled over onto her back, staring up at the blue sky, coughing and spluttering, her heart pounding hard in her chest.

"Negative!" she yelled then. "There's no one here!"

* * *

Martin gave the thumbs-up as Dea and Liam returned to Johannes's living room.

"You're onto something with this slurry tank, Dea."

Martin waved them over closer. Spread out on the dining table in front of him there was a big map of Funen Island. Five colleagues were clustered around the table with glowing cell phones and laptops.

"We're working on locating every tank on the island that could match what we know about the size of the space where they're confined."

"Primarily slurry tanks?" Liam said, surveying the map. There were already a number of markings.

"Old slurry tanks, wastewater holding tanks, sewage treatment plants, et cetera. We're looking for a tank that's eight to ten meters in diameter, probably rounded on top, made of concrete and with some sort of cover over it."

"How far have you gotten? Can we send people out?"

Martin nodded hesitantly. "There are an awful lot of slurry tanks, but we aim to have a rough list within the hour."

"They could be dead within the hour," Dea exclaimed.

"Do it yourself then!" Martin said, exasperated. "We're going as fast as we possibly can."

"What about that old amusement park, Fun Park Fyn? That place must have been closed for over a decade now," Dea suggested.

"That's pretty far from municipal Assens, where we were told to start."

Dea looked at Liam. "I remember that place from going there when I was little. There was a kids' swimming pool. That could be the right size."

"You're right," Liam said, turning quickly to Martin. "Send a team over there right away."

"I'm going to go with them," Dea said.

Liam shook his head vigorously. "We can't personally check every tank on the island!"

"No, but I'm going to go with this group right now to that fun park, and then we'll take it from there, OK? I have to be out in the field. I can't bear to sit here and watch people die." Dea left the room.

Liam bent over the printed aerial photo Martin had on top of the dining table. It showed a section of Funen with each parcel of land enlarged and clearly marked.

"How many tanks and pools do you think there are?"

Martin ran his fingers through his hair and shook his head.

"If we include all of them, then there are probably over a thousand, but if we start with tanks in places that are no longer in active agricultural use, then it becomes highly unlikely that they're in a slurry tank. And then we focus on the covered tanks, which makes it somewhat more manageable, since most slurry tanks are uncovered."

"Can we start dispatching teams to the ones you've marked?" Liam asked impatiently. "We're still going to be moving the tank teams from place to place, so we might as well get them out in the field right away, right?"

"Agreed." Martin glanced at his watch and then pointed to the map. "We'll start there, there, and there."

A technician interrupted them from over by the door.

"We tried mounting one of the little cameras we found in the office upstairs inside the slurry tank outside to test and see what it looked like on the screen. And there's significantly more light coming down from above than what we're getting in the feed in the live stream." He pointed upstairs. "So we don't think the tank we're looking for has a soft cover."

Liam quickly turned to Martin and the others who were pouring over the map of Funen.

"What does that mean for us?" Liam asked everyone in the room.

"It means that we've narrowed down our points of interest quite a bit. Good work!" Martin said, giving his colleague in the doorway a thumbs-up. Then he pointed to a young officer standing nearby holding a cell phone. "Notify the flyover team lead that they should pay extra attention to round tanks with any sort of solid roof structure: metal, wood, hard plastic, concrete."

* * *

The light coming in from outside tinted the dusty room orange. The room had been searched top to bottom for evidence and everything had been secured, packed up, or sent off to Forensic Chemistry. There was an enormous amount of data, and Johannes had done extremely thorough work, researching his victims for a year. He had even planned the wild goose chase with Peter on Thorø, and unlike Beate, Johannes had very quickly discovered that Peter had taken over his grandmother's little snail business. Johannes had taken the time to keep close tabs on his victims and their families. He had watched them and rehearsed their habits and patterns.

Liam exhaled tiredly and looked around the secret room. It seemed likely now that Johannes could have discarded Beate's cell phone out on Thorø Island to lead them astray and induce them to go after Peter. Just like he had done with Charlotte's bicycle when he'd removed it and then later placed it out behind the athletic center.

They had chosen to use his upstairs room as the center for all their IT work because of the rolling live stream. Word was that it was too risky to move Johannes's setup.

"Lene!" Liam nodded to the head of the computer team from the national office. He could see the feed running behind the people sitting around the desk. It did not make for pleasant viewing. "How far have you gotten?"

Lene gave him a gloomy look. "The stream isn't coming through his PC, as we expected. It's being shared directly to the screen on the left from a cell phone."

"What does that mean?"

"That means that there's no signal going into or coming out of the PC. So to trace the signal, we need find the unit that's sharing the feed. It could be an iPhone or an iPad."

"But can that unit be traced?"

"We're probably talking about an alarm system camera that's operating via an app, and if we find the unit that's sharing the feed here, then there's a real chance that we can also trace our way to the place where the nine people are located, but I'm pretty worried that we'll find the signal is obscured by a VPN and we'll end up somewhere in the US."

"Boss!" One of the experts at the desk held up a hand behind her.

Lene walked over to him. "Yes, Piil?"

"It's a cell phone that's sharing the surveillance footage, and it's located inside this house."

"We've searched everything thoroughly," Liam exclaimed. "Are you sure?"

Piil nodded confidently. "We can't be positive that it's that specific cell phone that's sharing the signal, but we can see that there's an active cell phone here in the house that's not one of our own. We have its number, and we know that the subscriber's name is listed as Mona Abelsen."

"We need to find that cell phone right now!" Liam exclaimed, and looked at Lene. "Tell me you can just track it, just like that."

"It emits noise when it's turned on, but it's far weaker than an electrical outlet or wires, so we're waiting for an emissions detector. When it arrives, we'll be able to track the phone by frequency fields, even if it's sitting in a box of oatmeal." She looked at her phone. "They'll be here in fifteen minutes."

"Perfect, I'd like to get . . ." Liam paused there in irritation to answer his phone as it rang. It was someone from the team he had dispatched to History House in Odense, where he had asked them to search the old newspapers and microfilm and set up full access to MediaStream. "Thanks. I need you to find everything you can track down about the case from forty-six years ago, and then I'd also like to know if there's been anything else at all in the papers about Ernst or Johannes for the entire rest of their lives. Put a hundred people on this if you need to. I know it's a big job. I want to know everything about their lives and about the assault case against Bent from back then. Find out if the judge from the old case is still alive, the defense attorney, old colleagues, whatever." He hung up and looked at Lene. "Are we sure that Johannes isn't still here in the house?"

"That's really unlikely after such a thorough search, but if he is here in a hidden room, we'll find him soon if he's with Mona Abelsen's phone."

Liam scratched his beard. "I'm going to assign a group to search the house again using thermal imaging equipment, and your radio engineer can join in once he arrives."

* * *

It was 5:46 PM. when Dea pulled into the overgrown parking lot of the long since shuttered Fun Park Fyn. The place had been doomed by a bankruptcy even before the financial crisis, and every attempt to reopen the park over the years had come to nothing. It was now a deserted wasteland of overgrown, dilapidated buildings, blighted county-fair-style rides, and big pools that were verdigris green with algae.

Even before she climbed out of her car, three more cars pulled in alongside hers with personnel from the search crew they were now calling Tank Group 1.

Dea was about to follow the first three people from the group into the park when yet another car pulled in. She gestured for the search crew to continue on into the area while she walked over to greet the canine unit.

"How the hell did you beat us here?" the dog handler exclaimed with a broad smile.

"No idea, Rolf, but let's get this dog to work right away!"

Rolf nodded and walked around to the back. "Thanks for the talk the other day," he continued. "You guys definitely have better coffee."

"Oh, is that why you drop by so often to take a break on my desk?"

The dog had been let out and was attentively scanning the parking lot.

"There. Ask and I are ready!" He sneaked a glance at her. "After this case is over, do you want to maybe get coffee together somewhere that's not the police station?" Dea didn't respond. He awkwardly looked down. "Sorry! That was out of line. I shouldn't have asked about that right now."

"Let's go in. We can talk about the coffee some other day." She smiled at him.

He smiled sheepishly and commanded Ask to heel.

A man from the search team came into view from behind the collapsed entrance. "There's a car parked in here, a grayish-brown Peugeot 205 . . . with license plates."

Dea followed him at a run and stared skeptically at the car. It wasn't a car they had encountered in connection with the case, but she ordered them to inspect it right away. She whipped out her phone and sent a picture of the car to Liam. Then she followed Rolf and the tank team into the wilderness of trees, crumbling buildings, and ragged awnings that had once been a cheery summer destination.

Heavy clouds had gathered over them, and the air already smelled like rain. She had lost sight of the others but followed the sound of their voices between the ruins and wildly overgrown grass and shrubberies. Nature was gradually reclaiming this space, and over the years the dilapidated food stalls, play structures, and bumper car ride had been increasingly covered by vines and moss. In several places a faded, rusting bumper car peeked out, its headlights broken and its red plastic seats facing the wrong way.

She followed the path under a dirty patio roof that was full of holes. The building's window openings stared vacantly into eternity. There was a lake alongside the path, where she spotted a large, filthy pedal boat shaped like a swan bobbing by the lake shore along with accumulations of plastic garbage.

Ask suddenly started barking loudly very nearby. Dea followed the sound, pushing her way through some overgrown bushes to emerge into a large open square with several filthy pools and a bank of multicolored water slides.

The dog had clearly picked up some scent. She and a couple of other officers followed at a run. They were heading toward the old pools.

The long plastic slides extended down a hillside, rising and falling, filthy and broken, down into the big swimming pool, which was filled to the brim with greenish water. Dea stared into the water and could see bumper cars and trash down on the bottom.

They continued past the largest pool and over to one that was a bit smaller. The dog stopped, barking at the top of his lungs.

In the middle of the pool was a little island with a hut about the size of a carport, covered in peeling white paint. All the windows and doors of the structure had been boarded up with black Masonite panels.

The dog was pulling, and they followed it to the other side of the pool, where a narrow footbridge led out to the hut.

Dea gestured for the two from the investigative team to move in close to the building and nodded to signal that they should open the door. Her heart was racing. The door was flung open, and they heard a squeal from inside.

Dea looked despondently at Rolf and pulled out her phone. *Forget the Peugeot*, she wrote. *It was just a couple having sex.*

We found the cell phone, Liam wrote back, *but the signal was obscured via a VPN, and there may not be much we can do, because we don't want to lose the signal by rebooting or bypassing or anything like that. Damn it. Come back after you're done shutting that place down.*

*   *   *

"OK, great! Sleep well, honey . . . Thanks, I love you too." Liam hung up and, embarrassed, and sat back down at the dining table with the big map of Funen. The map was full of pins. Every tank and pool in the municipality of Assens, which covered approximately five hundred square kilometers of southwestern Funen Island, had been marked with a red pin, the ones in the rest of Funen with blue. They had no markers outside Funen in the rest of Denmark, and if their search took them that far, all the people in the water would be dead before they reached them anyway. It was clear that their conditions were becoming increasingly critical by the hour.

"Was that Helene?" Dea said.

Liam looked at her with a distant, remote smile. Then he nodded. "Yeah, they won today, my son."

"His water polo game?"

"Yes . . ." The words stuck in his throat. It was almost seventy-two hours since he had slept more than a fitful hour here or there.

"We need some fresh coffee," Dea decided, and stood up.

Liam stared vacantly at the steam rising from the brown liquid as she poured into the cup in front of him. They were out of cream, though, and suddenly he didn't really want it.

Martin spoke on the phone and then placed green markers at three locations on the map.

"They weren't there either," he muttered, discouraged.

Liam brought the cup to his lips anyway, mostly for something to do. The coffee tasted terrible. They had nine investigative teams in the field, drones in the air, dogs on the ground, thermal imaging flyovers with a helicopter, and still they were barely inching along. Even a small municipality like Assens could feel as big as the moon.

Dea flopped down onto the chair beside him. He had hardly registered that she had left. She pushed a container of cream over closer to his cup.

Liam gratefully poured a sizable amount into his coffee and took another sip.

"I should have been the one down there in the water instead of Nassrin," Dea said almost inaudibly. "I don't understand. This is my family, damn it!"

Liam turned to her with a look of concern. "No one expects you to have seen this coming." He flung up his hands. "That man spied on you for a year. That is so messed up!"

"On us, you mean. He spied on all the people he had on his list." She fidgeted restlessly. "But I did know that Johannes is an odd bird, and Ernst . . . Well, it's like he was pulled right out of some sort of fundamentalists' handbook."

Liam nodded. "According to his records, he had intended you as his eighth victim and Ernst would have been number nine. But then, doesn't it seem like he changed plans and went after Hayyan instead?"

"I don't think Hayyan was planned," Dea said. "I think he was a spontaneous victim, because Johannes read about Bent's attack on him, and he was able to figure out from the articles that Hayyan must have been the man he believed had raped his mother. Ernst did tell Johannes that Mona had been raped."

Liam had pulled a piece of paper over to himself. He started outlining the Quran verses they had up on the board back at the station.

"What the hell made the man launch into all this insanity in the first place?"

He drew circles under each verse, and then out along the margin, he started on the Ten Commandments.

Dea folded her hands in front of her. She seemed washed out with fatigue, but now she straightened up and reached for the piece of paper Liam had pushed away.

"Ernst has always been one of those strong, ancient Christian figures in the local community in Tommerup, so the shame must have been unbearable to him when Mona gave birth to a biracial child out of wedlock whose father was Muslim. I imagine that Ernst has had a hard time loving his own grandson for all these years. He might even have considered him an irredeemable nonbeliever because of his father's Muslim heritage." Dea shook her head. "Johannes has spent his whole life trying to please Ernst, but nothing has ever been good enough. So then when Ernst was lying there on what he presumed to be his deathbed, he apparently decided that that was the time tell Johannes what he thought was the truth—in other words, that Johannes was the result of a rape. Why he did that, I couldn't tell you. Maybe he felt a need to explain his own shabby behavior for all those years that had passed."

Dea inhaled and continued.

"Then when Johannes realized that the reason Ernst had never been satisfied with him was due to something Johannes couldn't even do anything about . . ." She paused for a moment, staring into space for a moment. "Can't you picture him deciding to take revenge against Ernst, to show him how much pain you can cause by using religion in the service of evil? You could possibly say that this whole crime was committed because Johannes knows the only place he could truly stick it to Ernst is through his faith. Just as Johannes had always been oppressed by his grandfather's faith."

Liam nodded, thinking this over. Dea slumped a little. Her eyes were tired, and there were two dark circles underneath them on her tan skin.

"And based on Johannes' protocols, Ernst should have been victim number nine, because his grandfather coveted the church, the faith, and Johannes himself, for that matter, as his own property."

Dea nodded now. "Exactly."

"But we still haven't figured out who the tenth victim is," Martin broke in.

There was a loud knock on the floor upstairs.

"That's the IT group," Martin said, getting up. "I told them to knock on the floor if anything happened in the water."

"It's Beate," Piil said, pointing to the screen as soon as they walked into the room. The night was jet black outside the windows now.

They saw Beate untie two pairs of pants that had been holding her to the pipe and allow herself to slide back down into the water. The woman next to her reached out a hand, and Beate felt her way forward to the hand. She grasped it and held it and clung to it for a moment. It didn't look like they were talking.

"That's Luna," Piil continued.

Then Beate let go of Luna's hand and moved over to a third person. She felt her way to his face.

"And that's Kasper, right?" Dea said, staring stiffly at the screen. Piil nodded.

Beate stroked Kasper's cheek. Then she looked over at Luna and said something.

"It's rare for their faces to be turned so we can see them on the screen," Piil said.

Luna untied the clothes that were holding her up and slid down into the water. She moved as if she were in pain. Then she felt her way over to Beate, and together they helped undo Kasper and let him slide into the water. He didn't move. Beate put his head against her chest so that he was resting with his head under her chin. Then she felt her way to his wrist and started bending and extending his arm.

"She's trying to keep him alive," Dea exclaimed, staring desperately at Liam.

"What about Nassrin and Hayyan?" Liam said apprehensively.

"Nothing yet," Pill said. "It's very difficult to recognize the silent ones in the dark."

Day 10—Sunday

A RAIN SQUALL HAD moved through outside, and the delicate scent of rain-drenched summer night wafted in the window, which was ajar. Liam had sat down on the blue sofa, and the instant his body hit the soft upholstery, his desire to sleep had felt like lead under his skin.

Piil sat in the low armchair behind the computers at the desk and kept a focused eye on the indistinct outlines of the missing people in the dark water.

Liam's head fell back against the sofa's backrest, and he closed his eyes and surrendered to sleep. He had no sense of time, no inkling that he had even been asleep at all when he was abruptly tugged to the surface again by a cry from over at the desk.

He sat for a second, squinting in confusion, then he was on his feet. He grabbed the back of Piil's chair and leaned in over his colleague's shoulder.

"What's going on?"

"Someone new just landed in the water!" Piil turned to him with a grim expression, which unsettled Liam.

"Who?" Liam yelled, even though he was standing right next to his colleague, staring at the screen, which was completely black now. He saw bright spots and felt incredibly dizzy. "It can't be! We have people everywhere!" he roared in frustration.

Dea had come over, wrapped in a blanket. She had curled up on the floor for a few hours of sleep while the other two had been watching the screen.

Piil got up and stood before them, his shoulders drooping.

"And the signal is gone," he continued grimly, pointing to the black screen.

"But you can connect us again, right?" Dea stared insistently at the screen, which had been their only link to the victims.

"One second," said Martin, who was sitting behind the police's own IT equipment. "I'll have that section of the recording for you in five seconds."

Liam looked over at the third screen, which had been set up to transmit their own recording of the surveillance, and he repeated Dea's question.

"Can we get the feed back?"

"No," Piil replied. "It almost seemed like the camera at the pool was pulled down when the person disappeared into the water. The connection has been broken."

A few seconds later, the video was running on their own screen. The room was quiet as everyone held their breath. Liam felt an icy shiver run down his spine as he leaned in closer to the screen, concentrating on the clip Martin had prepared for them.

"It's sixteen seconds," Martin explained. "After that, the signal is lost completely."

Liam glanced from the black screen over to their own recording. The connection had been lost at 12:12 AM.

Martin started the playback. From the deep darkness there was the sense of a trapdoor or hatch being opened. A faint light spread and grew clearer, and a figure came into view in the opening and stood backlit in the moonlight. In the blurry recording of the feed, it looked like a slim man. A black silhouette in the moonlight.

Liam was so focused on the figure, who had stepped all the way up to the edge of the open hatch, that he hardly even noticed the movements down in the water. For a brief instant, the figure was lit by moonlight reflected off the water below. He grasped something that looked like a big metal hook, like the ones from a slaughterhouse, just inside the hatch. The whole thing happened so fast. A second later he disappeared down into the hole, and then the screen went black.

"Play it again!" Liam didn't take his eyes off the screen, and Martin replayed it. "Stop there! Back up a little . . . Can we zoom in?" Liam's dizziness had passed, and he fidgeted impatiently.

"Yes, just a sec."

Piil had also come over to stand behind them.

Liam stared at the still image that came into view. It was the second after the man's feet had left the edge, when he was suspended in the air—the instant right before the connection was broken.

"It's Johannes!" Dea stood as if turned to stone, staring at the frozen image.

Liam had straightened up, and he gave Martin an appreciative pat on the shoulder.

"I wonder if that's been his plan the whole time, that he would be the tenth victim?" She turned to Liam.

"It definitely makes a statement, anyway," Liam said. His tiredness was gone, adrenaline surging through his body as he tried to grasp what they had just witnessed. At the same time, he tried to understand the consequences of Johannes having broken the connection to the missing people in the pool. Liam was determined to find them, even if he had to dig up all of Funen by hand.

"I think this whole performance was done entirely for Ernst's benefit," Dea said in a monotone, looking as if she was thinking like crazy. "I think Johannes wants to tell Ernst what the outcome can be if your faith in God is stronger than your faith in people. Like we talked about earlier, Ernst has never been satisfied with Johannes. You remember?"

Liam nodded somberly. Dea continued.

"In Ernst's eyes, Johannes was nothing but a bastard, a mongrel, with Muslim blood in his veins to boot. And because Ernst has been the only father figure in Johannes' life, Johannes has dedicated all his energy to pleasing Ernst. I can remember that from when we were kids. Ernst was never satisfied with Johannes. He was verbally abusive to him, putting him down all the time, and I can see now that it must have been the very existence of Johannes colliding with Ernst's fairly strict interpretation of Christianity. Maybe that's the conclusion Johannes has reached too? That all his attempts to earn Ernst's acceptance have been wasted?"

Liam nodded thoughtfully, voices humming around them. People had come up to join them from the command center downstairs. A live connection had been established with the police station. Information was being exchanged. He noted Dybbøl's voice talking to the head of operations in Odense. The intensity in the room was palpable.

"That's why Ernst was meant to be the ninth victim, based on what Johannes said in his journal. Johannes wanted Ernst to be in the water already when Johannes threw himself in. They were both supposed to die down there. Together." Dea looked plaintively at Liam. He nodded again.

They stood for a moment in silence with all the commotion buzzing around them, and then Liam turned to Martin.

"Go through all the recordings. Focus on the pool and the hatch that leads down to it. I know it's probably impossible to find anything useful, because we only have the feed from inside the pool. But try. We need to get that out to the investigative teams as soon as possible."

He looked at his watch and then pulled Dea with him toward the door.

"We need to talk to Ernst."

* * *

"I don't know what you imagine that I could contribute at this hour of the night," Ernst said indignantly, and carefully tied the belt of his brown-and-blue-striped robe around his waist before he lowered himself a bit stiffly onto a chair at the kitchen table.

"Anything at all that could help us find Johannes," Liam said nonchalantly, sitting down across from Ernst.

"Just what do you think my son is involved in?" Mona asked. She had also been roused from sleep and stood disheveled in her bathrobe, supporting herself on the kitchen table. She crossed her arms nervously and defensively in front of her chest.

"It's looking like Johannes abducted all the people who have disappeared over the last nine days," Liam continued, diving right in. He looked straight at Ernst. "We know for sure that he intended you as his ninth victim, but his plans must have changed. We also know that he leaves his victims in a water tank where they slowly die."

"Oh my dear Lord," Mona exclaimed, hiding her shocked face in her hands.

"What am I supposed to say to that?" Ernst said, without looking at either Liam or Dea. "We can't do anything about that. We don't know where he is!" His face was as hard as if it were chiseled in stone.

"Johannes jumped into the water himself an hour ago. We need your help to figure out where this water tank is located. We've had units scouring Funen Island to locate the place, but we still haven't had any luck finding it."

"Oh God!" Mona started wailing loudly. "Dad, you have to help them! You can't let Johannes die."

"Sit down," Ernst thundered authoritatively, nodding to the empty kitchen chair. "Getting hysterical never helps." Mona sat down in the chair, sobbing. Then Ernst looked to Liam. "Does that mean that this Hayyan is in the water now too?"

"Yes."

Ernst leaned back, staring straight ahead with a bit of a vacant look in his eye, as if he was trying to picture the scenario.

"We need to know if you can think of any sort of slurry tank, disused water tank, or something along those lines that you could imagine Johannes using," Liam said, and explained that they had already searched the old Fun Park Fyn amusement park.

"Johannes and I have both seen a lot of slurry tanks," the old pastor grumbled. "We have one ourselves, but I don't know that Johannes has a particularly strong attachment to any of them."

"The one we're looking for is covered," Liam contributed. "Probably with a metal cover."

Ernst hesitated for a moment, then shook his head.

"Unfortunately, I'm afraid I can't help you." He turned to Dea, only a little twitch by one eye revealing that maybe he wasn't quite as unaffected as he appeared to be. "You've known Johannes ever since you were kids. So you know how unlikely it is that he would be behind such an evil deed. He can hardly accomplish the slightest things on his own, so it honestly seems inconceivable that he could have orchestrated all this all by himself. Tell them! I'm simply having a hard time believing that this could be true."

"But unfortunately, it is," Dea said tersely. She had put an arm around Mona, who was sobbing inconsolably into her hands and had started rocking back and forth in her chair. Ernst made no move to comfort his daughter.

Dea caught Liam's eye and nodded toward the door. "We'd better be getting back."

"I'll walk you out," Mona said, wiping her tearstained face on the sleeve of her robe. In the front hall, she grabbed Dea's arm. "Do you think Johannes is going to die?"

"I don't know," Dea replied honestly. "But if we don't find that water tank, I'm afraid they'll all die."

Mona looked as if she were on the verge of a nervous breakdown.

"It would all have been better if I'd insisted on staying with Hayyan back then."

It was hard to hear what she said as her words squeezed out through a throat thick with tears. She pulled herself together, wanting to say something more. She took a breath as if preparing to speak, several times, before her last words finally slipped out.

"But I didn't dare. I didn't dare, because they were both so furious, Hans Henrik and Dad. Dad would have disowned me forever . . . and Johannes was so little."

* * *

"Status?" Liam boomed with renewed energy to the assembled crowd the second they set foot back in Johannes's house. In addition to Martin, there were five people sitting in the command post. IT still had a couple of people upstairs, even though the live feed had been lost. They were still struggling to catch a signal on the mobile but so far without any luck.

Martin raised his hand in greeting and pointed to the map of Funen that was spread out in front of them. "We've searched a few more locations, but unfortunately without positive result. We've had the film clip analyzed, and based on that, we're still working with the assumption that we're dealing with a covered tank with a massive, heavy cover."

"Couldn't it almost just be an old slurry tank with a metal cover?" Dea said. "If we assume that, that would narrow down the number of places we need to search quite a bit, wouldn't it?"

"Yes, that's right." Martin nodded. "It's likely to be a slurry tank. Other types of tanks and pools are less likely to have such a heavy cover. But right now we just don't know the first thing about which tanks are covered. The drones are no use until it starts to get light out again. The thermal imaging flyovers also haven't paid off yet. It'll get easier in a few hours, once we can see the ground from the air again. We're getting a little help from Google Earth, but the pictures there are several months old, so we're working with the military to establish a live signal."

"Perfect," Liam said. "Are we close?"

Martin nodded intently and leaned closer to his computer to see if there was anything new, but then he shook his head.

"Why would any tank at all have a metal lid?" Dea said.

"It must be to prevent animals—or people, for that matter—from falling in," Martin said.

"So that means we're probably talking about an underground tank?"

"That would be logical, yes. But we don't have any sort of list of which tanks are below ground or above ground, and it's really hard to assess that from a satellite image."

Liam interrupted them. He held up his cell phone and explained that the group doing research at History House in Odense had emailed. They were going through the old articles.

He quickly skimmed through the email. Their colleagues had found an old interview with Ernst Abelsen. A profile piece that had come out in 1971.

"It's about his childhood and his father, Church of Denmark provost Abelsen, who was responsible for several parishes and their pastors," Liam recounted. "And it says that Ernst had a little sister who died in a tragic accident. She drowned in a slurry tank when they were kids!" Liam looked meaningfully from Martin to Dea, his eyebrows raised.

"What?" Dea exclaimed. She looked like she wanted to yank the phone out of Liam's hands. "Are you sure that's Ernst?"

Liam nodded and continued. "Ernst and his little sister were playing at a neighbor's house in a field behind the neighbor's farm. It doesn't say here exactly how the accident happened, but the little sister fell into the slurry tank. Ernst, who was only a little boy, couldn't get her back out, and no one heard him yelling for help. So he had to watch helplessly as his little sister sank down into the slurry and disappeared." Liam looked up. "That was almost eighty years ago."

"I've never heard that story," Dea said. "I knew that they had a sister. But I didn't realize that she had died in such an awful way. I don't think my father knew that either. He hadn't been born yet when that happened. He and Ernst had a pretty strained relationship with each other for most of his life."

"But of course Ernst can remember it," Liam said. "And it's probably not inconceivable that he's told Johannes the story."

Dea was standing completely still, her arms hanging at her sides. She looked as if she were thinking carefully, and then she began to recount:

"When I was a kid, I spent a week of vacation almost every summer with my grandparents, my dad's parents, at the parsonage. Johannes was often there too, and even though he was younger than me, we played together and had fun."

"So you're familiar with the area where Ernst and your father grew up?"

Dea nodded.

"My grandfather was a lot like Ernst. I didn't care for him that much, and we were never particularly close. But my grandmother was more like my dad. She was loving and great with kids. I liked spending time there. There was this place out behind their farm where our grandfather wouldn't let us go. Otherwise, we were allowed to run around and play wherever we wanted to, but we were strictly forbidden from being in that one particular spot that he had carefully pointed out to us."

"And that was because of the sister who drowned?" Liam guessed.

"I have no idea, because I've never heard about that accident. But we went there anyway. Because Anna, the neighbor who lived at that farm with her husband, used to make us bread with honey on top. They kept bees out back. I always thought we weren't allowed there because of the beehives."

"Was there a slurry tank?" Liam asked, so eagerly that his words nearly tumbled over each other.

"Yes, I'm pretty sure there was. But I haven't been there in so many years."

"Do we have an address?" Martin impatiently broke in. "I'll send a team right away!"

"It should be easy to find. It's the Kærum Church parsonage," Dea said. "It's one of the farms right behind it."

"On Kærumvej," Martin said, pointing out the church on the map. "We have a number of slurry tanks around Kærum Church."

"Can you get coordinates for all the tanks we know of that are close to the church?" Liam looked up from the map of Funen and over at Martin, who nodded intently. "We need to get crews out lifting the hatch on every tank located anywhere near the parsonage there." Martin nodded again. "And the two of us"—he looked at Dea, who stood silently, staring straight ahead—"we need to go talk to Ernst again, so that he can show us exactly where the accident happened."

*   *   *

They could still see lights on in the kitchen windows when they found themselves in the courtyard out front once again. Dea pictured Mona sitting in the kitchen, probably beside herself. She probably should have stayed with her, she thought, and hopped out of the car as soon as they came to a stop. But there was no time to look after your family in a situation like this.

Dea knocked hard on the door, then let herself in and went straight into the kitchen. Empty. She walked through the house once, calling to Ernst and Mona, but received no response. She was heading for the bedrooms when she heard Liam behind her.

"Their car's gone. They're not here!"

Dea kept going anyway, through the living room and yanking open the doors to the two bedrooms, only to ascertain that both beds were empty. Mona's light-blue robe had been tossed over a chair.

"Come on," Liam yelled from behind her, and Dea quickly ran back through the house. They both ran back over to Johannes's house and quickly got into the car.

When they arrived in Kærum, Liam passed her the map Martin had given them to bring, which showed the local area and the farms surrounding Kærum Church.

"Do you recognize anything?"

She was so tired and so hopped up on adrenaline that she started laughing loudly, feeling a sort of near hysteria.

"Recognize? No, not really!" she laughed shrilly, trying to stop herself. Liam smiled at her empathetically. "How the hell am I supposed to recognize anything here? It's so dark out that I can't see my hand in front of my face, and it's been more than thirty years since I last came out here on summer vacation," Dea said, wiping away the tears that had accompanied her laughter. But then she pulled herself together and turned on the car's overhead light. They could see the church tower now. She leaned over the map. "Wait a minute . . . We always went across the fields to Alfred and Anna's place, but . . ." She studied the map thoroughly. "If the church is there, then . . . yes, it must be down that gravel road there!"

The clock on the Passat's dashboard said 2:27 AM as Liam and Dea drove down the narrow gravel road near the church.

"Are you sure the Map Team marked a slurry tank on this road? I think the ones on the map are a little farther out," Liam said.

"I don't know about that, but this is where our grandfather wouldn't let us go. I'm positive." Dea stared out into the darkness and pointed eagerly ahead. "Anna and Alfred's farm is at the end of this road."

Liam drove carefully down the uneven, potholed gravel road until they came to a farm. The farm was well hidden behind thick clumps of old trees.

They kept quiet with the headlights on as they tried to orient themselves. There was a large courtyard in front of the farmhouse itself, and then the gravel road continued around the farm.

Dea got out and looked around. The house was dark, but in the glow of the car's headlights, she could see the wide tire ruts delineated in the soft gravel.

"The slurry tank was out there behind the barn." She gestured familiarly with her hand.

"There should be an old man living here now," Liam said behind her. He had turned off the engine, but the headlights were still on. They cast a sharp light on the whitewashed brickwork.

They walked up to the front door and knocked. Nothing happened. Liam knocked again, hard.

"I don't remember it looking like this at all," Dea said, peering up and down at the front of the house. "If the man inside is in the same shape as this property, then he probably can't hear or see."

Liam looked around. It started pouring, quickly transforming the courtyard into a muddy mess. His hair was wet, and rain dripped steadily from the tip of his nose.

"I'm going to walk around behind the barn and see if I can find the slurry tank on my own." Dea turned on her flashlight and ran off around the corner of the house.

*   *   *

Liam gave it one last shot and pounded on the door again. He was about to follow Dea when a light came on behind the little pane of frosted glass. A moment later the door opened and an ancient man peered out at him.

"Police," Liam said.

"What?"

"Police!" Liam repeated louder, holding up his badge.

The stooped man opened the door all the way and took a step toward Liam.

"I can't see that without my glasses," he said, "and my glasses . . ." He put his hand on his forehead and then shook his head, puzzled. "What's going on?"

"I'm sorry that we need to bother you in the middle of the night, but we're searching for a slurry tank."

"A slurry tank?" the man repeated, not understanding. His speech was slurred, as if he had trouble forming the words. It occurred to Liam that the man had probably taken his teeth out for the night.

"There's a major police operation underway in the area. Is there a slurry tank on the property?"

The man nodded but didn't seem to understand the part about the police operation.

"There's a tank around back, but there hasn't been any slurry in it for years," the man mumbled, gesturing loosely with his hand. He looked at Liam. "I'm afraid I can't help you." He shook his head for a long time.

"Have there been any people you don't know driving by your farm in the last couple of weeks?" Liam continued. There was something frail and indifferent about the old man, but his cracking voice took on some strength now.

"Yes, they fish back there," he said with conviction, once again gesturing with his hand.

"Behind the farm?"

"Yes, there's a big lake a good way out into the fields. You go around behind the barn and follow the lane out there."

"And people you don't know go out there?"

The man nodded. "People like to fish down there."

Liam felt his pulse rising with impatience. "Do you know anything about a drowning accident that took place here around eighty years ago?"

The man squinted. "The little girl?"

"Yes, exactly. A little girl," Liam said eagerly, wiping the rain off his face.

"A girl drowned here at the farm back in my father's day," the man said, then studied Liam with his watery eyes. "But that was years and years ago. My dad had a metal cover put over our slurry tank so that sort of thing couldn't happen again . . ."

Liam didn't stay to listen to any more; he simply took off running around the corner that Dea had disappeared around. He was fumbling with his flashlight in the pitch-dark night when Dea came over to him. Her hair was drenched and plastered to her forehead, and her eyes shone white in the darkness.

"It's here!" they said, talking over each other.

"Ernst and Mona's car is parked over by the barn," Dea continued, out of breath, pointing into the darkness. "And I definitely recognize the spot."

"Have you seen the tank?"

"Not yet, but it has to be here."

"Have you seen Mona and Ernst?"

"No."

Around them, they heard only the hissing sound of the rain hitting the leaves of the trees.

"We need to turn this whole place upside down. Call in a tank team," Liam said tensely in a voice that seemed brutal in the silence.

Dea was already calling Martin.

"Crime scene investigators, ambulances, Forensic Medicine. We need him to sound the alarm. All hands on deck," Liam added as he tried to see into the darkness.

* * *

Liam followed Dea at a run along the old low barn. The whole area out behind the farm was overgrown with tall trees with big leafy crowns, now interwoven together. Only the slender beams from their flashlights cast a little bit of light into the rainy night.

Liam could see the car parked alongside the barn. He ran his beam of light from the barn over to the trees, where he could discern a wall in the darkness between the tree trunks.

"I'm going to take a look in the trees," he said, and started walking toward the grove.

"Yes!" Dea was heading over to the barn's rotten wooden doors. The weeds grew tall along the wall, and big flakes of the whitewash plaster had come off in several places.

She listened attentively for a moment into the building behind the door. Then she grabbed the rusty handle. The door slid open with surprising ease, and the first thing the beam from her flashlight hit was the hood of a car. There were multiple cars parked inside in the darkness. Her heart pounding, temples throbbing, she ran her light over the old Granada. The Peugeot was parked in there too, as well as Johannes's Volvo.

"Dea!" Liam called to her from not far away.

She left the barn door open and ran back into the night. She had trouble orienting herself and was unsure where Liam's voice had come from.

"Coming!" she yelled back, and ran toward the trees, the light from her flashlight dancing in front of her. "Where are you?"

He shined his light at her from the grove of trees. She could see him standing, bending over a large, overgrown slurry tank. It wasn't underground, but it was completely hidden under the trees' leafy canopy. She could tell right away that this tank wouldn't appear on the map Martin had made. This tank hadn't been used in decades, and its location would make it impossible to see from the air. She pushed her way through the undergrowth and immediately spotted Mona, who was sitting hunched over on the ground, wailing.

"Is this it?" Dea yelled, even though she was standing right beside Liam now. She put a hand flat on the concrete wall and bent forward again, gasping for breath.

Liam lit up the side of the tank and heard Dea following as he started running around the curved wall. Thorns dug into his jacket, but he yanked himself free. Then, as he continued through the dense brush, he held his arms up protectively in front of his face. On the far side of the slurry tank, the light from their flashlights caught a stack of pallets supporting an old conveyor belt that led to a manure pile. He felt Dea bump gently into his back as he abruptly froze.

In the white glow of their flashlights were clear traces of blood on the edge of the tank's concrete wall. Liam felt the heat from Dea's body as they leaned simultaneously over the dried, reddish-brown smudge spread across the worn surface.

Liam quickly hopped up onto the conveyor belt and ran the last bit of the way to the top of the slurry tank so that he was standing on the rusty iron cover. He grabbed the handle on the hatch and yanked, but it wouldn't budge. He put his legs and back into it and tried again, but with the same result.

Dea had made it up on top now too, and she ran her light over the hatch to see if there was something holding it shut.

"There's more blood here!" she cried, pointing to the large smears on the rusty iron.

"Hello?" Dea yelled at the hatch. She had dropped down onto her stomach, her face so close to the wet iron that she could taste rust.

"Is anyone here?" Liam called out from above her. His voice echoed in the night, and he hammered on the iron with the butt of his flashlight, making the light jump in the treetops.

Dea got up onto her knees and lit up the bloodstains on the edge of the hatch.

"This can't be! We saw him fall in the opening!"

"Grab hold again," Liam ordered.

Dea set her flashlight down on the iron, and together they both pulled as hard as they could on the handle. The hatch hinge rattled a bit, but it didn't budge even a millimeter. The iron tore at the skin on their hands. If there had been any prints on the handle, they were long gone now.

She let go with an angry groan. "What the hell do we do?"

Liam put his cheek right up against the edge of the hatch.

"Phew, it stinks down there . . ." Suddenly he stopped, having caught a sound, a faint cry, a vague voice from inside the tank.

"They're here!" He jumped up and started tugging on the hatch's handle. He yanked and shook and yelled desperately to Dea, telling her she should call for emergency responders who could get into the tank.

Dea could still hear Mona's sobs from down in the bushes. She ran down the conveyor belt, using her flashlight to look for something to pry underneath the hatch so they could force it open—a shovel, a flat piece of metal . . .

There was nothing.

"I'm going to run back to the barn and see if . . ." Dea stopped as the sound of a powerful, rumbling engine reverberated through the night. Liam, who was on his way down to her, stopped abruptly.

The noise was coming from the farm, and it grew like a roar in the darkness, heading straight for them. Even though Dea could see the outline of the big tractor, it took her a minute to understand what was happening.

Liam stood still, frozen on the conveyor belt that led down to the old manure pile. Then he slowly raised his flashlight and lit up the tractor's driver. Ernst sat up straight atop the rusty red tractor. The tractor had enormous dual tires and a metal bar across the front of the grille. An instant later they were blinded by the tractor's bright headlights as the old pastor straightened out and rammed full force into the slurry tank.

The tank shook so violently that Liam lurched on the conveyor belt. He could hear water start gushing out below him, and a nauseating stench of rot and sewage spread through the darkness.

The tractor rumbled as Ernst backed the huge contraption away from the tank. The machine's headlights bathed the tank in light.

Liam held his hand up over his mouth and nose. The stench was overwhelming.

"Send Martin our exact coordinates immediately. We need multiple ambulances out here," Liam exclaimed, then he jumped down off the conveyer belt.

*   *   *

The rain and the muddy water from the slurry tank blended together around their feet into a reeking puddle. Over by the ruptured tank, Dea leaned in and yelled into the crack in the wall. The hole was nowhere near big enough for them to pull out the people who were trapped inside, and no one could get in either. Dea yelled reassuringly into the hole, explaining that help was on its way.

Behind them the tractor's engine roared again. Ernst was revving it up. Liam ran over to the narrow opening and yelled to the people inside that they should move away from the hole.

He had only just managed to jump to the side, landing and rolling in the stinking mire, when the tractor rammed its metal bar into the same hole as before. The ground shook, the gash in the wall grew bigger, and even more rotten water glugged out. Liam got to his feet and started slipping, flailing his arms wildly. The tank's concrete wall crunched. For a minute he was afraid that the whole structure would give way.

Ernst backed the tractor away again. Now there was a hole in the concrete from the ground up to the iron lid. The old man left the tractor's engine running so the headlights lit up the slurry tank.

Dea gasped for breath as she came over to stand beside Liam. She felt his hand on her arm and heard him ask if she was OK, but all her attention was focused on the figure slowly coming into view from the darkness.

With a protective hand in front of her eyes, Luna stepped forward on filthy, unsteady legs. She was soaking wet, covered in muck, and squinting in confusion into the light. She wasn't wearing anything besides a tank top and underwear. Dea quickly stepped forward and took hold of her. She pulled the young woman to her and ran a soothing hand over her hair, which was caked to her skinny face.

"It's over," Dea said, trying to avoid touching Luna's bare skin, which was red and swollen with open wounds in several spots. Luna grabbed hold of Dea and clung to her, sobbing, as her legs buckled beneath her.

* * *

Liam stepped in over the frayed concrete edge of the hole. The stench tore at his nose and turned his stomach. He reached out a hand to Beate, who was on all fours, trying to crawl out through the hole.

Her pregnant belly was exposed, and she was smeared with stinking sludge from head to toe. She precariously attempted to stand up but didn't have the strength for it. Liam leaned down to her and carefully took hold under her arms to help her over the lip of concrete. Her soaked nightgown was ripped the whole way up the front and clung to her body; her skin was greasy and in even worse condition than Luna's, with suppurating pink sores. Beate turned her face to him, and her eyes were two swollen cracks with big clumps of discharge stuck to her eyelashes.

"My daughter?" Her words were barely audible.

He squatted down beside her.

"Silje is fine. She's with her father," he said soothingly. "We'll make sure they're informed. And Peter is fine." He neglected to mention that her boyfriend had been assaulted by Claus and that right now he was in the hospital where she would soon be brought herself. "He will be so incredibly happy to see you."

Beate put her arms around his neck and hugged his chest. She reeked of excrement, but he put his arm around her and rocked her comfortingly. Over her shoulder, he saw that Mona was helping Dea bring Johannes out. He seemed limp and lifeless.

Once they had him out on the ground, Dea leaned over him and placed her fingers on the side of his throat. She looked up and caught Liam's eye. Then she nodded to him and gave him a thumbs-up. Somewhere in the distance a chorus of sirens began to wail.

Liam carefully let go of Beate and rushed back to the hole and shined his flashlight into the tank, where several lifeless forms hung tied to the rusty iron pipes. He pulled up his shirt and pressed the fabric tightly over his nose and mouth before stepping over the lip.

The sound of his movements echoed dully in the rounded concrete space. One of the people on the iron pipe moved, and he called to Dea. Two more people hung farther in.

Dea appeared in the opening. She pressed her arm over her lower face with very evident disgust and stepped inside so they were standing close together in the dark space.

"Luna says Kasper and Hayyan are still alive," she said hoarsely from behind her arm.

"What about Nassrin and Charlotte?" Liam asked.

Dea shook her head. "She didn't know. But Hayyan is with Nassrin."

Working together, they untied Kasper from the pipe. He sputtered, making a gurgling sound, as Liam carefully put him over his shoulders in a fireman's hold and carried him out into the fresh air.

Beate had stood up and staggered over to meet them. "Is there anything I can do?"

Kasper shuddered, and Liam asked her to stay with him. Kasper moaned but seemed unconscious.

The sirens sounded closer now, and they could see the bright blue lights flashing through the air. Liam quickly ran back to the tank and was met by Dea and Hayyan, who were carrying Nassrin out.

"She's barely alive," Dea whispered, choked up, her face contorted.

Liam faltered, then closed his eyes for a second and took a deep breath. He concentrated and steeled his resolve. Right now, he needed to finish this job. He would process his emotions later.

"If there's a chance that Charlotte is still alive, we need to get her out," he said roughly to hold himself together. Hayyan had collapsed beside his niece. He clung tightly to one of her hands.

On his way back to the tank, Liam felt Dea's hand on his arm. There was no mistaking the despair in her face.

"That should have been me!" she said, looking over at their young colleague.

*   *   *

The first patrol car came racing around the corner of the barn now, its blue flashers spinning furiously in the dark. It was Thorbjørn and another extremely young officer, fresh out of the academy.

Thorbjørn stopped abruptly at the sight of Nassrin and put his hand to his mouth in horror. He looked at Liam, shocked.

"We'll talk about it later," was all Liam said, and he waved him over to the crack in the wall of the tank. "There are more inside. The ones who are tied up to the pipes might still be alive."

"Here's hoping," Thorbjørn said, and sneaked a peek at Nassrin before following Liam in.

Dead, bloated bodies hung along one side of the tank. Thorbjørn and the young officer got to work untying Charlotte from the pipe. Her body seemed stiff, and Liam studied it in the beam of light, searching for signs of life, but she hung with her eyes closed and her arms slack. More ambulances pulled up outside.

"Is she alive?" Luna asked as they carefully lay Charlotte on the grass. The young woman was still shaking, her whole body shivering. She couldn't even keep her hands still, and her teeth were chattering so hard she could barely speak.

Liam searched for Charlotte's pulse. He closed his eyes and tried to focus. He convinced himself that her body was warm, but he wasn't sure.

"Sit here and talk to her," he told Luna. "Just keep talking."

Luna nodded and started to stroke Charlotte's blond hair, which was plastered together in clumps. Then she turned her face up to Liam.

"We thought you'd found us when Nassrin almost got us out. But then we realized that she had been captured too."

"But she fought him?"

"Yes, she fought with him up there; she got the hatch open and kept him away. Kasper almost managed to crawl all the way up. He wanted to help the rest of us. We really thought we were going to make it out." Liam could hear Luna's teeth striking each other. "We could hear them fighting, it went completely quiet, and . . . and . . . and then she was thrown in the water with us." Luna's voice cracked and she grew silent. "When the hatch opened after her, we were sure we were going to die."

"Did you hear her say anything?" Liam asked hopefully.

"No, it happened so fast."

Liam grabbed her shoulder as she started tipping in front of him.

"Johannes didn't say anything either when he came down to us. And he wouldn't answer if he had blocked us in somehow up there so the hatch would stay locked when he jumped into the water. But I think he did, since you couldn't get it open. He didn't talk to us at all. Beate said he seemed drugged. They know each other really well from the church. That's where I know him from too."

A stretcher was placed on the ground beside Charlotte.

"Her first?" asked an ambulance driver in a reflective vest.

Liam nodded and pulled back a little, out of the way. He hadn't noticed the ambulances arriving. He watched as Nassrin and Charlotte were carefully transferred onto stretchers and into ambulances.

"Come on," Dea said, putting her hand on his shoulder. "There's still more inside . . ."

* * *

"I want to see my husband!" A high-pitched voice cut through the noise of the emergency responders and the first two ambulances, which were just pulling away with their sirens wailing and Charlotte and Nassrin inside. "Where's Kent?"

Liam was helping a paramedic haul Verner out. According to Luna and Beate, the old grocer had lived for just under a day after being tossed down into the tank. Kasper had told them that. Kent had been dead when he arrived. Both deaths had happened before Beate and Luna were dumped into the water themselves.

"How the hell is that possible, for her to suddenly show up?" Dea exclaimed sharply from behind Liam. "Don't they live in Haarby?"

Liam left Verner to the paramedic and joined Dea. Thorbjørn had his hands full up by the corner of the house, restraining Maria. Her voice sounded scared and angry, and she swung her arms around trying get by him, but Thorbjørn put his arms around her, trying to talk her down.

Liam and Dea reached them.

"This is Kent's wife," Thorbjørn said, and they both nodded. Maria reached out to them. "She was in Ebberup at her sister's place, and then all the emergency vehicles freaked her out," Thorbjørn continued.

"Kent is still missing!" Maria howled. "I've asked so many times if you have any news, and then I got scared that maybe this had something to do with him."

She started to cry.

"We know Maria," Liam told Thorbjørn, and refrained from putting his manure-smeared arm around Red Kent's wife.

"I want to see my husband!" Maria pleaded, stepping over to Liam and Dea.

"I have made myself very clear that this is a crime scene," Thorbjørn declared with authority. "So you can't enter." He moved to stand in front of Maria.

"Is Kent dead?" Maria ignored Thorbjørn and looked into Liam's eyes over Thorbjørn's shoulder. There was fear in her eyes.

Both Dea and Thorbjørn looked expectantly at Liam, and Maria immediately picked up on the vibe that arose between them.

"Is he dead?" she demanded stridently.

Liam reached out, deciding he didn't give a damn about the manure, and pulled her to him.

"Yes," he said. "Your husband is dead. You can ride in the ambulance with him if you'd like when they drive him to the hospital in a few minutes. But I can't allow you to get any closer to the scene than this. An officer will come and wait with you."

"Is he really dead?" she repeated more quietly now, choked up.

"Yes, unfortunately." The ambulance was already being readied. Kent was on the stretcher, and his face was being covered with a white cloth.

On the ground next to Kent's stretcher lay Lone and Verner. They were both dead. Lone had longer gashes and wounds on her head and her arms than the others did. Beate had explained that Lone had been delirious and hysterical with panic from the instant she came down into the water. She had scratched at both herself and Kasper whenever he tried to help her by lifting her up over the surface of the water. In the end they'd had to give up trying to help her, and she had died in the water. She had been in the filthy water for six days without a break. Her skin was porous, with large holes in it.

Kent had been tied up so that his face, chest, and arms were above water, but five days as a dead body in the semi-rotten water had left awful marks, marks Liam wasn't sure it would do Kent's wife any good to see.

The paramedics were wrapping Lone up not far from them.

* * *

Dea was sitting on the ground, leaning against the tank. She stared vacantly at Hayyan, who still sat slumped. The whole thing felt unreal.

Ernst had eventually abandoned the tractor and come to stand behind Mona and Johannes. Dea watched him take off his windbreaker in the chilly night air. Then he stiffly leaned down over his adult grandchild and carefully placed the jacket neatly over him. She watched how his big hands tenderly and lovingly touched Johannes's forehead and how he meticulously tucked the jacket in around his neck as if it were a blanket.

Mona turned around and looked up at her father. For a second Dea thought Mona had been moved by Ernst's rare display of care and affection and wanted to express her sincere gratitude, but then she stood up and shoved her dad in the chest, hard, so that he stumbled backward. She stiffened in the middle of the aggressive gesture and glanced in disbelief at Hayyan.

For a second, she stood with her mouth open as if frozen, then her legs gave out beneath her and she sank down and sat on the ground. She covered her mouth tightly with her hand, as if she were trying to hold a whole life's worth of grief and despair back with that gesture. Her brow furrowed and she shook her head almost imperceptibly, then she seemed to snap out of it and her eyes darted back and forth between Hayyan and Johannes, who lay on the ground beside her.

"Mona?" Hayyan stood up and took a tentative step toward her.

It looked like Mona was trying to say something. She absent-mindedly reached her hand out and put it on Johannes's chest, as if seeking strength from her son.

"Get out of here," Ernst let loose in a roar. He had regained his balance and turned angrily toward Hayyan. "Can't you see we're grieving?"

"Shut up, Dad!" Mona hissed in an unfamiliar voice, so full of scorn that it silenced Ernst in surprise. Hayyan came a little closer, and Mona did not deign to look at her father as Hayyan knelt down in front of her.

He reached out a hand and touched her cheek. "It is you, isn't it?"

Mona put her own hand on top of Hayyan's and held his hand to her cheek.

Johannes made a sound. It wouldn't be long before it was his turn to be taken away.

Hayyan's brow furrowed, and he gave Mona a questioning look.

She nodded to him. "Yes, he's your son," she said without looking up.

*   *   *

The rain had subsided by the time the last ambulance departed from the farm. Enormous floodlights had been set up. The Home Guard was on its way with tents that would be set up around the slurry tank to secure whatever might be left in the way of evidence. At the moment, the technicians were working on the conveyor belt and the hatch that led into the tank.

Liam came over to Dea and sat down, leaning against the tank next to her.

"I need you for the case against Johannes," he told her without taking his eyes off the concrete tank, which had now claimed more lives than that of the little girl who'd drowned in it so many years ago.

Dea's voice was hoarse when she answered.

"I'm the last person you need on this case, don't you see that? There's going to be a lot of hoopla about why I didn't figure it out much sooner. Liam, he's my first cousin once removed. For crying out loud, we played together as kids!"

She felt a wave of fatigue roll over her. It had been so long since she had last slept that she could fall asleep sitting up in a second. She thought about Nassrin and recalled them lifting her body onto the stretcher.

Hayyan rode in a police car, and Aldar waited at the hospital to meet him. No one had told him yet that it had been his own son who had hurt Nassrin.

Dea watched Liam as he wiped his face with a wet hand. Surely he must see that she was done.

"That day when we couldn't find Nassrin," he said then, "and you asked about her? I found her down at the beach in Assens. She'd been out on the water, even though it was incredibly windy."

Dea smiled sadly. Nassrin and Johannes were both being lifted onto stretchers. Mona followed Johannes.

Ernst was left standing all alone. His old, wrinkled face was brightly lit in the glow of the blue and white lights that illuminated the area.

Liam patted Dea on the shoulder. "I'm going to the hotel where Helene and the kids are."

Dea nodded, and they started walking through the muck back toward the cars and the farm.